Ascension

Ascension: A Novel

Steve Tomasula

The University of Alabama Press
Tuscaloosa, Alabama 35487-0380
uapress.ua.edu

Typeface: Whitney

Cover design: Daniel Warner

Ascension is made possible in part by support from the Institute for Scholarship in the Liberal Arts, College of Arts and Letters, University of Notre Dame.

Cataloging-in-Publication data is available from the Library of Congress.
ISBN: 978-1-57366-195-9
E-ISBN: 978-1-57366-897-2

For Maria, Alba & Ava, as in the past, in this, the year of the plague, till we are one with nature.

Also by Steve Tomasula

The Book of Portraiture
VAS: An Opera in Flatland
IN & OZ
TOC: A New-Media Novel
Once Human: Stories
Conceptualisms: The Anthology of Prose, Poetry, Found, Visual, E-, and Hybrid Writing as Contemporary Art (Editor)

www.stevetomasula.com

Ascension

IT

didn't

have to happen

this way (or at all), the way we say

now, how it happened then, a catch
in the cosmic dust, the way the first grains of a future dune snag and pile. All in motion: Stardust, particles, motes clumping in space the way droplets form from O and H, the way clouds form from droplets, snow from clouds and flake binds to flake in freefall, becoming a snowball, rolling downhill, gathering more of itself to itself, growing larger, rounder, as does this cosmic stuff, rolling not downhill but around the gravity of a forming star, this globe becoming one of eight, compacting, growing, crunching itself tighter, tighter, so big and tight, and planet-massive that the weight of itself presses in from every side like hands squeezing for heat, more heat, heat enough to melt rock, its size, temperature, gravity, and mass all growing until all the dust-elements-hunks-mountain-sized-chunks that can be drawn in have been added—astronomical collisions—one so violent that it breaks off a piece that becomes this infant planet's moon—the molten ball that's left not so heavy that it ignites as nuclear fire—like its sun—nor so small that its own steam escapes—like its moon—its crust cooling as a glaze forms over this nameless planet, whipping around its sun—its orbit not so close that its forming oceans broil away, nor so far off that it becomes a world of ice; no, the new planet is just the right size and distance from the sun for further drama: cracks form in its crust, spewing magma, creating plates, geysers of vapor condensing as clouds, and rain and rivers and oceans, erosion, particles dissolve, wash downstream, carve ruts. All the while acids come into being. The first cells. The landmass cracks. Cell joins to cell and finds release as larger patterns: The first algae; dots of moss; then the first blade of grass. Blade adds to blade, and are joined by leaves absorbing, innumerable exhalations creating still-larger arabesques in air, in land, in water. Landmasses tear apart, grind back together, or drift apart. The Earth heats; ice melts; sea levels rise, melting calcium from shorelines, the calcium transforming the water so much that creatures begin to develop shells, bones. Trilobites, backbones, the first fish. The greening continents give rise to mountains that shape weather while flying, crawling, walking creatures come into being and pass out of being, the crust of the earth shifting: millenniums of eating, suffering, breathing, birthing, living, mating, dying, decaying, composting, sprouting—all life—playing out, becoming this thin earthen skin, the cracks in this skin widening, plates pulling apart, seas pour in: what had been a single landmass, now in pieces, on the move, two continent-sized islands emerge, opening new possibilities, narrowing others. Alternate histories.

WHO KNOWS THE RACES OF ANIMALS THAT CAME BEFORE US?

WHO KNOWS THE RACES OF ANIMALS THAT WILL COME AFTER OURS?

EVERYTHING CHANGES, EVERYTHING PASSES. ONLY THE TOTALITY REMAINS.

—D'Alembert, Diderot's Dreaming Philosopher, 1769

Chapter I: Transformation

Above, a flock of parrots, brilliant green in morning sky. They swept by as one, the entire flock changing direction with a single-minded ease that made Raul sigh. You've never held a world in the palm of your hand, have you? he asked them. Maybe a fledgling that had fallen out of its nest, making you the god who would lift it home or let it die? The parrots vanished into the trees without answering, leaving him with the *curepí* he said he would guide, scribbling away, as always, in that notebook he carried.

Raul continued helping the Indians prepare the canoe, stripping bark fiber with his teeth, as they'd showed him. Near the huts on shore, a trio of naked boys practiced shooting toy-sized arrows at a lizard they had tethered to a stake, just as their fathers had learned, and fathers before them. When Raul had been that age, he'd been learning from the mission priest that Cristóbal Colón had defeated an entire island of Indians, the priest swelling with pride and looking down on the class as if from a horse. Unable to believe the story, Raul later asked an old Guraní if it was true. Yes, it was true, the old man confirmed: Cristóbal, the first *curepí*, greeted by thousands of Taíno. Confused, Raul asked, Why didn't they just kill him? The old man looked down .

Would it have mattered? The Indians were so enmeshed with the forest that to kill it would be to kill them, and so it would never occur to them to think of themselves as masters of any Garden, never mind beings given "Dominion over all the earth." The *curepí* did, though. Having grown up among them, Raul knew well how deeply they believed this, their growing settlements pushing tribes ever deeper into the forest, often forcing these people into wars with the tribes that they encountered there, so remote and isolated that they had no idea there was another world outside their own. But looking down at his own mestizo skin, he knew that there were many ways for a people to vanish, and his maté-color—a history lesson in flesh—wouldn't let him shake the sense there was a reason fate had placed him between the *curepí,* who Raul had hired himself out to guide, and the deeper forest, the way La Malinche had found herself between Cortez and the Aztecs—the way the decision of life or death falls to the person—and no one else—who comes upon the fallen bird, or holds the fish gasping in a net. Maybe it was the man's sudden appearance in the cantina to find someone who could guide him at the very moment Raul had been preparing to go up river in search of his wife. Maybe it was guilt over the money. Still, he couldn't release the thought of just abandoning the man—just slip away—and let the forest, the jaguar, the fire ants, determine his fate....

What to do? he asked the river. In the time of high water, it was impossible to paddle upstream. But flat as it was now, the river was smoothing the way in either direction...

Watching how effortlessly a company of parrots could fly as one, the Professor sighed. Christ on a cross. What design or defect made it so easy for the arabesques of men to instead form the face of death? he wondered: thousands of healthy young men coming together back in the States not as a flock, or school of fish, but as maggoty mosaics of battlefield aftermath. Just before departing Asunción, the Professor learnt that the war he couldn't believe would ever break out had.

The voices of the Indians preparing his canoe were muted by the surrounding forest and the serene manner in which they worked brought to mind the cheers—*Huzah!*—that surely went up back in Dixie as men put off academic robes for gray uniforms, enlisting both God and Nature into The Cause. Oh, he could hear them lecturing students on the ferocity with which the races of red and black ants fought to keep one another in their place, using powerful mandibles to tear limbs, sever heads—sacrifice themselves if need be to preserve the Purity of God's Plan.

God's Plan. He watched the Indians bringing his gear to Raul, standing in what looked like a floating ox cart, only narrower: a coffin of cigar-box wood, Spanish Cedar (*Cedrela odorata*), that he had had them make in order to travel tributaries narrower than those that could be navigated by the rafts that the natives themselves used. Raul pushed off to test its draft in the deep water.

As obvious as the devil's prick, the Professor thought, the tapestry embroidered by modern stitches would overrun even the eternal world of the forest natives, as surely as it had all but erased the World he had been born into: an Age when the study of Nature was inseparable from the majesty of Nature and the majesty of Nature one with the Divine. Instead of looking to ants to justify the slaughter of men, the Natural Philosophers who had been his teachers would have seen the industry of ants as one more

tease, seducing them closer, inviting them to discern the pattern in a colony, which was a wondrous thing to behold. For they knew they were witnessing the handiwork of their Maker, which was, for them, true knowledge: naked science stripped of philosophy was of no more use to those men than a description of the inner workings of a clock by someone oblivious to its hands. But that way of the world had been dying for some time into the birth of another more hard, more measured—just as the ages of the ancients had devolved from a golden time of noble intentions to one of brass, then lead. So why did he, a mere mortal, have so much difficulty believing it could happen to him? Would, in truth, happen to everyone?

This I do know, the Professor wrote in his journal,

today we depart for a place where the air is ruled by the birds, the earth the worm, and no army can overthrow the flea.

Standing within the foyer of a great, unknown forest—continent-wide and as virginal as the forest that once carpeted the United States—some men plunged ahead as eagerly as the enslaved who finds the door to Freedom left open. Raul seemed to be one of these—and certainly the Rev. Eastwood, Miss Eastwood's missionary uncle whose clues he was following. But this leafy, heaving sea made the Professor cling to what guidelines he could: his Moroccan journal, telescope, shaving kit, a selection of books.... While securing provisions in São Paulo, he'd bought a pistol.

He touched it, secure in a canvas bag that hung from his shoulder. Adam and Eve before the snake. That's how the natives seemed to him, with him as the snake and the steel hatchet head he'd brought to trade for the canoe as the apple. A squat-line of muscular men stared with their Asiatic eyes at the hatchet head as though it were an idol. Black hair shaved into identical bowl shapes, their bronze, expressionless faces gave away no more than masks. What boon they thought this idol might bring them, the Professor could only guess because the surrounding forest seemed to be waiting with that ancient knowledge that all it had to do was wait long enough and he, Raul, and their hatchet would vanish as surely as a sea surrounds a sinking ship. The forest would always restore itself, they said, although no one could ever predict how. In the meantime, the Professor watched over the hatchet head as the squat-line watched over him. Other natives stacked the maté pots they used for small trade, as oblivious to the changes that were sure to come as those poor buggers in Atlantis must have been, living out their last days in the Mediterranean Valley, never once considering that the thin dike of land between them and the Atlantic Ocean would one day break—until it did—breached by earthquake, or the relentless centuries of pounding waves—or call it the Hand of God—and the terrible sea came pouring in

through a rupture that sailors today call the Strait of Gibraltar, transforming the peaceful farmland of the Mediterranean Valley into the Mediterranean Sea. Which radically altered the patterns of life—like colonies of frogs gathering around a puddle as Plato put it—and so gave rise to different worlds: farmers replaced by Phoenicians, then Venetians, and all of that...

Truly, all landscapes are sacred landscapes.

An odd insect lit upon the page. Hello, little fella.

Don't believe any of that hoodoo about the impenetrability of Nature, my little friend, he told the insect, beginning to sketch it, Terrible is God's clarity, matched only by that of Mother Nature. The insect looked back, shifting from side to side. And our place in Her—and His—pattern is revealed when we least expect it.

He gave a chuckle to imagine the faces of those first Spaniards who encountered these tribes and learnt how they lived in fear of spirits that pushed men out of trees or took the form of a Giant Terror Bird.

Given the fossilized femurs of Goliath-sized men, shrunken heads, snakes large enough to swallow a conquistador whole, and all the other marvels they'd already discovered, surely this thought entered their minds: Why not?

The insect crouched into the aspect of a tiger about to pounce—a comical pose, given its tiny size.

The ferocity of a flea.

Yea, why not? the Professor told the insect, for truly, there are things beyond the mind's ken in both Heaven and Earth: The End of Time—and The Beginning of Time, for that matter—The Resurrection of the Dead.... Even the fact that a creature such as a professor could be standing here in a vast alien forest thinking these thoughts was more bizarre than the existence of any Terror Bird.

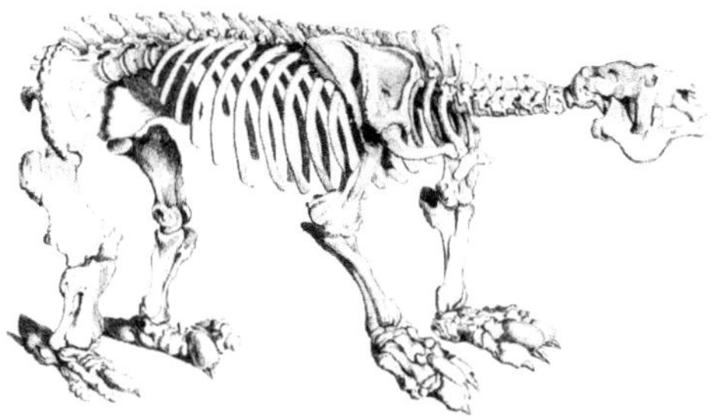

October 15, 1859

Nothing. More nothing. Still nothing. Then something: Goliath's skeleton, stumbled upon by Spanish explorers. Back in Madrid the bones of this puzzle were assembled into what Juan Bautista Bru claimed was not a member of Goliath's race, nor a dragon, but an unknown beast that walked the earth until Noah closed the door to his Ark, leaving it outside. Megatherium (Great Beast) they christened it—and thus man reveals bone by bone and stone by stone the shocking truth that a different world once covered the earth we now inhabit, believing, even as we sleepwalk over the graves of billions, that the world will always be just as we find it today.

Gently, the Professor touched the insect with the tip of his pencil. When he did, it shot up into his neck.

"Jesus!"—So piercing hot was the bite that it made him cry out, his journal and pencils flying in all directions.

At that same instant, the canoe rocked and all was confusion: the Professor thrashed about in pain. Raul called to the Indians for help, some of whom were hopping in imitation of the Professor, pointing and laughing.

"Minga! Pysyrô!" Raul implored, stripping off his boots in order to go after the gear. Only one native rushed to the bank, his naked body painted to look like the suit of a Spanish caballero, complete with lapels and silver buttons. As the pain subsided, the Professor became more fully aware of the argument the Indian on shore was having with his guide out on the boat though he was only able to understand one word of it: *piranha.*

Raul suddenly stopped arguing and stood motionless in the canoe, looking back at the Professor rubbing his neck. A worrisome look came over Raul's face. He raised the small black fist, carved from *azeviche*, that he wore on a thong around his neck as a charm to ward off the *Ojo malo*, and kissed it in prayer.

Bubbles rose from the river where their provisions had sunk.

My "guide," the Professor mused, rubbing the pain in his sweaty neck.

Paddling at the front of the canoe while Raul drove from the rear, the Professor had an unobstructed view of the river, each bend revealing one new vista, then another.

With every stroke, he could feel himself drawing nearer to the fossil he had devoted his life to finding. The date he had opened his journal to that morning—*October 24, 1859*—seemed out of place here, as did its entry:

Both saint and scientist agree: who we are, and what will become of us, is written in the book that is the earth.

Back in Massachusetts, that statement had driven the Professor on as fervently as if he had been a zealot and it his holy writ. But after a year of fruitless effort, the bramble of handwriting came to him as a loose thread that if worried too much would unravel the entire garment of belief, and he had to take a breath to compose himself....

In his mind he began to compose:

So this is a story about Nature but it won't seem that way since I am writing it. And you are reading it. And whatever I write won't be 'it' and whatever you understand won't be what I meant: All Life is here, but it has nothing to do with us.

Leave it be, he told himself, putting his back into a stroke, the river, the Paraguayan jungle around, wild, impassive, seemingly impenetrable, the bird cries and hum of insects speaking, if what saints and scientists said was true, a language that while incredibly complex was not unknowable, its alphabet more enigmatic than runes, but an alphabet nonetheless.

Fewer and fewer faces had poked out from the bush to look upon them as they moved up river. A lone man emerged to stare, motionless as a Greek statue and naked as one too. Then there was only the forest.

Would the trees welcome him when they arrived? Raul wondered as they glided past a man standing in full view on the bank: a shaman, maybe, who wanted them to see him and know that he would transform into a jaguar or a bird as night fell, and in this form follow them stealthily through the trees. Raul's father had forbidden his mother from going near her home forest to keep her from entering that world though she'd always told Raul that the trees were his family too—she had told him so many things—but surely her people were all dead and the trees and animals had changed so much that he wouldn't even recognize them. Or they him.

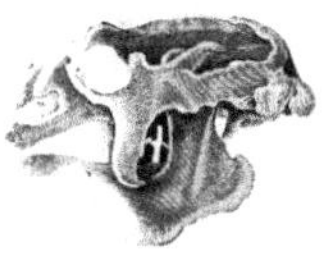

Raul did have a distant memory of headdresses and robes woven from the brilliant yellows and reds and blues of different birds. His mother had shown him how they would weave basket-like lean-tos that looked to him like giant bird nests—sturdy enough to stand for the few days that the tribe would rest near the river before moving back into the forest.... Though he'd worn pants and spoke the Spanish of his father, he could imagine himself as one of the boys he had seen learning to hunt.

The Professor retrieved from his vest the best map he had been able to secure. Unlike the intricately detailed maps of riverways in Europe, where all was known and etched into copper plates, this one had been given that snakelike shape mapmakers gave all unknown, jungle rivers: a blue squiggle, as if drawn by a child, across an empty green blotch that was supposed to be Paraguay. Yet a grid had been laid on top of this fancy passing-as-a-map the way new plants were given Latinate names—*Apocynum cannabinum*—to imprint upon them a whiff of Aristotle.

So this is a story about nature....

Holding up this ridiculous cartoon to the actual labyrinth of waterways—as though comparing a portrait to its sitter—the Professor saw how naïve he'd been for believing in it, back in his study. And how small he was now. But also how lucky.

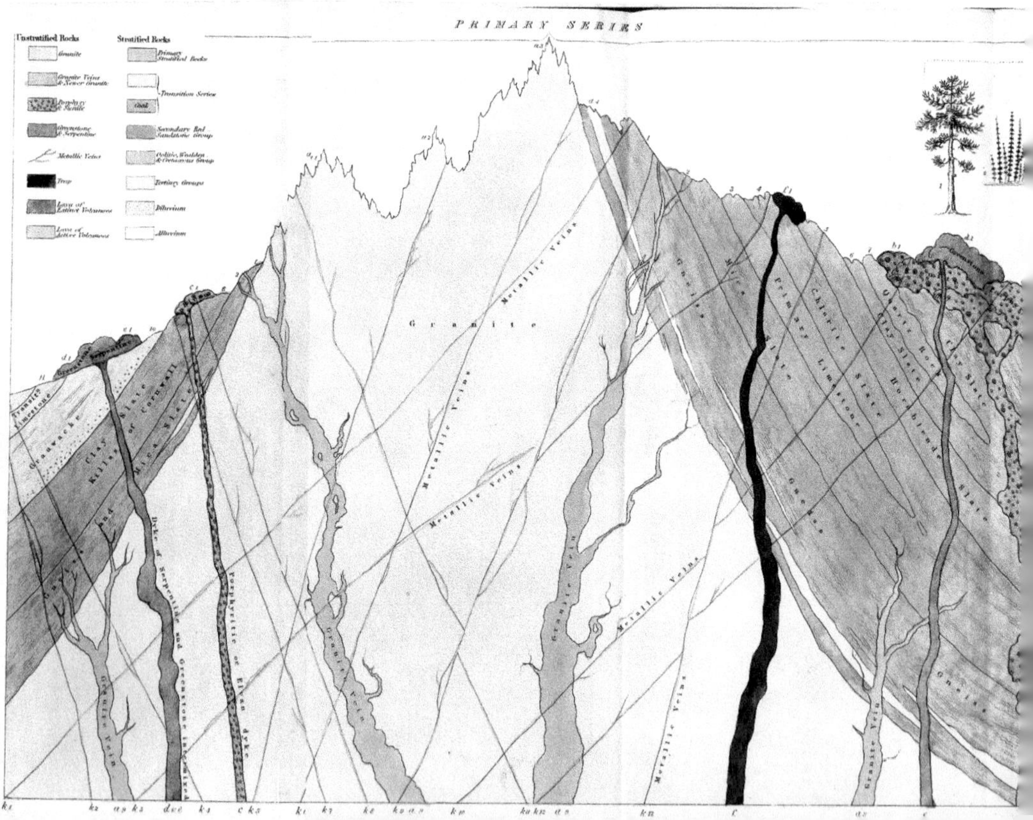

He had lost the bible of Natural History that he had carried all the way from Massachusetts: Humboldt's *Cosmos*. Also lost was Mr. Darwin's *Voyage of the Beagle*, a book that was nearly twenty years old but still the best record of South America. He had bundled these prized possessions into a large, specially made haversack with a waterproof lining and buckled flap, such as Union soldiers used, but all had been lost when Raul stood, clumsily rocking the boat.

Now his books lie at the bottom of the river. Along with: six cans of hard tack or ship's biscuits; 12 cakes of desiccated vegetables; 10 lbs. of jerked beef; all of his extra ammunition; a sack of dried beans; 1 pound of tea (Chinese); 5 pounds of bacon preserved with saltpeter; an oilcloth groundsheet; a poncho; blanket; tin cup; tin plate; a knot of tobacco; extra pair of shoes; and two changes of underwear—all of which Raul dismissed as needless weight.

And yet, by the grace of God, he still had in his possession the Moroccan journal in which he recorded his observations, and which he always carried on his person. And his brass sextant.

The Professor looked upon it in its case between his feet on the floor of the canoe; the map may not be more than fancy, but the invisible lines he could draw to the stars with this instrument could well be his only lifeline back should something happen to his guide.

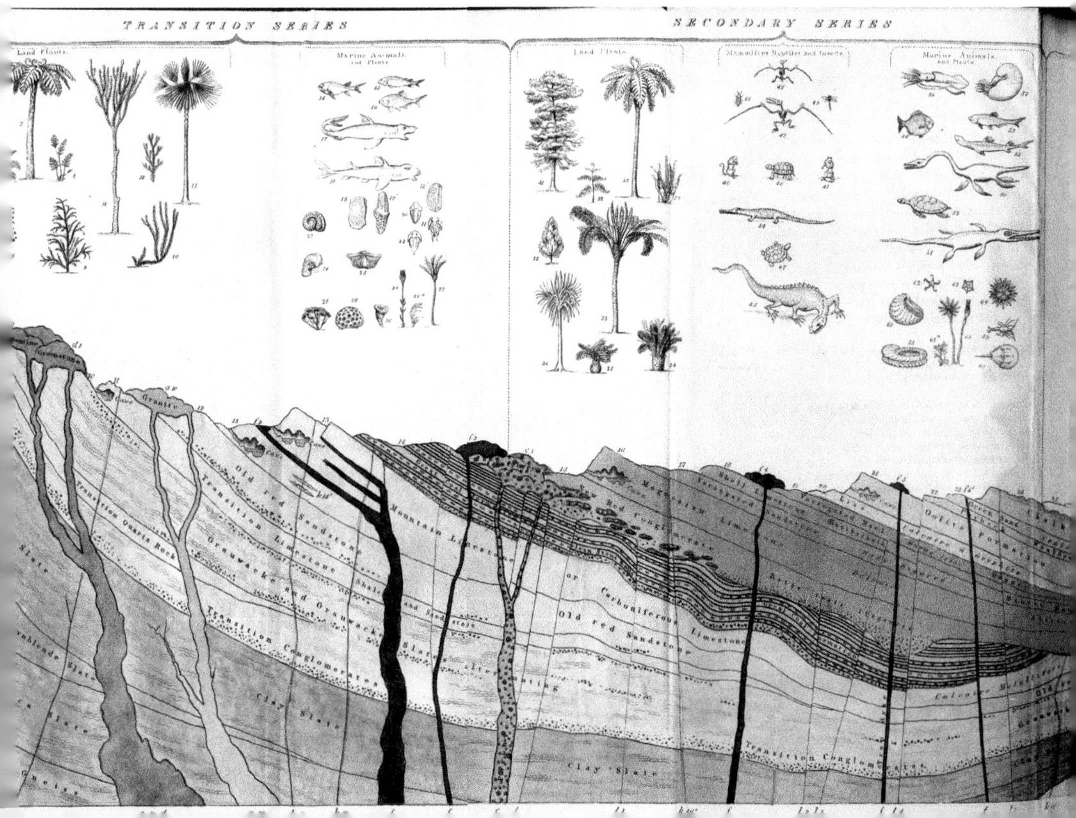

He glanced back over his shoulder and was surprised to see the man, looking steadily at him. His long hair hung around bare shoulders, the light reflected off the dull, flat river illuminating the undersides of his mestizo features. Dressed in Gaucho pants in the cantina where they had met, he had seemed more Spanish than Indian, but out here the Spanish effort to burn the Indian out of him seemed to have only annealed it, as an iron bar that had been heated red-hot hardens as it cools. As the canoe plowed on, the Professor resolved to hold the sextant close, as closely as he guarded his journal.

Watching the Professor from behind, Raul could tell he had fallen into dreams of the riches he would find.... When they first met, he had described an ancient bird that once lived in an ancient land. The way he described the land—a forest even more lush than the one that grew there today—made it sound like the Garden of Eden which the Indians always understood to be the *curepí*'s corruption of *Ywy Mará Ey*, or what the Spanish called *la Tierrra sin Mal.* That was why he agreed to be his guide—in the hopes that guiding this white man to where he wanted to go would deliver them both to the Land-without-Evil. But why exactly, did he want to go there? What was he really after? Gold? Bananas? Souls? All took souls.... For a time, after the Professor

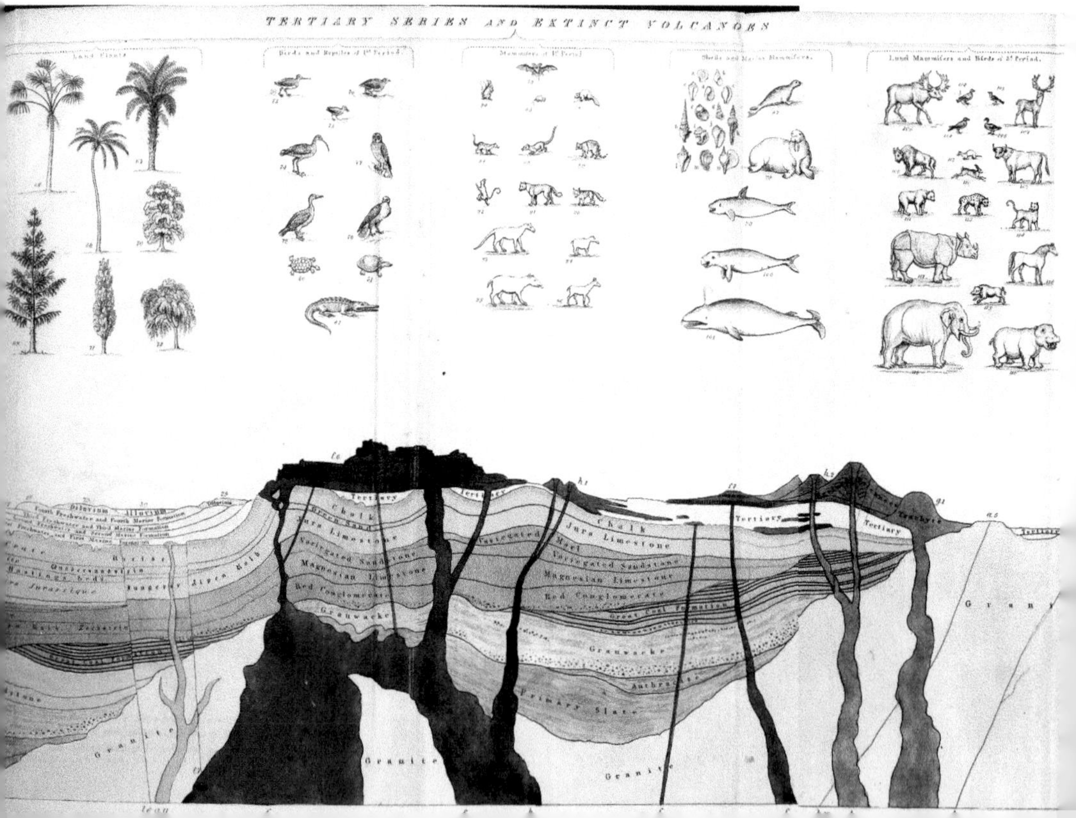

had shown him his rubbing of a gigantic bird feather, Raul thought the man had come to hunt the Terror Bird. But instead of packing a rifle that could kill a god, he only brought a pistol. When Raul saw that he also had a hammer and chisel, he thought he had come for *caucho*—the sticky, white pus that oozed from trees and that the Indians used to catch parrots. Why did foreigners suddenly have such a need to catch parrots? he'd asked himself, after the second, then third party came in search of *caucho*. But when he and the Professor paddled past a grove of what they called India Rubber trees, the Professor didn't even notice. What? What did he really want?

The air was filled with the sounds of birds and insects but none were visible in the wall of green on either side of the river. Suddenly a clearing of savannah grass and blue sky. A single hawk circled high above. So pristine and isolated was this land, it was easy to believe, as did Columbus, that Eden was here somewhere, just around the next bend. The Professor could tell that was what Raul was most interested in—the Land-without-Evil—*la Tierra sin Mal*. And while the Professor didn't believe, as did Columbus, that he'd ever find an Adam's Peak, it would be a lie to say he didn't harbor similar demons: a burning desire to find a Rosetta Stone in the form of a fossil

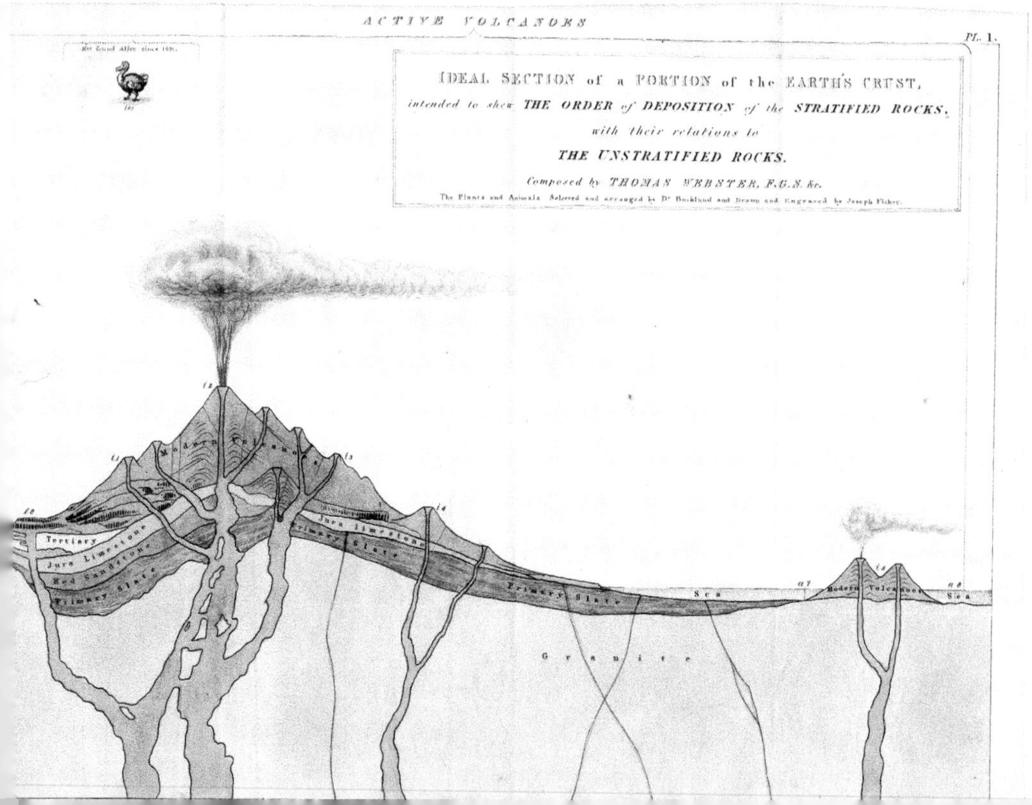

of a bird—proof that species were continuous—and thus unlock the shared language of Nature, God, and man.

Divus sive Nature, he often wrote on the blackboard of his classroom. God and Nature: One. If the next month went well, he would be back before Christmas. If his college would have him. Most of his colleagues believed he had either lost his mind or his discernment, clinging to the tenants of Natural History like an aging prophet, sure that, despite the lateness of the hour, his messiah would yet come. "'And God said,'" they would quote to him, "'Let the skies be filled with birds of every kind. The fifth Day.' And yet, we find nothing of the sort in the fossil records. Mammals, yes; sea creatures, yes. Birds, no. Not on the fifth day, or even the fifty thousandth day. Not for thousands of years."

Crap. To them he had no rejoinder. Entire seabeds of fossilized fishes and snails had been discovered. Quarries of plants, and reptiles—representatives of every animal kingdom—as well as creatures more bizarre than Ovid could imagine—trilobites and ichthyosaurs and Megalosaurus.... But no birds. The 2,000 pages of fine gothic print in Prof. Bronn's *Handbuch einer Geschichte der Natur* cataloged every known fossil—even fossilized dung—but it didn't list a single bone of a single bird.

As for the evidence of the living.... The chorus of birds along the river mocked him with each stroke of his paddle. Even in the U.S., the approach of passenger pigeons could be heard as distant thunder that grew to the deafening level of millions of threshing machines. A single flock could take hours to pass, darkening the sky as an eclipse, and leaving in its wake towns coated in white. Men killed birds by the hundreds by simply hitting the lower edges of the flock with rakes but the effect on these birds was akin to spitting into the ocean.

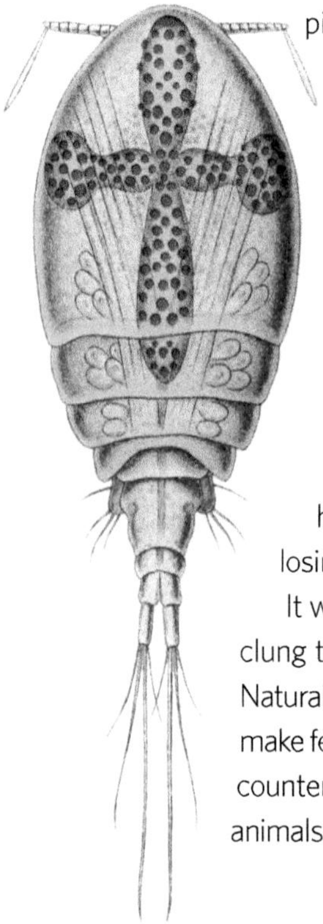

Where had they come from? If not from one eternal type present in the Garden, from what animal could so many types transmute?

He had even less of an answer, sitting in a jungle, empty-handed: no fossilized bird; no Rev. Eastwood, Anne's missionary uncle whom he thought would lead him to one. If his colleagues were right about him losing his discernment, how in Christ's Kingdom could he discern that?

It was certainly true that there were plenty of otherwise sober men who clung to erroneous beliefs with the tenacity of martyrs to a false religion: Natural Philosophers who in this modern age still proclaimed that if God could make ferns and fish, then the devil, who excelled in lies of all kinds, could make counterfeits of stone, never mind if it was more logical for God to make the animals and let natural processes make their fossils, dung and all....

Never had he thought he would, in turn, become one of those aging prophets—shouting into the wind ideas about the humours of the body, the transmutation of lead into gold, and other philosophies that had come into being, flourished a while, then vanished as does the morning mist, as do the men who dream them up. In fact, when he was young he thought he would grow into one of the venerable old oaks of academia, surrounded by students competing for his attention: a family man basking in the love of his children—many children—and loving wife. But then, his firstborn had died after taking only a few breaths; Elizabeth, his wife, passed a few hours later. Now, eighteen years after that, the gray hairs that heralded his coming winter found him awaking each morning to a cold and empty house. No clamoring students. No wife. No children.

And then, Darwin's Volcano erupted, proclaiming death and extinction as the engine of transmutation, and burying his life's work in ash. The Professor had thrown himself ever more passionately into the side of the debate that maintained that though the core of a species was present in the Garden, its variations were mutable: The fact that snakes had tiny vestigial feet showed that each generation had inherited shorter and shorter limbs to make it easier to crawl—snakes becoming more perfect snakes. Horses, more perfect horses.... And despite the claims of Darwinian evolution, there was a far simpler explanation for the fact that cats mummified by ancient Egyptians were exactly the same as modern cats: Cats had achieved their perfect cat form before the time of the Pharaohs.

Species change, he and other Natural Historians agreed, but the one tenant that they could not abandon was the fact that these changes are but variations of one everlasting TYPE—for if anything was given, it was man's final transformation. To believe otherwise, to believe in the victory of the grave—Elizabeth moldering in her grave.... All graves, including those of his daughter and other innocents.... The notion that all of the countless souls born of Eve did not count, or even exist, because they couldn't be measured was more bizarre than anything he could fathom. And it was the beauty of the sky at night that convinced him so; as well as the thunder of a waterfall; the caress of its mist as he stood looking down into its roaring churn, or the chill that issued from the mouth of a cave on a hot day.... No one would ever write an equation to explain the dance of a bumblebee, he knew. Nor the delicacy of a cantaloupe's yellow blossom in a farmer's calloused hand. Or the warmth of the sun on his face as he stood in the heat and buzz of field grass, trying to observe the recoil of a grasshopper before it leaps. He knew these things were real not because he could measure them but because he could feel them in his breast.

And truly the book that was the fossil record was not yet closed. A single fossil of a beak or wishbone would be as disruptive to the Extinctionist's version of Natural

History as the discovery of a pocket watch inside the wrappings of an ancient mummy would be to the history of civilization.

"Did your books speak of the children?" Raul asked. The steady, rhythmic work of paddling the canoe was meditative exercise, and Raul could see that his voice startled the Professor. He'd meant the race of fish possessed by the souls of drowned children that were said to live upriver. Their inconsolable weeping could lure even the strongest man into its depths, it was said.

"No, nothing about the children," the Professor said, paddling.

"What about the emeralds?" Emeralds and other gems were the common river gravel of Eden, all Christians knew, and still washed out of The Garden's overgrown ruins....

"No, nothing about the emeralds either."

Raul said nothing though finding the emeralds had lured more men to this river than any bird fossil. Before El Supremo closed Paraguay to the rest of the world, the Spanish colonials had fought over the rocky highlands where they believed minerals were to be found and mines established. The Indians only valued the lowlands for their game. Thus the two groups remained separated; thus the two groups lived in

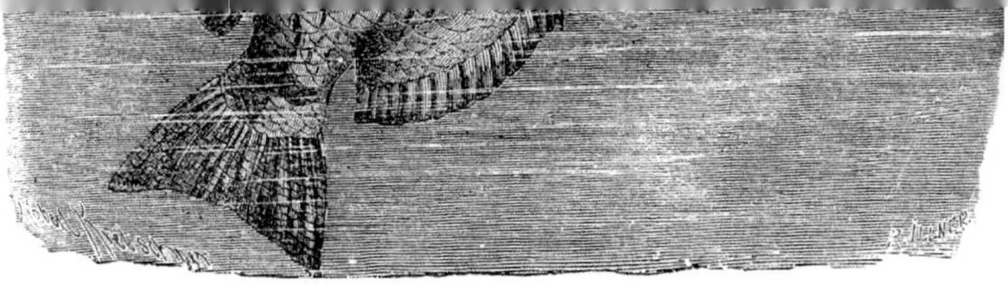

different worlds. Then the colonials wanted the lowlands too, and even foreigners had begun to lust after the white, oozing blood of the trees. Was that the real reason this one was trying to find *la Tierra sin Mal*? To stake his claim?

In the cantina where they had met, the Professor had shown Raul a rubbing of the fossil he had come to find: an enormous pennaceous feather from either the wing or tail of a bird far larger than any known on earth. But instead of shock, or even disbelief of the enormous size of the animal it must have come from, Raul said flatly, "You have come to hunt *Guyra Kyhje*," using the name that Anne's missionary uncle said the Indians had for a Terror Bird said to stalk their forest. The Professor tried to explain that he was not after a myth, nor a living creature, nor lost world, but evidence of an ancient bird frozen in rock: fossils of a prehistoric bird. Raul had muttered, "Why come so far for a rock?"

Why indeed? The Professor's mind often moved over the steps that had led him here: the arguments with colleagues over "the testimony of the rocks": they argued whether strata, such as those bared when Noah's Flood cut the Grand Canyon, could say anything about their age or only reveal the order in which layers were laid down; which meant that they argued over the Rev. James Ussher, Primate of All Ireland, who by totaling the ages of Adam's descendants calculated that the Earth began on October 23, 4004 B.C.; which meant they debated whether or not Noah's Flood was general over all the globe or only the result of a giant wave that inundated the "world" of the Old Testament as indicated by Prof. Winslow Wilson's discovery that seashells found in Noah's desert all pointed in the same direction; which meant that, given the fact that 40 days and 40 nights could not furnish rain enough to create a wave able to circle the globe, they appealed to geology for exegesis.

Three times, a world of plants and animals had flourished. And three times, all of earth's life had been extinguished. So clear was the book of bone and stone on this point that all agreed upon the Earth's three distinct chapters: Ancient (Paleozoic) Life; Middle (Mesozoic) Life, which in its turn vanished and was replaced by New (Cenozoic) Life. He could almost be convinced that the lineage of some animals present in The Garden ended forever in The Flood. But what confounded all sides was this question: Where did the new animals come from?

Some imagined a Divine Creator stepping in at the commencement of each Geological age. But the Bible only mentions one Garden, The Garden—and one mass extermination, Noah's.

Those who left out Scripture were even less convincing, using purely organic means—and the aide of galvanism—to explain how plants and animals might spontaneously arise. The evidence they accumulated was sound, even persuasive, but in total, to say that different plants and animals arose by their own nature was to believe that a castle could result from an avalanche of stones falling into place.

In any case, their materialist explanations did not eliminate the need for the Divine, for any series, no matter how long, has a beginning.

Wrapped in his sarape, Raul watched the Professor tossing in his sleep on the other side of the small fire they'd made to burn throughout the night. The howls of monkeys, rustle of raccoons, and hoots of owls calling to the souls of the dead kept him awake but Raul knew how foolish this was; it was when the animals went silent and the forest held its breath that some danger was present. Foreign *curepí* like him were a mystery: this one claimed parrots could become ducks, just as the Jesuits would have had him believe water turned into wine, bread into the flesh of a god, when one clearly remained water, the other bread. What was even more confusing was their insistence that their god could turn mud into a man while denying that men could become animals or animals men when, if left alone, the carcass of an armadillo would become a mound of maggots before their eyes.... When she was young, the Jesuits whipped his wife to force her to believe in their invisible sky god while right here on earth, the spirit of a murdered enemy often possessed a scorpion in order to seek revenge by burying its stinger into his victim as he slept....

That same old Guraní who had confirmed how few Spaniards it took to defeat the Indians had also told Raul of La Malinche, Cortez's concubine and translator who bore him a son, the first mestizo, like Raul—this detail had focused his attention—the spawn of an invader and a traitor to her people, vilified by all history for being a Judas—worse than a Judas, as Judas only betrayed their shaman, while La Malinche had sent generations to their crucifixion.

Before hearing this story, the people that Raul had seen on the street were just that, people. But as he grew older, he began to understand that Spaniards meant children like him when they said "Mestizo"; he began to see others for the creatures they were in the eyes of men like his father: the son of a Negro and Indian was to the Spaniard a "Wolf"; a Chamizo and Indian bear "Cambuja" fruit; the offspring of a Mulatto (little mule) and Mestiza was a "Wolf-Suspended-in-Air." "Zambrona," "Wolf Again," "Morisco," "Moor," "Cambujo," "Albarazado," "Barcino," "Chino...." The Spaniard who marries a Mestiza produces a "Castizo," while the Mestizo—as Raul was—who mates with an Indian—as his wife was—produced, in the eyes of Raul's father, a "Male Wolf-Return-Backwards." They, he and his wife, had named theirs "Christian."

To break the power of the Colonial elites, El Supremo had forbidden them or their land-inheriting descendants to marry each other, leaving Spaniards to either leave the country or marry mulattoes, mestizos, or natives. And though he had no proof, Raul always thought his father had traded a horse for the Indian who became his mother. Still, he didn't believe his father to be cut from the same cloth as the wealthy mule breeder who married the fairest Indian he could find, casting her aside the moment an even more light-skinned "Castiza" came to his attention. But Raul often wondered if his father would have had that in him had he had more money. Only the mule breeder's

fairest infants lived to be children because, people said, he simply murdered those that did not look enough like him. The other mule breeders thought that was 'natural.'

Christ's nails!—it was hard to sleep at night; a fluttering on his face made the Professor realize that he'd been awoken by a bat delicately biting the tip of his nose. The fire having burnt low, he found the heat of day replaced by a bone-chilling cacophony of monkey shrieks, insect clicks, and howls. He cinched his blanket around his neck to bar any snake that might be attracted to bed down against the warmth of his body.

Rubbing the insect bite he had received on his neck, he could feel that it had swollen to the size of a boil. Hot. It felt hot to the touch. "Raul?" he called to Raul's form, bowing his own hammock. Before wrapping himself in his serape, Raul had performed a night-time ritual, first praying a *Pater Noster* in Latin while placing the mystical beads of a rosary around his neck; then he repeated an incantation in his Indian tongue as he rhythmically kissed the small black fist he wore as a totem.

The Professor knew Raul was awake from the sound of his breathing; he was probably listening for the telltale snap of a twig, or a human cough that would give away one of the animals he believed men transformed into as the sun set. It was the reason they kept a fire burning all night. That and the jaguars. But the Professor had written in his journal *"The greatest danger to a colony of ants is another colony of ants,"* and man was the animal he most feared. Sometimes prospectors made up stories like those of the Terror Bird as a way to scare off competitors who they would otherwise murder. But Raul's stories were clearly more ancient than that, and so seemed to bode well for the prospects of finding in their settings the fossils of an ancient bird. "Tell me again about the Land-without-Evil: *la Tierra sin Mal*."

The question startled Raul. For the moment he continued to feign sleep. Missionaries were only interested in knowledge that seemed to confirm their own myths, like the story of Iporun, the great water that inundated the forest because people had stopped caring for it. In this story, torrential rains drowned all but the son of Irin-Magé, Tamendonar, Arikut, and their wives, who survived by climbing the tallest Genipa trees in the forest—much taller than those that exist today. When the flood receded, they descended to repopulate the earth.... The Tupinamba, Tamoio, Tupí-Guaraní and their other descendants all called that original forest *Ywy Mará Ey* or *la Tierra sin Mal*, as later generations called it: a land where there was no death and food grew without effort. But unlike the Christian god, Monan was not without pity; so once or maybe twice a century, He would inhabit the dreams of a chosen one to tell him where this land they all had originally come from might be and often an entire village would set out in search of it. Tribes they met along the way would as often as not join in, the pilgrimages gathering to them thousands of people, traveling for years, following the prophet's dreams, fasting to feed them, engaging in the great religious dances: as many as five thousand pilgrims would dance into the trances that would cleanse them, make them worthy of entering *Ywy Mará Ey*, until fever and exhaustion left them spent. One migration made it as far as the ocean; another to Maranhão; always the journeys had ended with pilgrims dying, the survivors returning, or being enslaved, or otherwise proving themselves as yet unworthy....

Spaniards like his father devoured these stories, believing the Indians were actually describing El Dorado—the land of unlimited wealth. The number of failed expeditions that these stories inspired led most Spaniards to give up, abandoning the places they described to myth. But the conviction of the Indians never waivered—*Ywy Mará Ey* remaining as real to them as the beating of their hearts.

Raul knew, because luna, his wife, or Lucia, as he still thought of her, had gone in search of *Ywy Mará Ey*—a prophet to herself. Like his mother, she had clung to the religious ways and dances, even when she had to perform them alone and in secret. Just as the priests were only interested in stories that corroborated their own, the Indians only pretended to believe the Christian corruptions of legends that had clearly grown out of the forest, and in this, displayed their truth: by feigning belief in fantasies like la Virgen Negra, they could both revere the animal spirt of ancestors and receive gifts from the priests.

After their child died of measles, though, Lucia—luna—drifted ever further from the ways of the whites to atone for the years she'd neglected Monan by pretending to be Christian. She increasingly talked about *Ywy Mará Ey*, and the kind of purification one must make to go there. He'd awake in the night to find her in the yard, in an *algarroba* trance, dancing in rotation with the stars, losing herself in the rhythm till there was no difference between the earth's turning and her own. He didn't think that

she believed that she was keeping their world turning in time with the earth, as the Tupí-Guaraní believed, or that she was performing witchcraft, as the priests would have said; rather it was that the dance kept *her* world turning, and her in it, and if either one of them stopped it would be a kind of death, or at least a world without her in it. Without their child. Then one day she was gone. And Raul knew where she was headed. But in which direction? Raul prayed for a sign—saying both a *paternoster* and a prayer to Monan.

Then this *curepí* appeared. And claimed to have some knowledge of where *la Tierra sin Mal* might be though he didn't use that name, and claimed to only be hunting for an ancient bird that had turned to stone. But Raul recognized his description of the land where he thought his stone bird might lie as what Christians called The Garden—and he suspected that the Professor didn't call it that because he didn't want anyone to know what he was really searching for.

"I've heard your Columbus believed it was here," Raul said, listening closely so he could note the man's reaction.

To his surprise, the Professor admitted it: Before the discovery of the New World, and even today, he said, many believed that The Garden of Eden was located at the antipode—the exact opposite point on the globe—of Mt. Calvary, where Christ was crucified. "Christopher Columbus spent the last years of his life searching tributaries of the very river we are on, looking for it."

"¿Aqui?" Raul, said, the quickness of his reply revealing that he was fully awake.

"Except Columbus died thinking that the Earth was round like an orange when it is actually more like a grapefruit—which meant that the antipode of Jerusalem is actually out in the Pacific. Maybe on some as yet undiscovered island. Like Tahiti, or a Galápagos, as Darwin thought."

Raul considered one pilgrimage that had ended at the coast, a vast ocean stretching before the people. They had thought that their prophet had misinterpreted his vision, and so continued up the coast where the few hundred who survived were put in chains and sold to a mine. But maybe the sea had been their final test. Maybe, if their souls had been lighter, they would have been able to fly across it. Or walk, as the priests claimed that the shaman Jesus had been able to do. If Lucia—luna—made it that far, how would he ever follow?

After Raul fell asleep, the Professor found his mind drifting to rosy-cheeked men lying and dying back home in America: maybe even men he once taught, and shared stories with, Professor Johnson and his son—men like him—swaddled like him in blankets that tomorrow would serve as their burial shrouds....

Cannon fire directed from balloons designed to study the atmosphere.... Lives extinguished by digital information: the dots-and-dashes issued by the fore-digit of military telegraph operators in offices too distant to hear the cries of those dying in the battles they ordained....

The America he would return to would be different from the one he left, he knew. Even before the war, the way of life he had known increasingly seemed to follow the fate of the old Woolfe cottage, not far from his college, erased a little more each year by field flowers and weeds and a thousand other tiny wedges that grew up through its floorboards. Vines pried its roof from its walls; frost and rain and seasons slowly but relentlessly reclaimed its wood and stone as their own. Years ago, Father Woolfe and his son had gone off to see one of the new "iron horses" that had begun to roar through the countryside. Standing on the tracks, they were unable to judge its incredible speed—35 M.P.H.—and were both struck and instantly killed. The news of their deaths was too much for Mother Woolfe to bear, and their home, the cabin they had built, fell to ruin. The land they had cleared went fallow, then wild. Already the ruin, built with fieldstone, notched logs, and other methods from the colonial frontier seemed out of place. The sight of it always put him in a melancholic mood, the way they say the silent ruins of Rome, or of a once grand castle or monastery can transport viewers to a world long gone. In not so many years, it would be hard to find any trace of the cottage. Or the people who built it. It would be as if they never existed. Even faster trains travelled those tracks now, racing to bring interchangeable arms to interchangeable men. Which side, other than the worms, was winning?

His thoughts were interrupted by the scuttling of an animal nearby in the bush, dragging the limp weight of some poor, lifeless and smaller creature....

Suddenly, the stars went black, then reappeared. In the moment it took for him to notice, a gust of wind blew up, whipping treetops and making the small campfire flicker. From deeper in the woods came the sound of splitting wood, then a piteous moan so human sounding that it filled the Professor with dread. Just as quickly it was all over. It was as though the stars had been obscured by a passing cloud when there were no clouds, as though the hand of God had passed above the trees, momentarily blotting out the stars.

Raul remained asleep on his side of the low fire. The Professor propped himself up on an elbow. Had he imagined it?—a gust of wind?—such as one that announces a storm, only a storm that was over in a single breath? A leaf—no, a feather—drifted down, was caught in an updraft from the fire, and then drawn in and consumed by the flames.

In the morning, Raul caught a swan. They had rounded a bend in the river when they spotted it, majestically gliding down to the water, wingspan of an angel. Raul motioned for the Professor's gun. By sitting very still and allowing the canoe to drift, they were able to get in close enough for him to kill it with a single shot. The gunshot was deafening in the quietude of the forest—like a rent in the fabric of reality—and sent up a tornado of birds from nearby trees.

On shore, Raul spoke to the swan gently; the Professor got the impression that he was saying a prayer over it. Or to it. Then Raul used his knife to cut off the bird's head. He held its beak shut and blew into its nostrils as the Professor had seen cockfighters revive their birds before sending them back into battle. Raul strung the head on a tong that he placed as a necklace around his neck.

As Raul dressed the bird, the Professor asked him, "Raul, where is your own gun?" Raul could feel the Professor's gaze bearing down on him. "Why did you need mine?" Raul kept working. "Tell me—did you lose yours when the canoe flipped?"

Raul shrugged to silence the man—let him think what he will—and when the Professor sulked away, Raul was glad to not have the *curepí*'s presence there to pollute his communion with the bird. Gently removing the swan's heart, he thought of the sad necessity, of the need to be pure of heart to enter *Ywy Mará Ey,* as both his mother and his wife had both told him, a land without evil where life was easy and where Lucia—luna—believed she would meet their son, if only she could find it. It was there, in The Beginning, that the owl called to Nhanderu to bring the night, and Nhanderu would bring the night. And when the dove cooed for Him to bring the morning, He would bring the morning. Hummingbirds fed people sweet nectar and manioc grew without labor. Then one day, an unknown animal arrived. He saw how lush the forest was, and said to himself, I would like to make this forest mine. But he was not quick enough to catch the swifts; and his fingers were too blunt to snag the coots. So he changed himself into an even fiercer animal—one that was silent, and stealthy, and had no name until the People gave it one: *Añag*—Jaguar.

The more birds *Añag* killed the more his kind multiplied. Together they killed so many birds that Nhanderu didn't know when to bring the night because the owl had been eaten, and the sun shone till it baked the forest dry. Another time, the darkness lasted almost 30 moons because *Añag* had killed the dove. With day and night confused, the banana and maize and manioc did not grow and there was much suffering among the People. They prayed to Nhanderu, and in reply Nhanderu girded Himself for another thing that the People did not know, war, and He did so by turning Himself into a bird no one had ever seen before—a bird larger and fiercer than *Añag*—a *Guyra Kyhyje*—a Terror Bird. In the form of the Terror Bird, Nhanderu set about cleansing His forest; whenever He killed an *Añag*, it changed as it died back into the man it had been all along, pale as a ghost. The greed, the senseless slaughter of the birds by these men caused Nhanderu's anger to overflow its banks, and He began to kill all men as He could not always tell the difference between those who were evil, and had come into His land as invaders, and the People who had always lived in His Garden in peace with the birds. And in fear, the People fled *Ywy Mará Ey*, what had been their home, this *Tierra sin Mal*, as those who came after them called it in the tongue that the invaders forced upon them. In the surrounding forests, they lived in fear of both the jaguar and the Terror Bird. And this is how they came to long for a return to their Garden; and this is how they came to their ritual: whenever they have the need to kill a bird for its meat or feathers, they wear it around their neck to ask forgiveness for the sad necessity, since the Terror Bird, which guards *Ywy Mará Eye*, could be watching them at any time from on high.... And Raul performed the ritual, as Lucia—luna—said anyone who wants to enter *Ywy Mará Ey* must, in order to keep his intentions pure. It—purity—was the reason that before leaving town, Raul had unpacked and left behind his gun, even his *facón*.

The Professor had never eaten swan before. Calmer now, he remarked upon how similar it was to duck. When he had been young, Raul said, sucking the marrow from a bone, swans had been plentiful. As he spoke, the Professor could see feather lice abandoning the swan's head and trying to find a blood meal, jumping onto Raul's flesh and hair. Inexplicably, Raul let them.

Indeed, so common was it to come upon a mating pair, Raul continued, that everyone used to keep a device for hunting swans in their kit: a leather thong with a wooden ball attached to each end. Swans had not yet learned to fear man, Raul said, so one could approach until he was close enough to throw his device in such a manner that the weight of the balls would wrap the thong around the swan's neck. Since the wooden balls could float, the swan couldn't escape by diving. Wistfully, Raul added that he wished he knew what hidden lagoon all the swans had retreated to, though in secret he was heartened by the realization that the sight of a swan was a sign that they may be approaching it—a lagoon remote enough to have swans that did not know man—and still moved between this world and *Ywy Mará Ey*.

The Professor had heard this lament before: in Rio de Janeiro they told of a whale fishery, once thriving, that had been forced to shutter after the whales left that part of the coast, and the story had brought to mind the 100 whaling ships that visit the tiny outpost at Galápagos each year: according to Darwin's *Voyage*, whalers used to only need a few hours to harvest 800 turtles, so thick were their swarms. But by the time he arrived, hunting parties required two days to obtain the same quantity. The sailors believed that the tortoises had retreated to more secluded spots, but Darwin speculated that the animals grew very slowly, noting the dates that previous hunting parties had carved into the shells of those too heavy to lift. One old tortoise, whose shell had a seven-foot circumference, had the year 1786 carved into it. Perhaps the recession of the animals was related to the vanishing of peoples? In answer to Humboldt's many questions about the strange names for landmarks along the Orinoco River he had been brought before a parrot. The parrot could say many of these names but no one could understand what else it said about them because it spoke the language of the Atures, an extinct tribe that the old bird was said to mourn in the words of the last Atures Indian who had owned it, and loved it, and cared for it, and had taught it to speak in a language that, when the parrot died, would die with it.

Even here, the Professor had overheard a Portuguese slaver bemoaning the diminishing number of Indians available for his trade due to their increasing ability to hide, a skill they had become so adept at that, he claimed, some tribes had learned how to make themselves invisible.

As they paddled, Raul could tell that they had entered an older part of the forest. Just as the river sounded different depending on its depth, so the symphony of leaves around them sounded different, smelled different, though he couldn't say exactly how. His mother would have been able to. To her it was as easy as it would be to him to find his way around town by estimating how far he stood from the church's bell tower. Yet whenever he would ask her how she knew where they were, she'd only laugh, saying it was too obvious to explain.

It hadn't been obvious to Lucia—Iuna. How he wished he'd never agreed to help her find her home forest. They had only been married long enough for him to know that he had married a virgin when she surprised him by saying that Lucia wasn't her real name. Her real name was Iuna. She'd told him how she had been a girl, just before her change, when she had been traveling through a part of the forest that her tribe often went to during the berry time of year. As they were picking *ñangapirí* berries, they discovered a rabbit in the bush that had died, and Mainumby, a cousin, fell into a profound sadness at the sight. Mainumby's brother had been named Tapiti, that is, Rabbit. Tapiti had recently died, so being in the presence of the dead rabbit had put Mainumby in the presence of the spirit of his beloved and gentle brother. As he was holding the rabbit, and stroking it, and telling it how much their family missed him, a *curepí* appeared, claiming that the dead rabbit was his: that he had wounded it, then tracked its blood trail here, and was now claiming its pelt.

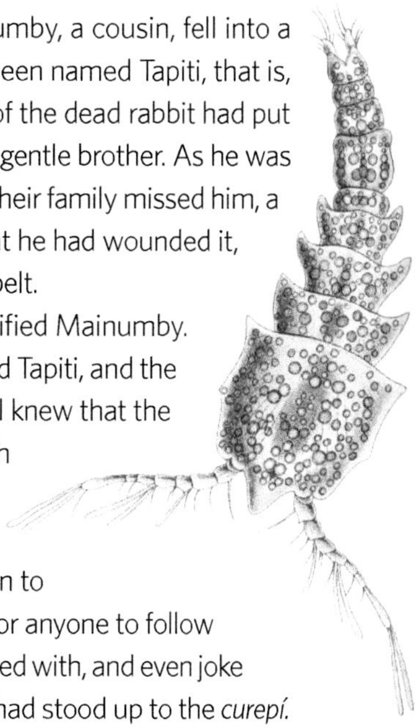

The thought of this monster skinning his brother horrified Mainumby. He and the other men formed a wall between the *curepí* and Tapiti, and the *curepí*, seeing that he was outnumbered retreated. They all knew that the man would be back, though, and that he would come with others, so they abandoned their berry picking and hurried back into the forest. After they thought they had gone far enough, they stopped to rest. By then it had begun to rain. And since it was raining, they knew it would be hard for anyone to follow them. They began to talk, and eat the berries they had escaped with, and even joke how Tapiti would have thought it was funny, the way they had stood up to the *curepí*. Suddenly there was a clap of thunder and Mainumby fell. It wasn't thunder. It was a rifle shot and it had killed Mainumby instantly. A second shot fell Mbyja Ko'ê but the bullet must have hit bone and ricocheted as it also fell Iuna's mother.

Everyone scattered, running in as many directions as there were people. Mbyja Ko'ê lie still, dead. Iuna's mother was only wounded but was unable to move. She begged Iuna to run, but Iuna refused to leave, instead draping herself over her mother, weeping, and praying until the *curepí* threw her aside. They fell upon her mother with machetes.

In their attackers' minds, Iuna's refusal to leave confirmed what they already knew, that Indian children were loyal animals. Like dogs. They gave her to a white family but because she was in such despair she never worked, or even spoke, and the family traded her to another family for an actual dog. This was the family that she was still living with when Raul found her.

She and Raul had been married for little over a year when she began asking him to find the church where she had been baptized to see if there were any record as to where she had been taken captive. She was hoping that this information might help her discover the location of her home forest, and maybe her People.

As though it were yesterday, Raul could remember going with her from church to church. In the neighboring province of San Prudencio, they entered a gloomy, stone church, squat as a chopping block. Politely, Raul introduced himself to the priest, and explained that Lucia was trying to find her first family, so she could thank them for the kindness they had shown her as a child.

Unable to read, she stood beside Raul, nervously fidgeting, as he turned the pages of the heavy leather-bound registers placed before them, running his finger down through the years they thought the murders might have happened. Thinking back on it, Raul could still hear her heart pounding with the rhythm of the names, *Isabella, Maria, Maria*.... Then her name jumped out: *Lucia*. The register listed the first family that had "taken her in," as the book put it. She had been rescued from a battlefield, the cramped note explained, after her rescuers had been attacked by Indians. The child was named Lucia, after Santa Lucia, whose feast day was celebrated on the date she was saved.

Does the world anyone thinks he lives in actually exist? the Professor wondered, the actual forest all around little like what he had thought a "forest" was before he came. Or does it exist in the manner of the equator?—a dotted line encircling the globe, made by men in order to guide men. From the Earth's point of view, there is no line, no division. Only Earth. And something similar was surely true of Nature. Instead of dividing the world and their lives with grids as did Europeans with their clocks and calendars, the lives of those who lived in it were shaped by the movement of its animals, the ripening of its fruits, the seasons of its fish, and in this they were all equals, and in this their lives bore as much relation to his idea of Nature as the river did to his map. And if this was true of Nature, then so the Cosmos? And if true of the Cosmos, then the division between the living and the dead surely begins to feel false, the bonds between people as strong, if as invisible, as the ether between planets.... Each star was a spirit waiting to be born, as Raul explained it, and accounted for the fact that the sleepy nature of the turtle or the industriousness of the ant could also be seen animating men. Spirts lived on by moving from one host to another, and the Professor certainly felt something akin to this from the strong emotion he felt toward Elizabeth, though she'd been gone these 18 years. Yet, he knew how this sounded to even his own ears, so asked, Was it so unreasonable to believe in an afterlife?—what were they, him and his colleagues, the creatures of the forest all around, Raul and the Indians—if not an "after" to whatever life had filled these spaces before? Who was to say this life, the one that filled the earth now, wasn't simply the life we pass through on our way to another? Why should such an idea seem implausible when, as the Indians believed, it was incarnate everywhere, a mother's life serving as the conduit through which the life of her child must pass to emerge into the life we call the world? Why couldn't the world itself be the mother we all pass through on our way to another? *Tierra sin Mal.* Was that idea any more bizarre than the fact that while we think these thoughts, we stand on a globe rolling around the sun at 65,000 miles per hour?

He gave a chuckle to think what his colleagues would think of him if they could hear his thoughts or see him now—The Last of the Mohicans—a living fossil as some Natural Historians thought of Indians: primitives who stood in relation to modern man as the woolly mammoth did to the modern elephant—a real antique—pushing a crude canoe against the current.

At meetings of the Science Society, he'd had the growing sense of his younger colleagues treating him as though he had arrived wearing a three-cornered hat. Talking to these men was to witness an entire way of life—his tribe of Natural Historians—dying out around him. He could see that discussion of Grand Natural History was of no more interest to this new generation than a grab bag of old legends.... He could see their minds wander as he spoke, their eyes move about the room for more engaging company, while each successive year brought students who knew less about the body of knowledge that the Natural Historians of his generation had spent a lifetime struggling to amass.

The age of the earth....

Granted, the world changes. Granted: all must be based on the bedrock of observation....

In his darkened office, he'd considered the years of deprivation, of sandfly bites he had endured to collect prairie dog specimens; he considered how the calluses on his hands matched the worn handle of his geology hammer; the hot library attics he had sweat in, laboring to wrestle into sense a jumble of curiosities. He had spent a lifetime to arrive at the point where he was able to understand how those before him saw each bit of nature as a portal to All of Nature, and then, just as he was able to add to this conversation, those around him stopped listening, narrowing the scope of their focus in the name of what they called 'scientific observation' until that's all they had: barometric readings; observations through the compound microscope; star positions.... But no History. No overarching Story of Stories that brought physics, astronomy, chemistry, geology—all the sciences—together, along with those of man and art and all the Cosmos.... It was as if he had spent a lifetime learning Greek so he could read Aristotle in the original only to have that held against him, once he was able to do so, as a sign of being old-fashioned.

Still, it was easier to imagine the earth slowing to a stop than to think he was transforming into the ancient parrot Humboldt had been shown, the last remnant of a whole way of life, the last remnant of his tribe: Φυσικοί ιστορικοί, Historians of Nature....

But on his desk was a book, *Photo-graphs of British Algae,* by a woman, no less. "The plates within this book are impressed by the agency of Light alone," it said, "'photo-graphs,' without any aid whatever from the artist's pencil." Looking at "photos" of algae, bones, and fossils, he felt he was looking upon his own death certificate, the accuracy of photos that younger naturalists heaped praise upon having nothing to do with their relation to the Cosmos, their cold, unthinking objectivity the very thing that made them shallow, brutal, in the Professor's estimation: still-lifes in the literal sense of the Latin, *natura mort*. They seemed especially dead when compared to those magnificent watercolors they were said to replace: Edward Lear's *Illustrations of the Family of Parrots,* or Robert Hooke's *Micrographia,* with its meticulously observed drawing of a flea. On the walls of his office he had hung hand-colored reproductions of Albertus Seba's shells with their bright striations no photo could ever capture—as much art as science. What "photo-graph" could ever understand the detail in an insect's leg minutely enough—dare he say it?—lovingly enough—to reveal the individual hairs seen through a microscope?—the artist-naturalists who created those drawings obviously combining specimens from dozens of expeditions into their single figure. Or hundreds of hours of looking: the way an astronomer gazes at Jupiter or the moon for nights on end to create a single sketch of its features, waiting patiently for the constant roil of humidity, temperature and turbulence in the earth's atmosphere to calm enough to give him a clear view of the planet—just a glimpse, just enough for a stroke of the pencil—then he waits, eye fixed to the telescope's eyepiece, waiting for nature to afford him another clear glimpse, another stroke; then another; and only by bringing together the totality of all of these fleeting glimpses, harvested over months of cold winter nights when the sky was the most dry and so transparent, was he able to make a drawing of stunning clarity that no single look, that is, no camera, would ever be able to convey.

This is something a Mr. Church, a Mr. Bierstadt understood, imbuing their paintings with the exact mood of the sky after a storm, or the blue glow of an iceberg that you know must be true for the way it transports you to that distant place. The blur of a hummingbird's wings; the metallic green-to-purple sheen of a mallard's head....

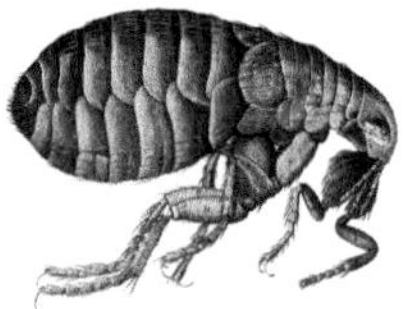

Unlike the lie of a "photo," these fleeting moments reveal a nature that does not stand still as a corpse but flickers into and out of being and gives an intimation of the world of becoming in which the beads of morning dew on a spider's web are in passionate communion with the sun, and as they evaporate, show our world to be ever changing and entwined, the forest, the glen, and indeed all the Cosmos, one living, breathing Being—the very thing these new scientists hope their photos will strip away....

The Indians understand this, the Professor thought, perhaps better than anyone. The names they used for themselves were the names they used for the animals they lived among, and ate, or were eaten by—*Chachugi* for white-lipped peccary; *Brioagi* for buzzard—and explained why they spoke of them as they would their family, while trading a tree for a hatchet could be as appalling as trading away a friend, say nothing of the commands, rules, sins, and laws the Spaniards wanted them to live by and which they would have none of....

An improved means to an unimproved end.

Then one day, that world of a Mr. Church, a Mr. Bierstadt, Audubon, Humboldt, and the Indians was no more.

He gave the paddle a rough pull.

What's more, there was no one left who could remember why it had mattered.

Through the shallow water, Raul and the Professor could see two fish moving in tune with one another, but also with the stream: their shiny silver bodies hovered just above the sandy bottom, held there by the slow undulations of their fins, but also it seemed by some contented hum within the earth. It made them easy to catch.

Raul had pulled over at a bend in the river where a large quantity of driftwood had accumulated. After a lunch of the two blackened fish, he sat smoking, opposite the small fire. They spoke little, both being tired from paddling against a current. The Professor offered a few tales of his tramps through the Connecticut Valley in search of bird fossils. He'd hoped that by talking about his own home, Raul would offer more about the Land-without-Evil, and maybe some clues as to what fossils it might contain.

The Professor told him of the steamer trip he had taken from New York to Rio de Janeiro, and then Santos. He told him of the ceremony held aboard the ship as it crossed the equator. He described the great gale that the ship had been caught in, accompanied by such lightning and waterspouts that even the saltiest of the sailors feared all was lost. In the morning, he and the other passengers emerged from below deck to blue skies, and what had to have been a sign of their salvation: the ship's rigging completely covered by the most beautiful butterflies, blown from the shore, which at that point was still more than 100 miles beyond the horizon.

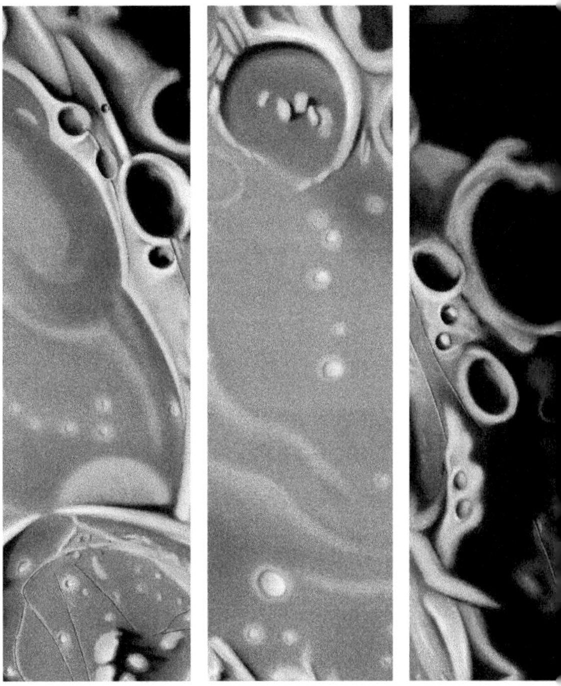

Approaching Buenos Ayres, what he had first thought were mountains in the distance revealed themselves to be, as they neared, enormous heaps of coal at the mouth of the harbor. So cheap was this method of importation, and so great the demand, that coal-burning ships bearing loads of coal were said to form a veritable wagon train across the Atlantic. "It won't be long before naturalists will be able to come up river on a fossil-hunting expedition in a boat fitted with a steam engine of English design," he said, "his teak cabin outfitted with all the books he could want, as well as a comfortable bed, crystal dinnerware, bottle of cognac, and a man servant dressed in white linen to pour it...."

The guide only grunted as though to acknowledge his reception of this information. To the question of whether he thought they would find the Rev. Eastwood alive, the man only shrugged. He didn't believe the rumor that the Reverend was living in the jungle with a "regular A-rabian harem" of women, as men in the cantina had said. When asked what he did believe, Raul made an eating motion.

The professor sat there puzzled. When it dawned on him what Raul had meant, he blurted out, *cannibals?*—the guide shook his head, then pointed to a boar print in the moist earth, followed by that of a jaguar, then a long line of scavenger ants.

Back on the river, they paddled in silence; Raul could tell it had rained up stream as the current had grown stronger, making it harder to push the canoe. The large *palo borracho* trees that lined both banks were thick as pillars in church. His mother could read a history of wet and dry seasons from the bulge in the belly of these "jug trees," as she called them. They raised an archway of vines over the river with the morning mist rising up into their branches as the incense that priests used to imitate clouds in their churches. Being back among people who called the forest home, he understood how his wife could have no god save one: Nature Herself, which was both omnipotent and omnipresent, as the priests claimed for their god. Source of wonder, source of fear. Reverence and terror. Temple and home, but also pantry, toilet, medicine, and war chest. The whites he lived among had the attitude that when they went into a church, hospital, or school they were entering three different worlds. But here there was only the forest, and it was all of these. And it was none of these. Unlike the Catedral de Asunción, which had been modeled on the priests' idea of their sky god—gilt angels and heavenly hosts on the ceiling, crypts forming an underworld of rotting citizens beneath the living who stood in prayer on the main floor—here, the organ and choir and all the rest were part of a living, beating body, the parishioners living the ceremony, not spectators to it. Last night, as he lay watching fireflies above, he'd seen one's yellow glow suddenly illuminate the face of a bat just as the bat devoured it. The bat's unhinged jaws and fangs gave its face the ghoulish aspect of a living gargoyle, reminding him how in this cathedral the monsters were real, and all around, not just outside on the ramparts, the sacred space undemarcated from the profane, its very life growing out of a compost of forgotten dead. The forest people feared the Terror Bird like a god; but he knew it could have many forms—a scorpion, a jaguar, a mosquito, man, or the measles that had carried away his and Iuna's son....

As they paddled, Raul's silence made the Professor regret that he had talked about coming up river in a steamboat. Talk like that was why the natives had been suspicious, suspecting as some did that he had come to hunt their Terror Bird—at least as Raul had explained it—and why some of them would have none of him or his hatchet head, that is, a thing with the power to upset their moral order, just as the steam engine, the telegraph key, had upset the moral order of his society. As soon as he handed it over, an argument had erupted, with one man accidentally cutting his hand on the blade. As the Professor and Raul paddled away, the Indian who had roughly grabbed it out of his hands used it to chop down a tree that they all once would have worked together to fell, causing the base of the trunk to smolder as they took turns chipping away at it with their stone axes. The scene had reminded the Professor of the story an explorer had once told him about the Indians of Greenland, and how the breakup of sea ice sometimes caused polar bears to come ashore, whereupon the Indians who lived there would band together to fight these monsters. Afterwards, at raucous banquets to celebrate the vanquishing of the bear (with the bear as the main course), the relish with which they recounted the acts of bravery, or cowardice, displayed in the fight made the explorer think that they actually welcomed these dangerous encounters: that something majestic, if terrifying, would go out of the world if these bears were to suddenly vanish: a loss we might feel, he said, trying to explain the story to himself, if every polar bear was suddenly taken from the world, though other kinds of bears yet exist.

A realization made the Professor stop paddling: Had Raul purposely rocked the canoe? Had he tried to sabotage the journey to appease the natives who were afraid that if he killed their Terror Bird, the only world they knew would die with it?—just as the preachers back home worried that Darwin would explain away their angry, vengeful God and thus diminish the world, the way storms at sea would lose their power to awe if they lost their power to kill, the "fury" of a nor'wester reduced to an inconvenience or irritation?...

When Raul spoke, he betrayed the fact that he had also been thinking about the forest and their place in it. But his fears were embodied at a smaller scale, the various parasites that lived in country: the Penis Eel, a worm rumored to wriggle its way into the bloodstream of a man by going up his reproductive organ as he bathed in the river.

Or the Werewolf Flea, which drove men howling insane by burrowing far enough up the anus so that the flea, and its incessant itching, couldn't be reached.

Such talk made the Professor think he felt something wriggle under the skin of his neck. Warm.

All morning, the insect bite he had received at departure had been swelling; now it was the size of a large boil. It did not itch, though it did remain oddly warm to the touch. Seeing him rub it, Raul offered to lance the boil but the Professor waved him away. "What, this mosquito bite?" he said, laughing off his "Paraguayan Welcome." Secretly, though, he began to worry, and took a sulfur pill as a precaution.

By midday, the swelling had begun to subside.

Later that afternoon he allowed Raul to lance the boil, which he did with the razor-sharp knife he always carried in his boot, heated over a small fire. The professor winced, but so deftly did Raul make the incision that the Professor didn't realize that the job was done until he opened an eye to find Raul standing there, examining the blade.

"Well?" the Professor asked, anxious.

Raul only shrugged, wiping the knife on his pants before returning it to his boot.

Using the rhythm of his own paddling, Raul marked the fact that the Professor's strokes were becoming fewer, and weaker, and the sight gave him strength. Before setting out, Raul had feared that his Spanish blood would be his Original Sin—his nature—just as luna, raised as Lucia, still had the Indian longing for *Ywy Mará Ey,* or the way a Christian, even if taken as an infant and raised as a Jew, will always harbor a taste for pork—even if he didn't know why. Was that why he had reacted as he had—shooting the swan before with no more thought? He tried to recall what the Indians said about *Ywy Mará Ey* and birds like swans. He also tried to recall more specifically the conversations his father would have with herdsmen about *la Tierra sin Mal.* From the first conquistadors to the present, expeditions to find those *'el dorados'* ended in disaster, the men becoming lost in swamps or mountains, or falling prey to malarial insects, starvation, snakes, or poison darts in the hot lowlands—proof to the Indians that *Ywy Mará Ey—la Tierra sin Mal*—could only be approached by the pure of heart while the forest would summon its tortures for the undeserving.... The thought made Raul pick up his pace. Like a river that quickens as it draws near to a fall, he could feel himself being drawn forward—forgiven, even welcomed—while their approach seemed to sap the strength of the *curepí* he carried along with him....

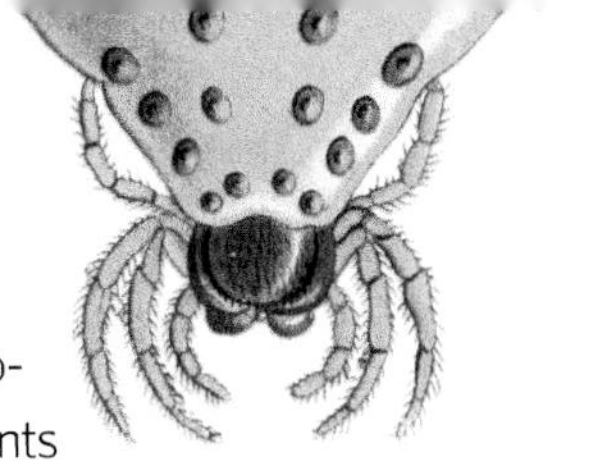

Lancing the boil seemed to make Raul oddly talkative, even invigorated; he described poison tree frogs, toe-eating fungi—all the torments Nature had in store for those who would play the part of Actaeon before he was torn apart by his own hunting dogs. By midafternoon Raul had said more words than he had uttered during the entire trip up to that point, at times growing excited, as though the exotic insect and snake bites he had witnessed, and the howling agony they caused, were adventure stories whose retelling he relished.

As Raul spoke, the Professor became hotter and hotter. His paddle grew heavy. Though back home he could row for hours without fatigue, here, he could feel his limbs grow heavy, making him wonder if being nearer the earth's equator somehow made the force of gravity stronger in this part of the world. He didn't think it was malaria as he didn't have any of its chills....

Existing only as a voice from behind, Raul's murmur worked as a hypnotist's bob, lulling the Professor toward lethargy. Raul related folktales about a jungle that could have come from a storybook, the methodic rhythm of his voice at times indistinguishable from the continual hum of the forest, issuing from the very air, from within the Professor's own head. The Professor could have been an infant in a cradle rocked by Mother River as Raul's voice droned on about forest people with strange, animalistic rituals and animals with humanlike cunning: here, there was no quarrel between the theories of fixed or unchanging species and those of monkeys that kidnapped children to raise as their own, or snakes that could hiss in imitation of human speech....

The Professor would have succumbed completely to drowsiness if the heat in his body didn't make him so uncomfortable. His shirt clung to his back. He looked up expecting to see a merciless sun beating down and was surprised to find only the deep green of the forest canopy. As though trapped in the restless sleep of a bad dream, his thoughts kept returning to the Terror Bird, to the increasing frequency with which it figured in the letters that Miss Eastwood received from her uncle, and, as she put it, how it became increasingly difficult to tell what her uncle meant by the "Terror Bird." Did he mean it as he originally had, as a figure of speech, like the Boogeyman, which he at first thought the natives used to frighten children or explain the disappearance of a tribe member taken by the slavers who roamed the forest and were a constant danger to wilderness Indians? For a while she thought it was a euphemism for the secret guilt that she suspected he hid within himself. But later she came to wonder if her uncle meant "Terror Bird" as the Indians meant it: an actual animal.

"...a huge black bird with the body of a jaguar. Eyes the yellow of an old wolf's canines," Raul was saying, "and a predator's single-minded, holy intelligence...."

The Professor tried to remember bringing up the subject of the bird. When he couldn't, he wondered if he had been speaking his thoughts out loud without realizing it. Then he saw that what he had mistaken for calmness in Raul's voice was actually a soberness about the giant bird that the Indians said guarded the inner sanctuary of the forest. As evidence, Raul related a tale of one lone prospector who had been carried off by the enormous bird as Sinbad had been carried off by a Roc in *The Arabian Nights*, then torn apart and fed to Terror Bird hatchlings in a nest the size of a thatched hut.

"And you have seen this bird?" the Professor asked.

The question silenced the man. Then he muttered, "Many have." He described glimpses of a huge black bird seen through a screen of trees. Hunting parties that had discharged their guns into the sky to no effect. Tufts of feathers snagged in brambles....

As the Professor suspected, the man had no more evidence than twice-told tales; shadows at night; or an odd, unidentifiable smell.... Still, he realized that such stories lived on for reasons: often to scare off others, but sometimes they were the narrative remnants of a past that may have had some actual fearsome creature at its heart. A disturbing thought came to mind: Symmes' Hole—the theory that prehistoric animals found only in the fossil record were not only not extinct but living in the subterranean chambers of a hollow earth. Symmes had maintained that an entrance hole must exist at one of the poles, by which he meant an inaccessible, and therefore undiscovered place. But wouldn't it make even more sense to be here?—in an equally inaccessible jungle? Had Symmes only been wrong about its location?

From between the pages of his journal the Professor retrieved the rubbing. *Orintho giganteus,* he had written beneath it. The creases of the folded paper made a grid across the veins of the enormous feather such as a scientific survey might overlay onto a plot of wild forest. Why had he decided it was thousands of years old? A sickish feeling came over him as he realized the answer: presumption. It was possible that the feather was much younger. Geology could only provide the sequence of events, not their ages, and depending on how it had been petrified, the stone might not be stone at all but hardened clay. Not an imprint laid down millennia ago, but only yesteryear: not the record of a monster from a remote past, but a living primitive.

Then he laughed. Laughed out loud at himself. If that lone prospector had been regurgitated into the hungry mouths of Terror Bird hatchlings, how had he told his tale?

The trek inland was slow going. The Professor had expected the mission to be on the river. Raul scoffed. A hunter sets his traps where his prey can be found, not where it is convenient for you to go, he said, and the Guaraní never stayed in one place. Not even for god. This was why strangers who entered the forest were as obvious to them as men blowing bugles, and how the Guaraní had managed to survive to this day: no matter how stealthily slaving parties slipped into the forest, sooner or later they'd discover that the Guaraní had set fire to the forest all around them.

"Cuidate," Raul said, leading him around a trail of warrior ants: an entire race of ants animated by the spirit of the fiercest fighter, he said. They bit with such ferocity that their pinchers would remain embedded in the flesh, even if the ants were decapitated. Natives used the ants as a kind of suture. And as a torture, and Raul wanted to give them a wide berth so as to not anger them. Then they lost time looking for the *achiote* plant Raul needed to paint red, serpentine patterns on their legs as a talisman against snakes.

The forest floor had a soft sponginess, a damp carpet of leaves giving way beneath each step, and the Professor realized he was walking on the dead: a layer of earth-in-the-making, the countless leaves, plants, insects, and animals that had once been alive now rotting beneath their feet. Green shoots rose from this grave. And he suddenly had the thought that we're all going to die. A fact that even children knew, of course. But moving through the dense fecundity around him, the realization came to him with a deeper level of conviction than he had ever known: an echo of the intimation he had once had holding a stone spearpoint in the collection of an amateur conchologist who had discovered it. It had been lodged in the rib of a mastodon: irrefutable proof that someone had come, struggled, and then died. The smooth stone had fit his hand so perfectly he could have been the spearpoint's author, and as he ran a finger along its tool marks, he'd thought, 'That man is I.' Engulfed in the superabundance of life around him now, he felt something similar, the relentless growth coming to him as a terrible thing: a wearying, relentlessness of life dying into life, only to give forth so much more life that it could only live by eating itself.

The tree canopy seemed to cast the day in a perpetual twilight and the gloom brought to mind Mr. Johnson, a colleague: Inspired by the early discoveries of mastodon teeth found by slaves in South Carolina, Mr. Johnson had set off for the South. The deeper into the South he traveled, though, the more horrified he was by the depth of human suffering. The daily beatings that everyone in the North had heard of, the tales of women abused by white masters who then tore babes from their mothers' arms to sell like cattle—children turned into animals by their own fathers— all of this came vividly to life around him—not as a lurid abolitionist pamphlet, but with the density and inescapability of Reality itself—for blacks, whose every breath was ruled over, and for the whites as well, who had transformed themselves into the kind of brute required to inflict such unrelenting misery on others. Projecting jaws with large, open mouths; bowed legs; and other repulsive features were common among the slave-owning class, Mr. Johnson had reported. The son of a particularly brutal, Irish slave driver had been born with semi-horny excrescences all over his body. But the excursion reached its nadir when Mr. Johnson entered Biggin Swamp, his destination, which he'd been told harbored a bonanza of ancient bones. There, he found a yellowed tibia within minutes. Then a fibula. Then a skull, and the truth of his discoveries sunk in: they were all human bones. Not fossils. That dismal swamp was a refuge for runaway slaves, he came to learn. Driven by hunger, the runaways would sometimes try to earn scraps of food from lumber camps by bringing out logs from places too mosquito and snake infested for the whites to venture into. Instead of being paid at the end of their labors, these runaways would just as often discover that the lumbermen had sold them to slave hunters who were waiting with shackle and whip.

Mr. Johnson had been interrupted in his work of searching for mastodon bones by cries so piteous that they sent a shiver of dread through him. Drawn to a clearing, he discovered there a group of white men abusing a runaway slave for his inability to get up and walk any further. Burn marks, from the firebrand that still smoldered nearby, revealed how the slavers had extracted the hiding place of others, who were chained, huddled in fear. Then, as casually as wiping a shoe, they held his head in the swamp water and drowned him.

When Mr. Johnson returned to the college, and described the world they'd made of interlocking cruelties.... His eyes misted up as he fell silent. He grasped the Professor's arm and implored, What god had heart hard enough to allow it?

Suddenly an orchid of astonishing pink.

The Professor paused, pretending to examine it though really, he just wanted to rest. Catching sight of the Professor suddenly motionless, Raul whirled about, machete raised, obviously thinking that the Professor had frozen at the sight of a snake. Not wanting Raul to think any less of him than the man already did, he picked up a rock, pretending to examine it for fossils. Raul tsk'd loudly, impatiently informing the Professor as if he were a child that there was no gold in this part of the country.

Raul took the stone from the Professor and used it to sharpen his machete, keeping an eye on him. A story was what brought the man here, he saw, as had been true for so many missionaries, explorers, adventurers, men of god and gold before him, the stories they created in turn bewitching their lives, even the very earth, as relentlessly, as patiently, as water....

His own story may as well stretch to the edges of the earth, he also saw, and somewhere within it was *Ywy Mará Ey*. Or so thought Iuna. He had tried to convince her that there was no *Ywy Mará Ey* or *la Tierra sin Mal*, Garden, El Dorado, or whatever a land without evil could be called, the illusion of words like 'miracle,' and 'Lucia,' and 'scripture,' and 'mestizo,' and 'nature' able to be spun into stories with the power of a spell to make people believe that things that had never happened had happened. He had hoped she'd see the truth in this by recalling the Christian myths that had been thrust upon her. But the more luna spoke of finding *Ywy Mará Ey*, describing how their son had begun to come to her in her dreams, the more she came to believe it was less of a place to go to as one that could be brought into existence.... Now she was out here somewhere, trying, while he was what?.... He looked at the Professor, breathing hard, rubbing the knot on his neck, and he felt foolish for once thinking that the man might lead him to her.

Even if they stumbled upon a *Ywy Mará Ey*, Raul realized, he probably wouldn't recognize it, not if it was more of a place that was made rather than discovered: luna and her people were as much part of the forest as its moss, as its vines, as the fish in its rivers; their being had knit with that of the forest since its beginning while he.... He wore boots. And therein was the divide—the stories he'd been told of creation and its flood coming to him as histories of people and places long dead, not prophecies of worlds to be—and there weren't any Genipa trees tall enough to climb to escape another cleansing.

He looked at the Professor sitting there like a sagging sack of sand. "The forest is making you ill," he said, throwing the stone back into the bush. But he also knew that they were making the forest ill and in response it was trying to purge itself by vomiting them out. Still, he kissed the charm he wore around his neck, then tightened the laces on his boots. He tried to purge his mind of the discouraging thoughts he had just had and replace them with what he had seen of all truth seekers, be they luna, the Professor with his rocks, priests, or men like himself: that they will see it when they believe it.

When they continued, the Professor wished he hadn't stopped walking. The pause had broken the rhythm of his step and now he could feel his body rebelling against the renewed effort. Instead of being carried by his legs, he felt as though he were dragging them forward with each step. He walked into a cloud of mites, swallowing several before he realized he had breathed them in, and coughed for several minutes, unable to clear their bodies from his throat.

Dark sweat stains gave Raul's back the patterns of a Castniid moth that, in order to keep up, the Professor pretended to follow. Cicadas buzzed so incessantly that the sound filled his head. Then the forest would fall silent so abruptly that it seemed it had all been a dream. Then the cicadas started buzzing, the buzz of one waking another, then dozens, and hundreds, and thousands.

He felt the Moroccan notebook against his breast where he always kept it and the sketches within were like a weight; the snails, insects, leaves, and sentiments he had tried to depict by his own hand such crude caricatures: together they were less of a map of observations than of him, a no-one, an everyone who ever returned from the seashore with a shell or wave-polished stone they had been unable to return. Or found the imprint of a fossilized fern, or insect entombed in the amber of its time and felt compelled to sketch it, to name it, and so name himself. He had loved the scent of lilac. Of her hair. Of woodlands. The feel of warm hearth stones on a winter morning, and the smell of bread baking. Of sweat and muscle ache too, tramping dried riverbeds and outcroppings, moved too easily by starlight, by music, by confusion at foreign tongues in the cantina, or humiliation from his colleagues, or fear of death during the storm at sea....

At sea, all sea stories are true, a deckhand had told passengers who doubted his tales of sea serpents. Now, weak with the sensation that he was being digested by some immense creature, the Professor saw how humans were always at sea. Isn't that why he had longed for some balloon, or better, some magic carpet ride to rise above it, above the forests and mountains and clouds, high enough to look back and see the earth as the blue marble depicted in mechanical planetariums. In the planetarium owned by his college, a candle could be put into the sun so that its warm, yellow light bathed earth, and cast a crescent shadow on the pearl that was its moon. And yet, anyone who has lived near a harbor has seen the sight of storm-battered sailors falling to their knees to kiss the earth the instant they stepped ashore.

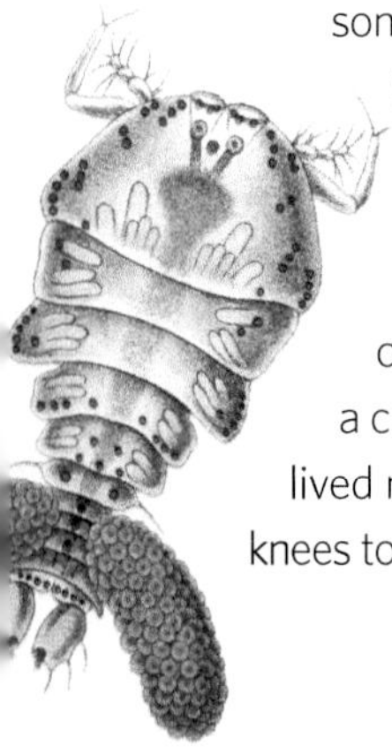

The next time they stopped they both had reason: a crease in the vegetation revealing where humans had trod.

The evidence of a human presence made the Professor's heart race. He suddenly had the sensation of being watched. They took turns in the lead, using a machete from time to time to hack through low hanging tendrils. But the effort drained the Professor. Every cut he made with the blade seemed to release more humidity, each stump exuding moisture, making the air as still and thick as wet felt. The smell of humus and decay was suffocating. Each turn he took slowed their progress so Raul began to extend his own shifts; after a spell he relinquished the machete only for as long as he needed to catch his breath.

The Professor half expected the jungle to howl in pain with each of Raul's strokes, so violent were they, so alive did everything seem, the tendrils that fell down around his head and shoulders immediately curling as though to strangle him in order to climb back toward the light. Since heading inland, they seemed to be going ever deeper into the belly of an immense, living organism. The mud was alive, sweating its moisture; plants seemed to grow before his very eyes. Though he had no barometer, he could feel that the air was beyond its saturation point with the sweat of birthing and dying, mating and decaying.... The air was as dense as it became before a downpour and yet the downpour never came because the density of the air was the result of humidity steaming up from the forest floor.

He kept thinking that he spotted a face deep in the bush, watching. But each time he looked directly at it, it only became a face-like arrangement of leaves, or a shadow. When he looked behind to the path they had just trod, he believed he could see the jungle closing in as he watched, plants writhing, fighting each other for the air and light admitted by the void Raul had just cut before they were choked off by their neighbors.

The gloom of the forest had begun to deepen long before they reached the point Raul had hoped to have achieved by now. He stripped creeper vines from their trees to weave into a crude hammock as the Professor gathered firewood. Returning with an armload of brush, he dumped it on the ground, then just sat there gazing vacantly at it. As Raul built the fire, the Professor's thoughts went back to the woman all of Santos had been talking about the day they'd left. As the cantina owner explained it, her husband, a robust man, had suddenly taken ill and died within the space of three days. As in many new countries where men greatly outnumber women and chastity is not encouraged, she soon remarried. This new husband also succumbed to a mysterious illness. As did a third. At this point, everyone was sure that some evil was afoot. But this did not stop a fourth man from marrying her, possibly lured by her ever-increasing wealth. As everyone in town predicted, and despite all of his efforts to remain safe, this man also died within a week of the wedding. Now nearly everyone in town wanted to stone her to put off the evil they were sure she invited. Just as they were about to act, the undertaker discovered a snake fang in the instep of the dead husband's boot. It was the same pair of boots that the woman's first husband had worn into the jungle, and that each of her dead husbands had in turn availed themselves of. To some, the simplest explanation was that the first husband had stepped on a snake, and the snake bit into the boot, piercing its sole with a fang that became dislodged and remained there in wait for the other men. Most, though, believed that the woman had been given the *Ojo malo*, and that was what caused the chain of events.

"And you?" the Professor had asked Raul after they'd heard the tale. "What do you think?"

"¿Qué es la differencia?" Raul had answered.

Once, he had come upon the tracks of a boy beside those of a wolf. Had the wolf followed the boy or the boy the wolf? Or had they been made weeks apart? He never knew.

September 30, 1859

So fixed is Divine economy that should a certain means be provided, certain ends must follow: out in the emptiness of space, nebulous matter must condense into planets should it reach a certain density; the turning of the earth produces winds, but if they come together in such ways as to compound one another, storms arise, and ships and lives are lost. We feel our insignificance in the face of forces of this magnitude; we feel a vague, terror-stricken sense of alarm when we recognize the possibility of a collision between celestial bodies, or the deterioration of our climate. Yet we also feel a sense of calm in the measured path of the sun, or the mutual attraction of the earth and moon, or the rhythmic ebb and flow of the ocean, and the procession of turtles as they come ashore to lay their eggs....

All of which reminds us that every organism is but part of a singular universe. That is, we are in Nature, not apart from Nature, and so live within an all-powerful unity of life, whether it be expressed as the unfolding of a flower, the ripening of a banana, or the rending of clouds by the wind. We may here trace the revelation of a bond of union, linking together the visible world and that invisible, spiritual world which escapes the grasp of our senses as those moving too fast are rendered invisible by M. Daguerre's camera machine. The two become unconsciously blended together, developing in the mind of man as a simple product of ideal conception, and independent of the aid of observation: the first germ of a Philosophy of Nature. We acknowledge the mystery of color shimmering through coral beds; of mountains, of course, but also the flea. They are of us and not of us, and we respond with confusion, even anger, when our dog bites the hand that feeds it. For we want animals, like all of Nature, to respond to us as if they are of us, and are flustered when they respond in ways that are animal. In this we are a mob of Ahabs, pursuing the great white whale as if it were a murderer, when for the whale there can be no such thing as murder. Or mob. Or whale, for that matter. All of Nature is whale, as is the ocean, as is land, though we alone play judge, jury, and executioner, and take the whale for its oil with no more remorse than we swat the flea. Yea, even if the whale could be given its say in court, it would be condemned to die, and go to its gallows as to its trial: mute. And even if a jury found it innocent, it would still be sentenced to death. For the scientist imagines that a fair trial depends on the gathering of facts, while facts, like light through a bottle, are bent by glass, which is to say, us, though we can no more say how than can the bottle. So we go on,

like Ahab, in the only way our language will allow, seeing the "greed" of pigs, or the "loyalty" of our dog, each our own Ahab though we may believe we've never stepped aboard a whaling ship, unable to think of—

"It."

What animal, or plant, for that matter, can ever gain a fair trial when this is the language of its court? And yet if we were to use "who" for "it," the outcome would be already determined, and so we refuse. Because Scripture tells us so—Dominion over all the Earth—but also because we know that the rights that we grant to ourselves—life, liberty, and the pursuit of happiness—would mean very different things for different animals: that a whale, to have a whale's life, needs very different conditions than that of a dormouse, though in our minds they both share one nature: "animal."

But must the rights of man and the mystery of Nature always be in conflict? Do not the Indians speak a kind of Truth in the kinship they feel with the rabbit, the armadillo, the hawk? Does not the horse whisperer who allows his horse its integrity elevate the human? Could not the same regard be given to the whale? The coral reef? The oceans and fields? Need it be asked?—our fellow humans?

Should the turning earth begin to wobble on its axis, say by shifts of sea ice as has been proposed, the seasons would be thrown into confusion and the species of men perish. Yet the earth would wobble on, and in this it must be admitted, there is constancy and so sagacity. What difference could it make to any single man? Be his life the span of the mayfly or Methuselah, wouldn't it be but a blink in the grand scheme of creation?

Fossils are Nature's memory, and remind us that there are many worlds, not just ours. The mayfly, playing out its entire life within the span of one of our weeks, experiences time differently than the man or woman of 100. As do the tendrils of a vine, slowly climbing a fence to reach the sun. While we cannot experience time in the same way as a river rock, or mountain face, can we not have sympathy, even love, for them?

In the Eternal view, then, do not the fears of men shrink to a narrow compass? Are the wars and other so-called glories that fill history but an aberration in a more general, natural law? An economy of Nature that is beautifully arranged and vast in its extent, and does not begin to satisfy man's idea of what might be? Wasn't it possible to believe this?

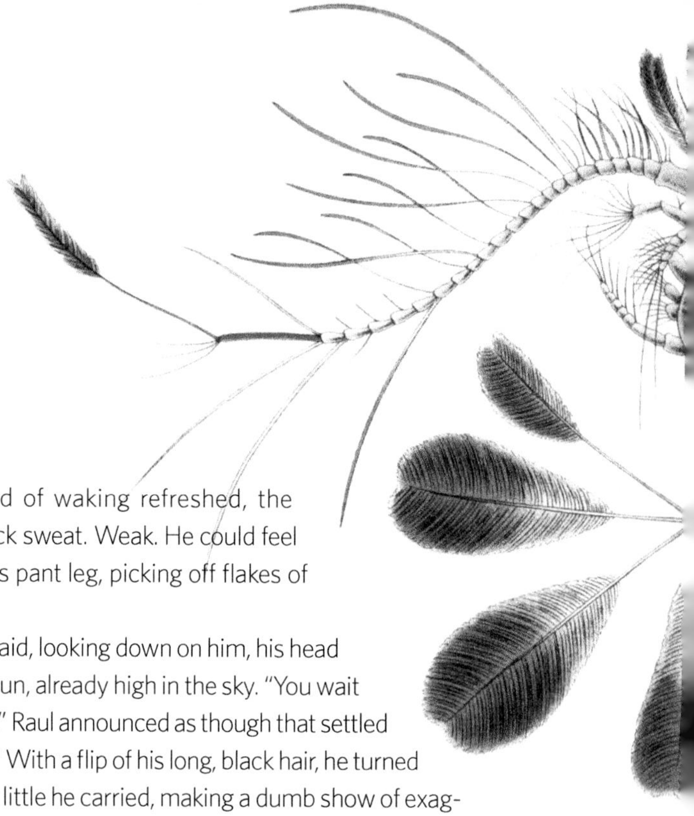

In the morning, instead of waking refreshed, the Professor awoke in a thick sweat. Weak. He could feel ants trailing up inside his pant leg, picking off flakes of dead skin.

"You are sick," Raul said, looking down on him, his head a dark orb eclipsing the sun, already high in the sky. "You wait here with the equipment," Raul announced as though that settled it. "I'll go on without you." With a flip of his long, black hair, he turned to divest himself of what little he carried, making a dumb show of exaggerated motions to proclaim that he was preparing to move on alone.

After coming so far, and coming so close to their destination, the Professor would have rather taken his own life than give up. And yet now, weary, he felt as though he was dragging himself onward because the world he had left behind no longer existed—Elizabeth was gone; unless he returned with a bird fossil, his reputation, even career would be gone as well. Even the very nation he had known may be gone by now.... If there was a future, it was only forward. Aware of Raul's critical gaze, he rose as steadily as he could, and began to gather his things, surreptitiously using the large, flat blade of his hunting knife as a mirror when he felt a shiver in his eye. There, reflected in the mirror of his knife, something wriggled beneath the membrane, a parasite traveling fast through his eye's white the way a gopher burrows across a lawn.

On the march again, he could tell he was noticeably sicker than yesterday. Raul had been right about his health. Instead of the restful sleep of the honest laborer who awakens refreshed, the Professor felt as though he had been wrestling with some immense beast all night, some creature that was too large for him to get his arms around, and yet too inert or lethargic to finish him, and so they struggled through the night and into this day.

He had no idea how long he and Raul had walked. It seemed all morning but was probably far less. The omnipresent gloom of the forest put him in the mind of those lost explorers who tried to walk out of a featureless desert or snowscape by strictly adhering to a straight bearing. Invariably, because one leg was always a little stronger than the other, they'd discover that they had walked in a circle by coming upon their own tracks. The Professor kept watching the ground, fully expecting to come upon his own footprints, wondering how many men like him had circled their own graves, unawares as water around a drain, while the ants, beetles, and other pallbearers waited to return them to loam.

Suddenly, they were able to explain the mystery of Rev. Eastwood.

Or so he had thought. At the spot where Raul believed the Reverend had kept his mission, they found a patch of new, green shoots that formed a perfect rectangle. Nothing in nature grew so regularly. Indeed, the corners of the green rectangle were the first right angles that the Professor had seen since they entered the forest, and they appeared so unreal, so out of place here that he gazed at them, bewildered, unable to comprehend what he was looking at.

Raul thrust his machete into the new growth. When he drew it out, the blade was gray. Ash. As though testing the depth of a pool, he walked around the green rectangle, sticking in his machete with always the same result. The ash beneath the new growth could have been the remains of a bonfire if it didn't so clearly demarcate what had once been a rectangular, one-room cabin, a log hut, nay, a chapel, its rectangular footprint already carpeted by new growth.

No bird had done this.

Another few weeks and it would be impossible to find any trace of the chapel. Exhausted, the Professor slumped down as Raul used his machete to sift through the ashes beneath the growth. Some time later he fished out a metallic button, then a melted figurine—Christ, posed as though nailed to the cross that had been consumed in the fire.... Then Raul fished out a blackened medallion, and allowed it to dangle from its chain in front of the Professor:

För att fira prästvigningen av de mest vördnadsvärda Johan Arnbjörg....

Swedish. It was an ordination medal bearing the newly ordained minister's name: Johan Arnbjörg: a Swedish name. Not the Rev. Eastwood. Not Anne's uncle. His guide had led him to a completely different missionary. He sputtered, "This wasn't an American! Not even English!"

Raul shrugged. "You wanted to find white shaman." He motioned toward the rectangle of fresh growth, which now had the aspect of a grave. "Here he is."

Suddenly there was a cracking of branches from the woods. A whoosh of a volume of wind, then heavy flapping—like wings or a carpet being beaten. Throwing away his machete, Raul plunged into the bush after the sound, and was immediately swallowed by the growth.

"Raul? Raul!" the Professor cried, the effort to stand making his head throb. No reply. The dense growth remained a closed curtain. Mute.

He staggered toward the curtain of vines, its tangles holding every whit of his attention, his heart pounding. Parting the curtain took the remainder of his strength, so weakened had he become from the effort to stand.

In a clearing just beyond, he found the amulet that Raul always wore around his neck, but nothing else. Nothing other than a scattering of feathers. Then an empty boot—and another. As though the man had been taken by a great mystery.

So this is one way a world ends, flickered through his mind. Not in ice, as the Poet had it, but fire.

As he fluttered in and out of consciousness, the entire forest seemed to be melting, trees going wavy in the heat that surrounded him as in a mirage, smoke making the honeybee groggy, and so dooming the flowers, the wilting flowers spelling an end for the meadow, and so its mice, and so....

Each geological stratum was a judgment, but all would return, one day, wouldn't they? He tried to take comfort in the thought of his place among them, among everyone who had ever stooped to retrieve a fallen leaf and tried to preserve it; who found a fossilized snail, marveled at its whorl and saw themselves, one of millions becoming one of the composted billions, mud that had for a time walked upright, and would return to take its place in the crust of the earth. Six miles thick....

Whenever he had come upon a dead butterfly, its legs were crossed as undertakers crossed the arms of Christians in their caskets.

Put aside your strife and come to me, saith the Earth. Standing before Elizabeth's grave one spring, he had opened his eyes to a storm of white pear blossoms so fierce that he'd thought it was snow.

Ash. Ash rose on the heat around him.

High above, a bird circled on an updraft, serene....

Chapter II: A Little Truth

No great and enduring volume
can ever be written on the flea,
though many there be who have tried it.

—Herman Melville
& Robert Traub, Miriam Rothschild, and John F. Haddow, Epigram to *The Rothschild Collection of Fleas, The Ceratophyllidae: Key to the Genera and Host Relationships with Notes on Their Evolution, Zoogeography and Medical Importance*

RABBIT OR DUCK? Lying on a mat-thin mattress in a Paraguay hotel, Jane stared at the drawing of a flea she had made in her notebook. It looked like a rabbit. She refocused: flea. But if she squinted, it snapped back to rabbit, the way that famous drawing of a rabbit could also be seen as a duck.... She pulled from her shirt the medallion hanging by the leather bootlace she wore as a necklace. Embossed on it was the skeleton of *Archaeopteryx*, the fossil some people saw as a bird and others a pigeon-sized dinosaur. Bird. Dinosaur. Bird. Dinosaur. Bird, definitely bird—she knew because the lice of a bird were unmistakably different from the fleas of a rabbit—and she'd say so, tomorrow.

Too excited to sleep, she returned, in her mind's eye, to jostling with tourists, bird and PBS watchers, crowding into one of those cavernous, new IMAX theaters being installed in museums across America. When she closed her eyes, the screen came alive with trailers in surround sound—previews in IMAX Vision of NASCAR races, then a polar expedition—Shackleton's 19th-century ship crushed by ice— rock climbers, then here it was!—*Our Feature Presentation*—a green carpet of tropical forest streaming below a camera's flyby as the voice-over described other biologists who had remade the world by getting people to see 'rabbit' where they'd once seen 'duck': Darwin, in the Galápagos Islands, with his *G. abingdoni tortoise*; her grandfather in his Kuala Lumpur field lab, deducing from the bodies of Stephanocircidae fleas the movement of continents—then zoom down through the tree canopy to her. "And now following in their footsteps—Call me Ahab—no, just kidding— *Jannnnnnne Korzeniowski!* Live! from the only remaining virgin forest of South America," Jane said, rehearsing for tomorrow's camera, trying to not let her game face melt into giggles. Yeah, no "girly" giggles....

It had only been a week since her real crew had mutinied; or rather she from them. Todd (an ornithologist), Christopher (ornithology again), Cristóbal (a local ornithologist), Wang (ditto the ornithology), and her (flies, fleas, and feather lice) had been at the Asunción airport, waiting for their flight back to the States, worn out from days in the bush, collecting bird and bird lice specimens. The expedition had been successful. They'd put in plastic baggies a number of blue-fronted parrots (*Amazona aestiva*) that they'd netted for comparison to their domestic cousins. William, their postdoc, would land on tenure-track; there'd be ink for all their institutions—and she, the lone paramecium tagalong, would have been happy too—if not for that brief glimpse of a feather louse she had gotten on their last day. She'd been looking through her field microscope, sketching the *Amyrsidea cracis* that she'd taken off of one of Todd's curassow specimens when another insect suddenly appeared in the aperture like a shadow puppet in the corner of a feature film. Instead of just blowing it off the microscope's stage, for some reason—call it fate, or okay, call it intuition if you insist—she pivoted the slide to bring the insect's tiny body under the lens. What she saw took her breath.

Just as quick it was gone. Blown out of the microscope by a gust of wind. She'd only seen it for a moment, but in that glimpse, the world moved: a louse with a head shape as distinctive as any prehistoric skull: unfused flagellum lengthening its antennae, generalized mouthparts, the distinctive characteristics of a louse too primitive to be alive yet there it was!

When she announced to the others what she'd seen, they all turned toward her in unison. "No shit?" Wang, who never swore, swore, breaking the stunned silence.

Then they jumped up around her, one's excitement adding an exponent to that of another—

Until she was unable to produce the specimen.

When she couldn't, they thought it was a joke. After her intensity convinced them that she was serious, they'd helped her comb the forest floor. Try as they might, the specimen was gone. "Or imagined," Cristóbal said.

"Are you sure you saw it?"

"What made you turn the scope on it?"

She didn't like the tone this was taking. "I don't know, intuition."

"Did anyone else see it?"

Head shakes all around.

Christian collapsed the antenna of the Manpack—his geo-positioning gear—as though that settled it. Their time in the bush was over. Flight reservations. On a plane that arrived only once a week. Plus it was about to rain, and if it rained, the roads could get so muddy they'd never make it back in time for—

"Oh my God!" Todd shouted, pointing into the bush. "I just saw a Bigfoot flea!" The first laughs.

"Listen," said Wang sympathetically, "it's not that we don't want to stay, it's just that we'd have to have more to go on than a woman's intuition."

"What's that supposed to mean?" Jane said.

"He means this is a birding expedition. It was always about the birds."

"He means that if we had some evidence...."

"...and didn't have jobs...."

"...or a fiancée back home and a wedding to plan...."

"Don't be mad," Todd said, as though to make up, though the others had already gone back to striking camp. "We all promise we'll come back next year to look for your louse."

"If you still believe you saw what you think you saw."

"Promise contingent on funding...."

SO CLOSE.... At the airport, Jane had sat in the shabby Asunción terminal with the others, an enormous, gilt-framed painting of the country's El Generalísimo Presidente scowling down as she fumed over how they had just blown her off. A flea in a gale. How could she have been so stupid as to ever think she could be one of the boys?

The coordinates for the spot they'd been at—24° 03′ 18.45″ S; 55° 23′ 53.60″ W—moldered in her like bad electrical wiring threatening to burst into flames and burn down the house. Then, just before boarding, their Air Paraguay plane developed some problem and the other passengers began to bunch up their laundry for pillows, take off shoes, settle in for a long delay, unaware that the gods of science had intervened to keep her in country.

Or at least give her time to think.

Through the terminal window, she could see the lone jet sitting out on the tarmac. Old. Its faded aluminum dully reflected the sun: the same kind of passenger plane, if she was remembering the news photos right, that the Russians accidentally shot down. Odd how totally unrelated events could combine to create consequences on the far side of the planet—Butterfly Effect—Russians accidentally shoot down a Korean airliner, so Reagan allows civilians to use GPS, and now here she was, in Paraguay, with a Manpack that she could use to pinpoint the location of a louse that could rewrite the Tree of Life. If only she could get to it!

Mechanics in sandals and coveralls crouched in the shade of the jet's wing, pointing at something in the hydraulics of a wheel while just beyond the tarmac was a clearing and beyond that a tree line, calling to her.

Widows in black weeds moved about the passengers, selling empanadas and oranges from the baskets they carried on their heads. If Jane had grown up here, she considered, she'd probably be one of them. Just as she'd look Canadian—a big red maple leaf on her backpack—if she'd grown up in Canada, or be British—with her tweed skirt—if she'd grown up in England. An American threw back her bushy head of hair to drink from one of those flimsy plastic bottles Coca-Cola had begun using—when had people begun to mimic TV commercials?—a bare shoulder exposed by the overly large neck hole of her tee shirt.

A coin toss: if the flight was cancelled, Jane decided, watching a feathered forest Aché enter the gate area, she'd stay; if not, she'd go.

Dressed in a ceremonial parrot-feather headdress and belt, he seemed to have stepped out of one of those antique paintings of Columbus's first encounter with natives. Logging was flushing tribes from ever more remote parts of the forest, and this one picked his way among the waiting passengers, sizing up each, stepping around the stoic Paraguayans with their bundles and yerba-maté horns to get to the German or Brit tourists in stonewashed jeans. Before a pair of hippies, he went into a dance: a little skip, then hop, then a rocking from one foot to the next. It was a ritual dance to ask forgiveness from the souls of the birds he'd killed, Jane realized, seeing that his necklace was a string of colorful bird bodies. As he danced, he held out his palm for a gratuity.

Frayed bellbottoms and dashikis.... One hippie wore a faded army jacket with an upside-down American flag patch. She and her tie-dyed old man looked like some sort of ghostship that had left the States during the 60s, gotten lost in S.A. ganja for twenty years, and now, for some reason, were drifting back—like those Japanese soldiers who sometimes stumbled out of the jungle on a remote Pacific island. Maybe they'd just now heard that Carter had given draft dodgers amnesty?

The hunter gave up on them, and danced over to a family with a teenage girl wearing a torn, lace glove on one hand, black, Goth eye-shadow, a heap of rosaries and crucifixes dangling as costume jewelry.

The indigenous people who survived must have had super-strong immune systems, Jane thought. Their descendants, like this one, were said to be immune to diseases carried by birds the way Europeans, living with their cattle, became immune to cowpox—tiny insects doing more to shape history than all the Napoleons and Churchills combined....

"Rad," the girl said, beginning to dance in time with the guy, as if that was what he'd wanted.

Unperturbed, the native danced on to others—skip, hop, bob-bob-bob—using gestures to hawk his wares: a blowpipe, arrows, his ceremonial cowrie-shell anklets and armbands.

When he got to Jane, she crossed her arms, shaking her head as others had to whatever he was saying in his odd-clicking language, something more remote than even the Aché that was used outside the Spanish or Guaraní-speaking areas. She wanted to watch the feather lice she could see on his string of birds but looked down to show that she wasn't interested. He persisted, shoving jewelry—a necklace with a single bead—into her gaze—

There she saw it: evidence that she HAD seen what she'd seen in the bush. Trapped inside one of the amber beads was an insect; when she held the bead to the light, she could distinguish the distinctive globular head and laterally semi-flattened abdomen of a primitive louse. Its head had clearly been more mobile than those of modern Psocodea but not as mobile as those of the older Liposcelis they could have evolved from; its jaw was not quite hypognathous but its gular and postgenal areas had not grown large enough to push the jaw forward into a configuration that could be called prognathous as in modern Psocoptera.... Jane bought the necklace without bargaining and called over the others. But instead of admitting she had evidence for what she'd seen, they only squinted at the amber bead, then exchanged silent, condescending glances.

"Just look at its labial palpus!" she blurted so loudly that a security guard looked over. "It's one segment!" She handed Christian the loupe she always carried in her shirt pocket and as he used it to examine the specimen; she did all she could to keep from pushing it into his face. "It has cerci for Christ's sake! No modern or fossil Psocodea has well-formed cerci!" she said, indicating small appendages on the abdomen of bark-lice species that had been lost in the line of parasitic lice well before the Permian. It was as clear an indication of its age as the ridge on the forehead of Neanderthal skulls.

He passed the bead to Wang who took his turn with her loupe. He shrugged, and said that the louse could have been deformed when the amber solidified.

"Hard to see anything through the amber," Christian agreed, squinting. "Hard to tell."

"What about its size?" Jane said in disbelief. "Did you ever see a modern louse this big?"

That was harder to explain, they admitted.

"Unless it's primitive!" Jane exclaimed.

Or wasn't a louse at all, Christian said, but some member of Thysanoptera or Hemiptera or maybe some other larger, undescribed species.

She couldn't believe what she was hearing!—laymen on lice lecturing her on what she was looking at—their ignorant opinions determining whether they'd stay or go!

An interesting and unusual specimen for sure, they said, but ultimately more puzzle than answer, more inkblot than evidence. If she really thought it was older than the amber that held it, she should bring it back to the lab. Do a thorough cladistic analysis, they said. "That is"—and here it came, just as she knew it would—"try to extract its DNA and draw up its phylogenetic character complexes using its genetic fingerprints," they said.

DNA, DNA, DNA. She was sick of the way these younger biologists threw "DNA" at the biologists of her generation—the way teenagers once sneered Rock 'N Roll at their parents.

Apply for a grant, Christian was saying, then come back. Todd added, Do it the right way—their way, in other words. Otherwise, the only thing the bug trapped in this amber would prove was that she was stubborn. Or hysterical, they may as well have said.

The airport P.A. crackled something and the locals began to rush the gate the way they turned every city bus ride into a phone-booth cramming contest.

Jane stood and announced to her crew, "I'm not going."

The words had just come out, surprising her as much as them. But once out, they became a battle line.

Wild louse chase, they complained. Obsessed. The P.A. called their seating section. They begged her to return with them—hysteric—now they were saying it. Or at least that's how she remembered it later: The scientific method vs. the female mind. But she knew what her grandfather would have done, back in the days before technicians and DNA sequencers took the place of scientist adventurers like him. And he was mapping new species before they were zygotes.

BACK IN THE HOTEL PARADISO, it began to rain. The road into the forest would be a sea of mud, so she lay in bed, staring at the ceiling, and wondering if she really was losing it. Or if not losing it, then, as Cristóbal had said, trying to politely tell her why he didn't want to go back into the bush, that she was trying to write a story that had less to do with science than science fiction. It was a possibility. She took out the drawing of the Evolutionary Tree for Lice that she had altered; the paper was so full of erasures and redrawn lines that it looked like some kind of crazy treasure map. Even crazier, the X she drew to mark the spot claimed that the lice that chewed feathers emerged 150 MYA before every other entomologist in the world said they did: bird lice that had, according to her sketch, emerged 150 MYA before there were birds. She'd drawn the X, then erased it and redrawn it, then erased it so many times that she'd worn a hole at the spot. An empty hole that she kept digging deeper and deeper....

Once, at an Arts & Science conclave for women faculty, a prof from the psych department told her about her own work studying the crazy things that intense desire made people see: God, UFOs, weeping statues, "a faithful spouse," she'd added bitterly, throwing back a swallow of cheap reception wine. No, Jane didn't need that example to know scientists weren't immune. Percival Lowell died claiming that the lines he saw on Mars were canals.

Truth always wins out, Wang and other scientists liked to say. But when she considered the failed theories that had been true only so long as the people who believed them were alive; when she considered all the pristinely crafted, and obviously expensive, oak-and-brass scientific instruments collecting dust in the basement of her university lab, equipment that had been custom built for purposes no one in her lab could even guess at, not to mention her own copious output of bygone state-of-the art artifacts—reams of tractor-fed computer paper, COBAL, punch cards, nongenetic cladograms, and all the out-and-out lies, wrong reasoning, mistakes, and biases contained in libraries full of journal articles no one consulted—the March of Science seemed more like a tangle of grand schemes by optimists and petty schemes by bureaucrats; the timid ambitions of pessimists and skeptics; the benevolent hopes of women with warm smiles; and the recordkeeping of men with limp handshakes; the hunches of schemers and dreamers, the constipated, bed-wetters, cheats, even thieves and murderers. That is, of people. That is, the fallacy of Wang and his ilk was that there was time enough—a.k.a., infinity, a mathematical fiction that cannot be measured—to arrive at a single, unchanging, and Eternal Story while she was HERE, at a particular place, NOW.

In the gloom across her hotel room, she could see the Manpack that Christian had pressed upon her as they said their goodbyes. Miles above, the first three of what they said would eventually be a ring of 21 satellites were in orbit and transmitting signals that allowed soldiers anywhere on earth to use Manpacks like this to locate their position within a few meters. To call in air strikes, liquid fire, and who knew what else.... Christian had gotten a loan of the new gadget along with his military funding, she suspected, because of some secret mission cooked up by the military to occupy their time now that Vietnam was over. He didn't ask, and they didn't tell, he'd said. And she'd chosen to believe him—the guy, like all the guys in the lab, enamored with every new tech toy. The Manpack weighed a ton compared to her nets and baggies—almost thirty extra pounds to lug in the field. But she knew he was right when he said that its solid-state accuracy gave her the best chance to navigate back to 24° 03′ 18.45″ S; 55° 23′ 53.60″ W, the exact spot they'd been at when she spotted her prehistoric louse.

Its army-green metal case, an industrial-strength keypad, and an antenna to communicate with spacecraft made her own leather-bound field kit look like something off of a 19th-century whaling ship. The Manpack had the same red L.E.D. digital readout as the DNA sequencing equipment every lab in the country was hot to get their hands on and she couldn't help but feel like a dinosaur, the relevance of her pencil sketches, nets, training, skills, and knowledge fading quicker than the half-life of an isotope.

Looking at her insects through their genetic sequencing machines, she understood how the critics of Galileo must have felt, refusing to look through his telescope: not because they were afraid that they would see what he said was there. Rather, those old priests knew that to look through Galileo's machine would be to admit that his way of seeing would bring their world to a close as surely as DNA sequencing was eclipsing her ability to sketch insects so as to place them squarely in the correct phylum....

Already, when she stood before the flat-files of drawings in her office back home, she felt like a scribe watching the library at Alexandria burn. Except she was inside the library. And the only one to smell smoke, the others too busy with their Commodore 64s to notice, let alone care.

She lay still, the amber bead she'd bought at the airport tight in her fist. Rain droned on the hotel's tin awning as she vacillated between doubt and anger: a woman with a sketchbook (images of dainty ladies painting watercolors of primroses) instead of an ABI sequencer (he-man science)—then *victory!*—the louse in her hand a Hail-Mary pass, a long shot at the buzzer—*swish!*—on her last chance, using her old drawings, and nets, and yes, punch-card programming, to leapfrog them all!

Then she'd imagine herself returning home, empty specimen baggy dragging behind, the bead in her fist containing a bug that wasn't even a louse, and the vision would throw her into despair.

The next morning she awoke to silence. She opened her shutters to see that the streets of Asunción were deserted, except for a military truck. Eerie. Like a scene from *The Twilight Zone*. A soft knock on the door startled her. "Teléfono," a boy's voice on the other side informed her.

Down at the desk, she discovered that the call wasn't from Cristóbal, as she had hoped, but from a film company and she knew, just knew, fate had intervened—yeah, it wasn't a woman's but a scientist's intuition that had won out—and now here she was, ready to go back into the bush, a camera crew in the next room ready to film her making her discovery. True, it was only a one-man crew—Arty baby!—though he told her not to call him that. And he was only recording tape that might end up in an educational video, not an IMAX theater. But still!...

The room filled with the growl of another one of those logging trucks outside, downshifting as it labored to the harbor....

[**ARTHUR SAT**] on the edge of his bed, sticky with heat. The hotel was situated on a street wide enough for trucks and now that it was night, the cacophony of daytime street noise was replaced by the solitary groan of a truck loaded with logs. Then another truck. Then another, and another—a train of trucks that rumbled past the hotel, the airbrakes of each hissing when they were caught by the traffic light right below his window.

In the silences between trucks, he could hear his "star" in the next room. *"Jaaaaaaaane Korzeniowski!"* Rehearsing again. He switched on the single bare bulb of his room, pulled back the mosquito netting then tried to position himself so the video camera he'd propped up on the dresser could see his face and the gecko on the wall behind him—local color; he hit REC on the remote, and—*bippity-boppity-boop*—the camera came to life. But instead of the clicking of film reels that used to give him such an adrenaline rush there was silence, a tiny red "record" light on its front blinking to let him know the zombie was awake.

"Where to begin," he said to the camcorder, trying to not fall into the clichés of Geraldo Rivera or any of those other trashy, spectacle chasers that cable news had begun generating. Infotainment. Then he grew angry at himself for only being able to think in their clichés—tan safari jacket, exotic, third-world backdrop....

But damn it, he was weary. Three changes of flights—Air Paraguay flying through a storm as if the pilots couldn't pedal fast enough to get above it. Strobes of lightning illuminated freeze-frames of terrified passenger faces with an intensity brighter than kliegs. *Flash-bang!* People screamed. A shudder through the spine of the plane as it began to descend. Lower, lower. Suddenly it was below the clouds, the jungle rushing up to the plane—Arthur sure they were all going to die in a jet scattered across miles of forest—when at the last instant, a clearing miraculously appeared, and the jet touched down. On a runway.

The other passengers cheered—because, he'd thought, they'd been as relieved as him to discover that there was a runway below the plane's descent. But as they taxied toward a soggy Paraguayan flag, hanging limply from the terminal, the cheering morphed into some kind of national song, emotion overwhelming the passengers; a flight attendant sang shiny-eyed like the guitarist in *Casablanca* when Victor Laszlo led them all in "La Marseillaise" as an up-yours to the Nazis.

A journalist, or professor, or someone who had been in exile for years, Arthur gathered as they deplaned, had been allowed to return, and it was just Arthur's luck to be on the same flight.

To get to customs, he and the other passengers filed beneath a huge, gilt-framed portrait of Generalisimo Presidente. There, an official in a mismatched uniform went straight for Arthur's camera equipment. Like a magician pulling an impossibly long scarf out of a hat, he pulled from the camera bag the nylon bandoliers loaded with 35mm film canisters and placed them on the counter beside Arthur's Leica. When he opened the other camera case, his eyes opened wider than those over-the-top, Hollywood eye-poppers they always used in B movies when Blackbeard or Ali Babba opens a treasure chest of glittering gold. Better than gold, Arthur's VHS camcorder was so new that its manual was still in the case. Excitedly, the custom's guy called over a second official. They'd never seen a camera that used magnetic tape, Arthur realized, watching them poke its buttons, one demonstrating for another how he thought the tape cartridge fit. Arthur turned the cartridge around for him so he wouldn't break the camcorder by forcing the tape in backwards. Ah, let them have their fun, he'd thought; everyone else was wowed by the latest gadget, why not them?—

But then the guards began to accuse him of trying to embarrass El Presidente by filming the anarchist's return.

He was here to film a woman, Arthur tried to explain—

Pornographer?

No! A woman scientist.

"And what does this woman you study," one asked sarcastically, "study?"

Arthur's hesitation made it look like he was lying, so he just came out with it: "Fleas."

One agent sniggered. The other's teeth clenched. "There are no fleas in North America to study?" They conferred among themselves, then it became surreal: they accused him, and his lover—the woman who was posing as a scientist—of being spies. He had come to film state secrets, they said, and to spread lies about their nation and its heroic leader's fleas.

In the end, Arthur wrote out his itinerary, and signed documents swearing that he would check in with the Departmento de Commerce once a week to prove he still had his "camcorder" (Christ, not even a real word!) in his possession. Then he stood there while the two officials debated what the proper processing fee should be. Three thousand guaraní, they decided, the exact price, he later learned, of a six-pack.

He swat a flea on his neck, afraid he felt a genuine case of the shits coming on; too late he had realized that the Evian he'd ordered at the hotel restaurant had been brought to his table already opened, a sure sign that the waiter was refilling bottles at the tap.

"I didn't want this," he said to his "camcorder," motioning in a way that he hoped conveyed the shits, his one-bulb room—his life.

The camcorder's autofocus tracked him....

If any shred of him still thought it was possible to get a little truth on film, he'd be making a documentary about the soldiers who hung about street corners, watching and being watched by black-market money changers, soccer hoodlums, street kids in cast-off American tees—*Compuserve*—a soundtrack replaying the groan of logging trucks hauling away their future. He'd do something with the guys in customs—life—like in the "actualities" from the early days of film, showing women picking cotton, or men leaving a factory at the end of their shift: ordinary people doing ordinary things where the real subject was the rhythm of the job, the unmediated truth of the mundane, the kind of art he'd longed to make as a student. His thesis film was titled *Puddle*, an unblinking look at the beauty and pathos of a puddle of rainwater as it dried. The test-of-concept film that he'd been able to make had looked great, but he'd never gotten the backers he needed to shoot the full movie because audiences were too stupid to sit there for the 27 hours it would take to watch it. To really understand. To SEE.

Since then, *Puddle* had taken on more significance than even he had foretold: given the hyperkinetic graphics that video allowed—BUY! NEW! LAUGH-IN! SOCK-IT-TO-ME! spinning out of TV screens in psychedelic colors—throwing the last heaps of dirt onto the corpse of the truth cameras had stood for from the very first time Louis Daguerre exposed the view outside his window to light sensitive plates: an anchor in Time that asserted that at least at that moment (open shutter), something (a man having his boots polished), had been before the camera's eye: proof of existence. Or at least that's the belief he had tried to cling to until the truth of the background made that impossible: all around the man had been the swirl of pedestrians and horses and carriages of a busy Parisian street; the only person in the scene who had stood still long enough for the long exposure needed by Daguerre's glass plates was the guy having his shoes shined; all the other people appeared as wispy blurs, or not at all, and more and more, filmmakers began giving up on Reality for "realities"—as many truths as there were times of exposure. It was as if each frame was that famous Duck-Rabbit picture—which could now also be seen as a monkey or bear and or unicorn or Godzilla....

Maybe the problem with *Puddle* wasn't the audience, but him?

The eye of the camcorder—The Future—stared back as stoically as an interrogator who refused to be lied to and he sighed.

"Who am I kidding?" Giving up on *Puddle* had only been his first surrender—before giving himself over to the making of *Improve Your Golf Swing*, and *Are Penny Stocks for You?* and a whole videography of other films that had buried his soul in ash. Not that it had been his fault. No, at least that much was true, he wanted the camcorder to understand, even if Sheila, his old girlfriend, couldn't.

It was the reason he gave up trying to work with actors and actresses—like Sheila—and started filming trees. And rain. Then raindrops. He hadn't been out of film school long when that epiphany came to him. And Sheila had had hers. They had gone to a movie—*Soylent Green*—set in a future where everyone looked out for themselves; apartments came with Hollywood-beautiful women, or "furniture" as the women were called. Suicide centers allowed people who'd had enough of this omni-polluted and depressing world to see a 10-minute movie in exchange for their bodies. It was this movie within the movie that had done it for Arthur: the movie that Edward G. Robinson, playing an old man, watches while the hemlock he'd drunk takes effect. High-chroma long-shots of sunsets and waterfalls transition into fields of wheat swaying across a superwide movie screen. It put on parade all the natural beauty that had once existed: natural wonders that had been extinct for so long that Edward G.'s younger partner, a gritty detective played by Charlton Heston, thought the old man's descriptions were fairy tales he made up the way old people always aggrandize a Golden Past that never was. Film makers didn't have IMAX back then, but that's what this movie-within-the-movie was, the screen wider than peripheral vision could see so the viewer had the sensation of being in the scene instead of watching a film.

Watching Charlton Heston watch Edward G. watch this movie-within-the-movie, Arthur felt as though the film was speaking to him personally; seeing the hardened detective from a super-polluted future moved to tears by those brilliant images of vast sunflower fields, stars on diamond-clear nights, Arthur knew he could never work on another fiction with actors and papier-mâché scenery again.

Seeing that movie, that is, the movie around the movie-within-the-movie, where beautiful women did whatever it took to survive in a postapocalyptic world, Sheila had had her epiphany too: go to Hollywood. And do whatever she had to to make it there. And though neither of them realized it then, it was there, in that theater, that he had seen 'duck' while she had seen 'rabbit' with the consequence that they had begun to live in two very different movies though they went on another year sharing the same set.

Soon afterwards, Arthur bought a macro lens so he could shoot a single dewdrop—unmediated nature would be the stars of his films—honest films that were what they were and forced viewers to see them as such instead of living within the illusions most people wanted. First he gave up flashbacks, plots, and all the other tricks that didn't exist in nature, for as every film editor knew, just putting objects in a sequence was to comment upon them. From now on it would be one camera, one scene, one take: the way Atget shot all those haunting photos of deserted Paris streets.

Thinking of those gray scenes, the color in his own films began to appear garish—fake.... This is when he first began to think of *Puddle*, or *Water*, as he first called it, as the way he had to go: an Atget in motion—pure cinema the way Atget's black-and-white images were pure photography. But of course, capturing Reality by getting rid of color in the age of color would be the most artificial move of all, and this is where the screen of Arthur's mind went black.

Paralyzed in the grip of this contradiction, Arthur spent increasing amounts of his life on jobs, putting in overtime as a grip and boom operator for an educational film company. Sheila was going to star in the movies they'd imagined while they were both in school, but she'd already moved to L.A. by the time he took on *Asbestos, Good for America*. He moved up to cinematographer on *Chicken King Industrial Fryer Operator Training*, then art director, script, camera, and director on *Army Training Film 10037: Keeping Your Feet Dry in Tropical Climates*.

Then, back when ma-and-pa video rental shops were springing up on every corner, cable TV was opening up new oceans of airtime, and the number of TV channels went from 3 to an unimaginable 50; back when the number of homes that had cable TV hit the 50% mark and even prisoners on death row were getting it; back when the industry was starving for content to fill these new oceans of hours—they even began to run the news 24 hours a day—CNN, with Darth Vader as its signature voice—and one, *The Weather Channel*, was actually that—a whole channel devoted to the weather report—day and night! What next?—*The Watch*

Paint Dry Channel? Everyone who owned a camera thought they could sell a movie direct to one of these markets—how could you not compete with weather maps!—and some friends from school offered him shares in exchange for camera work on a film backed by their rich parents.

"Are you nuts?" Sheila had asked long distance from L.A. when he told her how much debt he had gone into to invest deeper in the film, the film that would allow him to make the movies he really wanted to make, the film that was, all along, a tax dodge for the rich parents: It was only later that he found out that his "partners" and everyone else on the inside had been betting against the film, taking out massive amounts of insurance against its failure.

By the time he found out that Sheila was sleeping with her agent, he was working full-time for Delta Film & Video to pay off the charge cards he'd lived on during "his stupid adventure," as she'd called it. Less than a year on that job and they took away his camera, gave him a "camcorder," and fired (or "downsized," as they called it) almost everyone else.

The fact that you have (minimum-wage) experience doing a variety of jobs (part-time, pickup work equals jack-of-all-trades) makes you ideally suited (master of none) for the new videotape (throw it together) economy, they told him.

Whatever.

He'd gotten the footage he'd needed for *Visit Montevideo!* and was about to fly home when he got a call from Delta. They'd been subcontracted to put together another educational video, *Careers in Field Science*, that would play on a kiosk at the Field Museum, and were up against the deadline when they realized they didn't have any women or minorities in the film. Deadlines. A one-"camcorderman"—him—budget. Frantic calls to universities dug up Jane, doing field research—on exotic birds in an exotic land—Perfect!—only one hop away on his circle route home. "So, okay," he'd said by phone to Heinrich, the producer back in Chicago. "Footage of female science geeks."

"The correct term is 'nerd.' Don't you go to the movies anymore?" he said, referring to the movie that made pocket protectors and speaking Klingon cool.

"I never was good with scientific terms."

When Arthur arrived, he discovered that Heinrich and the others had screwed up even this detail: she was a flea nerd, not a bird nerd.

Whatever. When he considered how long it had been since he'd made an art film, though, when he thought how long it had been since he'd even thought about *Puddle*, let alone actually try to shoot the full version, he wondered if picking the low fruit day in and day out didn't make him a phony, as he liked to believe, but a true hack. Everyone knew the effect of a camera on the subject—point a camera at Sheila and she'd flash that Farrah Fawcett grin as automatically as a knee jerks when tapped. But who thought about the effect of the camera on the cameraman? What would those smiles become if their owners could look back and see, truly see, that their smiles were turning the camera into a cage with a small furry animal trapped inside, and that animal was his head?

Duck or Rabbit. He'd wake up in the wee of the night, his legs twisted in ropes of VHS tape he'd shot of cheering employees waving banners at motivational conventions, as well as the billons of miles of tape shot by every joe-shmoe now that moviemaking was so cheap—no kitten shall go undocumented—all tangled with the endless reams of tape he had shot on jobs from places like Delta Films and Acme Films and General Films and Standard Films. A little voice had begun to whisper that the best creators of hack work—and he WAS good at it—would be those who actually thought in clichés—those who, when put on a film about endangered species, immediately thought to shoot a candle flickering in the wind, or who, when sent out to film a lady bird-expert, immediately imagined a young woman in a park ranger uniform, jaunty ponytail, head cocked to exchange a kiss with the cockatoo on her shoulder—not because they could think of nothing better, but because—

Using the camera's remote he pulled in for a tight, confessional shot, wondering if all the trade shows he attended, the cramped rooms with folding chairs, discussions with clients and associates like Heirich showed in his face.

Was that the real reason he couldn't figure out how to remake *Puddle*?

This last thought saddened him most of all for it made him understand why his old mentor, Prof. Godmilow, an old-school, avant-garde, doc-film maker, would go mental on any student who wanted to use a camera to make product instead of art. He could still hear her calling after them, "Don't shit where I pray!" as she banished them from the velvety night of the screening room into the common day.

Somehow, he had become one of the shitters, crapping out a whole resume of clichés in one educational, training, gov-propaganda video after another....

On the nightstand beside the bed, the black metal body of the Leica he'd brought to shoot stills looked ponderous: an antique machine with a film advance like the crank on an antique phone in a world of sleek, ergonomically molded handgrips, plastic buttons, oceans of instantly viewable, reusable tape....

Then he gathered himself, and said aloud, "Well, okay," confronting his own reflection in the black eye of the camcorder, "If your world is dying, maybe you ought to die with it." The black eye of a camcorder was more magic mirror than any witch ever had. "But for the moment, you are the undead. And you've got a job to do. A job with fleas.

"Ow!" He swat another of the tiny bastards.

[THE SCENE OPENS]
WITH VARIOUS SHOTS OF ASUNCIÓN:
THE BIG CITY

In the morning, Arthur stood across the street from the hotel, his camcorder camouflaged in a newspaper so he could catch Paraguayan yuppies with their cowhide briefcases, tooled like saddles. He wanted to get one of them in the same frame with an old grizzled onion vendor—or maybe even an Indian in feathered regalia like he'd seen at the airport.

[PAN LEFT] He sighted down the dingy beach umbrellas shading garrapiñada vendors.

[NEW ANGLE] Up to crisscrossing power lines juicing signs for Interfarma and Toyota and SHOPPING and Super Pancho....

[PAN TO] Paradiso Hotel.

[CUT TO] Jane's hands, inside her room, packing (shot earlier).

CUT BACK TO OUTSIDE OF HOTEL.

Where Old & New Worlds Collide, ran the subtitle in his head, the jumble of electric signs jutting from both heavy Spanish colonial buildings with their wedding-cake facades and those crumbling, high-rises: poured concrete boxes of Soviet design relieved by pastel blue and pink trim. Actual Soviets went by as well; you could pick them out by the knockoff Converse All Stars they wore, a hammer and sickle where the star would be on an American pair. At the far end of the street he could make out a patch of brown river. He'd hoped for Paraguayan music, pouring out of a record shop, maybe. But the street just sounded tired: the lament of a cargo ship's horn; the groan of cranes loading the ship with lumber from the trucks that had kept him awake last night. Heinrich would have to dub in something upbeat later.

JANE EMERGED from the hotel, rolled sleeping bag under an arm. She looked up to the sun, striking the Jane Goodall hero pose she'd practiced last night, and held it long enough for him to capture with his camera. But when her eyes adjusted to the brightness of the day, she found Arthur still across the street, his camera hidden in a newspaper. What was with him?

For Christ's sake, he thought, turning away. She waved to him again—"Hey!"—when he was trying to be inconspicuous. "Hey! Hey Arthur!" she yelled, "I'm over here!"

She skipped down to the car she'd rented from some fly-by-night outfit: a Brasília, with cardboard where there should have been the glass of a vent window.

The duffle bags and that GPS that she was transferring to the car had drawn the attention of street kids wearing Ho-Chi-Minhs, or whatever they called hemp-and-tire sandals down here. They kept drifting over to help, or to make off with a bag. Arthur never found out which because the guy from the hotel kept popping out like a cuckoo from its clock, shooing them away. "Excuse me, señor, you are lucky they did not arrest you," he'd said, leaning forward from his post at the front desk when Arthur first arrived, complaining to Jane about the hassle he'd had at customs.

Then he told them about the roundup of suspected coup plotters a week earlier.

"Oh wow," Jane said, remembering the morning she'd woken to deserted streets; going down to take Arthur's phone call, she'd found the lobby filled with people watching some somber general on the communal TV. "I thought it had something to do with soccer."

"Soccer?" Arthur said in disbelief, imagining the footage he could have gotten. "Were there tanks in the streets?"

"Maybe a troop carrier or two." Was that the reason Cristóbal didn't want to go back into the bush? "But the next day everything was back to normal."

"Shopkeepers who did not open for business," the hotelkeeper explained, "would be accused of striking in sympathy with the coup. If there was one. Sometimes the government stages fake coups for their own reasons."

He offered to draw them a map around that day's military checkpoints all the way to the road that would take them out of the capital, out to the village at the edge of the forest where they would leave the car.

THE [O]PEN ROAD PUT them both in a better mood, a warm breeze blowing in through the windows of the car. Framed by the windshield, the sky was a blue screen above scrub trees. The bright day washed out the camcorder's built-in monitor, so Arthur used its gun site to pan over to Jane, the flat landscape passing behind her like one of those panoramic scrolls that Victorians used to slowly unroll in theaters—the first "movies"—artists rendering trees and waterfalls instead of saints....

"So tell us..."

"...what's so fascinating about fleas..." her cameraman asked. Finally. The black lens of the camera stared back at her like the lidless eye of a cobra. But also one that spoke, and this is what it said: 'Don't screw up.'

As a girl, she'd had a poster in her bedroom: Jane Goodall, alone on a hilltop, binoculars in hand, jungle canopy below.... The camera had caught her in the moment just before she made first contact with her apes and revolutionized primate study. Before hearing about Jane Goodall, it never occurred to Janie—for that was what she was called back then—that she could become a scientist. Or a judge or an astronaut in a world where women scientists, judges, or astronauts didn't exist.

It wasn't that she thought she couldn't be one, it was just something she never thought about—Duck or Rabbit—the way a person never thinks about opening a bank account in sand dollars. If her future did come to mind it was always like some movie where she was the mom or a cashier or one of the other real women she knew. Her grandmother stayed home—not dress up in judge's robes, not even for Halloween—while men, like her grandfather, were the ones who went on insect safaris, not even imagining a girl like her would like to come along even though he was always happy to give her tours of his specimen collections.

Then, in 6th grade, the teacher showed the class a filmstrip about Jane Goodall and Janie's world was rocked as a canoe that tips one way then the other until it settles into a new steady state: upside down. She came across the poster of Jane Goodall in a record shop and put it up where she could look upon it as she drifted off to dreams of apes using tools, apes living as families instead of alone in cages.... Awake, her math scores shot up because she had some vague idea that math was important to science—all her scores went up as she worked toward becoming the Joan d'Arc of Science, laying waste to the eye-rollers that the real Jane Goodall must have vanquished too—and not by discovering a new kind of ape; the apes she studied were the same apes anyone could have seen. All she did was show how they could be seen differently, and that made them different—not even the same animal.

Now, here was little Janie. Camera on. Hoping to do the same with lice. She imagined some young version of herself as a girl today—trying to get her neighbors to put their newspapers out on the curb so she could collect them with her wagon for the paper drive instead of the landfill—it's called "recycling," she explained, before they closed the door, snickering as though she were trying to convert them to a new religion—and maybe reusing a newspaper was laughable against the immensity of the earth—but the girl had to do something!—and she knew, just knew that if she kept at it, one day they would see the 'rabbit' as a 'space ship earth' and together they'd save the planet. Then, there she was, the little girl standing in the great hall of the Field Museum, eyes fixed on Jane in the video Arthur was making—the woman in the video—her!—seeming to speak directly to her, and Jane took a moment to compose herself.

The story she was about to tell would transform how people saw lice—not even the same animal—and so transform the dinosaurs they lived on—not even the same animal—and so transform the people who studied them—women, like her, not even the same animal. Jane knew because she was one of those animals—but not the one that she'd grown up thinking she'd become, though as often as not the world around couldn't see it: feeble old men holding the door, or giving her a seat like she was a baby animal too weak to stand; department heads giving her a pat on the head like the retriever who'd brought back the right answer; PIs with their condescending understanding that she, the only woman in the lab, would have to turn into a werewolf once a month; the world around her casting her as the character who was too emotional, too childlike, too illogical, too impulsive, attracted to shiny things....

One day, it wouldn't be like this. There would be so many women in labs that all of them, those in the lab and those outside, would be different animals than what they were today, and the only discovery it would take would be to find a new story to tell about them.

She lifted her chin into the Jane Goodall pose: pensive, yet confident, her face tilted toward the sun—if only she had that horsy jawline!—her eyes trained on something in the distance: the Future!

She got that spaced-out look again. Arthur hadn't seen a chick zone out like that since art school when the ganjapreneur he sat next to in his 2D class would forget where she was, drifting off into 3D, then 4, 5, 6, 7, 18D?—who knew how many dimensions the psychedelic world had?

He pulled in; the weird thing about keeping a camera on someone was that it always made them want to talk. And not just talk. Confess: focus on what was important to them and so reveal who they were. "Is there a problem?" he asked, trying to figure out how to cast her. She had her shit together too much to be the nutty professor type, and her lack of glasses worked against the female nerd he'd imagined he'd be shooting. Black hair, a short, no-nonsense cut, she sort of looked like one of those tough chicks, a woman cop or marine. But her voice and mannerisms were too suburban nice for him to frame her that way. Girl Jock, Mother Theresa of the Fleas, Betty Boop, Xena.... Nothing seemed to fit. Maybe if she'd at least take off that Olivia Newton John headband.... He considered "a woman of contradictions" but that was too messy to get across in a few frames—but maybe more Indian Jones-ish?—just as John Huston didn't get Katherine Hepburn to be a good spinster in *The African Queen* until he told her to play it as if she were Eleanor Roosevelt.

"Actually, I study Lice," Jane began.

"Huh? Could you speak up? More like you're an explorer in a lecture hall." He clipped a directional mic to her collar so he could catch her voice without the road noise.

"I do study fleas, but my specialization is lice. Feather lice. There's a big difference: feather lice have powerful mandibles to chew feathers, to cling to the hot, twitchy body of the bird they live on...."

As she spoke, the transparency she would show in class during this part of the lecture seemed to fill the hazy, sun-streaked windshield of the car; it even had the same creamy white as the light of an overhead projector. She'd given these introductory lectures so often that she could repeat them in her sleep, and she sometimes did, thinking about all the things she had to do after class while her mouth continued on autopilot. During one such lecture, her mind had drifted off into an argument that she'd been having with an RA over whose duty it was to wash the petri dishes—the nerve of the guy!—assuming that the only female RA in his group was supposed to, naturally, do the dishes!—and she'd become so incensed by what she should have said to him that she'd come to, in mid-sentence, and been shocked to find a classroom full of undergraduates before her.

But when it was good, when the students cared and really paid attention, she'd fall into another kind of trance: God, how she loved the language!—the music of the Greek names—the Ceratophyllidae and Leptopsyllidae—the names coming together as stanzas—the Order of the Phthiraptera—stanzas forming poems—the modification of Siphonaptera during the switch from a hair host-environment to a feathered one—invisible worlds living in the underwing of a gull; the underwing of the gull giving it lift; the lift allowing it to soar above the sea, spot fish below; fish and water and gulls and wind all combining to make a shoreline different from a forest; forest and shore combining to make a coast; coast line and fields and mountains and deserts combining to make.... Pass out the syllabus, an invocation to the Muse of Evolution.... Standing before a class of majors, she could feel like a Homeric Bard reciting the *Iliad*, no, reciting an epic greater than the *Iliad*, which, after all, only had a single war, while to declaim the epic of 3,000 tribes of lice—warring across millions of years—in struggles of total annihilation or victory for every cell, every mutation, every bud, branch, and limb on The Tree—as they evolved from bark-chewing lice, to skin-chewing lice, to feather-chewing lice—was to chant the epic of the world. *The Greatest Story Ever Told.*

"...the legs of feather lice are weak, while fleas developed powerful legs so they can jump on and off their host," she said loud enough to peg his sound-level meter, "a dog, for example, that begins to scratch itself...."

Lice and itchy dogs. And he was supposed to make something heroic out of that? He turned down the gain, and then panned from her to the landscape scrolling by, grainy and pixelated in his viewfinder. "So okay," he said, stifling a yawn, "tell the kids of America what's so fascinating about lice."

[**DRIVING ALONG**], it amazed Arthur how little they had to travel to not only get out of the capital, but out of the 20th century: it were as if there were the grid of streets, then there wasn't. Two wires ran out of the capital, one for phone, the other for power, reminding him of those 19th-century paintings that showed Native Americans and buffalos fleeing before The Goddess of Progress or some such, unspooling telegraph wire as she went along and leaving in her wake farmland where there had once been prairies and forests....

But while North America had been settled by trading companies back in England—a long commute—the land here had been shaped by soldiers who built haciendas: self-sufficient militarized compounds, whose generals broke away from the mother country to become nations unto themselves. So North America transitioned from farms to agri-corps, paving the Midwest with corn; miles of trees had been planted along the highways of Virginia to block views of mountains whose tops had been blasted away for their coal—it was hard to tell any difference between nature and commerce—while here, generations of generals-turned-dictator parceled out the land to favored officers who cut their ties to the mother country since going back meant hanging for treason. They took indigenous wives and established their own haciendas, laying down an infrastructure that shaped the country to this day. Even the wealthy suburb they passed though on their way out of Asunción showed it: each house walled off from its neighbor, broken glass embedded in its adobe to prevent outsiders from scaling the walls; a metal ranch-style gate that could be

rolled open with the solemnity of a drawbridge; a water tank on the roof, electric generator out in the yard to make each dwelling, out of necessity, out of habit of mind, as independent of the iffy police and city services as possible....

A motor scooter shot past, the Virgin Mary emblazoned across its rear fender making its driver invincible. A walled, ranch house stood alone against an expanse of horizon like those first haciendas—mestizo children out in the yard. Arthur turned his camera on them, waving to the kids to prompt them to wave back.

"...fleas are descended from lice, so lice are a far more ancient than fleas," Jane continued, knowing what an uphill battle she had making lice fascinating to laymen. At a party last year, she'd started telling a group of people what she did, their initial jokes and exclamations becoming frozen smiles that wilted before she could get past the preliminaries they needed to understand the really cool stuff....

If only she'd specialized in fleas! Fleas were always the golden girls of the paramecium world what with their plagues and all—*Bring out your dead!* "The louse may be the oldest living parasite," she said now, trying. "Generations live and die on the same animal, as if it were a small tropical island.

"In the world of feather-chewing lice alone, there are 8,500 'Islands,' that is, species of birds. Like Darwin on Galápagos, we've identified over 25,000 species of 'tortoises'—that is, feather lice—each one specialized to the particulars of its 'island,' that is, its respective host: *Ibidoecus bisignatus* has a broad head to accommodate

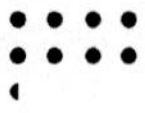

8,500

bird species

25,000

feather lice

the large mandibular muscles it needs to chew through the tough neck and head feathers of the glossy ibis, but were it to stray...."

"...to the wings, its size would make it easy to pick off," she was saying, and he wished they were at a party instead of caged together in this car. Class would be better if he could get a beer. He tried to follow her dry explanations, but she may as well have been going "meow, meow, meow." He adjusted the white balance of the camera, and she suddenly looked ghostly in the little CRT screen in the viewfinder. "...there, thrives *Colpocephalum leptopygos*: a smaller louse that can flee quickly across the wide feathers of wings...." Framed within the tiny TV-screen of a monitor-viewfinder, Jane's ghostly image could have been any number of the talking heads Arthur had shot in the past: spokeswomen addressing fund managers, or the narrator of *The Judicial Process*, or an actress knocking herself out to pump some interest into *Your Phone Bill Explained*. He seemed to hold them all in the cup of his hand, curved around the monitor to keep day shine from completely washing out Jane's video image, a whole crowd of ghosts bleeding through her head bobs, voice modulation, and the other tricks narrators used to transform something dutifully good for you into something fun and exciting.

"Meow, meow, meow...."

More often than not the actors and actresses couldn't save their subject. Nothing could. But the artifice of the attempt still made him marvel at the thousands of things the same "thing" could be. Once, he'd seen an actress stare at a single word in her script—"No"—trying to puzzle it out. When her opposite teased her she said, "Give me a cue." Then she proceeded to make "No" mean like 40 different things by the way she said it. And the same was true with a camera, a looking glass that....

—Yeah! Alice through the looking glass!—a way to cast Jane suddenly opened before him: he'd shoot her as Alice! Not the wide-eyed Alice everyone thinks of but the Alice at its end: the Alice who had already downed the Drink Me potion, had been into the microscopic world of fleas and back, and was confidently giving her recitation to the adults, sure in her knowledge of things the adults would never see, and wouldn't understand if they could.

As the miles went by, she explained how to a louse, the microenvironment of a bird's body remained constant—even if the bird migrates for thousands of miles, suffering drastic changes in climate and diet. "The important point is that parasite evolution runs counter to evolution in general; every evolutionary step for people, for example, has made us less dependent on a particular environment. The more a louse evolves, though, the more dependent it becomes on its host. That's why entomologists say, 'Show me the louse...'"

"'...and I'll tell you its host,'" she said, just as the camera slipped, and focused on his crotch. The sight gag was so stupid it made him laugh.

Finally! she thought, a show of interest. "It's also the reason there's an excellent chance that primitive forms are alive today," she said, excitedly, "living in some hidden microclimate."

"Microclimate," he sniggered. "Like in *The Lost World*?" Claymation dinosaurs roared at explorers on an inaccessible plateau full of pterodactyls....

"Exactly like *The Lost World*," she said, throwing fuel on his fire of curiosity, "only in miniature."

"In miniature," he repeated flatly. "The Galápágos island we're going to see is in miniature—a bird with lice."

She nodded excitedly. Each animal a lost continent; each parasite evolved to live there and nowhere else. She hesitated, because what she was about to say sounded so crazy. Then she blurted out, "Or a feathered dinosaur!"

She glanced over at him, expecting him to be agape at what she'd just said. Feathered dinosaur! Didn't he get the bombshell she'd just dropped?

"You meant we're going to a jungle—"

"Forest."

"—to look for a flea—"

"Louse."

"—that chewed on the feathers of a dinosaur?"

She nodded excitedly.

"Dinosaurs don't have feathers."

"That's what everyone says!" she shouted, slamming the VU to max.

["...LOST WORLDS are real," she said, sitting with him under the single tree some farmer must have left for its shade when he clear-cut the rest, the poor soil not good for more than a few seasons, and so now abandoned and full of savannah grass. "Australia used to be one: a land cut off from the rest of the world. Back in Europe, people thought that descriptions of kangaroos and wallabies were a lot of crazy sailor stories…."

Arthur handed her one of the empanadas they had bought on the way out: chorizo baked in buns and wrapped in tinfoil. "Lost worlds still exist today too, it's just that they keep getting smaller. We might be sitting on one." She pointed out how spongy the ground was around them. How many passing drivers had stopped to squat behind the tree they sat under, uric acid altering the microbial food chain of the ground? "I'm sure that the millions of insects eating microbes eating organic matter is what's aerating the ground here, making it more porous than over by the road."

He stood up. "Oh, that would make a great movie: *Lost Latrines*."

It would, she knew. But then she decided that he was probably being sarcastic, so moved on: "Maybe. But most of the lost worlds that still exist are harder to find. When the last ice age began, sea levels dropped, and exposed land formations, like the ones we now call the Bahama Islands. The ocean water trapped in their caves became lost worlds of aquatic life with animals like Remipedia: an underwater centipede with poisonous fangs that was alive before the dinosaurs and living in this lost world, unchanged, for 300 million years.

"Who knows how many other prehistoric insects are hiding in permafrost and seafloor sediments."

"You ever see *The Andromeda Strain*?"

"Every time one of these pockets gets exposed it's like a doorway onto the ancient world opens up. And out walks a prehistoric life-form."

"Still sounds like a movie." He balled up the tinfoil from his empanada, and hit it like a home run into the far weeds.

With one easy motion, she slipped her head out of the cord she wore as a necklace, pulling from within her shirt a medallion, then a large orange bead that was also strung on a cord. "Some movies are more fantastic than others—especially when they're true."

The medallion was the kind sold in museum gift shops and bore a bas-relief of that famous bird fossil: the skeleton of what looked like a chicken flattened by a truck before it could cross to the other side of the road.

"*Archaeopteryx*," she explained.

Its wings were spread the way eagles were always posed on national flags. But its head was bowed, as though it had died while praying.

"The oldest bird." But she wanted him to look at the bead: a honey-colored blob of amber.

"That little blob in your hands contains an animal as momentous as *Tiktaalik roseae*, the only known link between fish and mammals. It's a prehistoric louse."

"Oh yeah?"

"Do you know how rare these are! Think how many insects have lived over the millions of years they have been on earth. Why, just the ants alive today weigh four times more than its 4.8 billion people." She pointed to a line of bird tracks in dried mud. "Those will be gone with the next rain; in the forest, where birds live, their paper-thin bones don't even last that long. They go right into the leaf litter where they decompose. When it comes to their parasites, it would take a miracle for one to be fossilized." She took a bite of her empanada. "No, only a dope would look for bird fossils in a forest."

From her breast pocket she produced a jeweler's loupe. "Look closer." When he trained the loupe on the amber, he could see a bug-like spec—or twig or something trapped inside.

"How old did you say this bug was?" He put down the loupe, picked up his Leica, and screwed its macro lens into the camera's body, a Noctilux 50mm f/1.2, that let him get close. He pulled in on the amber as tight as he could, the yellow blob going in and out of clarity as he worked the focusing ring: he could see something but not the detail she was describing: "Its head is more globular than a modern animal louse, but not as rounded as bark lice, the nearest and oldest ancestor on the evolutionary tree. Unlike those primitive bark eaters, this one's body is flattened dorsoventrally—you know, like a dinner plate—so it could run between hair or feather shafts. But it's not flattened enough to live on modern birds and doesn't show any of the other evolutionary developments that allowed Late Triassic lice to exploit their new habitat—bird feathers. Its thorax is more rounded than a modern feather louse; it's covered with simple setae of various lengths; it still has a primitive number of instars, indicating that it had a longer immature stage than modern lice..."

She may as well have been reading tea leaves compared to the black speck he could see through the macro lens.

"...its antennae consist of a scape, pedicle, and three-segment flagellum like modern lice, but the last two segments haven't evolved to the point where they are fused like in modern Amblycera, so its antennae are still longer—all of these things indicate it would be more vulnerable to preening—at least that's what most people would say. But what if longer antennas helped it survive on an animal whose mouth hadn't yet evolved to have the tweezer-like precision of a beak? An animal that had—"

"What's that other thing in the amber?"

"A sliver of feather," Jane said reverently. "It's almost too beautiful to be true. Under a microscope you can see it's a particle of the red feather that the louse was attached to when they were entombed together...."

When he switched back to the loupe, he realized that he'd been looking at the wrong thing—the insect itself was only a tiny mite attached to a sliver of feather that he'd mistaken for the bug itself.

"Wouldn't that explain why this louse has generalized mouth parts but sharp, apical toothed mandibles that are parallel with ventral surfaces of the head like in modern Amblycera?"

Even so, even though he now realized what he was looking at was a sliver of feather with a bug attached, she still seemed to be reading a whole Jurassic world into a black speck. "How do you know the bug isn't flat because someone stepped on it?

She sighed. "Do you see the fierce, T-Rex-like teeth of the louse?" she said slowly, a kindergarten teacher at Show and Tell. "See how ferociously they've bitten into the feather fragment?"

"I don't see any teeth."

"Don't you see that serrated edge protruding from the head?"

"That's a head?"

Using a twig, she etched into the earth the features he was to look for: VVVVVVVVV.

"Under a microscope it's possible to tell that the sawlike teeth were made to nibble through both feathers and skin. Most entomologists would call this a lack of specialization, proving how ancient it is—it hadn't yet had time to evolve into the more specialized feather-chewing lice we know today. Or—and here's where it gets REAL interesting—OR it's not undeveloped at all but instead is highly specialized to live on an animal that had both reptile *skin* and *feathers*." She sucked back a drool of excitement over the thought.

"Look at its abdomen. See that little bump? That's called a cerci. A cerci is to lice what the sloped forehead is to a caveman! It's the louse version of the feature that showed *Archaeopteryx* was between modern birds and dinosaurs, or swimming *Dorudon* were between modern whales and land-walking anthracotheres, or australopithecine were between modern humans and monkeys!"

She gave a laugh at the reaction other etymologists would have if they could've heard the outrageous thing she'd just said. Outrageous but nonetheless true!

"Believe me, that little guy's going to blow the collective minds of the entomological world! Any entomologist worth her salt would have to admit that it's at least from the Cretaceous Period, from the time that most people say birds were descending from dinosaurs, 60 million years ago—but it could be—no, I'm certain—that it's even older: an extinct ancestor of Permopsocida, one that morphological comparisons have always predicted, but has never been actually seen. Till now!"

[WHEN SHE WAS YOUNG], Jane used to get lost in the woods near her parents' house the way others got lost in a book, its leaves, its bugs, absorbing her with their endless plot twists. Actually, what she and the other kids called "The Woods" was one of those patches of land that stayed feral because no company wanted it: an old hilltop cemetery that had served the neighborhood 100 years ago but fell into neglect after the descendants of those venerable dead died themselves, and the city used the remaining space to bury those too poor to bury themselves. The back side of this potter's field dropped off to a strip of swampy wasteland adjoining a little-used railroad siding.

Tangles of ivy, tree roots that had grown thick enough to topple weathered tombstones.... Brambles, sticker weeds, and snot flowers covered the slope of the hill down to the tracks: an algae-filled marsh that was a Garden of Eden to her. Pristine. Devoid of school rules, or any rules except those of the wild: there were always bedsprings to jump on. Untamed: a place of muddy edges, oozing with tadpoles. At any moment she could come upon a lizard sunning itself on one of the warm rails of the railroad siding, or a nest of hornets that had made a home in a heap of bricks. More than once, on the eroded side of the cemetery's hill, she'd found human bones.

Depending on how much rain there had been, the hillside would erode and the swamp that gathered at its base would expand and contract. One spring it was deep enough to force kids to build a makeshift raft to navigate the channels between its cottonwood trees and bushes, and the occasional TV cabinet or cushionless sofa. The following year it had dried completely, leaving only a weedy field of junk. The first time that happened, she'd cried for the minor miracles that had vanished with the pond—exotic pond striders, *Aquarius remigis*, she'd later call them, that could walk on water and dart sideways quick enough to dodge her spit, or the tiny black leeches, Hirudinae, that would rivet themselves to her white legs.

But then, miraculously, the next year they were all back—as if the rain had generated snails, mosquito larvae, and even tiny fish right out of broken glass and couch grass: farmer ants and mayflies, or Ephemeroptera, as she'd latter learn to say it, termites, or Isoptera, as she'd be told they were called, Odonata, as she'd put it in her adopted language, along with Plecoptera, Coleoptera, culturing Plecoptera in vitro, charting negative binomial distributions of Neuroptera, Thysanura, graphing the transmission synchronization hypothesis of Lepidoptera, or the sensillum coeloconicum on each of the last two segments in the five-segmented antennae or two on the terminal segment in the forty-segmented antennae of Menoponidae, Boopiidae, and Ricinidae, respectively, the A, B, Cs, from Amblycera to Zoraptera, composing her new mother tongue.

When she closed her eyes and tried to breathe in the scent of that place—its brackish, stagnant water, sunlight, aphids, and simple answers to how elements came together to form life—she could only smell computer paper. How large her stories had made that puddle back then, inflating garden snakes to water moccasins, stink bugs, and earwigs, and centipedes, into the beasts of an Everglades. How narrow her stories made it now, turning an Amazon of exotic beasts into bar graphs of Dermaptera, a census printout of Anoplura, making a brief encyclopedia entry out of Mallophaga, Diptera, Psocoptera.... How expansive her drawings of insects seemed compared to the strings of genetic letters that biology was starting to turn every animal into.

WHILE DRIVING IN THE STATES, you could tell you were approaching a lake by the pleasure boats, dripping wet, being towed in the opposite direction. Here, Arthur could tell they were headed toward a forest by the logging trucks: flatbeds loaded with tree trunks and rumbling toward the port in the capital he and Jane had come from. The heads of the drivers appeared tiny behind their windshields, like determined worker ants, their dashboards an altar of deedle balls and religious icons, the trucks' undercarriages orange with the clay of unpaved logging roads.

As Jane turned off the main road, the car that had been behind them continued on toward the waterfall that was the focal point for the few tourists in the area: Cola de Caballo. The terrain became more hilly. The road became narrower, passing not towns but signs to other towns, then there weren't even signs. Just an expansive prairie, cut by an orange clay road still slick from rain, its shiny parallel tire ruts winding like twisted railroad tracks up then down low hills, toward a tree line that looked like a cloud front or mountain range on the horizon.

"I thought we'd be there by"

"...now," Arthur said

[1970]

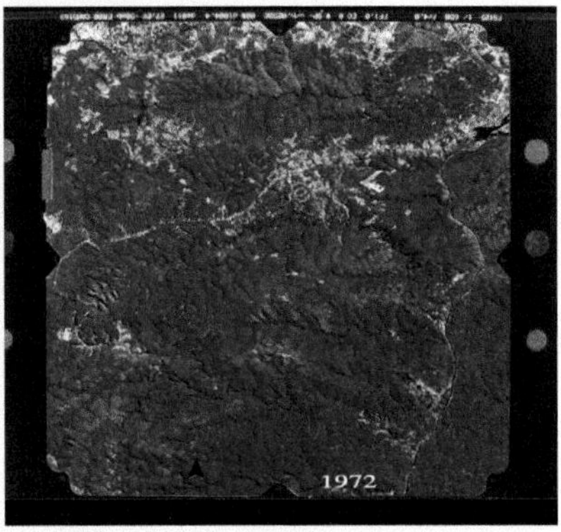

[1972]

[THE FOREST]

"The Interior Atlantic Forest used to fill South America," Jane said, navigating the bumpy road. "Home to sixty-one mammal species, and over four hundred bird species, including the endangered rufous-faced crake, the endangered helmeted

[1975]

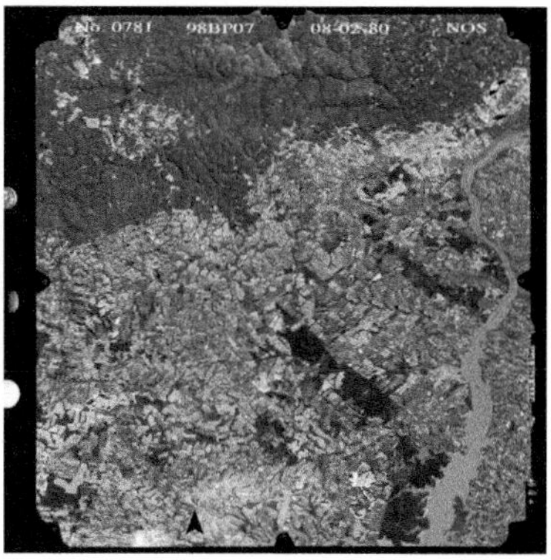

[1980]

woodpecker.... The endangered giant river otter, the endangered collared anteater.... The endangered kirandy.... More plants, and more prehistoric plants, than anywhere else, from ferns the size of your pinkie to ten meters tall. And who knows how many species we'll never know about because every year the Atlantic Forest loses an area the size of Connecticut. Gone. Vanished." The thought brought to mind the look Cristóbal had, as though he were describing a loved one not expected to make it out of intensive care, while he explained: "Forests like this aren't as sexy as the rainforest, so they don't get the pub those places do. No pub, no donations, no celebrity to tell their story. Mostly they just slip away...."

"I thought we'd be there by now," Arthur said, looking at her map.

"Maps go out of date before they can be printed. Old Professor Hauser, an emeritus who used to hang out in the lab when I was a doctoral student, used to tell us stories about traveling through Paraguay by boat. The place was a web of tributaries, but they all dried up after the river that fed them was dammed for a hydroelectric project.

"The forest has been shrinking ever since Europeans landed," she added, wishing she'd taken more time to talk to Old Professor Hauser—instead of always feeling like she had to get back to work, "but there was always so much forest to shrink that no one cared—the way nobody in Arizona cared about water rights until they had to jump down from their piers to walk out to their boats. But the effort wasn't to save the forest; it turned into a gold rush to cut down what was left.

"In the '70s the road we're on was cut, opening up the forest to industrial logging. General Stroessner?—the guy whose portrait you saw at the airport? The Protector of the Motherland gave away huge tracts of the forest as bribes and payoffs to army buddies. All they had to do was drive out the Guaraní who had lived in the forest for thousands of years, foraging grubs, hunting monkeys or armadillo—basically living as they had before Columbus invaded."

"I heard about that."

"Yeah, it got international attention fifteen years ago. Cristóbal, our local partner, was here through it all. No one used the phrase 'ethnic cleansing' back then, he said, but that's what it was. Only it was more like economic cleansing, given that half the people doing the cleansing were part or full Indian themselves. The Aché used to rely on firebrands."

"Like in *Quest for Fire*?"

"Yeah. Except they had to go up against soldiers with rifles. Talk about one-sided. As far back as colonial times the locals would kidnap Achés, keeping them as slaves. Guayakís was their name for them. It means 'rabid rats'—torture, rape—you name it. They used steel traps.... After the ex-generals got involved, it became

systematic. You see the results around you," she said, the road they were on surrounded by waist-high weeds except for a single tree, every hundred feet or so, stripped of its branches so it could be used as a utility pole. The forest itself was still a formless shape in the distance.

"It's unbelievable how recent this all was," he said, imagining dense jungle where they now drove, soldiers with modern rifles ambushing forest people who fought back with blowguns and stone axes....

"It's only been six years since the last of the Aché survivors gave up and came out of the forest. They live on a reservation near the pueblo we'll use as a base camp. The missionaries are trying to teach them to farm. But the long-range planning that a farmer has to do is as alien to them as flying a spaceship would be to us. An international court gave them the right to hunt and forage for their needs, provided they only use traditional methods. If it wasn't for that, they'd be extinct by now too."

[BIENVENIDOS]. In the fading light, a cloud of gnats buzzed around a plywood sign cut in the shape of Paraguay. The single phone line they had been following since the capital ended up ahead in a compound of cinderblock buildings surrounded by a ranch-wire fence. The place had the look of an outpost. Jane liked to think of it as a French village in an occupied countryside, the villagers going about their business during the day, but coming out at night to misdirect road signs, or do anything they could to keep the logging companies from bleeding them dry. But Cristóbal explained how they were more like collaborators, pressed into service by trying to live on $5 a week.

She eased the car down into the area that served as a town square. A couple of footpaths radiated out toward other buildings. The square itself had the essentials: adobe mission on one side, adobe cantina across from it, its windows flickering with the gray light of a television, a gasoline generator chugging along beside it. Every time Jane saw one of these juxtapositions—like a *curendera* in the *mercado* using a calculator to add up the prices of her potions—Jane felt a wrinkle in time.

Faces began to appear in widows—Guaraní features—as Jane drove up to what seemed to be part general store, part garage. A Brasília like hers rested on blocks out front as though it had been waiting so long for a part that it had become part of the landscape. A man in work clothes rose from a car seat that served as a couch out on the porch.

"That's Felipe," she told Arthur, pulling in behind a pickup truck parked under a corrugated lean-to. "He'll watch the car for us while we're in the bush." A water tower supported by legs that could have come from an erector set leaned like the Tower of Pisa. "Hola, Felipe," Jane called to him, killing the engine.

IN THE MORNING, Arthur was woken by the crowing of a cock. He smelled car smells, his face against the pleather of the Cadillac seat that served as the couch on Felipe's porch during the day but had been his bed last night. A big mongrel stirred beside him, exhausted from running with the dogs he'd heard last night, no doubt. "At night they get brave," Felipe had said, talking about all the dogs that could be seen sleeping in the village during the day but returned each evening to the forest to run as a pack, to howl, hunt, fuck, and fight.

Arthur got up, stretched, checked on the extension cord that had been run out a window for his benefit and plugged into the converter that was doing the translation of South into North American electricity. The light on the battery charger was green. All systems go. He used the towel a boy had laid out for him the night before and washed at the pump. Then he tapped a Paraguayan Palermo out of its pack, and lit up, wondering if he could get ahold of some homegrown, or wild, around here. Ganja grew like weeds throughout South America. That's why they called it weed, he figured. And someone surely had to have a drying operation. Was it too early to ask around at the bar? He unpacked his camcorder from the black foam that protected it in its case, looked around for local color....

IN THE MORNING, Jane was woken by the hubbub of a playground. At this distance, the kids sounded abstract, a collection of laughter and cries that all sounded as happy as the morning chorus of birds. For a moment she thought she was back in her own childhood, but then she opened her eyes to a gory crucifix hanging on the wall of the spartan bedroom she'd been given by Felipe and Marga for the night. And she remembered what childhood was really like—the schoolyard fights, the playground tears of defeat and humiliation—and she remembered what the morning chorus of birds was really made of—as much aggression as happiness, as many threats to stay out of each other's territory as calls for sex.

Was Arthur awake yet? Getting into her jeans, she could see through the window ESCUELA NO. 823: a low building with a corrugated metal roof. In its clay yard, kids played on a sphere of rusted pipes—monkey bars in the shape of a globe—a rusted-out planet.

Beyond the school was a large area that had been cleared of brush. A bulldozer stood abandoned in the field, a pile of broken trees pushed to one end like a gigantic beaver dam. The field would be an airstrip one day. Now that the forest was supposed to be protected, someone in government had gotten the idea to turn it into an eco-tourism destination. But construction of its resort had been abandoned. Still, she could see that there was government money involved, so maybe it would happen yet, the forest and waterfall linked by air to spins of a roulette wheel.

The sizzle of an egg hitting a frying pan came from the kitchen. "Señora, el

desayuno," Marga called.

FELIPE GAVE THEIR [EXPEDITION] a ride in his pickup truck to the trailhead at the edge of the forest: Jane and Arthur in the cab, and the two teenagers Arthur had hired to be bearers rode in the bed with her gear. Did they know?

Before leaving, Felipe and his wife Marga had tried to dissuade her from going back into the forest. They described the tensions that had been building again between the settlers and the Aché. When the government began clearing for a landing strip, the Aché were convinced that it would sweep away their right to hunt and forage in the forest just as the first roads had brought laws making it illegal for them to live there. Except not being able to hunt would be a death sentence—or so they thought. And what Jane thought was that they knew better than anyone else. Your taxon doesn't make it into the modern age without knowing something about survival.

"Caníbales," Marga had said, biting her fist in a gesture that needed no translation, getting in the way of homesteaders or logging jobs that turned waste-land—how they saw the forest—into cash....

A bulldozer operator had been badly wounded by an Aché arrow and the entire reservation fled into the forest, sure that soldiers would soon use the skirmish as an excuse to finish them off.

Stay or go, it would not go well for the Aché as planes sometimes spotted even more primitive tribes. Sometimes, when logging drove one into another, war would break out, and the loser would stagger out into the space-age to die. Some of these peoples—a diaspora of ancient civilizations—had originally retreated into the forest hundreds of years ago to escape Spanish conquistadors. They had lived there so long that the outside world only existed for them as myths of *Tierra sin Mal*, as this Eden was called in the language of their conquerors: The Land-without-Evil. Some didn't even know there was a world outside their territory, let alone that it was inhabited by hairy, dead-white, manlike creatures that would come after their trees with bulldozers and guns.

"They say they—" Felipe shadowboxed a one-two punch. "This time they fight—for their lives. Their home. The forest."

"O morir," Marga added.

Jane could tell from Felipe's tone that he was warning the boys through the truck's missing rear window to be careful of any Aché they might come across. "Y si tu estás en peligro de los indios, huir." Or at least that's what she imagined he was saying. They didn't even seem to be listening, hunched as they were over the bleeping of a Game & Watch, a Russian knockoff of one of those new Japanese handheld electronic games that looked like a calculator and sounded like crickets. Kids went nuts for them.

"How much are you paying these boys?" she asked Arthur, debating whether or not to tell him about the Aché. She herself didn't know if there was anything to worry about: she'd heard so much B.S. about the Aché that she knew not to believe 90% of it. Still, when she'd gotten Felipe alone, and asked him if there really was anything to be afraid of, he'd simply shrugged. "Don't worry, be happy," is how she'd interpreted that shrug, wishing Cristóbal had been there to confirm. But he wasn't. And this hardened her resolve.

But then she would think of Dian Fossey battling poachers and corrupt officials in Rwanda to keep them from killing the gorillas she was trying to study. Murdered for her efforts, she was. Still, Jane thought, they were more likely to get hurt driving to the forest than walking in it—a minimal risk to reach a habitat that might well be disturbed by the time she could return again. No landscape was truly the same even two days in a row, and that was the real danger, she knew. Why, just within her own university she knew of three archaeologists, two zoologists, and a conservationist whose careers had been strangled by civil wars: archaeological digs looted in their absence, delicate permafrost destroyed by snowmobiles.... The U.S. boycotts the Olympics to protest Russia's invasion of Afghanistan, but who was there to protest the destruction of habitat? Unable to do fieldwork, there was

a whole generation of paleontologists who had spent what should have been the best years of their research life waiting for politics to change....

"Look!" Arthur yelled.

Above, a flock of parrots headed for the forest—an island of green that grew ever larger as they approached. The parrots, with their bird's-eye view, could see the truth. They must have been flying along and then suddenly found themselves, like fish thrown out of water, out of the forest. Just in the week she'd been gone she could see that its edge had been chewed at some more. Distant smoke signaled brush being burnt to clear another field for farming. The parrots were making a beeline back to what was left. As was she.

THE DIVISION BETWEEN FOREST AND NOT-FOREST was as stark as if they'd crossed an empty room that dead-ended into a green wall. "Estamos aqui," Felipe announced, pulling up to it. When they got out, she could smell its freshness, hear a kind of white noise of animal, leaf, and water gurgles. Arthur chattered away happily as Roque and Jacinto got the Manpack and the rest of her gear.

The strain of lifting the Manpack showed both of them as just a little too thin, or maybe their tee shirts were too baggy—*IBM Typewriters* on Jacinto's shirt—the kind of shirts that were made in sweatshops in China to be given away at conventions in the U.S. before making their way back down the Salvation Army-UNESCO pipeline to here. Arthur had wanted them to come along to make the trip look more like an expedition: "Can't you see how great they'll look lugging your stuff?" he'd argued, "with you cutting a path with your machete?" He raised his arm in pantomime.

After what Felipe and Marga had told her, it didn't seem to be a bad idea to have a bigger group. Especially since Cristóbal wasn't there. But she always hated the way photos of archaeologists, biologists, and other field researchers—Westerners—always had their local "partner" in the front row, even if they left his name off the study. And if Arthur thought he was going to turn her nature film into a cartoon of a safari....

When she complained, he raised his eyebrows, "Nature, is it?—you want documentary?—like those ones that have great photos of an owl hunting a mouse? The photographer who gets those kinds of shots must be incredibly lucky," he scoffed, "he just happens to train his camera on the exact spot where a mouse would walk. And his strobe fires in the exact microsecond the owl's claws open...." As he spoke, he kept getting more and more worked up... "...only a hack would think to put a deer carcass where a tiger and a lion will find it at the same time...."

The boys had stood there silently, looking down at their feet, obviously clueless about what the argument was over but knowing the lesson that had been ground into generations of *campesinos*.

[TRICKS]

Someone must have taken that photo of Jane Goodall, of course, and deep down Jane must have always known that no professional photographer would go into the bush to get a hero shot of a nobody. Maybe the photo wasn't even shot in Africa. Maybe it was all just fake, an illusion that Jane had turned to for solace whenever she was passed over for a grant, mistaken for a secretary, or the wife of one of the "real" biologists, or ran into one of the old-boy networks all the way back to the high-school lab where even the kids were old boys.... Still, she didn't want to admit that making up stories like he did was anything like what she did even though she knew how often conclusions were watered down, or amped up because of the dollars riding on demonstrating why smoking was good for you; then at least not harmful; then finally, not as bad as the government regulations claimed—and that didn't include plain old mistakes, or muffed calls. Well-intentioned errors in interpretation: attempts to clean up data to make the results clearer. The shadowy areas where she and her colleagues often found themselves was so full of lapsed judgment, data that was discarded because it contradicted earlier findings, or out-and-out lying—even if the liar was only lying to himself—that she was almost glad so few cared whether or not Anoplura and Rhyncophthirina formed a monophyletic group that she may as well write a poem about it. Most of all, his words brought up something she couldn't even let herself think about: that she could be wrong. That the truism that had the most truth was *I'll see it when I believe it.* More and more people seemed to invent their own facts these days, even whole histories. A geologist friend worked for years at ExxonMobile, documenting how carbon was heating the earth. She'd assumed that the company would take her research seriously—which it did, redesigning oil platforms to account for future sea-level rise—then setting up the Global Climate Coalition to feed lawmakers, journalists, and everyone else "information" to undermine the very climate science she and her department produced.

What if everything Jane said about the louse in the amber was the result of wanting to see what she saw so bad that she did see it, as Christian and Wang said all along?

"...those lemmings jumping into the sea in *White Wilderness*?" Arthur was saying. "Pushed."

His lip began to quiver, making her think, Geesh, what's with him?

"They had the lemmings run across a spinning turntable that was out of the frame; when the lemmings stepped onto it—*whoosh!*"

"Okay, okay, I get it," she said to shut him up. "All I want is a little truth."

[STEPPING INTO THE FOREST]

Arthur could feel the change as immediately as if they'd stepped from a hot, Arizona parking lot into an air-conditioned lobby. The explosion of green, of bird calls.... The trees muffled their voices as though they'd entered a felt-lined sound booth, and the quiet let in the voice of the trees and flowers and vines. Whatever mental picture he had had of the forest before was just a flat storyboard—not this total immersion—and he suddenly knew how he'd shoot the opening to *Puddle* if he ever got to remake it: just bang!—jump right in, no intro, no credits....

They all seemed to be moved, the way even tourists in a cathedral are hushed by sacred space. Walking along, it felt like going back in time; maybe not back into prehistoric time, but at least back into pre-fax machine time, or even pre-telephone time, which they had, actually: the end of the phone line was literally back in the pueblo.

They walked along, single file in their thoughts, Arthur's mind ablaze with how free shooting here would be. On the last indie he worked, the director wanted to reenact a kidnapping scene where a girl gets pulled into a van at night. But they didn't have the two lighting trucks and major generators it would take to light up the half block that a scene like that would need. So he and John, the director, drove down Clark, shooting with his 16mm wide open until they found a stretch where there was enough light from store signs and windows to make the sidewalk two f-stops brighter than the street. A friend of a friend was willing to lend them a pair of 2Ks for side lighting if they paid the $700 in insurance that had to go with them. But then they discovered that to get far enough back to shoot the scene, they'd have to set up the camera on the street's median, a patch of weeds and litter that was taken care of by the Clark Street Association, which wouldn't let anyone set up a camera on their median without paying them $500 for a piece of paper that the director could show in case some cop came around asking for permission slips. Every city seemed to be getting that way: Nobody lets you light anymore. Or shoot. Every square inch owned. Regulated. You can't even put a tripod in an alley without spending three days at the mayor's office listing your locations, filling out forms about what you're going to do, how you're going to get there, who gave you permission, which is nobody unless you pay their user fees, which they won't let you do without first proving that you're carrying a million dollars of liability.

But here!

He wanted to beat his breast like an ape man!...

The tremolo of a lone tinamou rippled through the leafy hush. Then it suddenly switched to the mouse-like squeak of a manakin and she wondered if she was hearing some South American version of the lyrebird—the bird that imitated sounds around it. An explosion of movement rustled the upper branches: Capuchin monkeys screeched, fleeing through the trees with the synchronization of a school of fish because one of them must have spotted a harpy eagle high above. Every time Jane entered a forest, or a jungle, or a bog. Or desert, or field. Or meadow, or swamp, or tundra or any chunk of untamed land, an excitement came over her that could build to an anxiety attack if she'd let it: a sense of freefall brought on by nature itself, its infinitely complex web of interactions so overwhelming it turned everything she said about fleas into an elaborate hoax, or at best a cartoon.

Nature. Forget about getting it down on film—when she thought of all the things "nature" had been to different people at different times she felt the vertigo of standing on the edge of a precipice. Just this one forest had been a myth of a distant Shangri-la; peaceful animal kingdom; dark, impenetrable mystery; terra incognita; adventure; laboratory; zoo; picture postcard; depository of wood, dirt, and genes with the stampede on to extract all of its useful value.

In the few seconds since they'd entered the forest, a dozen birdcalls she couldn't identify reminded her how inadequate all the charts in the world could be. Even *The Rothschild Collection of Fleas, The Ceratophyllidae: Key to the Genera and Host Relationships*—the massive volume she carried around—was a lie in that it depicted its fleas like butterflies pinned to a board instead of interwoven with the grand scheme of Species, Genera, Families, Orders, Classes, Phyla, Kingdoms, Domains that had been going on long before they were separated by labels. And all based on the logic of the optometrist: is the eye chart clearer when you look through Lens A or Lens B?—what a story!

When she considered the relentless and haphazard strings of extinctions, the chaos of detail around her—no, not chaos, for surely the innumerable factors followed constraints of their own, even if they were too subtle, too multifarious for her to recognize as pattern. Say rather, when she considered how hard it was to say any A caused B, she couldn't even begin to imagine an equation that could describe all that goes on when a woman's high heel breaks off on the stairs and she tumbles backwards—let alone all of the chains of accidents that would have to happen to get from worm to woman. Then there was the epic that man told himself to explain how he got to the top of the food chain, a.k.a. Dominion over all the Earth, a.k.a. the right to peel back mountains, cork rivers, to rub out species as though they were the butt of a cigarette that had been smoked to its end....

What was needed was a theory of chaos, not cause-and-effect. Assuming there was any "there" there to begin with and not just the semantic differences everyone used to distinguish 'dog' from 'cat,' or 'fact' from 'fiction,' for that matter, 'religion' from 'superstition,' 'history' from 'story,' never able to come any closer than a series of approximations, an overlaying of Venn diagrams, when it was more like the story of the turtle that can never get to the pea by continually halving its distance to it. But when she tried to think of another way to proceed other than by noting that Anoplura lice were more like Rhynochophthirina and less like Amblycera lice, and then concluding that Rhynochophthirina was a closer relative to Anoplura than Amblycera, she sighed.

She had Roque take the Manpack off his back, and place it on the ground so she could get a GPS fix of their starting point. She unsheathed its telescoping antenna from its green canvas case, and extended it, then took the hand control from its pouch, and uncoiled the cord that connected it to the main unit. When she switched it on, the little electronic bleeps it gave off jarred—like one of those pagers that doctors began to carry going off in the audience at a symphony, the symphony here played by instruments of wind, of leaves, of birds, of insects.... 23° 00′ 0.45″ S; 54° 21′ 12.12″ W, said the Manpack's L.E.D. readout.

"This way," she said pointing.

Jane in the lead, Roque and Jacinto lugging the Manpack between them, her mind drifted to the Rocky Mountains where she'd once tried to explain the value of scientific cartoons to a woman she'd met off-trail. The woman had been in an environmental science program, she said. But she'd dropped out to chop her own wood, drink from springs, live among the wild flowers; to walk valleys and high country, feel the bite of winter on her nose rather than become part of the lie where temperature was a red vein trapped in glass. While Ms. Natural looked back with that simpy, God-loves-you smile worn by flower-peddling Moonies at airports, Jane tried to explain that she knew that the degree lines etched on a thermometer were only a picture of temperature, that temperature itself was shorthand for what they both felt on their noses in the winter. She knew she was inventing dots that could be connected to form a picture, but that the picture, once it emerged, would have the same relation to a nip in the air as a landscape painting of a field has to the field itself; the same relation of a quadratic equation to the ellipse it describes and the ellipse it describes to the orbit of Mars. If the dots gathered on observation nights were accurate, observations of Venus would supply coordinates for different dots, which, if the math was made to be a true mirror, would describe a different equation, a different ellipse, a different orbit (depending on how you defined orbit). A man-made thing. Like photography. Or logic. Not the thing itself.

Simple to say when you were in the lab, the woman noted, standing before a scene that could have been a vivid postcard if the mountains and their snow-capped peaks weren't a 360° panorama all around; if the clear blue sky wasn't so fresh in their lungs, the sun so comfortably warm on their faces; if the ice-water runoff from those snowy peaks didn't form the ice-cold river rushing over boulders at their feet....

Her reply bugged Jane long after she returned to her lab because she knew its truth: that it was easy to prefer the painting to the field, the aquarium to the sea, the equation to the orbit; so easy to confuse the simplification for the nature it describes, treat it as if it were a real entity, as solid and present as those stepping stones they used to cross the mountain stream, or the path leading deeper into the forest before her now. When had the idea of 'ecology' replaced 'nature'?

She hitched the strap of her rucksack up higher onto her shoulder, took a deep breath, and told herself, Okay, I'm over it now.

For a while, Jane carried the Manpack while the brothers humped her tent and rucks on their heads, as Arthur had asked them to, their faces fixed with a stoicism that said balancing gear on their heads for a boss was no different than digging an irrigation ditch, hauling bricks up a ladder, burning brush to clear a field, or any of the other jobs they had ever done to earn battery money for their Soviet Game & Watch....

Late in the afternoon, the boys wanted to gather some *Ilex paraguariensis* leaves to chew—for a caffeine boost while on the trail, to later dry for maté. With them carrying the equipment, they'd covered more ground than Jane had planned, so she let everyone break off for the day, and set to making camp before they lost the light.

Arthur slumped against her gear; the corner of a book in one of the nylon bags poked him in the ribs. Roque and Jacinto climbed a yerba tree. In Iran, Arthur knew, kids their age were being told a story about Paradise before they were told to hold hands and run across a field that needed to be cleared of landmines. *Ali Ali Ocean Free Free Free....* Roque slipped from the smooth bark of a tree, and Arthur winced when the kid's bare foot came down hard on the ground. The boys laughed.

Back in the U.S., the news had been full of pictures of Rumsfeld shaking hands in one of those gilt, Baghdad palaces, chumming it up for the toe-poppers and other weapons America was giving to Saddam Hussein, and Arthur wondered what else was behind that handshake: I'll trade you one shipment of Dow Chemical sarin in exchange for two ExxonMobile drilling rights once you've "depopulated" those parts of Iran? Rumsfeld didn't go all that way just to say hello.

Resource wars suck, Arthur thought. He got out the Palermos he'd bought in Asunción and pulled the red line to strip away its cellophane wrapper. *Bajo Tenor De Nicotina.*

He tapped the pack to make the tip of the first cigarette pop up. "You got a knife I could use?" he asked Jane, going to where she was messing with her equipment. She handed him a Swiss Army knife. He saw the X-Acto she used on her specimens and said, "A razor would be better."

X-Acto in one hand, cigarette in the other, he went back to where he'd been sitting, then dragged over his hard-shell camera case to use as a worktable. The complications of the world were almost enough to make him nostalgic for the good ol' days when grainy photos of some loser hijacking a plane to Cuba was big news. Carefully he slit the cigarette paper with the X-Acto knife, humming:

...I don't want to die in a nuclear war.
I want to sail away to a distant shore
And live like an APEMAN*....*

He sliced open the cigarette and blew out its tobacco, then flattened the paper on top of his camera case. Then he took the grass he'd scored in the pueblo out of his shirt pocket, an envelope made of old newsprint—and shook out a line onto the cigarette paper.

What if they had a war and nobody came—hippies and acoustic guitars. He rolled the joint, twisting the ends shut, then gave the whole thing a suck to seal it with saliva, and he wondered how everything had gotten so tangled up with everything else—if a butterfly farts on the other side of the world—butterflies on opposite sides of the earth now up in each other's grill; they transplanted the heart of a monkey into some kid; tiny margins of error in every part of a rocket add up until—*KaBoom!*; the U.S. wouldn't even let its athletes go to Moscow because Russia had invaded some tiny speck of a country he'd never even heard of before. Afghani, he thought it was called, named after the weed?... "*...live like an Apeman....*" He got up to help Roque and Jacinto gather dead brush. As a precaution against jaguars, werewolves, the Loch Ness Monster, and whatever else might be out there, they'd planned to keep a fire burning all night.

A supper of reheated rice and beans, and the ever-present Ilolay Dulce de Leche. Roque and Jacinto laid down the large palm leaves they'd picked to use as mats. On top of those went the NASA-like thermal blanket Jane had loaned them—soft cloth on one side, some kind of thermally reflective foil on the other—big enough for them both to sit on. They got out the maté gourds and bombillas they'd brought along, and used her camp pot to heat water. After dinner, they chewed leaves like chaw, each boy growing a wad packed into his lower lip, as they had a serious conversation about something: "¿Crees que Padre que lo robamos?"

"Nosotros no lo robamos. Nosostros lo tomamos."

"What were you humming a little while ago?" Jane asked. She'd finished hoisting the backpacks with their food up into a tree away from where they were sleeping, and had switched off the miner's light of her pith helmet as she came over to sit down with them.

"You know, *Apeman*. By the Kinks."

He looked at the joint, wondering if he should roll some extras while the fire was still bright.

"I love that song!—but now I can't get it out of my head," she said, and she started to hum it, then she saw his stash. "What are you doing?"

"What'd you mean?"

"I mean I didn't know you were into dope."

"I'm not into dope!"

"Then what's that?" she said, pointing at the joint.

"Well, I'm not *into* it. Not the way stoners are into it; I mean, it's not like I know the difference between Columbian and Mexicali or could tell you which years had the best crops of Aussie Blues the way wine connoisseurs can wax poetic about grapes. I couldn't tell you any more about Amsterdam Gold than its name, let alone offer an opinion on if the buds grown in California have a more orangey aroma than the ones from Holland; or if the taste of Afghani is so heavy it tastes like cough syrup; or if the high from AK-47 lasts longer than Black Jack; or if White Queen is a better hybrid than Early Girl, or White Widow or Super Skunk or Easy Rider or Louis XIII; or if Bubblegum is a better homegrown than Flo; or if Blue Velvet or Blueberry or Buddha smokes smoother than Green Spirit, White Shark, Early Pearl, or Northern Lights; it's not like I could rank the different grades of Special K, Caramelicious, Ganesha's Dream, Hindu Haze, Kush, Waikiki, Marley Mist, Yoruba, Shiva, Red Hair, Tanka, Ganja Dwarf, L.A. Lowrider, Ice, Four Way, Swiss, Wonder Woman, or Rhino...."

She was already back with her own trowels and towels, and he wondered how long he'd been talking to himself. He lit up, took a drag. Just Say No, Nancy. Held it in as long as he could, then exhaled. Not bad. Not as rough as he thought it'd be; the guy in the cantina he'd bought it from probably just drying whatever he found growing wild. Though he did wish Jane would join him. Mary Jane. The joke would be funny if he had someone to tell it to—the reason toking alone was always sad, especially compared to passing a doobie around a circle of friends the way they used to in college, the stereo blaring—Janis—a lot of heavy metal—good stoner music. They'd have the TV on but sound off, its flickering glow more lava lamp than TV....

He sighed. That was over too, he knew, MTV setting music to videos that people actually watched instead of tuning in a vacant channel, nursing a mellow to the Om of white noise. Seeing how locked-in Roque and Jacinto were to the tiny screen of their Game & Watch, he could tell things were going to get a lot worse. It was the ease of editing videotape, instead of cutting and splicing film, that made all those psychedelic graphics possible—the electric drug, they called it. There wasn't much crack around back then either. Everything was getting harder. An iron age.... Full of shitty videos.

As much as he used to crab about his fellow students in film school being nothing but trust-fund babies, rich kids being the only ones who could afford $60 for every reel, $120 to process a single reel, $200 for every fifteen minutes of film—$260,000 just in film to shoot a short.... As much as he used to crab about the cost of film ensuring that you had to make something simple enough to appeal to the lowest common denominator to recoup that cost—he never imagined that putting movie-making in reach of everyone would be even worse: with videotape, everyone in America was suddenly cameraman, director, editor—no, not editor, forget editing—a Niagara Falls of footage overflowing its millions of banks.... Every wedding, graduation, grade-school concert monumental enough to preserve on magnetic tape; Uncle Joe Blow taping every cat stuck in a tree. Every kid who ever slipped and cracked his nuts while climbing a fence; or cracked his nuts on a bike's crossbar; or cracked his nuts trying to execute a kickflip on his skateboard; *America's Funniest Home Videos*—they actually made a whole TV show of the stuff!—and people actually sat there watching the home videos of total strangers!

His high coming on, he could see a future galaxy of stupid pet-tricks and videos of my awesome garage band and videos of baby ballerinas crashing into the living room lamp—*ha! Ha! Ha!*—the whole home-movie industry redux only on steroids and growing like weeds that choked off the flowers, the sowers of weeds unable to recognize a flower if it sprung up among them, which it wouldn't, weed growers pulling up what flowers might have bloomed not because they couldn't appreciate them, but because crap becomes its own good—as the connoisseurs of TV commercials or bubblegum music showed every day: American Studies, he believed the professors called it....

Rage, rage against the dying of the light, he told the "camcorder" at his feet: an executioner of light. He pried it from the foam hollow of its carrying case. What would happen to art when everyone was an artist? he asked it.

The silence that was its answer gave him a shiver for it seemed to be the sound of a world without the mechanical purr of a film projector: as impossible to imagine as the silence of your own grave, or books without the rustle of pages. To imitate the purr of a projector, he riffed the corner of Jane's book: *Prrrrrrrrrrrrr*.... At least that sound would always be there to remind him....

Bleeeeeeeep! went the Game & Watch, Roque going limp like the air had just been let out of him. Jacinto offered the game to Arthur for a turn. электроннка NM 02 was embossed on its metallic case, a stick figure man and alligator drawn with the same kind of pixels used to make calculator numbers, the curves having jagged stair-step edges.

He was higher than he thought, he realized, from the effort it took to sit upright, and he begged off, motioning for them to continue playing as he took up his camcorder to try out its low-light mode.

...*teek-meek / teek-meek / teek-meek*.... The game sounded like some kind of electronic tree frog—and it seemed like real tree frogs were adjusting their rhythm to it.

The camcorder was pretty amazing, Arthur had to admit. The faces of the boys were bright in the viewfinder though only lit by the light from their game. As was Jane, further off, lit only by the fire though even at 800ASA the scene would be completely black if he was using film. "Action," he called to her, like a director, when she noticed him taping her.

She mugged for the camera, then came over to where he had laid out the sleeping bag she brought for him. "Guaraní for your thoughts," she said, flipping him a coin.

"That's funny, in North America they're only worth two cents." She laughed, obviously getting the *Casablanca* reference.

He put down the camera, and offered her a toke, the way Humphrey Bogart had poured Lauren Bacall a glass of champagne, but she took a pass.

"What makes you so sure that this is the place where you'll find your missing link?" he asked, sweeping his arm to indicate not just the jungle but all of it, the stars, the heavens, the earth beneath their feet.

That smile came over her—the one she got, he was beginning to learn, when someone doubted something that was as obvious to her as the sun. She sat down beside him on his sleeping bag, rubbing her legs to warm them. "I mean," he explained, "of all places on earth, what would make you think your Lost World was here? And even if it is, it's still like finding...."

"A needle in a hay stack?"

"Worse: a flea in a jungle."

Her smile faded, the fire's glow squaring her jaw line.... If he was more ambitious, he would have pulled out his Leica....

"There had always been signs that birds were related to dinosaurs," she said solemnly, "for those who were willing to see. As far back as 1859, a professor of Natural History, as they called our field back then, thought that the dinosaur tracks he discovered in Connecticut had been left by giant ravens that never made it onto Noah's Ark."

Author laughed. "Crazy, huh?"

"But it shows how much the foot of a theropod looks like a bird. *Bactrosaurus* means 'duck-billed' dinosaur. *Psittacosaurus* means 'parrot lizard'; Ornithomimosaurs means 'ostrich mimic'.... People have been looking at birds and calling them dinosaurs for so long that you have to wonder if they were under some kind of mass hypnosis.

"Let me show you something," she said, rocking up.

She crossed over to the side of the fire where the brothers had laid out their own palm-frond mats. "Donde esta," she stammered, trying to get her smattering of Spanish to connect. Roque handed the Game & Watch to Jacinto, getting up from the pack he'd been using as a seat. By firelight she rummaged though it till she retrieved a rubber-banded stack of papers. She thumbed through them until she found the one she was looking for, then sat back down beside Arthur to show him.

A watercolor depicted a birdlike creature with red feathers and a lizard-like head: *Archaeopteryx*.

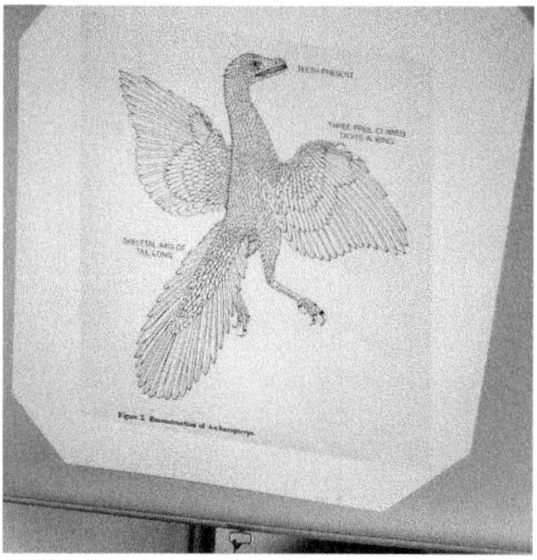

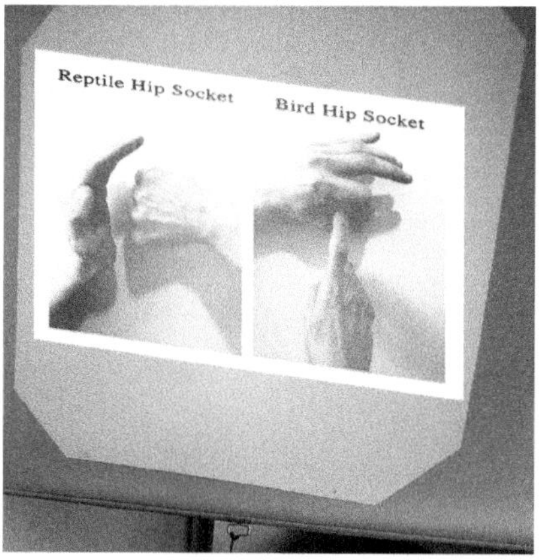

"Look, what's the difference between a reptile and a dinosaur? Let me rephrase that: why is one creature called a dinosaur and another a reptile?" She couldn't wait for him to answer. "Because we say so! We define animals with cuplike hip sockets as reptiles," she said, using her hand to show how a cup-shaped hip socket lets a leg move horizontally. "Those with open hip sockets," she said, illustrating with her hands, "we call dinosaurs. An open hip socket allows the legs to extend vertically, like the leg of a human. Or the leg of a—" Using light from the fire, she made a shadow puppet of a bird, hopping along on the ground, her fingers-legs twitching with the furtive, quick motions of a bird.

Shadows, he thought. Something about shadows kept shadowing his conscience, shadows of leaves, shadows of sand, shadows of water, of puddles. Shadows on puddles, but why?

"You see, don't you?" she said. "You must see it!" she cried, her voice shocking him back to attention the way she often jolted freshmen nodding off in lecture halls. "*Archaeopteryx*—what they call the first bird—has modern feathers...." As she spoke, she could feel herself slipping into the familiar tracks of one of her lectures, writing on an overhead projector. She didn't have an overhead projector. But she could pretend.

"Its common ancestor—*Compsognathus*—supposedly, the 'wolf' to their 'dog' line of *Archaeopteryx*, was smack in the middle of the Jurassic period, about 170 MYA."

"But you have a problem with that," he guessed.

"Drawing *Archaeopteryx*'s lineage this way can't account for the time it would take for an aerodynamic feather to evolve. Or flight. My louse, the feather louse I saw, is way older than *Archaeopteryx*'s modern feathers."

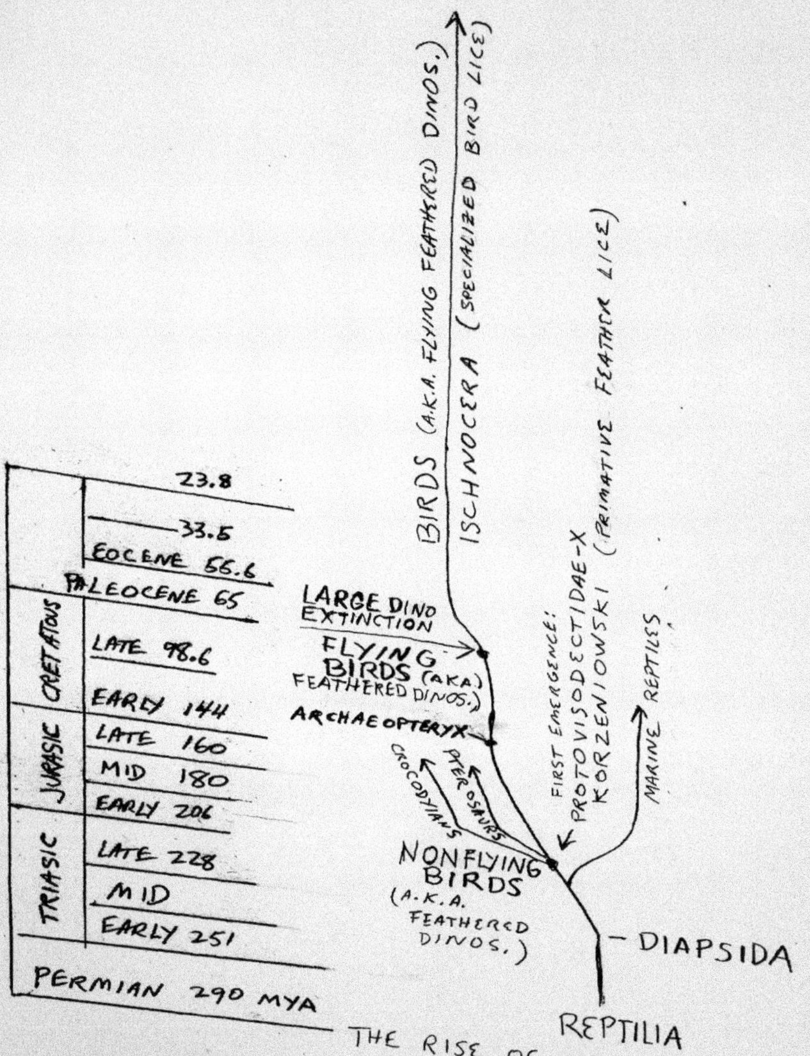

THE RISE OF WALKING, THEN FLYING, FEATHERED DINOSAURS, A.K.A. BIRDS (ACCORDING TO FEATHER LICE EVOLUTION)

"And you're saying that where there's smoke there's fire."

"I'm saying there's two kinds of smoke: Feathers for flight, like those on a hawk; and feathers for warmth, like those on a penguin.

"The shape of *Archaeopteryx*'s feather—a feather designed for flight—is the thing that finally convinced enough paleontologists to reclassify *Archaeopteryx* from pigeon-sized dinosaur to bird: Why would an animal that couldn't fly develop feathers designed for flight? Conversely, covered with feathers that create lift, how could it not fly?

"But answer me this, 'How could this 'first' bird have modern feathers?'"

He thought a moment, then answered, "There must have been older birds?"

"Bingo," she whispered, reverently. "And so older feathers."

He got a confused look on his face. "On a dinosaur?"

"That's my point!—a dinosaur with feathers is a bird! Open hip sockets, three primary fingers, air pockets in the skull: Give these characteristics to an ornithologist and he'll say you're describing a bird. Give these same characteristics to a paleontologist and he'll say it's a dinosaur. Thing is, they're both right!—and the fossil of one of these creatures is a Rabbit-Duck drawing in stone!" She folded her hands and brought fingertips to lips as if in prayer. "Oh, it's so obvious that sometimes I think I'm losing my mind. If feathers are what make a dinosaur a bird, then a bird is a dinosaur with feathers!"

"And this is where lice come in."

She gave a slow serious nod. "There's no such thing as a feather without a feather louse." She opened her field journal to a pencil drawing of a family tree, so smudged by erasures that he could tell she'd spent hours reworking its lines, even wearing a hole in the paper at one point.

If we trace the line running from Amblycera to the point in the tree where this group branched off from its sister order Liposcelididae, we would say that bird lice are no older than late Cretaceous, say 65 to 100 MYA to be generous. In other words, feather lice came into existence about 70 million years ago—right when everyone says dinosaurs went extinct and birds came into existence."

"Makes sense. Lice of a feather evolve together," the rhyme struck him as funny, funnier than it should be, he realized, a sure sign that the grass was having an effect. So he tried to cork his giggles by saying, "Birds appear, so do their lice—check." But she was soooo serious, it made him want to giggle again.

"Yeah, wraps up real nice. Call it Theory 1. Except you and everyone else in the world are forgetting the little thing we just pointed out: that *Archaeopteryx*, the so-called first bird, had modern feathers."

He looked back, tried to puzzle out if she'd just told him something or asked him a question. But before he could make a stab, she said, "Let's see what the lice say."

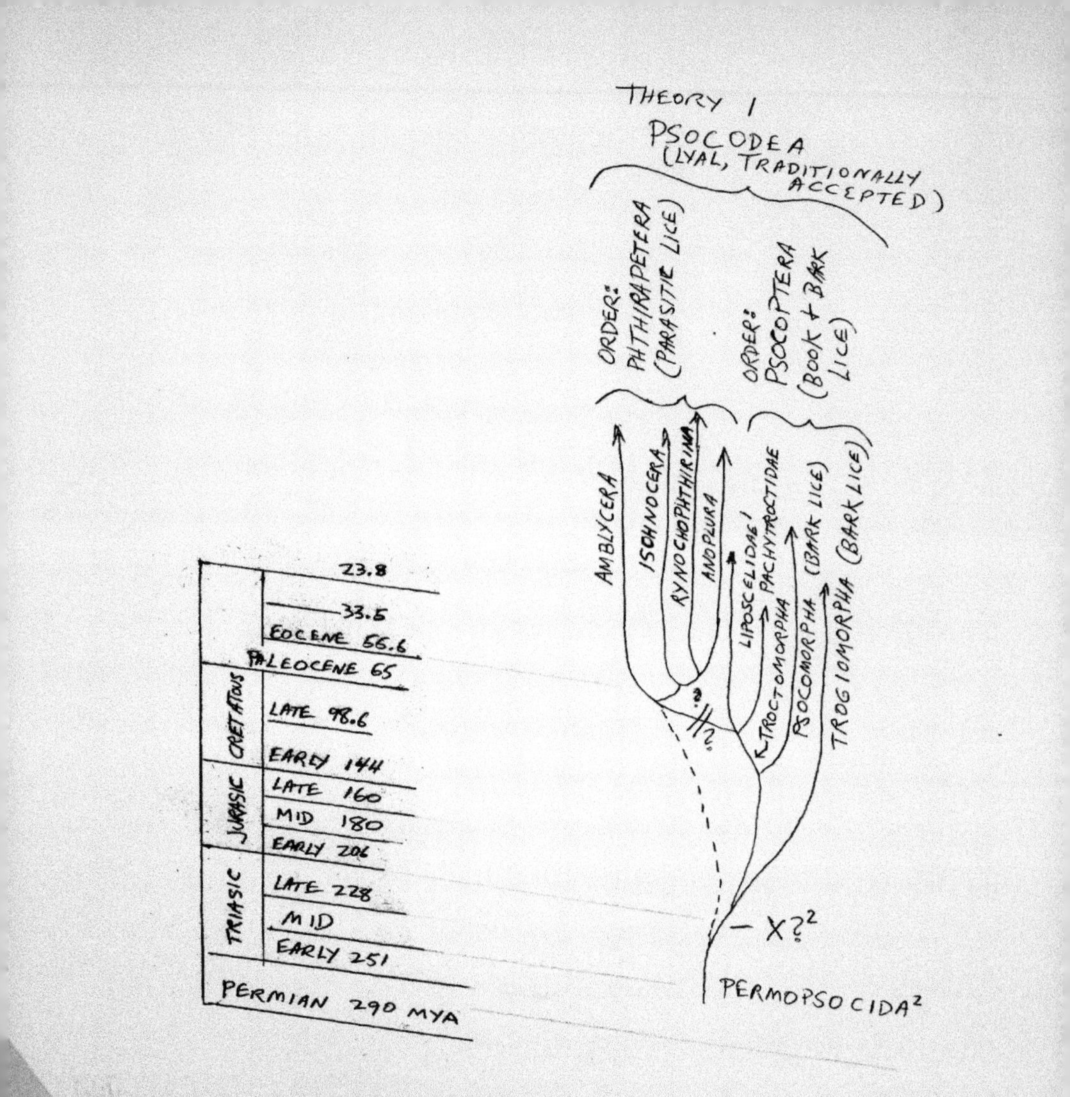

<< Theory I >>

She thumb-pumped a mechanical pencil to bring out fresh lead, then drew a question mark on her drawing near the base of the family tree. "Let's make a new theory, call it Theory 2." She broke the link between Amblycera and Liposcelidae and drew a dotted line directly to her X. "What if feather lice descended directly from their common ancestor?

"If modern Amblycera lice are SISTERS of modern book and bark lice, instead of DAUGHTERS, then parasitic feather lice have to be much older—from the Carboniferous or Permian or Triassic age, 280 million years ago, not 70—not when dinosaurs went extinct; instead, the earliest feather lice would have emerged right when the dinosaurs were beginning to proliferate.

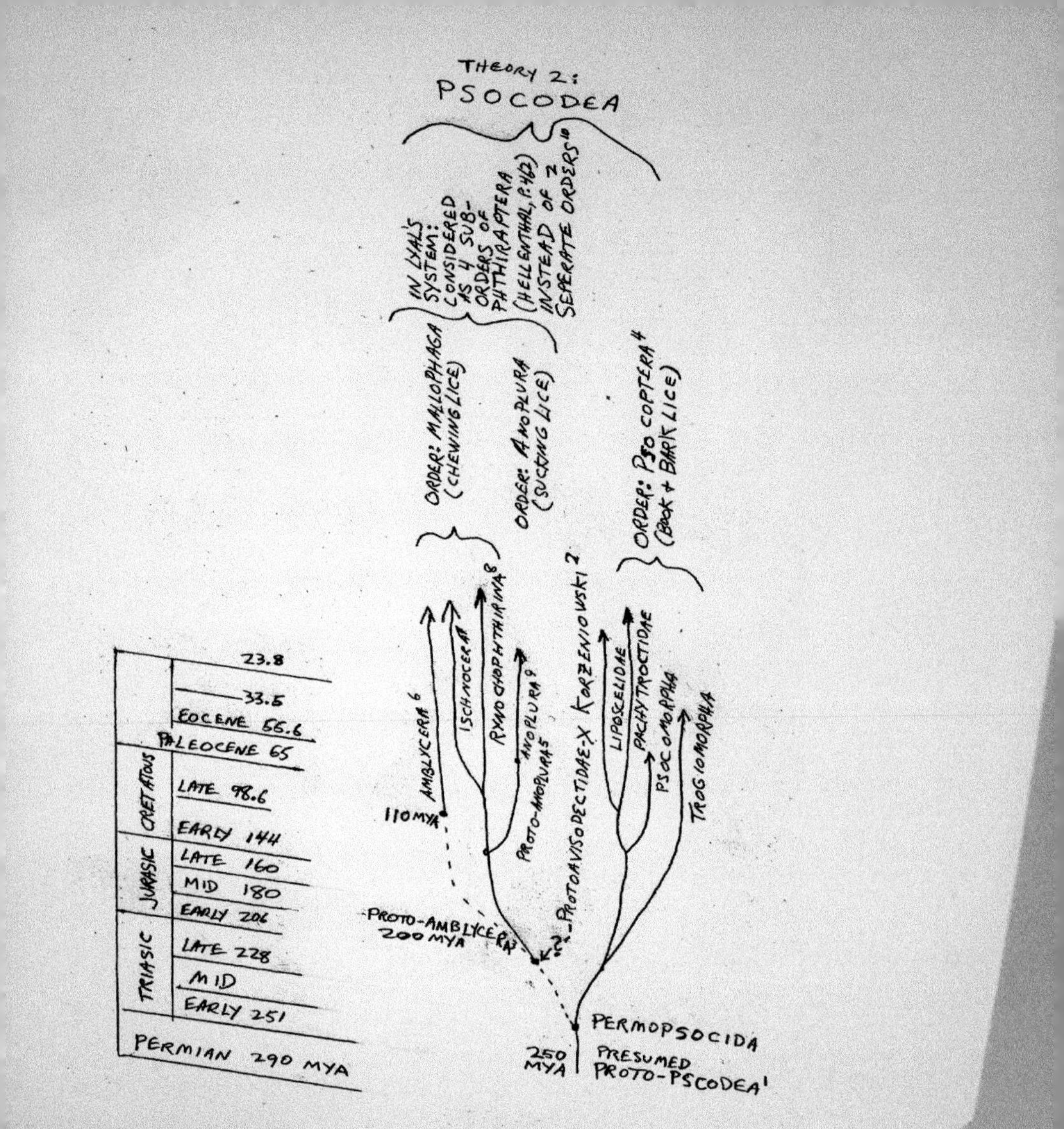

«« Theory II »»

"Think about it," she continued, "at that time, trilobites were more common than snails are today. But then something happened to the oceans and they all died."

Puddle....

"Ecosystems everywhere collapsed; sea levels fell, shutting off currents and changing the temperatures and the chemistry of the oceans and the plants, gastropods, bivalves, fishes, amphibians, crocodiles, and insects of all taxa went through mass mutations in response to the planet's catastrophic change: massive chain reactions with feedback loops of every sort raged throughout the environment, transforming the planet into a different place: after some 300 million years of slow,

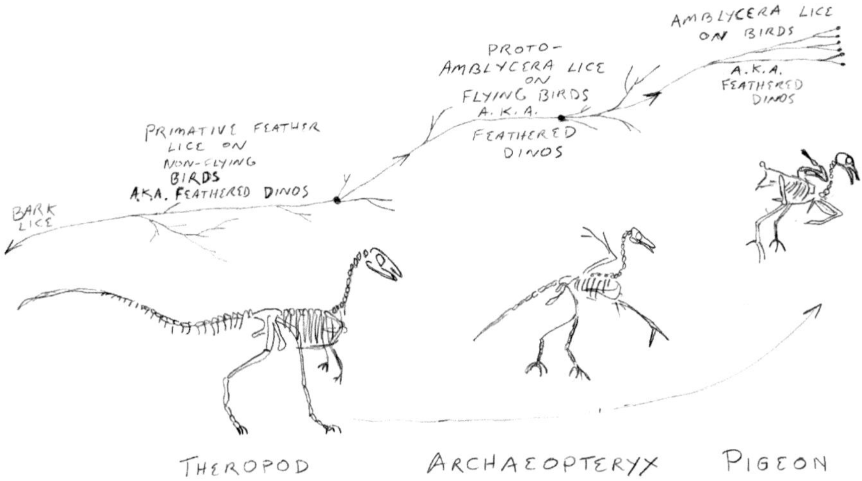

gradual change, the heavy finger of eco-destabilization pressed the fast-forward button of evolution. Life-forms of all kinds died off. Different life-forms radiated into new areas: insects of all kinds mutated into different wing geometries, or vein arrangements—and for survival, some insects began to adopt dinosaurs as hosts; they became Triassic lice."

She pulled out her amber bead and gave it to him: "Primitive lice like the one in your hand. Lice with generalized mouthparts to chew reptilian skin, and then reptilian feathers." She sat back with an I-told-you-so sort of smugness, and repeated, "Reptilian feathers" for emphasis. "Makes you look at that speck in your hands with a little more respect, don't it?"

He gazed into the bead, feeling the mellow of so many late-night discussions he'd been a part of as a student when they used to toke and talk about God or Sartre. Everything seemed profound back then, no matter how stupid it sounded in the morning. The grander the better. "Wow," he said, the god-talk she was laying on him making him even more nostalgic for those bygone days.

"So you're saying," he asked, trying, really trying, "that birds didn't descend from dinosaurs?"

"Or dinosaurs always had feathers. Even 280 MYA."

"Dinosaurs always had feathers," he repeated slowly, trying to make it look like he was absorbing what she said.

"If you follow the lice," she said, tapping on her sketch, "this is what the lice say." She took out a drawing of dinosaur evolution and laid her louse evolutionary tree on top of it, then shined her miner's light through the back of the paper to superimpose them.

The evolutionary tree of the dinosaurs and her new evolutionary tree of feather lice matched hand-in-glove. Or, rather, like a branch and its shadow.

"There had to have been an earlier bird," she said more soberly, "one that flourished before the continents drifted apart. A bird—or call it the other way around, a feathered dinosaur—that flourished all over Pangaea, and allowed its descendent, *Archaeopteryx*, to be found in both Europe and China—exactly as my grandfather saw that both New and Old World Stephanocircidae fleas had to have emerged from an earlier ancestor in Pangaea."

He laughed just because it was hard not to, given the mood he was in. "I'm sorry, the whole thing just sounds so damn crazy—birds turning into dinosaurs turning into birds...."

"Is it? People in the hard sciences always turn their noses up at paleontologists or other scientists that deal in stories instead of repeatable experiments. But once in a while we get a chance to predict something with our stories too."

She told him about Elpistostegalia, the missing link between animals that lived in the sea and those that crawled onto land. For years it was just speculation. Practically a mythological creature. Then a team from the University of Chicago figured out where, if true, this story would most likely have happened. Like sailors in search of the Golden Fleece, they set off to the Canadian Arctic, which the story of continental drift said would have been at the equator in the time of Elpistostegalia. And lo and behold, after five years of digging in ancient riverbeds across 400 miles of frozen tundra they discovered complete skeletons of a prehistoric animal with both mammal and fish characteristics; Elpistostegalia, in other words. Then there was....

The dying firelight made the monsters she described seem believable, and he had an intimation of what it must have been like sitting around a fire telling stories back when that was the only way people had to explain the world. Maybe that's all we ever had, he thought, the forest around like a darkened movie theater, early audiences running in terror from a locomotive coming straight out of the screen, or able to believe that an actual gigantic ape had been filmed to make *King Kong*.

On the other side of the fire, the boys were asleep, worn out no doubt from lugging the Manpack. The weave of the palm-leaf mats they'd made looked primitive as a stone ax compared to the thermal blankets; they'd turned the reflective silver-linings inward to conserve heat, the serene expression on Jacinto's face poking from that NASA blanket reminiscent of an astronaut floating in space.

"If I was going to predict where we'd find a bird older than *Archaeopteryx*," she said, "I'd let the feather lice tell me where to look and they'd say it's right where we're at—in a forest that's survived from a time when birds ruled the continent, a forest that to this day has more birds, and more different kinds of birds, than anywhere else on earth. A forest where it's still possible for a lost world to exist."

"And you think you'll find the first true bird here?" He tried to calculate the years but his head was too hazy, so he just said, "One from the start, not the end of the dinosaur age."

She looked down, shyly, a schoolgirl about to open her diary to him. "There's more. I never told you the whole story about that amber," she said. "I didn't want you to laugh. You won't laugh, will you?"

Why did he keep feeling like he was slipping into some kind of movie with her?

"Well," she said, scooting closer, as though what she was about to say bound him to her in some soon-to-be-revealed intimacy, "Remember how I said that the feather louse trapped inside the amber was from the Cretaceous Period? Well I wasn't completely honest. I mean, I'm sure that the louse inside is at least that old, 280 million years old. But get this: almost all amber is only about 90 million years old; either this is the oldest piece ever found or the insect inside is like a Neanderthal that suddenly showed up walking down a street in Cleveland."

"Wait. You're saying?..."

She bit her lower lip in hesitation, then added, "It gets even better. I saw one—alive."

[IN THE MORNING], she paused to take a bearing. She understood, of course, why her colleagues had begun to avoid her. After Alfred Wallace turned to ghostly photo exposures to prove that the spirit world was a continuation of the evolution he and Darwin discovered, he probably had the same problem. But still, the water-based eyeball independently emerged more than 40 times, so why was it so hard to believe birds did it twice? Laying her compass on a topographical map, she triangulated to where she thought they were, as sailors, soldiers, explorers, and others before her had done for centuries to make their way around the globe. Unlike them, she checked her work with the Manpack: She had the boys place it on the ground below a thin spot in the tree canopy, extended its antenna and switched it on. Its red L.E.D.s blinked as it ran through its self-check.

When Jane handed its hand-control to Roque, his face lit up as though she'd just handed him the best gift a boy could receive. She showed him how to use the keys to select SETUP, then DEG so that their angle would be displayed in degrees and MAG so it would provide the same data as her magnetic compass. Jacinto, who'd been patiently waiting his turn, entered '0' for ELEV, then '-4,' the number of hours they were behind Greenwich Mean Time. She got out the paper manual, limp with humidity.

Trained by hours on the Game & Watch, Roque's thumbs moved over the control buttons of the Manpack as fast as Jane could lead them through the steps, and it was easy to imagine him as an engineer. "Switch on ERR," she said pointing to the picture in the manual. This would allow the display to show them the degree of error they could expect their location to be within. She let Jacinto select the NAV-SLOW mode, since they were navigating while walking. The L.E.D.s began to list the satellites it was able to pick up: SVN01, SVN02.... They needed all three to get a fix, and after a pause—it seemed to be thinking—it added Satellite Vehicle Number 3. Then, just as she was about to go to the next step, SVN04 appeared. Since she'd left the states, the number of satellites in the sky had gone from 3 to 4.

"I think I might have seen one last night," Arthur said, watching the L.E.D.s form numbers. All over the world, the painted numbers of scoreboards, alarm clocks, and gas pumps were being replaced by blinking lights. He had thought that when they reached the last village served by the phone line, they would have reached the furthest outpost of sprawl. But out here, watching the Manpack talk to satellites, seeing the tiny computer that the boys carried into the woods—and that's what their Game & Watch was, a "computer" though when most people heard the word they thought of the TV-sized appliance hogging their desk at work—when he thought of all the red L.E.D.s spreading like a rash all over the globe, he understood how the idea of borders was going extinct, the way all the mega-suburbs back home had spread so much that they'd begun to connect. Already, a person could drive from Indiana to Wisconsin without thinking they'd ever left town.

"The march of progress," Jane mumbled, her attention on the arrow keys she used to page through results on-screen:

NORTHSTAR002 +-30m
TRK 305.3M
AZ 311.3M
STR >6 P
Then:
RNG 12.55km
TTG2AN 00480:05
ELD -00050m
MMD2 30m P

They were less than 38.62 kilometers from the destination she'd entered, which was 50 meters lower than they were—they'd be walking downhill—toward what had probably once been a river—and it would take them a little over 480 minutes to get there: if they were in a treeless land where they could walk as the crow flies. Which they weren't. If they were machines that didn't have to rest. Which they weren't. In any case, they'd make it to the target before nightfall. It gave their position as 24° 03′ 18.45″ S; 55° 23′ 53.60″ W. Plus or minus 20 meters. Right where she'd figured with her compass, which didn't weight 27 pounds.

"Hmph," she snorted, switching off the ManPack. Roque collapsed its antenna, and the boys hoisted the machine between them.

She gave the wagons-ho sign, and the brothers fell in behind, Arthur a few paces behind them, single file as a precaution against stepping on snakes, though the "trail" was more like "stepping stones" of thin patches in the growth, and often disappeared completely beneath prehistoric ferns.

Walking at the end of the line, Arthur mostly saw the boney shoulders of Roque and Jacinto, the Manpack swaying between them. When Jane looked back, it was at the moment he looked up—as if he were watching her. She let him see the smirk she always got whenever he said something that would send her off into some private joke. "Tell me a movie," she called back to him over her shoulder.

"What?"

"Tell me a movie," she repeated, using her machete to give the brush a whack. "It'll give us something to think about," she added, though he could hear the sarcasm in her voice.

"All right." They walked in silence except for the few words that the brothers passed between them—"Padre...Game & Watch...alma...infierno..."—their voices dampened by the forest. Arthur wandered the vault of his memory, looking for the opposite of a silent movie—one to hear but not see, like radio. So many: film canisters on shelves to the horizon.... It made him wish he'd been born early enough to have witnessed the origin. The world of movies had been black-and-white back then—until Dorothy's house landed on the Wicked Witch of the East and Munchkin Land suddenly turned lollipop red, blue, and green. The audience gasped—then broke into wild applause when they realized that they were seeing the world's first color movie. It was the kind of Huh?-Wow! moment he'd always dreamed of: an audience too confused at first to know what they were looking at, and then, Pow!—Wow!

To capture a little truth before that, all you had to do was take the cap off the lens: people leaving a factory gate.... Then it kept getting more complicated—*Nanook of the North*—and the first rapid cuts of a city—*Man with a Movie Camera*—and he began describing *Woman of the Dunes*, a movie whose first few minutes he'd been thinking of stealing for *Puddle*: the contrast between a noon-bright beach and its deep shadows were really hard to work with, but the movie was full of close-ups of this fine, powdery sand moving in very Zen ways. Hiroshi Segawa got the Japanese equivalent of an Oscar for his exquisite sand photography—even better than *Lawrence of Arabia*. The audience Arthur had been in when he first saw it knew about playground sand, and beach sand, and sand for concrete, but sand as philosophy didn't exist until Segawa made it so....

"It begins with a guy living alone," he said, "a no-one, an every-one, who goes bug hunting in a desert at the edge of a salt sea. Lots of beetles live in the sand, and the guy—an amateur beetle collector—hopes to discover a type no one had ever seen before. If he did, he thinks, then he could name it and its name, and also his, would get put into books about beetles. Forever."

This part got Jane's attention, he could see.

"Wandering the dunes, engrossed in looking for beetles, he doesn't realize that he's lost his way until night falls. He's stumbling around in the dark when he's discovered by a group of what?— Bandits? Armed with shovels? But they offer to take him to the hut of a woman who would put him up for the night. He's suspicious. But sure enough, just as they had told him, there is a woman, and a hut, at the bottom of a deep pit in the dunes. As they lower a rope ladder so he could climb down to her, relief comes over him to realize that these simple sand dwellers were, in fact, just helping him out.

"In the morning, though, the ladder is gone. That's strange, he thinks. But the woman is pleasant enough, about his age. She even makes him breakfast. He doesn't want to seem rude by rushing off. But whenever he says anything about leaving she falls silent. Eventually, enough is enough, and he begins to insist on leaving. Instead of showing him the ladder, she starts filling sacks with sand. He gets more and more agitated, then angry. He shouts for the men. Silence. After a couple hours of this he slumps down, exhausted by the idea that is sinking in: worse than bandits, they are kidnappers! And he's the woman's prisoner!"

"Ha!" Jane said. "That's how the antlion beetle—Myrmeleontidae—catches its prey: it makes a hole in the sand so smaller insects can fall in!"

Whatever. Arthur continued: "The woman explains to the guy that her fellow villagers have delivered him to her so that he could help her dig the shifting sand, which slides into her hole so much that she has to dig all night to keep her home from being swallowed up. And not just her home: if her sand house caved in, her neighbors' houses would follow, one by one, like dominos.

"But he doesn't care. He wants out!"

"Wait a minute, did you say this was a documentary?"

"Si," Roque said.

"No creo," Jacinto answered, seemingly to Jane's question. But they were off in their own conversation, switching positions to reposition the sling they'd made to carry the Manpack. "Padre nos va a golpear si acaso se da cuenta...."

"See what you think," Arthur said, loud enough for Jane to hear. "Maybe it's even about us." He hurried up ahead of the boys so he could tell her the movie without shouting: "At first the guy tries threatening her, then cajoling her. He refuses to work and deprives them both of the ration of water they get paid if they do their job. Water being the most precious commodity in this desert world, they nearly die of thirst. Gradually, he has to bend to his fate, just so they can survive, and they fall into a kind of mundane rhythm, sleeping during the day, digging out the sand at night.... Always and everywhere there's the sand: it marks their time more than the rising and setting of the sun. The camera, and so we, never leaves the hole, so it's our reality, as it is for the man and woman, shaping their labor, their thoughts, their very selves. The man can feel his grip on his old self weakening so he tries a different tactic, telling the woman about how great his life had been in the city.

"He can see that she's intrigued; they even begin to get along. One hot day, he happens to see her sleeping nude, her muscles glistening with sweat as if she were in a sauna. He goes to her, and she clutches him to her. Afterwards, together in bed, she says, 'I suppose there are restaurants and movies that are open every day in Tokyo,' trying to imagine a world that's as alien to her as her world of sand had been to him.

"He redoubles his efforts to convince her to go with him to see those restaurants and movies. Over months, he tries reasoning with her, then threatening her again, then begging—everything he can think of until she finally gives her reason for not leaving: 'If I wasn't here, no one would care about me, including you.'

"The sand continues to be the real star of the film with its ridges and shadows, its ever-shifting shapes, folds, curtains of grains.... Dune grass bends under its own weight, and the camera pulls in on a blade pirouetting in the wind, its tip drawing arcs in the smooth sand as though Nature herself was raking it into those symmetrical patterns Japanese gardeners make as an aid to contemplation. The sand turns dark when moist; as it dries, it becomes a light beige, then bone white, bleached by the sun. But mostly it's the sand's power to shape their reality, as patiently, if relentlessly, as a river smooths the hardest stone, continually burying them and her home as if they were at the bottom of an hourglass. If they didn't keep digging themselves out, they'd soon become a microcosm of those lost civilizations: the once busy marketplaces of Ancient Egypt buried in sand; abandoned mining towns; Mayan temples buried in vines. Who knows how many Atlantises there are at the bottom of Time?

"In secret, the man makes a trap—'my last hope' he calls it—a wooden bucket that he camouflages in the sand. His plan is to catch a crow, then tie a rescue note to its leg. Months turn into the first year, and he and the woman continue their routine, sharing the work to get their daily water ration from the other villagers, gradually living as husband and wife: Mr. and Mrs. Sisyphus, digging out the sand each night only to do it again the next day. As time passes into the second year, and the man tries to catch his crow, he discovers that moisture condenses in the buried bucket. He works out a way to use the bucket to extract water from sand. At about the same time, the woman becomes pregnant. One night, when she's in danger of losing the child, he screams for help and the villagers come and take her to a midwife, but in the heat of the moment they leave the ladder down.

"The man climbs out.

"He walks to the beach—the sea is enormous before him. He gathers a handful of sand, thinking of the centuries of wave action it took to grind mountains into the grains he holds. He lets them run through his fingers, remembering Tokyo where everyone scurries about like workers in an ant farm; he remembers his own apartment, the size of a cricket cage; he thinks of the numbing bureaucracy and the cramped life that had made him dream of discovering a new insect so his name would appear in a book....

"He realizes that if he doesn't take his chance to escape now, the villagers will return him to the pit. But if he does return to Tokyo, the woman, and his child, and the others will never know of his discovery: that their dry, sand world was permeated by water.... Water: the most precious thing in the world....

"The movie ends with a police report in Tokyo, a hand closing his missing-person file since he has been gone for seven years, and we, the audience can see how the story of his life is very different depending on if it's written in the language of sand or bureaucracy with its list of 'facts': height, weight, length of hair, color of jacket.... We realize how many others had been writing the story of his life: the police, the woman, his boss and coworkers in Tokyo, the systems that created his job, the dunes, the villagers—even us viewers.... But here's the most brilliant part: Segawa lets the camera pull back to show that the cop writing his life is an actor on a movie set made to look like a police station. As the camera keeps pulling back we see the crew around him shooting the scene, the grips and gaffers, the lighting racks and umbrellas, the boom mic and operator, sound mixers, best boys, and continuity women, while the camera we are seeing this all through swings around to look back into the camera shooting the scene and behind it, looking back at us through the lens of the number one camera is a shadowy, enigmatic figure—Segawa?—the black eye of his lens grows larger and larger till it fills the whole screen as though it's absorbing the audience, as if to remind us that seeing is what makes the movie, but it's the movie that makes the audience."

They walked in silence. "That was pretty great," Jane said, after a while, thinking how the man's last hope had turned out to be exactly that, though not for the reasons he'd thought. And Arthur said, "Yeah," though his mind was on the enormity of the ocean, and the ocean of sand, and how small—ant-like—Segawa—the camera—had made the man, standing at the edge of the sea while in the hole, full-screen close-ups of their faces made him and the woman fill their world. "I thought you'd like it." Especially the part I added, he thought.

AT AN INTERSECTION OF TWO TRAILS, they came upon a soldier. At first, Jane thought he was a boy playing solider. A teenager in a military uniform. He had wadded a plastic grocery bag into a ball and was playing hacky sack with it when they startled him as much as he startled them. He stopped to quickly button his collar. But then, seeing that they weren't whoever he thought they might be, he grabbed his rifle.

"*¿Quiénes son?*" he demanded, swinging it around, though he kept its barrel toward the ground.

Jane looked to Roque, then Jacinto to explain, but they both lowered their heads as though they knew all too well the drill.

"What? What's he want?" Arthur asked, readying his camera, but keeping it low.

"He must be some kind of checkpoint."

"Here?"

She couldn't tell him about the Aché uprising, not now, so her mouth raced with other reasons she could think of: to guard against poachers, to keep the campesinos from squatting....

"Well tell him we're not poachers. We don't even have guns."

The soldier's face was so young, he could have been a freshman in her BIO 101 classes, his eyes ping-ponging between them and the Manpack—a military-green piece of hardware. He seemed more scared and confused to see them than they were to see him, and Jane wondered what would happen to him if this didn't go according to some script. She only caught the last part of his rapid-fire questions in Spanish: "...mercenaries...."

"He thinks we're missionaries," she said.

Roque and Jacinto remained frozen, eyes squeezed shut as though praying to become invisible.

She could hear the nervousness in Arthur's small laugh. "Go with it," he said, "talk to him."

She knew Arthur was worried about his camera, about the papers he was carrying that gave him permission to film in the capital, 200 miles away but not here; the stash in his gear wouldn't help. She saw her own project come to nothing, joining the innumerable expeditions that never happened because of border wars, epidemics, boys with guns.... This one held her discovery hostage, she suddenly realized, making her willing to say or do anything to save it, and she lied, "Si—ah, ah, yo soy," and she motioned to indicate both her and Arthur, "mersenarios."

The boy soldier swung the barrel of his rifle up at them. Both Jacinto and Roque fell to their knees, Jacinto, the younger, beginning to go weepy, his brother pointing at Jane and Arthur and emphatically saying, "*No es mi culpa*" or something that Jane took to mean he had no idea who they were, the soldier shooting back his own questions, Roque claiming that they were only along for the trabajo, or some such plea and Jane suddenly realized her mistake and cried out, "*No! No! No soy mercenarios, soy mission—Missionarios. Missionarios!*" she said, indicating both her and Arthur, frantically waving her hands 'no' to indicate that the boys weren't part of their plan....

The soldier squinted, eyes giving her a quick up and down before he demanded, "*Papeles, andele!*"

"Oh Christ, now we're screwed," Arthur said. He raised his palms slowly to indicate he was reaching to get them from his pack, pausing to make sure the solider gave him permission to dig out the sheaf of documents that the custom guards had given him at the airport.

Watching the boy, rifle balanced in the crook of one arm as he went through her passport, something about the unsure way he turned each page told her that he was looking for stamps. That is, pictures. He couldn't read, she realized, and it gave her the oddest sensation—not fear—rather envy—envy for his utter freedom from evidence, supporting material and reams of data.... No matter how many degrees she had, he would be the one who determined the outcome of her study because he was the one with the gun: all over the world the truth was being made by boys with guns.

Apparently, what government seals he did find were official looking enough. He handed their papers back, then said with a nod that they could go—but not forward. He motioned for them to turn around.

"Nooooo! We have to go that way!" Jane cried. "Permopsocida is over there!" She pointed down the path behind the soldier.

He stiffened, tightening his grip on the rifle.

Arthur took her arm, tried to pull her back, "Don't argue with the man. We'll find another spot."

Jane could feel herself beginning to lose it. "We have to get back to that part of the forest! The microclimate we're looking for might only...."

Arthur stepped between her and the soldier. "It doesn't matter!" he said, gripping her arm.

And she saw he was right, the guard holding his vintage rifle across the path, his face hardening, becoming older. Jacinto and Roque were already hurrying back the way they came, the weight of the Manpack between them tugging them this way and that.

They walked so far that Jane thought she'd missed it before finally spotting a dense stretch of firecracker vines that Cristóbal had pointed out earlier. Machete cuts showed that someone had passed through them not long ago. "Okay, here it is." She motioned for Roque and Jacinto to put down the Manpack, and switched it on. They extended the antenna, uncoiled the cord to its handheld controller, and Roque handed it to her as the red L.E.D.s blinked, the GPS trying to locate the satellites above.

"Do you think that had anything to do with the coup?" Arthur asked, waving his canteen back toward the soldier.

"Who knows," Jane said, weighing whether or not to tell him what she knew. "Back in the pueblo," she said, cautiously, "Felipe told me that an Indian shot an arrow at a bulldozer operator. The tribe fled into the forest." She studied Arthur's face for reaction. None. "The army was probably called out to arrest them," she said, realizing as she spoke that she was trying to convince herself that she hadn't led Arthur and the boys into an Aché uprising. "Or maybe you're right, maybe they're tracking down the last of the soldiers who were part of the coup," she said, coming up with reasons she could believe. "But by navigating with this," she said, holding up the Manpack's hand control, "it shouldn't be hard to just loop around him."

"You're not serious."

The brothers looked worried, their eyes searching the trees for Aché, rebels, jaguars, or soldiers, whatever.

[WITHOUT ROQUE AND JACINTO], camp seemed tiny in the huge woods. The tree frogs and howls were louder, a completely different ecosystem taking over at night. She'd never been alone in the forest. Or even with just one other person. The sense of it, its immensity, made her understand how her grandfather must have felt, running back to the wilderness every chance he got. She and Arthur stayed up late talking. Partly because she was excited—tomorrow they'd be at 24° 03′ 18.45″ S; 55° 23′ 53.60″ W—and partly, she knew, though neither would admit it, because the soldier had them spooked. But not as much as the skinned monkey: They had only walked a couple of miles into the bush, following more fresh machete cuts, when they came upon the "voodoo."

"It's not voodoo," Jane said, sarcastically. "The Aché don't practice voodoo."

"Yeah? Well somebody does," Arthur said, terror frozen on the monkey's face, as though it had been skinned alive. Back in the mercado, he'd seen pig heads hanging from hooks, flies buzzing around the fresh meat. But this monkey had been crucified, its long arms and legs stretched into an X above the path like those ape hides set up as 'Keep Out' signs before the Forbidden Zone in *Planet of the Apes.*

"Maybe the guys are right," he said, nodding toward Roque and Jacinto, hanging back as though he and Jane were tourists stupidly walking up to the mouth of a volcano to get a better look. "Maybe we shouldn't go this way."

Using her weight, she tested the soundness of one fallen tree lying in the crotch of a neighbor, then she walked up it, as on a tightrope. The porta-potty smell of the dead monkey grew stronger as she neared, its head wearing a crown of bright green bottle flies: Lucilia sericata. "Maybe there's an amber mine around here," she called back. "We must be nearing the spot where my amber came from. Maybe whoever works the mine skinned this monkey to scare off trespassers."

"Maybe." He zoomed in on the monkey's eyes, which had been sewn shut, then gave the camera a Dutch tilt so the monkey's face would have a cocked, horror-movie look.

"Maybe it was put here by Greenpeace. Dian Fossey used to set up voodoo warnings to scare poachers away from the gorillas she studied."

"Yeah?" he said, eye to viewfinder. "Or maybe we'll all wake up as zombies."

She ignored him as she tried to read the flies to determine how long the monkey had been dead. Sarcophagidae, flesh flies, the vultures of the insect world, always arrived first, and she could see them here with their red eyes and checkered bellies. But she could also see a few adult *Piophila casei*, cheese skippers, that only took up residence after the corpse had gone beyond cheesy, beyond gooey. Sepsidae came to drink during caseic fermentation of the eyeballs but before ammoniacal fermentation....

A minor miracle. That's how she thought of the symphony of insects ravishing the corpse, each filling its niche to melt the body back to the essences from which it came—just as necrophagous insects would do with her and Arthur, and the boys too, one day....

Transubstantiation, they called it in church—water into wine, bread into flesh....

"*Argghhh, argghh,*" Arthur moaned, his tongue hanging out in imitation of the monkey. "Ever hear of *The Serpent and the Rainbow*?"

...Dermestid beetles crawled in and out of corpse's ears.... He wouldn't let it go—describing a documentary about a medical student who went to Haiti to learn how witch doctors turned their victims into the walking dead, and got turned into a zombie himself.

"...back in the '20s, the Haitian-American Sugar Cane Plantation had hundreds of zombies working its fields," he said, adjusting the contrast to bring out the gloom of the forest and turn Jane into a creepy silhouette, the way evil clowns, or chainsaw murderers were always silhouetted against fog at night. He turned to tell the boys to climb up beside Jane so he could get a shot of them with her and the monkey—

"Hey! Where are they?"

Gone. The Manpack lay on the ground by itself as though Jacinto and Roque had vanished.

"Oh, that's just great!" Jane said, "Now you've done it!"

Now, the forest seemed colder than last night. "Do you think they knew what we were saying all along?" Arthur asked.

"Probably more than they let on." They sat closer to the fire, and, as though to tighten their pack of two, closer to one another, talking about nothing, about lots of things—ex-hippies who now dressed preppy; how every single tech in her lab kept a *Star Wars* action figure taped to his PC, and how dumb TV shows were, always putting in things like computers that could talk or cars that could drive themselves. One subject jumped to another as though they were having a sleepover. Music—bands and the best LP art: Pink Floyd's album with two businessmen shaking hands, one of whom was on fire, or the crowd of characters tricked out in primary-color regalia on the *Sgt. Pepper's* album.... Reducing LP art like that to the tiny size of a CD's jewel case was like putting the Sistine Ceiling on a postage stamp, Arthur insisted.

"Times change," Jane said.

But he was off in the weeds about the new Compact Disks and how they would never replace vinyl because vinyl sounded better—no matter how many engineering nerds claimed they couldn't tell the difference with their meters. Even if they were right, Arthur said, trying to convince her, that didn't mean the vinyl-heads were wrong. Jacket art like the *Ramones*—too cool for school in shades and torn skinny jeans—made you feel like you weren't just buying music; you were buying into something bigger than yourself. You'd argue about guitar riffs with your friends, and that was part of the music too; you worked extra hours at your stock job to pay for a preamp and that became part of what you heard; you and your girlfriend, if you had one, drove your beater out to Sound Trek, or Hi-Fi Buys, and that was part of listening, as was the chemical odor of new circuit boards the first time they warmed up....

"That smell made the music sound better just as radio was better back when people had to wait for a DJ to play their favorite song." He cracked his knuckles. "Just before flying out here," Arthur said, "I saw some guys on a road trip, each plugged into their own Walkman when the best thing about any road trip was the talking; the joking; the songs on the radio...."

She saw what he meant, and added, "Yeah, labs used to be real social places, like Leonardo da Vinci's studio, I used to imagine. But more and more everyone just has their nose buried in e-mail."

"E-what?"

"Electronic mail. It's this new thing where you don't need a stamp; you just send your letters by computer. They say it will kill off the post office." She told him how Bell Labs was working on a way to send pictures through the phone lines too; if it works, instead of getting a newspaper delivered to your door, it would automatically update on your computer screen.

Men in lab coats reading newspapers printed in the gray-green of cathode-screen light.... Would people miss strolling down to the café for a bagel and the morning paper? Nah, stories about the future were really about the present, and given enough time, people of the future wouldn't even be able to imagine what a simple pleasure that had been....

"Well they can have it," he concluded.

Jane still listened to radio, she said, when doing something repetitive in the lab. She was almost on *Science Radio* once; an intern had mistaken her for her famous grandfather.

She told Arthur how she'd gotten into etymology, and asked how he'd gotten into film; he told her of other shoots he'd been on, asked her about other bug hunts, and why she sometimes thought it was all a mistake—having to live up to her grandfather's name—a giant in the flea world (irony not intended!): everyone knew everyone else so the jealousies were all magnified. And that on top of the normal pettiness in academia, the politics of getting an article published, or a grant. "You're lucky you don't have to deal with any of that."

He gave off a sarcastic laugh. "Oh yeah, I'm as free as a monkey in the trees," he said, motioning back toward the skinned monkey. Then he found himself telling her about the film he thought was going to let him make the movies he really wanted to make, the film he couldn't let go, escape, or get around because the disaster that it was set the course of his life: a commercial indie that two friends from film school got their rich parents to back. Seventy percent of their budget—a hundred grand—went into hiring a marquee name—Rutger Hauer—because that's the only way an indie film can get distribution: "a hundred grand for his marquee face to say one line in our film." They'd let Arthur in by trading camera work for shares. "I mean, it's Rutger Hauer—a month after they sign him, *Blade Runner* goes into production."

"Wow, you had the star of *Blade Runner* in your movie?"

"Not Harrison Ford—he would have been a hundred times what they got Hauer for; Hauer was the android, the tough guy. But suddenly *Blade Runner* is a sleeper hit and he's a huge star too, and they have his next film. So I borrow every cent I could, and maxed out a dozen charge cards to buy into their film as deep as they'd let me.

"Six months later we're set up to shoot Hauer saying his one line—his hundred-thousand-dollar line. It's a dinner scene, and Hauer's sitting at the table. Only from the perspective of the camera it looks like one of the candles on the table is sticking up his nose. I didn't say anything because it's not the cameraman's job to direct, and I figured they were going with Camera 2. The director didn't notice, he said, because he's not looking through the lens; he's sitting next to the camera." Or else he set it up that way on purpose, Arthur thought but didn't say, his stomach knotting at the memory. He'd never been able to piece together with any certainly what was Rabbit and what was Duck in this disaster. That is, he couldn't tell for sure if they set fire to the film because they had bought all that fire insurance, or if they took out all that fire insurance because they smelled smoke. Bottom line: Hauer says his one line with a candle up his nose. "It's not that we didn't get the shot; we didn't even get the scene! You can't cut around him. He's only in that one scene!"

As Arthur spoke, he got more and more heated.

"He's getting a hundred thousand for one line but you can't put a candle up his nose because he's got millions riding on that tough-guy face, his lawyers tell us, and they'll sue because we're degrading the earning potential of his investment by making him look stupid sitting there with a candle up his nose."

"Couldn't you?—"

"No, no do-overs. His contract didn't obligate him to do retakes and he was already on another movie whose contract wouldn't let him even if he could. They wanted Hauer's next film as bad as we did." He slumped back as if the weight of that past had suddenly landed on him all over again. "I lost the scene! The whole fucking scene! A $100,000 scene! The whole fucking movie!"

He was breathing hard. "Worst of all, they tried to blame me—the camera-man!—when anyone who's been within a hundred miles of a set knows that's the director's job." He snorted. "And I thought those guys were my friends," he added.

She didn't know what to say. So she said, "You have any more of that cannabis?"

"Huh?" She bounced her eyebrows.

"Yeah, I have some." He got out his baggie—one of her specimen bags. But instead of chewing him out for sneaking it, she got out her X-Acto knife. As he had last night, he slit open a Palermo and blew out the tobacco, continuing, "You go nuts worrying about the little stuff. And the big stuff. And the in-between stuff. Is the gate clean, is the light working, can you get any closer?" He replaced the tobacco with the grass, tapping the bag to shake out a line. The ritual of rolling it, sealing it with saliva calmed him. "The director's getting lousy sound so the sound guy wants to get closer, but you can't get your camera in any closer without skewing the shot and all the while the director's having an argument with the lawyers of the guy who owns the property you're shooting on. Then an actor has a hissy fit about something, maybe there's no toilet paper in his dressing room, and your consciousness can't be everywhere—maybe it really was an accident.

"In any case, at the end of the day, that candle looks like it's up the guy's nose, so what's the dif?" He held the rolled joint by its tip and tilted it to her. "Pretty good job for not having any papers."

Passing the blunt back and forth, they sat there in human silence, forest racket all around. "Everyone was so into drugs when I was in school, but I never did any of that stuff," she said, trying to observe if the marijuana was having any effect. Didn't seem to. "I always had the feeling that I'd missed out on something."

"You got to inhale deeper," he said, demonstrating. She took a drag, the tip of the joint flaring orange, then held the smoke in till she had to cough it out. "If we had some Altoids, you could suck on one to make the smoke taste sweeter."

"A couple of chem majors I knew got expelled for making L.S.D. They weren't even stoners—just nerds who wanted to see if they could make it."

"Yeah, a lot of stupid shit went down back then. They should have transferred to my school."

Then she asked him what kind of film he'd make if he could make any movie he wanted. "Something with huge special effects, I bet."

"Nah, those kinds of movies are just eye candy. But with everything going to magnetic tape, I don't know how long it'll even be possible to make the kind of film I'm talking about."

She looked at him, confused.

It was hard to explain the way working with film was not just part of the process, but part of the product the way throwing a pot was a meditative act. That's why master potters in Japan were considered philosophers. Take away the process and it's just product. Not handmade. Not philosophy. "Unlike magnetic tape," he tried, "to edit film you had to physically cut it up. You had to physically tape tiny pieces together. It was all about labor, labor, labor, physical and mental." There was something religious, too, about a wall in a dimly lit editing room, little pieces of film hanging from pins, like milagros in a church, that you had to sit with as you worked. "If you cut out 8 seconds here, 3 seconds there, 5 seconds someplace else, you had to keep it all straight: You had to have the whole movie in your head, the parts you shot, the parts you didn't shoot. A Moviola only lets you work with 2 audio tracks but everything's separate—pictures, sound effects, music, voices—so you had to build up an idea of the movie in your head."

"Doesn't tape make it easier?"

"Yeah, but the things you can't do are what make a movie too. Just like the things you can't do in poker are what make the game.

"With this," he said, lifting the camcorder, "I just press a button. Instead of 2 audio tracks, I can work with 50 and I don't have to wait until I go into mix—at $800 an hour—to hear it. There's no need for a Mozart to compose the whole symphony in his head. Any kid right out of film school can do it all on magnetic tape—technically, that is. But do they have any film sense? No. Do they have an idea that's fresh? No. Do they have skills? You better fucking believe they have skills. But the movies they make come from a completely different mindset. Instead of having to gamble on a shot, you can run over to the video deck and see what you got every other minute; tape is cheap, so you just keep going. Synching is easy. You can shoot with half the people and cut in one-tenth the time. And since every movie is made with borrowed money, every moment that money isn't repaid comes out of the pockets of investors. So the forces aligning to kill off film are many and powerful," Arthur said. "It's a matter of when, not if, film goes extinct.

"The mindset is what I'll miss most, though...."

He didn't know why he wanted her to understand what he'd meant—maybe it was because she was the first to ask—but he did, so he tried to explain how working with a limited number of frames shapes your mental space, organizes your mental furniture, makes composing a way of life that forces you to be in the moment instead of just shooting a bunch of stuff and then picking out whatever looks good. As he spoke, his fingers remembered turning the crank on his old Bolex, the tension of its spring-wound motor stiffening, a fully compressed spring giving him 28 seconds of shooting time.... One reel, 100 feet of film, 3 minutes of movie. Opening the camera's body to load film had been like opening the back of a pocket watch, its interior simple as a mousetrap, a poem of loop formers and precision sprockets.... Threading the film through the gate, getting the right amount of slack in the loop so it wouldn't jam.... Closing the back of the camera, then tightening its latch so light couldn't leak in had always been exciting—The moment of truth....

Now, they said, Game & Watch companies like Sony were experimenting with cameras that could store a picture like a number in a calculator. And it didn't take a Sci-Fi writer to imagine what kind of future there'd be once some company won the race to stick a camera on a calculator or Dick Tracy's wrist watch—or shoe, toilet plunger, or telephone, for that matter—what difference would it make?—even if toilet-plunger cameras were "better."

"Once at this silent-film festival," he said, the grass mellowing him out, "I'd fallen in with these critics who'd been around forever, real old-school guys. We were in this Italian restaurant and they started arguing about what had happened in a Mel Brooks movie that played at the festival as a gag: *Silent Movie*. A really dumb piece of shit, shot as a silent movie, but it had one good joke: there's only one word of dialog in the entire film. And it's said by a mime. But they couldn't remember what the word was. Suddenly they burst into laughter—as if they simultaneously realized the same thing. 'We're getting old,' one said wistfully. 'And senile,' another added. They *were* old too: white hair all around. But then the oldest of them said, 'Nah, that's not it. I just wasn't paying attention. There's too many distractions at these festivals to watch even a dumb movie like that anymore and I knew that if I had to, I'd just rent it on tape.' Then they started talking about the old days when people really paid attention to a movie because they knew that they might not ever see it again. One of them had written an entire book about a couple of films that he'd seen only once at an open-air screening in Palermo. He'd been one of 800 people gathered in a field and all silent, watching. Movies were precious. Events. Watching a movie meant something different to them just as reading a book means something different to us than it did to those medieval monks whose monastery might only see one new book a year. One monk would be picked out to memorize it so he could recite it for others after the book was passed on to the next monastery.

"Oh yeah," Arthur said, taking the joint from her for his turn. "There's a big difference between 'watching' and 'seeing.'" He took a pull, then exhaled. "And I'd rather give people a different way to see than a different thing to see, if you know what I mean."

She said she did, and she seemed to mean it. So he hesitated a moment, then told her about his student project, *Puddle*, and how if he could find a way to make a full-length version, he'd be happy if he never made another film. Others had already done stuff like it: Yoko Ono and her film of naked butts, or Joe Jones's film of smoke or Andy Warhol's *Empire*, an eight-hour film of the Empire State Building. "But I don't know.... My film is different, somehow. Warhol's long shot makes the building look like a mountain, or monumental, like it'll be there forever. My *Puddle* is more meaningful. Or more something. At least to me."

She should have said something like that to that Earth Mother she'd run into up in the Rockies, Jane thought: not that you could make up whatever story you wanted about nature, or confuse marks on a thermometer with temperature, as Ms. Natural insisted, but that without an accounting system, or grid, there'd be no "nature" and so no "us." It was the reason she'd been so pissed at the roommate she'd had, long ago, she realized. Back then, Jane had kept an aquarium full of slime in her room—until her roommate threw it out, her roommate unable or unwilling to comprehend how its stench held the beauty of the Earth generating a bubble-thin atmosphere that made flowers and blue skies and stench—and roommates and their arguments—possible too....

They'd had a bitter fight, her and her roommate. But Jane had grown more subtle about such matters since then, considering how often she'd seen a clear thought of her own twist into a knot of prose as she tried to translate it into the medium of her pen. This was why, during the oral exams of her doctoral students, right while they were in the thick of giving their explanations of phylogenetic mutations of Psocodea taxa or cladistic hypotheses using autopomorphous characters or whatever, she liked to trip them up by asking the simplest of questions: What, exactly, do you mean by 'Life'? Or, Define 'species'? Everyone knew what 'Life' or 'species' was of course, which was precisely why they didn't really know, the way alchemists didn't need to think twice about witches, miracles, or any of the other 'facts' of their lives.

In a way, the film Arthur was describing—a movie of a drying puddle—was a lot like that. She thought of an article describing an acre of rainforest vanishing every second; she thought about Dr. Thompson's 1,500-year-old ice cores and the story they told of ancient seas warming, then dying, and taking with them the Trilobitomorpha and most other life too. She thought about her grandfather, arguing from the anatomy of Stephanocircidae fleas that the separate continents must have all been together as one—this back when the very idea of continental drift was crazier than canals on Mars, her grandfather using fleas, the smallest of bodies, to explain the movement of continents, the largest of bodies, and she hadn't realized she had committed to memory the epigraph to his book until it came to mind now:

Flower in the crannied wall,
if I could know you
all in all,
then I would know all:
you, myself,
the cosmos,
God,
all in all in all....

"I'd love to see your movie," she said.

Somehow, he knew she meant it. In fact, she struck him as the ideal viewer—the unknown audience of one that had always been there in the dark theater of his mind, waiting for the show to begin while he was up in the projection booth, struggling to get his 16mm film to thread onto the theater's 35mm sprockets.

He handed her the joint. "How about you?" he asked. "If you could write any journal article, what would it say?—Woman entomologist puts living primitive on display at the Bongo Room? A really loud jazz band.... It's easy to see you in *Mighty Joe Young*, a King-Kong-sized louse chained to pillars on stage."

"Nah, that's the cliché—some scientist in a pith helmet..."

"Like yours," he said, pointing to the one she wore.

"...goes out into the jungle..." She sucked in a deep drag, then held it.

"Like this one," he said, sweeping his arm around.

She coughed out, "...and brings back the missing link."

"Like the one you're after?"

The cannabis making her light-headed, happy, she cried, "You ought to film me shouting 'Eureka!'"

"Scientists never shout Eureka?"

"Eureka! Eureka!" she laughed—such a funny word!—suddenly having that flash of joy that accompanies a mental block suddenly dissolved. When she was younger, she used to have those moments often: insights that had filled her with the same buoyancy she got recognizing how the grammar of the periodic table organized its elements so poetically that it didn't have to be memorized any more than you had to memorize *do-ray-me-fa-so-la-tee-do* to sing a scale, or the graceful way her pencil pirouetted about the point of its compass in geometry class, pencil lead tracing thin gray arcs, like a figure skater on ice, to bisect her first acute angle....

It was different now. Even if the same, the way a mature love is different yet the same as a young love, and she calmed herself to answer, "Yes. Scientists say Eureka. If only to themselves. But usually they're at home instead of in a jungle. In bed, drifting off to sleep when the light comes. Or in the shower. Or while looking through the dusty box of rocks in the basement of some university, trying to figure out why the fossilized arthropod they've turned over and over in their hands doesn't have segments like all the other arthropods they'd ever seen when they realize that the arthropod wasn't an arthropod at all and had only been classified incorrectly forty years ago. And because of a wrong initial classification, the decades of stories that had been built upon it—by people who only read the journals because they were too busy, or couldn't get travel funding, or were too lazy, or for whatever reason never looked at the actual fossil itself—were also wrong. Or maybe you're the one who sees how the Rubik's Cube that everyone wrestled into single-colored sides can also be seen as a completely different puzzle—one whose solution was checkerboard sides—why not?—and means that *Opabinia* isn't an arthropod as everyone made it out to be, but a completely unknown species. Then someone else who assumes that *Opabinia* isn't an arthropod sees that the whole branch of the tree that had been created around it has a hollow core, and if the branch breaks, a third and fourth realize, working on their own puzzles, then the tree needs to be rethunk, as does the structure of the sea and how life was formed....

"Now that moment—the one way back there with our paleontologist bent over a drawer full of dusty fossils?—that's a Eureka moment. But at the time, she'd have no way of knowing it. Her grandchildren might get the satisfaction," she said, thinking of her own grandfather. "More often than not, you'll be a box of bones yourself before anyone gets to shout Eureka."

The thought of working for years on a movie you'd never see finished, or worse, one that couldn't be finished. She seemed to be talking about his movie, *Puddle*, and the way his brain would freeze up every time he tried to imagine a way to shoot it.

"Why do you do it then?" he asked, hoping she might explain him to himself.

"I wish I knew." She shrugged. "Because the stakes are so small?" She burst into a hissing laugh, handing back the joint. "Sorry. It's an old entomology joke." The M.J. was definitely mellowing her out, making everything funny, her mind going to a small turtle walking to a pea on the horizon, halving the distance to it each day but never reaching it. She tried, "I guess the smaller the world gets, the smaller its truths become? Maybe we come to accept that, and it's okay?" She thought a moment, then continued, "Whenever I have a student who's thinking about going into the field, I tell him to run the other way. To join the Foreign Legion or a pharmaceutical company. Do something else, anything. Then, if he finds he can't forget his first love, to come back to it: the life of a flea holds more secrets than all the sphinxes of Egypt, and if he could contribute just one line to this epic poem, he'd—

"That's all Darwin did," she said, as though the idea just came to her, "make a new story out of all the snail shells, bird wings, and other stuff naturalists had been collecting for decades: no math, no experiments, just his reading the earth's fine print and then telling a story with more layers than the Bible."

"Is that what this is about? Writing a new bible?"

"Nah. A prophet in the age of these gadgets?" she said, giving the Manpack a poke with her foot. "But that's science's dirty little underbelly: people seeing what they believe. 'I'm too busy in my lab,' one of my colleague once said, blowing me off the time I tried to bring this up during a tenure-denial hearing for a junior colleague. 'And talk about the 'opera of science' will never help us discover the cause of AIDS,'" she added in a mock male voice. "But when it was called GRID—Gay Related Immune Deficiency—when their story said that only Haitians or gays got it, there was no political will, and so no funding, and so no known cause.

"Point this out, though, say, 'Hey, maybe instead of scientist-heroes scaling mountain peaks, we can be more like women in a quilting circle,' they whip out their hundred-million-dollar particle accelerator and ask if there is a 'female gravity' or 'female quadratic equation.'

"But yes, I want to say, yes, actually there is.

"At a Women in Science Conclave, I met an engineer from JPL. When she was hired, the good ol' boys were trying to send a rover the size of a pickup truck to Mars. After a while she asked why it had to be so big. Why couldn't it be miniature? A great idea—until one day at lunch she let slip the fact that she got the idea from playing with dollhouses. Suddenly, they started finding all sorts of reasons why it wouldn't work.

"I mean, Jane Goodall gives chimps names instead of numbers, something any mother would do, something guys with their clipboards and cages never thought to do, and just by seeing them as characters in a soap opera instead of numbers on a spreadsheet she turned them—and us—into completely different animals: primates with families and culture and war. Look here. You want to see a picture of male science?"

She pulled out that fat book she'd hauled along and opened it to a map of the world. "The shaded areas are places where the flea population has been inventoried. Take a guess why so much of the flea world is Terra Incognita."

"Because it hasn't been studied?"

"Well, duh, but why?"

"You mean?—Why is it unknown or why hasn't it been studied?"

She waited for him to answer his own question.

"Money."

"At the first university I had a regular job at, I was dating another assistant prof—a guy in History. One day he shows me a composite map he was making of all the wars the U.S. had been in from 1945 to the present. At first I thought I was looking at a map of world flea distribution. Vietnam, Nicaragua, Cambodia, El Salvador.... All the places where the flea population has been studied overlapped exactly with the places that the U.S. had boots on the ground.

"And guess who was the only one in my field to get an NSF this year: the one who's doing sand flies, in Afghanistan. They don't give a rat's ass about the lice on Bedouins, but if U.S. soldiers are there arming Taliban Bedouins to fight Soviets, the money for fly bites comes flooding in. And he knew it too; when I made a snide remark about knowledge for knowledge's sake, he answered, 'Did you know that Napoleon's Grand Army lost more soldiers to parasites than Russian bullets?'—that was the first line of his grant proposal. Next time he'll write up a grant to study the flies in whatever other desert or jungle or Arctic tundra the U.S. thinks it can use to block Soviets."

They both looked into the fire, letting the mellow that enveloped them deepen. There were over 250 definitions of 'forest,' Jane thought, but none of them captured the sense of what it was like to be out here high, every part of the forest more alive than ever though she also knew that some of the trees were too valuable to survive in a country where people lived on $200 a year, the wind in their branches as mournful as the violins that would be made of their brazilwood (*Caesalpinia echinata*), the trees already playing their own requiem.

"You know," she said wistfully, "the Tevatron particle accelerator cost $120 million to build." She motioned toward her nets and ziplock baggies. "Do you know how much flea research $120 million could buy?"

"That's how much they spent to make that piece-of-shit movie *Towering Inferno*," Arthur echoed. "A movie about a New York skyscraper catching fire, then collapsing."

"But I got news for them," she added defiantly. "What I do, out here in the bush with my nets and specimen jars, is science too. The story Darwin told was science too. And yeah, that's what I'd want my dream article to do too: give the world a new *way* to see, not a new *thing* to see.

"So what? Your dream article wouldn't prove that dinosaurs had feather lice?"

"My dream journal article is the one you're making a movie about." She took a drag on the joint, surprising him with how like a pro she exhaled the smoke through her nose as she said, "Here's its abstract: There were no such things as dinosaurs."

"Huh?" He laughed, taking the joint from her. "Maybe you ought to go easy on this stuff."

"Don't you see?" she said. "Darwin WAS right about the tree of evolution. But he should have drawn it like a conifer: lots of branches at the bottom that get fewer the higher up you go. A Big-Bang of life that rapidly spreads into empty continents and empty oceans and empty skies. Room enough for every freak combination of fin and claw to thrive—here comes everyone!" she laughed.

"It's only later, after oceans and fields start to get crowded that competition begins to winnow every limb, every twig, every bud in the branch....

"But to say that there never were any dinosaurs.... It's like.... Like saying that people didn't come from apes."

"We didn't."

"Oh, the Flat Earth Society will love you."

"We ARE apes, silly!" she laughed, pushing against him. "Just as birds didn't emerge from lizards with a pituitary problem, they were dinosaurs all along—at least some of them—at least that's the manifesto I'd like to nail to the church door: a redesign of the evolutionary tree to account for the evolution of feather lice: some dinosaurs were never dinosaurs. They were birds all along: sisters, not daughters, of the theropods. Or have it your way: some birds are as old as the dinosaurs: feathered, nest building, two-legged, dinosaurs. Take your pick, I don't care—Or knock yourself out waving a flag that says 'dinosaurs' had feathers. Whatever. It's just a word, like 'Earth' or 'Natural.'" Or 'woman,' she thought, but didn't say.

"So how come no one's ever seen this before?"

The question was an electric current up her spine, the stranger that quickens her step. Already there had been articles that referred to *Archaeopteryx* as "an early bird," not "the first." "When Is a Bird Not a Bird" was the title of an article about the birdlike skeletons that had begun to come out of Liaoning, a place that politics and language had kept out of bounds—till now.

"Because there's no fossils?" he asked.

"Fossils." She gave a condescending snort.

"Do you know how much of the Evolutionary Tree is based on fossils? It has gaps of millions of years. So many lines of animals are based on a single tooth that paleontologists make jokes about teeth mating to produce other teeth. No, my friend, you can take fossils and make a million stories out of them. This one is confusing because birds emerged twice. Or maybe a hundred times if you bore down to the level of the cell. I'd bet that the proof of dinosaur feather lice is laying in a collection somewhere, unrecognized by the paleontologist who put it in a box years ago, not realizing that he'd been looking at a louse's fossilized chew marks or eggs because he'd never had a class in entomology—why should he?—and so didn't know squat about ectoparasites, let alone how to recognize the remains of a fossilized *Protoavisdectidae-X-avis korzeniowski* exoskeleton in a partially preserved if distorted foregut within the abdomen of a fossilized bird that he sees as a featherless theropod dinosaur.

"Just look around today to see how it works: after farmers exterminated western wolves, the whole ecosystem was thrown into chaos. Elk populations exploded. Deer populations exploded. Bear populations shot up. Other species collapsed. The deer consumed all the blueberry bushes and so butterfly and bee colonies collapsed. With no insects for pollination, entire spectrums of field flowers and fruits slumped. Elk ate willow shrubs so songbird populations declined. Without willow bushes to eat, beaver colonies collapsed, and without beaver dams, streams ran faster, rivers cut deeper. The water table dropped below the level that roots needed. Erosion set in. Now, even if you put the wolves back in, that part of the world is gone forever. Every creature in it was interlaced with every other creature, and every creature had to scramble to change or die, and every change caused a cascade of other changes—without salmon, bears start eating more elk. Throw a rock into a pond and watch the ripples; now throw 2 rocks, 10, let it rain rocks, and try to chart the ripples.... But still, we describe this 'evolution' in terms of 2 animals mating to produce teeth; and we line up those teeth on a chart as clean and organized as a corporate command structure instead of the messy biological weave that it is, woven with everything around it, and everything around that, and everything around everything around everything—"

"How do you draw that?"

"I don't know. But I do know that those first Natural Historians didn't need any new information to see this 'dinosaur,'" she said, holding up the replica of *Archaeopteryx's* skeleton on her medallion, "as this," she said, tapping it against the picture of *Archaeopteryx*. THE FIRST BIRD. She held up the amber with the louse trapped inside and gazed into it like a fortune teller. "One day, we'll see that the story of evolution is far too messy to be shoehorned into the 19th-century, linear plot Darwin gave us. Or even represented by a cloud, or squiggles, or—I don't know—a tangled ball of yarn. Maybe the best way to represent the Evolutionary Tree would be to knit it like a sweater. And once people see my feather louse, they're going to have to come up with new ways to tell stories, not just come up with new stories to tell."

"The Jane Goodall of the lice," he said, letting out a low whistle. Though she waved off his joke, he could see how much pleasure it gave her. Still, he meant it: the thing he had burst out laughing at a minute ago now didn't seem so crazy. Especially when he tried to imagine how he would have depicted *Archaeopteryx*: a fierce bird-dinosaur—using the claws in its wing tips to fight—instead of scratching its lice.

"Yeah, why'd the artist make its feathers red?" he said. "You can't tell the color of an animal from its bones, can you? Or did the artist just figure that a ferocious bird must be fire-engine red?"

Exactly! she wanted to cry, resisting the urge to hug him—finally—someone who understood instead of—

A dinosaur: that's what her and her way of thinking were becoming to junior colleagues, sliding cursors around with a gadget called a mouse, the strings of DNA data that they were beginning to compile, the glossy pictures of jewel-beetles made possible by the graphics cards in those powerful, new computers—a massive 128K of RAM compared to the 64K of memory in the Eagle moon lander.... Even if their animations were more of a fiction than her drawings, they looked so much more contemporary than her drawings that she couldn't help but remember what her scientific illustration prof used to say: A thing better expressed always wins out over one more true.

This was why she used to keep the pieces of three or four different jigsaw puzzles spread out on the table in the communal lunchroom shared by her graduate students. She'd mix the pieces together, dump them on the table, then turn them upside down so only their gray, cardboard backing showed. It was fun, trying to put them together, something her and her students would do during breaks, or while waiting for an assay to run: good practice for imagining what a flattened fossil of an insect might look like in its living 3D form she'd tell them.

Any longer though, hardly any of her students wanted to play. And given the growing emphasis on data sets, DNA stains, government grants, and pharmaceutical patents, she herself had begun to think that *Monopoly* would be a more fitting game.

"Ha!" she cried out, though not beat yet: "Their high-tech images are going to look as realistic as Mothra once my louse proves dinosaurs looked more like parrots than snakes!"

He was smiling.

"They laughed at Jane Goodall too," she said, pouting, conscious of herself playing a role. But somehow she didn't care; the Mary-Jane mellow they were riding giving them both all kinds of permissions.

She flipped through her book, looking for something among the schematic diagrams of lice. To his eye they looked identical, but each louse had a balloon drawn beside that showed a magnification of?—

"Man, they have weird tongues," he said, tapping one of the magnified curlicues. By the light of the fire, they seemed to waggle.

"That's the male organ."

He looked up quickly to her.

She nodded.

"All of them?" He rifled the pages, fat as a phone book. There must have been hundreds, no thousands, of different complications of the crotch: the baroque church-steeple architecture of *Perineus concinnus*'s shaft, and *Galliphilopterus brunneopectus*'s fleur-de-lis prick, and other arrangements beyond phantasmagoria.... "Their penises, right?"

"It's the most distinguishing feature of each species." She moved closer so she could share the book with him. Turning pages, her hand brushed against his, and she seemed to let it linger, her face in soft focus because of the weed. "Sex is what defines a species—each kind of key fits one specific shape of lock. It's what keeps an elephant from mating with a mouse. But what if mice were the same size as elephants?" The image made them both burst into laughter. "How... How..." She could barely get the question out. "How could Mother Nature prevent their mating?"

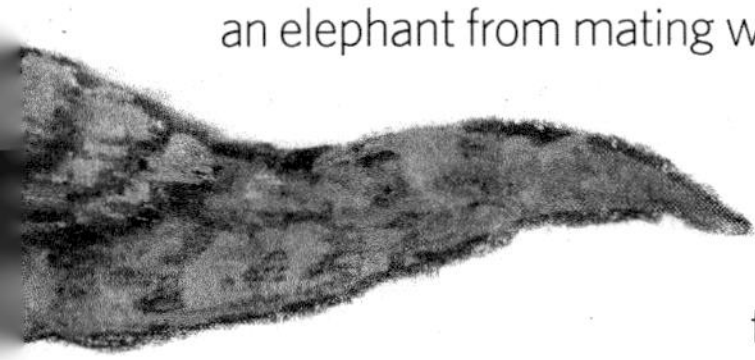

"Round pegs and square holes?" His answer made them both laugh again.

"Check out *Eucolpocephalum femorale*," she said turning the page to it. She had the rough hands of a carpenter. Not the soft ones of an academic. Or cameraman. "This little guy's got the most complicated organ on the planet." She leaned closer so he could see a wanger that looked like it had been drawn with a Spirograph. Her thigh was against his own, smooth with its muscle. She didn't move away, her voice becoming a little breathier as she explained how complicated their mating could be.

"Good thing people aren't like this, huh?"

"Oh, I don't know," she chuckled wistfully, "humans have their own complications." She never could understand why breaking up with that history prof shook her up so much, even though she never really liked him, him and his Kennedy accent, Ivy league manners and anal-retentive bowtie. A guy who didn't like movies. What kind of man didn't like movies? Then there were all the married guys she'd liked and the guys who turned out to be divorced jerks. But she didn't want to sound the way she sounded when she heard herself say these things. So instead she said, "Did you know that we're the only animals to have sex face-to-face?" When she looked up, she saw how close her face was to his, his eyes huge, dilated. Neither of them moved. "To develop pair bonding," she said, considering his face but not moving away. "There's volumes written on the evolutionary function of why women respond to candle-lit dinners and flowers while for men it's all about the body."

"Well not all men," he said in a stage-defensive way. Then more seriously, "At least not always."

"Oh really?" she said, rocking to bump against him, kidding him back. "Then why have thousands of years of evolution made our bodies the way they are?"

"Hmm?"

"Men say lots of things but biology doesn't lie. The female of our species is the one who ensures that the genes of males who are patient and caring, who have imagination and empathy, get passed on. With men and lice it's all below the belt." She turned to a drawing of a long, skinny louse: *Columbicola columbae*. "This guy uses his antennae to hug the female to him during copulation, which can go on for days."

"Days?"

She shivered. "Why did it get so cold all of a sudden?" she asked, briskly rubbing her upper arms.

An invitation? "And your louse?" he asked. "What does its penis look like?"

"Still terra incognita," she said dreamily. "But it'll tell the tale...." Her face really was handsome.

He leaned in closer to her. Her eyes closed, her hand falling limp on top the page as he—

"What was that? Did you hear something?"

"Hmm?" she murmured. "I didn't hear any—"

Then it sounded again, a low groan. Then the babble of the night forest closed in again.... "Must have been an animal," she whispered. "Survival of the fittest, 24/7."

"No," he said, getting up, adrenaline suddenly focusing his attention. "It sounded more human."

"Human?"

He stoked the fire to make it burn brighter. Shadows of the trees twitched by its light, as though animated.

She stood up as alert as if she'd had cold water thrown on her. Aché? The firelight made tree shadows jump back and forth. And she could have sworn she saw a face duck behind one. "I saw someone!"

"What? Who? The brothers?" He switched on the low-light setting on his camera and in its viewfinder the forest appeared dimly, with a weird yellow cast. No shadows. He used the camcorder as a soldier would use night-vision goggles, panning across the density of the brush, with the center in focus but his head fog surrounding it with a blur as though he were looking through a tunnel-vision lens. "Roque? Jacinto?" he called.

"Shhhh! They'll hear."

"Who?"

"Whoever might be within hearing distance."

"Soldiers?

"Worse."

"I thought you didn't believe in voodoo," he said. "I better go have a look." Something primal—fear?—in her eyes made him realize how stupid he was for falling into the role of 'the male.' But still, if there were someone out there he'd rather know now, while he was awake and clothed instead of bundled up like a mummy in his sleeping bag. Dian Fossey. He kept his camera trained on the tree Jane had pointed to, the daytime in his viewfinder an unnatural blurry yellow, an artificial, shadowless daytime.

"With that?" she said, nodding at the camera. She unsheathed her machete. Trying to walk as straight as he could, he could feel her fingers light on his back as they approached the tree where she'd seen the face, his heart so still he could hear the tiny motors of the camera's autofocus working the lens in and out. What would he do if there were someone there? Go out with his boots on like those cameramen who kept filming as their canoe went over a waterfall?...

The brush smushed loudly under their feet, their eyes trained on the tree. How the hell did he slip into a dead-teenager movie? ...alone with a girl in the woods, a conversation about sex.... Well, flea sex. No classroom, cafeteria, gratuitous nudity, or party at the parents' house scene, either.... Still, slasher-movie images of axes swinging down, limbs being hacked....

As he neared the tree, he realized its trunk was too narrow for anyone to hide behind.

Her hand still on his back, he could feel her tension through her fingertips, keeping him no more than an arm's length away. As a joke he suddenly stopped and said, "Boo!"

She jumped. Then whacked his ass with the flat of the machete blade.

"Owww!"

"You scared me, asshole!"

"Sorry. False alarm."

"Real funny." But she could see from the relief in his voice that he'd been scared too, the absurdity of the situation striking them both at the same time, making it impossible for either of them to be angry or scared, or be anything other than appreciative of the joke, the joke being, I'll see it when I believe it.... They walked back toward their fire, his camera on pause, her machete swinging at her side like a field flower she'd just picked....

"I guess we should turn in," she said, her pulse returning to normal, "instead of poking around in the dark."

What did she mean by that? he wondered, sweeping his sleeping bag with the flat of his hand. The scare must have brought her down some, just as it had him, he thought, as she got her own bedroll ready. He always had been proud of how he was able to fight through a weed high when he had to drive or study, but he still felt good.... Was she going to invite him in? For a sec he thought so, the way they both just stood there awkwardly hemming and hawing in front of her tent. But then no, she didn't, and he wondered if he'd imagined that moment back with her flea book too. Had it just been the Mary Jane talking? Or a spontaneous thing, now over? He didn't want to push it. Maybe there was nothing to push. The female of the species were funny creatures, he thought, watching her get into her tent as she had last night, sitting into it backwards. A million years of survival of the fittest making them cautious. Inclined to keep their house tight. But he could tell she was still high too from the way she flopped back a little too hard, then just lay there for a minute, her feet sticking out. When she moved again, she had a harder time kicking off her boots and sweat socks than she had last night, to keep from tracking insects into the tent.

The sight of her bare white feet emerging from those big-ol' clog-kickers she wore, then sweat socks, was sexy, the way Sheila used to look wearing one of his baggy shirts for pajamas. Zipped up in his sleeping bag—which was actually Jane's—he chuckled at the thought of him sleeping in Jane's bag the way Sheila used to sleep in his shirts—and he twisted in it so he could watch Jane's silhouette, cast on the wall of her tent by her flashlight. Did she keep the light on for his benefit?

Her shadow ran her fingers through her hair as women did in harem movies, *The Thief of Baghdad* and *Arabian Nights*, the folds of silk tents in those movies like folds of a belly dancer's balloon pants, concealing even as they invited. Her tent had a zipper. Then it went dark.

Through gaps in the tree canopy above, he could see the night sky, black.... No stars. Overcast. He hoped it wouldn't rain. There was a breeze up there, he could tell from the swaying of the highest branches, though it didn't reach him here on the ground.

Then he heard it again—a low groan—a growl or whatever the noise was that he'd heard before. The light came on in her tent. She'd heard it too, this time.

The fly of her tent unzippered. Her head emerged. "That wasn't you playing around, was it?" she whispered.

He shook his head.

Her head popped back in, then her feet emerged, her hands pulling on her boots again. Without lacing them up she came over to him, her legs muscular as a rock climber. She was in her underwear and tee shirt, a flashlight in one hand.

He was getting out of his bag when they heard it again—a groan, or something that rose slightly in pitch. They went motionless, listening intently, trying to discern the clues. Then he got the rest of the way out of his sleeping bag and stood in his boxer shorts beside her. They heard it again. "That didn't sound like an animal to me. Not human either, but human made." They stood listening—nothing but crickets and the hiss of the trees moving high above in the breeze, a wavelike sound that, if he closed his eyes, would make it easy to believe they were standing on a beach. "It was more of a pounding. Like drums. Log drums or something. Maybe they're listening for an answer too."

"You've seen too many Tarzan mov—"

There it was again. A faint groan of something just beyond hearing that grew barely audible before dying away again. "That was definitely an animal," she said. "Oh, I wish Roque and Jacinto were here to explain it."

"Yeah, like they explained the voodoo. Listen." Faintly, it sounded like the hokey roar Godzilla made. "It isn't possible that there's a dinosaur out here, is it?"

"Don't be stupid."

"It sounded like a truck. Or some kind of machine."

"Your mind's playing tricks on you again; you hear a jaguar and think it's a truck because you wish it was a truck."

Back in the hotel the groan of trucks had been so constant that Arthur continued to hear them even in his dreams. "Yeah, you're probably—"

"Shhh. Listen." But this time it did sound like a truck, then the wind shifted and it sounded like a groan again. "Maybe it's an animal in pain." It sounded again, fainter this time, though they were able to pick it up because now their ears were attuned to it. "Maybe whoever crucified that monkey is making that sound."

This time, he could tell from the tightness of her expression that he'd gotten her attention. She shined her light into the forest, its beam sweeping the trees like a searchlight, washing out their color, turning them into ghosts. "Whatever it is, it's still far off. Out here sounds can carry for miles. Especially at night."

"That time it sounded like it was moving away, too."

They stood close to one another, listening for the noise. Nothing. Nothing for the longest time. Then they gave up listening. They said goodnight again. Then they thought it best to build up the fire in case it had been a jaguar. They piled up enough wood to make it burn bright and long, and there, in its orange light, she shook his hand goodnight. Then she got back into her tent, and he returned to his sleeping bag. The sleeping bag was waterproof, but he thought he'd set up its hood anyway, since it was starting to look like rain. But before he could finish, the zipper on her tent went down and her head emerged again.

"Maybe it would be better if you slept in here tonight," she said. "I mean, wouldn't we be safer if we stayed together?"

The tent was small. He struggled to stuff his sleeping bag into a slit of the tent opening, and needed her help from inside. Then he passed her his camera—always his camera got the best care. He followed it in, lying beside her, her body soft, the scent of her hair in his face. The interior of the tent was aglow, reminding him of commercials for camcorders that showed how they could record even if the only available light came from the candles on a birthday cake....

She could feel him against her, getting hard, like those guys slow dancing at the prom. Is that a pickle in your pocket or are you just glad to see me? the girls used to laugh in the washroom, and lightheaded, she bit her lip to keep from bursting into laughter, her mind filling with *Columbicola columbae's* sexual marathons, the male's antenna wrapping around the female's body, and she arched back against him, that ancient cliché, his mouth finding the back of her neck as the camera panned to the trees....

HE WOKE GROGGILY TO SILHOUETTES OF LEAVES against the ceiling of the tent, dappled light playing against the fabric like shadow puppets in those theaters that preceded Kino. Name of the play: *Morning in the Forest* with—

Jane. Back to him, soft against him, her hair was disheveled. Did women feel the same things as men? Or did men feel the same things as fleas, as she claimed? He'd be a liar if he didn't admit to a little envy as she described the Ichi-o-whatever-it-was, going at it for days.... Neither of them had meant for last night to happen; it just did, just like....

Put a male and female of the same species in a box, Jane thought, and what else do you think is going to happen? The cannabis probably didn't help—even though she knew that this evergreen, stoner excuse probably didn't have any clinical basis.

Outside, the birds were going at it, squawking and waging wars for territory and sex. Nature had seemed so huge last night that she didn't even think to not let it take its course—two people on this spinning globe—why not?—having no more importance to the grand scheme of things than a couple of fleas humping on a dog that was humping another dog on an earth that was going to keep on spinning no matter how hot and bothered its parasites got....

Some of the men she'd slept with had thought it weird that her mind went to fleas during sex, even though the male entering the female was such a classic parasite-host relationship that she couldn't believe it didn't occur to everyone.

She untangled herself from male legs. After her grandmother died, and her mother had to get the house ready to sell, they'd found dozens of photos of her grandfather in his field labs in the Babuyan Islands, and the Brazilian rainforest and other unidentified places, and in all of them he had had a female assistant. Always they were beautiful, she'd thought, remembering one photo in particular from his army days in the Philippines: his hair thick and black, back then, combed into an Elvis wave. A real hunk, he was, dressed in his khaki uniform, handing a specimen bag to an assistant seated at a microscope: a Filipina with the striking looks of an actress. Whoever shot the photo had also been seated so the perspective of the camera was up, his 6′2″ height caught in a hero shot, while his assistant looked up to him dreamily, a long, model-delicate hand reaching up to him so languidly that even to Jane, at age nine, there seemed to be something illicit about the photo. Her mother had sighed, putting the photo in a box, telling Jane that while he was in the bush, her mother had had her own adventures. Janie had imagined her grandmother in a pith helmet. But older, in sociology, she'd learned that 30% of all infants were the children of men other than the man listed by the mother as the father on the birth certificate, and she suddenly realized what her mother had been trying to tell her, back there in that attic.

Did this one think it was more than that?

...it was like being in a movie. Point a camera at people and they smile: the camera itself part of the world, not just some mirror held up to it.... When he got back, Arthur thought, he'd reshoot *Puddle* with the sun setting behind him: a cameraman who appears in the film but only as a shadow on the puddle he's filming.

The idea jolted Arthur awake: *Eureka!*—he'd film a dying puddle for as many hours as it took, but as the sun bore down, he'd keep moving so his shadow protected the puddle from its glare: that is, he'd be on both ends of the camera—making the movie but the movie revealing its director, the sun, always at his back because that's where light places a cameraman to get the best shot, and he moves there—a parasite as Jane would say—the earth in its orbit and the needs of the camera making him move between sun and puddle and so allowing the puddle to last as long as it can. He protects the puddle and the puddle keeps the film going. In balance. They keep each other alive. Until they don't. Then we're both done, Arthur thought, because there was no Nature without humans, just as there were no landscapes until Dutch painters trained people to see fields and rivers as "picturesque." He'd shoot with his old Bolex—not magnetic tape—because film needed the thing itself to happen in front of it—and even that wouldn't last forever: nothing mortal does—the film deteriorating in its canister as all film does, a failing effort—that is, a human effort, melting into another strata of deep time—and this simple truth was so liberating that he could feel the logjam that had been his life begin to break....

He squirmed to free his arm, numb from being under her so long that the circulation coming into it ached as trees must when the sap begins to flow after a long, dormant winter....

She suddenly sat upright. "Do you smell something?"

A cigarette? Someone was smoking. He unzipped the tent to look out and there, a short distance away, a forest Guaraní looked back stoically. "We got company," he said, getting into his shorts, a surge of adrenaline tightening his voice.

"What!" But he was already out of the tent. She hurriedly groped through the sleeping bag till she found her pants, pulling them on, buttoning her shirt as she emerged to find him standing before a nearly naked man, his body painted black, small patches of white feathers glued all over in swirling patterns.

"Hola," Jane said. He just sat there. Motionless as a photo if it wasn't for the smoke curling out of the pipe that stuck from his fist. Jane tried hello in the three dialects she knew for the word. Nothing. She thought he was an Aché tribesman because she recognized his lip plug: a kind of war paint for those who were always at war. A dead parrot hung by a cord around his neck.

When he stood, his penis dangled like a sausage in a shop. He held out his parrot to Jane, saying *"C'ho apa oma kaji,"* speaking a dialect even more ancient than the one she'd heard in the airport, infused with clicks and whistles that had developed to blend in with the forest so that hunters could communicate without alerting animals to their presence.

When he finished talking, he raised a hand to his face, formed a rectangle with his fingers: an imaginary camera, she realized when he pumped a finger, using the click in his language to imitate its shutter.

"What? What? He wants my camera!" Arthur said, moving it behind his back.

"No, I think he wants you to take his picture."

"Do I!—that's the first thing I tried to do but the battery's dead. Tell him to wait till I—"

Jane grabbed his arm. "Not so fast," she said to Arthur, smiling at the man but not taking her eyes off of him. "I think we should wait to see what he really wants."

Her words precipitated a long monologue with lots of gestures at Arthur and his camera which made her think that the man had heard that there were white people—eco-tourists?—out here who would pay to take his picture. That's why he's all dressed up. The black resin he'd painted himself with and feather polka dots—vulture feathers, she could see, *Coragyps atratus*—were for the traditional club fights, though there was no club fight, hadn't been any for years. The forest was alive with people like him, Felipe had said, on the move, like rivulets coursing toward the city.

The man shook his head, a gesture that must have meant yes, the way he thrust his open palm at Arthur again.

"Oh, right." He began to dig in his pocket but Jane told him to stop, to not show how easy it was for him to fork over the 5 guaraní bill.

Too late.

The man took it, and held it up to the sky to examine its watermark. After a moment, he grunted in approval, then held out his parrot to Arthur.

"No gracias," she answered for him, pushing Arthur's hand down.

The man thrust it toward her, spreading its feathers to show her their quality.

"Just take it," Arthur said.

"No, you don't understand. If we take it, we'll have the whole tribe trying to sell us dead parrots tomorrow."

She pulled the medallion she wore out of her shirt. "This is the only bird I'm interested in," Jane said, slipping her head out of its string to show him the engraving: the fossil remains of *Archaeopteryx*.

As though it was a language itself, the man studied its image for the longest time. Then he motioned for her and Arthur to follow him. They just stood there.

But the man was persistent, a river of language pouring out of him as he gestured for them to come along. His own parrot was on a string, like a necklace that he put back on. Then he took Jane by the upper arm, and pantomimed walking, nodding his head in the direction he wanted her to go.

"You? You know this bird?" Jane asked, holding up the medallion. "*Archaeopteryx*?"

"*Ñandejára avei oiporu chupe oñe'e oê hag^ua hérape....*" He kept up his stream of language, pointing at the medallion and her, saying, "*Ywy Mará Ey*." But he wasn't pointing at her, she realized. He was pointing at the amber bead she wore on a bootlace around her neck. When she gave it to him, he put it together with the *Archaeopteryx* medallion, repeatedly making a pair of them, and then pointing out into the forest. "*Ywy Mará Ey*."

"*Ywy Mará Ey*." Jane repeated. "I think that's his word for *Archaeopteryx*. I think he wants to show us one."

Arthur snorted. "Yeah, right."

Jane got out her compass to verify what she already knew: the same direction she needed to go.

"For real?" Arthur said.

Lugging the Manpack, camcorder, and other gear they couldn't leave behind, they struggled to keep up with their new guide, dense growths parting before him to reveal footpaths that Jane would have walked right across without noticing. Where Arthur saw compositions in green and vine, where she saw habitats of Calopterygidae or Carcinophoridae, their guide saw highways and overpasses and intersections. Twice they took shortcuts across creeks, using bridges that were invisible until their guide plunged across them, each bridge consisting of a submerged log for the feet and a sapling, bent from birth to grow from one bank to the other at just the right height to use as a handhold.

Every time Jane checked her compass, the hairs on the back of her neck tingled. He was leading them—as the crow flies—to 24° 03′ 18.45″ S; 55° 23′ 53.60″ W, and like a marathon runner sensing the finish line, Jane could feel her steps lighten. But it was as much from anxiety as excitement.

The entire time, she felt as though she was running toward her last and best chance to get people to see lice differently, and so see dinosaurs differently, and so see all nature differently—including her—and maybe women like her—and women after her, working in labs as if labs were their natural habitat, which one day they would be, if women like her didn't give up. That's why being in Arthur's stupid little educational video had become so important to her, she realized—obsessed, as the bird boys would put it.

It started to rain.

Jane frowned, looking up to the overcast sky. The rain wasn't that bad but Arthur kept complaining about his camera so they stopped to break out the ponchos, and their guide led them under an umbrella of Butiá Palms. As Arthur fiddled with his camera, their guide used a hand ax made of sharpened bottle glass to dig grubs out from under its roots.

The first time she'd seen one of those Stone-Age tools, made from the glass of a modern wine bottle, it seemed to come out of a time warp. But watching him work, his tool made a lot of other things visible—the way the cow paths that originally formed the roads of a village could shape a city like Boston, or the way the tribesman who sold her the amber could walk around in an airport, wearing a necklace of dead birds. From an anthropologist, Jane had learned that forest Aché initially wore the corpses of the birds they hunted as a way to ask forgiveness for the sad necessity. Was there only one reason left for them to do so now?—so tourists could take a picture?...

If only there were a way to keep all ways of being alive, Jane thought, leaning back against the tree as their guide did, dry in its rain-shadow. At the first bridge, she and Arthur had followed his lead, talking off their shoes, and she realized that that's why the Aché went barefoot through the forest. Doing so made them seem primitive to outsiders. But to them it was ignorant to not go barefoot across the submerged logs; barefoot, the Aché would feel the snake they accidently stepped on in time to react, unlike her and Arthur, who wouldn't realize they'd stepped on a snake until it bit them. Was that also how the forest Aché avoided some of the diseases their city cousins suffered?

As their guide stored some grubs in a Pepsi bottle, Jane could see feather lice hopping back and forth between the parrot around his neck and his long hair.

They were abandoning the carcass of their dead host, she knew, biting anything they could get their mandibles around in the hopes of finding a new host. Virologists thought hunters like their guide had some natural immunity to diseases because they were exposed to low doses of the disease; but Jane wondered if it was the delivery system itself—the lice—that were doing the job. She made a mental note to look into this later.

Oblivious to the bites, he popped a handful of plump, white grubs into his mouth like popcorn, watching them as though they were a movie.

"This is weird," Arthur said, his hands inside the poncho, manipulating the camera. "First a fresh battery goes dead, then a new tape runs out."

"Maybe you just didn't put a blank one in."

"I distinctly remember seeing the counter when we were checking out that noise last night. It had at least an hour left just before we went into the tent." The neck hole of his poncho was stretched wide so he could see down into it as he messed with the camera.

The tape finished rewinding and the screen flickered to life with replay: more darkness, but it was the dark gray of recorded night, not nothingness, and its soundtrack was the music of night crickets and tree frogs. Then there was a moan from the camera. A woman's moan.

The picture lurched, the scene suddenly shifting as though the camera had been kicked; on-screen were mountains and valleys—no, they were folds in cloths—shot in close-up—and with the orange cast that the fire light and low-light mode of his camcorder gave everything. Arthur recognized the glow—after the scare they'd gotten last night, they'd built up the fire and for the first hour or so, its orange glow had filled the tent with enough light to read by. They hadn't been reading though. Lapping sounds? A brook? No, the sound of kissing. Auto focus sharpened the folds and he could see they were folds in her sleeping bag.

Then there was blurry movement. A flash of bare skin—his leg—tinted by the warm candlelight glow. Another mummer—a man's voice this time—and it dawned on Jane what they were looking at.

"You filmed us having sex!" she shouted so near that his ear rang.

"It's not film—"

"But there it is!" she yelled, pointing down into his poncho at the screen.

"And I didn't *film* anything!" A rustle of cloth as it dragged across the microphone. The breathing became heavier, more rhythmic. Another kick to the camera and the scene got a Dutch tilt. "It was an accident. With everything going on I must have— Anyway, you're the one who put the camera down by our feet."

"I didn't know you left it on!"

"Sorry!—I was distracted at the moment!"

They stopped arguing, distracted by blurry glimpses, shadowy outlines....

He hadn't intended any of this but—the shock of it was a *Wizard of Oz* moment in reverse—the audience gasping as the movie switches to gritty Reality. And an idea came to him—

She reached into his poncho to erase it.

"Wait a minute," he said, leaning away. "Let's think about this for a minute."

She stood upright. "There isn't anything to think about. You've got to erase that right now!"

He tried to slow her down, tried to get her to see how the accident might have created something special, something spontaneous that couldn't be captured again even if they tried. Instead of the voice-of-god narrators and stock scenes of most nature shows—*Just as the mother lion protects her cubs, you can protect your family with Mutual of Omaha*—they had something real. He could imagine an audience settling down to watch a regular, clichéd nature show and having the film open with this instead. No one would ever see a nature show the same again and it was the camera that made it possible.

"Last night we might have stumbled into one of those accidents you were telling me about—like when a tech connected the wrong wires and invented the transistor. Without planning, or trying, or even being aware of it, we created a scene that doc-filmmakers have been dreaming about since the creation of film: no mic-boom to spook the subject; no light-meter readings to kill the moment.... There wasn't even a cameraman. But we went where no camera had been able to shoot before: the dark!"

And for the first time in my life I was in the right place at the right time, he thought. But he said instead: "And what did it show?—that the people that make the show are animals too; that the only difference between the nature before the camera and the nature behind the camera was that one got to define the other."

Jane stood there, arms crossed, looking back at him as though studying a strange object as he explained why it was no accident that the first documentary about indigenous people—*Nanook of the North*—was shot out where you could use a dogsled to haul around the cameras of the day, which weighed 120 pounds. The thought had come to him as they ran through the forest, following their guide across streams, the camcorder letting him shoot more promiscuously than anyone could with film, and maybe changing the way people saw nature as Leacock had changed the way people saw politicians just by doing what the first shoulder-mounted Éclair let him: follow Kennedy, the ordinary human, from his hotel room, to his car, out of his car, through a maze of basement hallways, then up a staircase, and out onto a balcony where Kennedy, the political rock star, looks down upon a sea of screaming fans at the Democratic convention....

He thought she was considering what he said, but when she spoke she said, "I'm not going to let you put a video of us screwing in this or any movie!" He tried to reason with her, he tried to point out that she wasn't even visible in the video—that if anyone's ass was visible it was his—which made it all the better: "If *National Geographic* put his ass in their magazine," he said, pointing to their guide, "no one notices, because him and Nanook, and all the other 'natives' are part of nature, but if you show my ass, and try to say we're part of nature too, they...."

She wouldn't have it.

"You can put your ass all over Times Square if you want but we're still making the movie you came here to make." His fists clenched. "Because we still might find my louse."

Their guide pointed up at the sky, then motioned for them to follow, saying, "*Ywy Mará Ey.*"

"Look, I really wanted to shoot you as David defeating Goliath. I really did. It's not my fault that your story morphed into Don Quixote." The guide pointed to the clouds ushering in worse weather. "All I want is for you to let me be your Sancho Panza—to show how the search for a little unvarnished, unedited, unmediated unqualified truth might be crazy in today's videotaped, everyone's-got-their-own-reality world...."

"My movie isn't...."

"...and we can still make your movie. And mine. We can make a hundred or a thousand different movies with the same footage. But isn't that the real story?—We eat Red Dye 40 and other poisons they call food; we burn down Vietnam for fake reasons. Whites Only water fountains, Men Only labs—isn't the telling at the heart of these stories the story we're both trying to tell?"

The guide motioned more violently for them to follow. "*Ywy Mará Ey!*"

"Even if there isn't a bird out there that roars like a dinosaur, gives birth to kittens, or shits diamonds?"

"Maybe. Maybe my louse was a windmill from the start—like everyone said—one big windmill.... But there's one thing I believe...."

"Yeah?"

"*Ywy Mará Ey.*"

"*Woman in the Dunes.*"

At first he thought she'd meant the ending where the camera turned around to look through itself at the cameraman, but the brusque way she gathered her stuff said she was moving on, 'with or without you.' But damn it, he was angry too, angry at her for thinking she'd seen through him, seeing through her seeing through him. Oh yeah, she knew everything about him even though she wouldn't even give him the chance to tell her the way *Puddle* could end, and how they were really both making the same movie.

Most of all he was angry at himself for not having her sign a release form before they started. "Look, I just cannot do what you're asking me to do. I just can't!" he said, but he hit the eject button and took out the cassette anyway. "My—no, our last hope," he said, agitated, handing it over. "In case you realize that we really did discover how to extract water from sand."

Less than an hour later they burst from the forest into a clearing that shouldn't have been there. Her hands shaking, Jane set up the Manpack to confirm what she already knew: 24° 03′ 18.45″ S; 55° 23′ 53.60″ W—the very spot she'd spotted her louse only a week ago. But the trees were gone. Vanished. She stepped out into the open space turning around and around, the vertigo of disorientation making her dizzy as the realization of what had happened began to sink in.

An enormous hole had been torn out of the forest as though the mouth of some immense monster had taken a bite from it, leaving a field of stumps. At the opposite end of the field, the tree line had been cleaved: a part in the tree line showed where a bulldozer had cut a logging road.

Jane dropped to her knees, hollow, as though her guts had been removed with the trees, her mind racing with the knowledge that the microenvironment was gone, the habitat gone, its animals gone, as well as any chance of finding her louse—gone—and then she realized she'd cut her knee on a jagged piece of metal.

Sticking out of the rut she had kneeled in was an arc of corroded brass. Like a brass porthole from a ship? How the hell did a ship get out here? Degrees of arc were etched into the corroded metal, and she saw that it wasn't part of a ship, but a ship's instrument—a sextant like she'd seen in museums—and the stupidity of it all—the absurdity of the vanished trees, the ruts torn into the dirt by a bulldozer's treads, the sextant of a ship, the sight of Arthur stepping into the field, turning around as though unable to believe the space he was in was real—made her dizzy.

"Are you sure this is the right spot?" he said.

She let her head drop. The Manpack lay cocked in a bulldozer track, mud splattered.

"But are you sure!"

She looked up into the black eye of his camera, trained on her. "Oh shut that damn thing off," she said, trying to keep it together as she slumped back onto her heels.

She looked miserable through the viewfinder of the camcorder, her hair wet and stringy, her lip quivering like the victim of a hurricane explaining to a news crew how her life had been washed away. Her knee was bleeding. If there wasn't a naked man polka-dotted with vulture feathers behind her, she could have been a video pietà of an Alabama trailer-court mother who lost her child in the storm. He couldn't tell if her face was wet with tears or raindrops, but to the camera it didn't matter. All he'd wanted was a little truth, and he'd ended up with a melodrama. "Oh shut that damn thing off," his heroine said on-screen, slumping back on her heels.

He panned up from her to the pitiless sky, gray and rainy.

"*Ywy Mará Ey! Ywy Mará Ey!*" the guide was shouting to the skies, a lament to an uncaring heaven. "*Ywy Mará Ey! Ywy Mará Ey!*" Thunder rumbled in the distance at just the right volume to lay under the man's plaintive cries, making a great sound track for the ending—as though he was trying to conjure the red lizard-bird from the heavens with his lament and the heavens answered with indifference—and Arthur kept the camera on the pitiless sky—hoping for a lightning flash. Then he saw: the man was emphatically stabbing a finger at the sky, pointing. "*Ywy Mará Ey! Ywy Mará Ey!*"

"Wha?—" Jane asked, turning, then rising to her feet.

"*Ywy Mará Ey!*" their guide continued to cry, pointing to the sky.

"You saw one? Where!" she excitedly asked, grasping his shoulders to speak directly to his face. He kept jabbing a finger at the sky behind them, rattling off a stream of words she couldn't understand. "Did you see it?" she asked Arthur. "You were facing that way." He shook his head, and all three of them turned to search the sky where their guide had pointed. Then Arthur remembered: the camcorder. "Wait! I might have caught it on tape!"

He rewound the tape to a few minutes ago then pressed the play button as they gathered around: there was Jane, on her knees on-screen, their guide standing behind her, his back to the camera, the sound of her sniffles coming from the tiny speaker on the camera. *Oh shut that damn thing off....*

Jane, Arthur, and their guide drew tighter together, the three of them hunched over the screen, trying to block out what light they could to make the screen show up better as its scene panned up to the gray sky. *Ywy Mará Ey!* The low rumble of thunder. *Ywy Mará Ey!* Between cries, in the corner of the screen there was a red streak—fast as a meteor shooting across one corner of the view.

"There!" Jane yelled.

Arthur rewound the camera and played the scene again, his finger on the pause button this time. Jane again. Pan up to gray sky again. *Ywy Mar*— PAUSE— the three of them hunched over the tiny image frozen on-screen, a red smear in the corner of the frame, too indistinct to make out as a red bird or animal or flea or speck or just static in the electronics of the camera, the tiny scene mute as an abstract painting of gray with a tiny red strike across one corner: a film reduced to its most minimal elements, one frame, the most minimal movie possible, the red slash a Rorschach inkblot—a streak that looked uncannily like the sliver of red feather trapped in amber when seen through Jane's loupe—the smear of red standing for everything, nothing, waiting for significance to be poured in.

There are things
We live among 'and to see them
Is to know ourselves.'
GEORGE OPPEN, OF BEING NUMEROUS

Chapter III: Ascension

-
- Read online
  @ www.ascensionnovel.com

Dave, I'm afraid, Dave.

HAL, 2001: A SPACE ODYSSEY

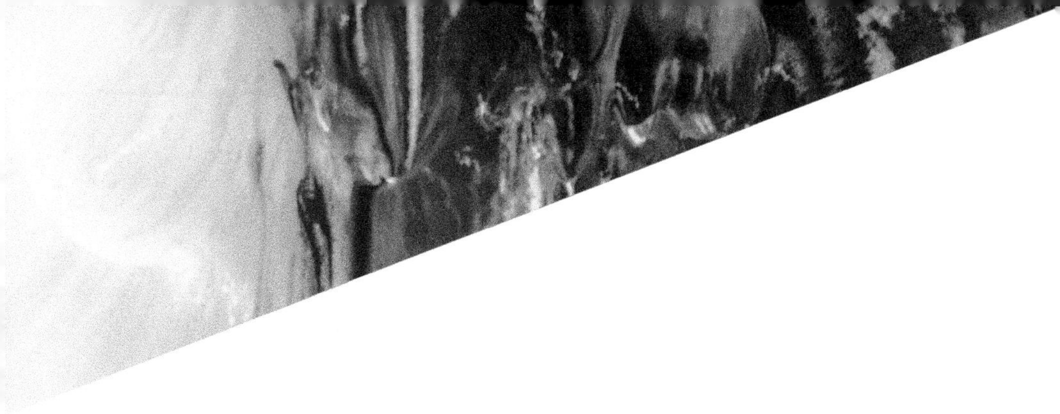

When the end came, *it came as resolutely as the sun, having as much choice, and giving as much warning as a predawn sky when there is just enough light for an imam to distinguish a black from white thread: the alba moment, when a convergence of temperature and pressure morphs dew to fog, and day's first gray warns lovers to part, the strengthening day quickening the rooster's circadian rhythms till its crow erupts and pricks the ears of thieves and betrayers.*

But few had been awake, not to this end. Not the imam. Not the lovers in their bed. Not the thief in his rounds. Even after artic ice began to pool, mirroring the rosy fingers of dawn, lovers sighed and returned to the dream of their embrace; even as the bottoms of those ice lakes cracked, betrayers denied the dawn thrice, then four and more times, dismissing as Chicken Littles the roosters who warned of rising seas.

Relentlessly, having no more choice than water over a fall, trickles of ice melt grew into streams. Soon circular Niagara Falls of melting ice were pouring in on themselves, their thunderous torrents creating rivers beneath the ice caps as a current undermines a foundation and causes a seawall to collapse; the Arctic shelves broke apart far faster than anyone had anticipated, and it wasn't until the sun was fully up that people noticed: the seas had in fact risen. Risen so much that low-landers who had been crowing for highlanders to wake!—to see!—were migrating from the rising water; masses of refugees—the Bottom Billion—who once inhabited sea-swept coasts, now moved ever inland while those nations that remained dry installed fences and cameras and guards and tightened the mesh of their electronic screens as if that would help when in fact it only made the whole world flat. A monotonous drone was everywhere. Animals that couldn't live everywhere with-ered. Malaria and poison ivies crept northward with kudzu and tropical insects proliferating in ever higher latitudes, the corrals built around refugees unable to keep out the insects that had begun to migrate upward, bringing with them diseases that had only been known in what had been the low, hot, and humid tropics....

Beeping...

The alarm on the humidifier that kept acting up went off again—and Gabe hit its reset button as lethargically as she might silence the alarm of her bedside clock. How odd it was to wake to a reality more Sci-Fi than her daydream.

Tired, always she seemed tired, as though coming down with a cold. The humidifier was blowing normally, according to the gauge on the wall—Paraguayan humidity—no danger to the lice colonies that she tended. She made a mental note to check the alarm's trigger later, a lack of energy making her put off everything—and she returned to the monotony of transferring blood-fed lice into OviPots.

As she worked, she tried to slip back into the graphic novel that she drew in her free time. But it was getting harder. Not harder to daydream, just harder to keep pace with banana trees that shed leaves of synthetic skin, mice that chirp, scorpions with the intelligence of rats and the rest of the genetic mess that the wild was becoming. How strange—after all the disaster films—*Planet of the Apes*—after the countless books, movies, video games, and scientific studies too—the *Club of Rome*—after all the denial, there was such an explosion of life just as the planet was dying.

Not dying. Still, it was hard to get her mind around the idea of an earth that all humanity had known becoming a place that none of those old-planet people would recognize....

NGers got tattoos of Red Marble Earth: that black-and-red cartoon meme of Earth boiling off its atmosphere as though it were a meteor. But maybe the best tattoo would be of a cargo ship the size of Kansas, traveling from China to America and passing as it did an identical ship traveling from America to China, and both loaded with cars. Whatever. The punks just got their tattoos then went back to their barista jobs. And most people didn't even do that much. They just went to work. They had their morning coffee, tucked in their kids at night, worried about house payments, and updated their software. Even the people she worked with here in the lab were more worried about the next outbreak of avian influenza, H5N5, the virus spread like the common cold and characterized by its sudden onset and internal bleeding. Rapid contagion, and a mortality rate that can approach 100%: 'The Big One,' they called it, the tsunami of bird flus that could make the Covid-19 outbreak—with its food shortages and outdoor morgues—look like the sniffles.

Who wouldn't feel run-down given that to think about 24/7. Working in the Insectarium all day didn't help. She sighed at the containers of sand flies, the wall of ducks, geese, and other birds in glass containment boxes like feathered fish in aquariums: Blue Fronted Parrots, captured in Paraguay, crawling with lice, specimens to generate the data Chen needed for his statistical analysis. Olympia, the PI directing the study, had had Gabe blunt the beaks on the parrots so they couldn't preen, allowing their lice populations to shoot up. Some of the birds scratched themselves incessantly. Others sat there enduring.

The room was sealed as tight as a walk-in refrigerator with industrial-strength doors—the perfect setting for one of those doomsday scenarios where someone emerges from a bank's vault, or fireproof storage room to discover that the rest of the world had perished in a nuclear blast. Or been overrun by zombies.... Should she put zombies in her story? Looking toward the listless parrots, she realized that they were already there....

Except instead of the supplies that would stock a real bomb shelter, the wire shelving of her vault held OviPots of the fleas, lice, and flies that she bred for the labs: Tupperware containers of Stage 1 larva and Stage 2 larva that she fed on the mold that grew on ground-up rabbit feces, nursing them into adulthood; she'd fertilize the disease-carrying adults, let them feed on the geese, then bear eggs that she'd nurse into Stage 1 larva, trapping her in a cycle that needed constant care, even on holidays—sauna-like heat and humidity, the mind-numbing drone of the humidifiers, and smell. Whatever was good for the lice and flies, she, their bitch, had to take....

Gabe selected a mouth aspirator, and threaded the business end of its rubber hose into the glass box she had filled with lice from the birds. She began to suck. The cage was suddenly a snow globe of bird lice and human shrieks, she imagined, her aspirator the Godzilla to their Tokyo. The lice fled to the white light that their neurobiology equated with escape but was actually the white cloth that she'd stretched across the back of the cage where their tiny black bodies would stand out, making them easy to catch.

If only they could step outside their own story for the god's-eye view of what was happening.

She was after the females that had taken a blood meal from the birds, their tiny bodies bloated with bird blood as compared to the more elongated males. As she sucked one after another into the tube, she made a mark on a scrap of paper for every 10 she caught.

Another Shitty Day in Paradise, said the postcard taped to the wall, its edges curled. If she used her imagination, its palm trees swayed in a beach breeze instead of the airstream of the humidifier. *Eden. Wish you were here!* It was from Guy. When his unit was called up, he was first sent to Bahrain, which locals claimed was the site of Eden, and he'd e-mailed everyone in the lab a postcard. Sunshine. The drone of surf. Heat. Humidity. Beads of sweat running down her back. She could almost imagine the rubber hose she sucked on as a straw in a piña colada—if it weren't for the stench of feces, if she didn't feel like the last woman on Earth. And this, a man on a TED Talk said last night, may well end up being the pinnacle of civilization. Whatever.

Two geese labored to gain altitude, one rising into place at the wing tip of the other, the pair joined by a third, and more, the geese languidly forming a V in the sky—not because of a leader but because patterns of behavior could emerge as surely as a convergence of light and moisture could throw a rainbow across the sky. The geese made their way south across a brilliant sunrise—each bird carrying the

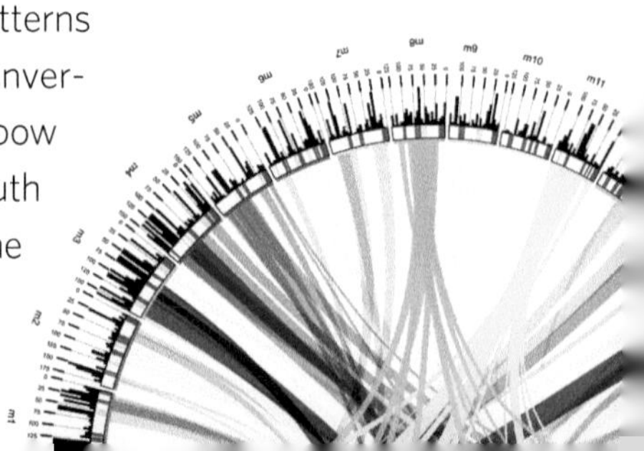

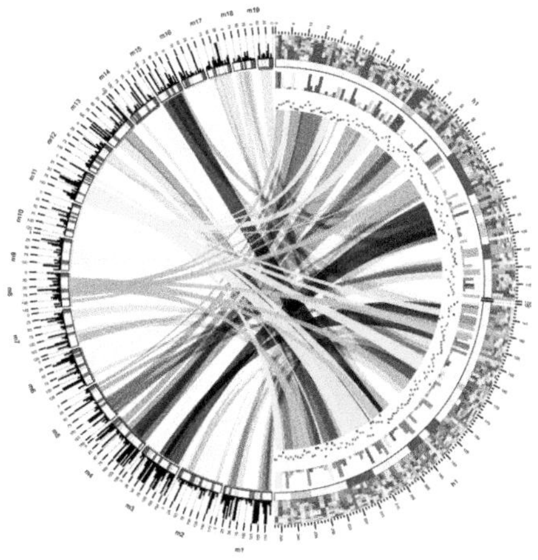

logic of the flock. And the logic of its lice. And the logic of the cells within the lice. And the logic of the virus within the cells, churning the tumblers on their biological locks. The odds of hitting the jackpot on a penny slot machine were one in a 1,000; a player pulling the handle 10 times a minute would hit the right combination every 100 minutes. But 1,000 players would produce 10 winners every minute, whether those players were people cycling through combinations on a slot machine, or the genetic stuff of a bird.

A flu infection can produce 200 trillion new viruses a week. Some combinations would be stymied, freezing into death as quickly as they were born, while others opened up new paths for life the way a single log in a jam can suddenly click out of place and allow a mighty river to flow within viruses within lice within geese within flocks—like these—all over the world, on the move, laboratories in the sky, crossing borders, landing in forests and public parks and backyards and waterways and wading pools....

What was she hiding? Or rather, what was it that made him think she was hiding something? Dan wondered, listening to Olympia talk to his boss. He'd seen it before: some professor discovers a protein fold, or useful fractal pattern or some other philosopher's stone able to turn academic research into dollars and—Voila!—another startup is born.

Before the meeting, IiM, InformationInMotion, the company Dan worked for, had GoogleSeurated her profile, of course: she didn't do FB2—and only

checked JoinApp to avoid flash mobs. But that didn't necessarily mean she was a loner. FB2 had been bleeding users for years. Not that it mattered: every time she updated any app, they would have downloaded her complete cloud—just as the 75-page privacy notice she probably never read said they would. Facial recognition tagged her galaxy of weddings and birthdays and vacation photos—and the man who used to be in all of her photos until he began showing up in the photos of another woman, posed with a different set of kids. Her toothbrush reported that it switched on twice a day (6 a.m. and 10 p.m.) and stayed on for an average of 2.3 minutes. Your Privacy Is Our Business. (*It really is!*) Just as her Fitbit used patterns of wrist movement to determine whether she was on an elevator, sleeping, eating, or driving over the speed limit, IiM extracted patterns from data traces to generate a portrait of her for its sales team: an ex-husband back in California, with her son (whose own FB account had tons of info on her). An annual spike in beer, hummus, and paper napkins indicated that she entertained her grad students once each year (the number of beers she bought having a high correlation with the number of grad students enrolled in her Lab Practices course, and indeed, the locations obtained from their phones showed that they converged at her house once a year), as though her annual party was an obligation, like going to the dentist (which she did twice a year).

The raw data from her car was so regular that its patterns could have been mistaken for those of a rat in a maze (she didn't like cruise control), though there was something going on with her Thursdays. Every third or fourth Thursday she deviated from her commute by driving to a different high-end restaurant in the Tech Corridor outside the city. But her charge-card history indicated that she never paid for dinner. She started taking these trips about the time that the word cloud they extracted from her email began to change: for the previous 5 years her N-grams had been dominated by work vocabulary—'parasite' 'protein' and 'DNA'—except for that period when she first moved to Chicago. Emails to her (then) husband bumped up the use of words like 'miss' and 'you' to 19.7% but took on a slope of -3 as the usage of 'apart' increased. It flatlined after 'seeing someone else' appeared. It was also during this time that her movie-watching history skewed toward chick flicks before dropping back to its annual average: 0.67 (what kind of person didn't like movies?). She began using the gym in her condo with the regularity of a boxer. And her Google searches became even more work intense.

Over time, a picture emerged from all the patterns she generated the way the rings in a tree could tell a story of weather. Or so claimed profilers. But anyone

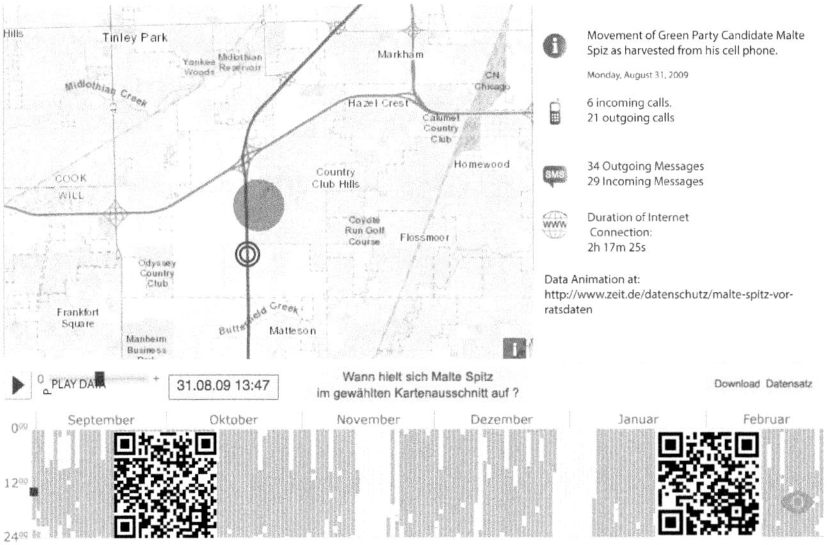

ascensionnovel.com/dan

who wrote algorithms knew that Big D portraits could be so much phrenology: determining moral qualities by reading the bumps in her Cloud. Meeting her in the flesh, Dan could see that there was something secret in her life that the data didn't show. Or so he liked to imagine. Maybe because of her glasses—clear frames with racy green pinstripes that whispered something not in her profile. Or at least the desire for it. Each time she leaned forward to point out something about bird lice, her lab coat stretched and he couldn't help notice a black strap though the report said she stayed squarely within the quintile that favored beige (SD-1 on the world map of Lingerie Use).

Back in the '80s, she was saying, explaining the background to the project she wanted to bring liM in on, a biologist in the last remnants of the Paraguayan rainforest noticed what indigenous people had known for centuries: that natives who hunted birds had some immunity to bird-borne diseases. The natives attributed it to the spirit of the birds themselves, but her guess was that it was the lice on the birds, not the birds, that gave the hunters immunity.

Instead of following up on her speculation, the biologist went down a research dead end about dinosaur feathers and lice. Olympia smiled wistfully. "The entomological community can be so competitive," she said, "because the stakes are so small.

"Sorry, it's an old entomology joke," she muttered, apologizing for the pun—which was Dan's Boss's cue to laugh—louder than the joke was funny—and nodding for Dan to join in. Thinning hair, portly build. His boss was obviously uncomfortable, stuffed into his business suit, more used to lounge-seats than the lab stools Olympia had offered them. Pants too short, his shins showed above the top of his socks.

"But there's evidence that her hunch was right," Olympia continued, "So that's the first of our goals: to find out which protein in bird louse saliva gives mammals some protection, if in fact that's what's happening. Our long-range hope is that this knowledge can be used to make a vaccine."

"A vaccine for birds or people?" Dan's boss asked, taking notes.

"Both," Olympia said. The answer just came out. But the moment it did, she acted as though she wished she could take it back. She stammered, "Eventually, I mean. There may be agricultural applications down the road but right now my lab is looking at antibodies in humans since that's the mandate given us by our funder."

By which she meant the military, Dan knew.

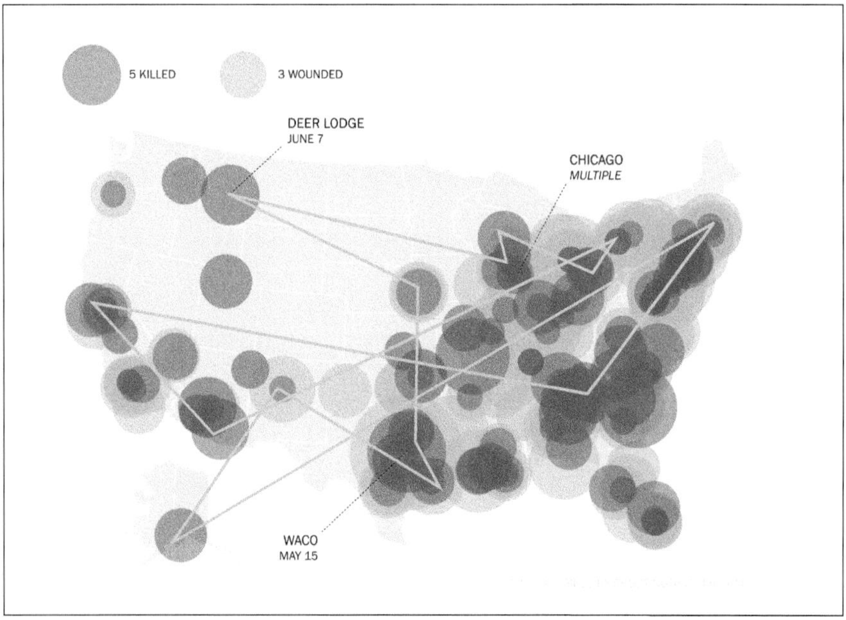

LIVE •
Annual Mass Shootings (U.S.)
shootingtracker.com

"But of course that's proprietary information," she said. Don't ask, don't tell. She breezed by the moment by going into some of the determinations they'd have to make, the first being the amount of genetic variability between different bird lice populations.

She pulled her chair closer to Dan and pulled up a sleeve of her lab coat, motioning for Dan to lend her his arm. "I'm a woman; you're a man," she said, pushing the sleeve of his suit up high enough to expose his forearm. Dan noticed his Boss frown at his tattoo, an NGer tattoo of the Red Marble Earth that he always kept covered at work. She laid her arm next to his on the desk. "Your hair is coarser than mine," she said, demonstrating. Had she noticed him looking at her and decided to yank his chain? "Within the human species, there's a lot of genetic variability. Same with lice: the geese in Venezuela may eat prairie grass, while geese in Bolivia might feed primarily on clover, or even bread thrown to them in urban areas. Their lice will be the same species, but their genetic makeup will have drifted in respect to one another. How much difference is there in their

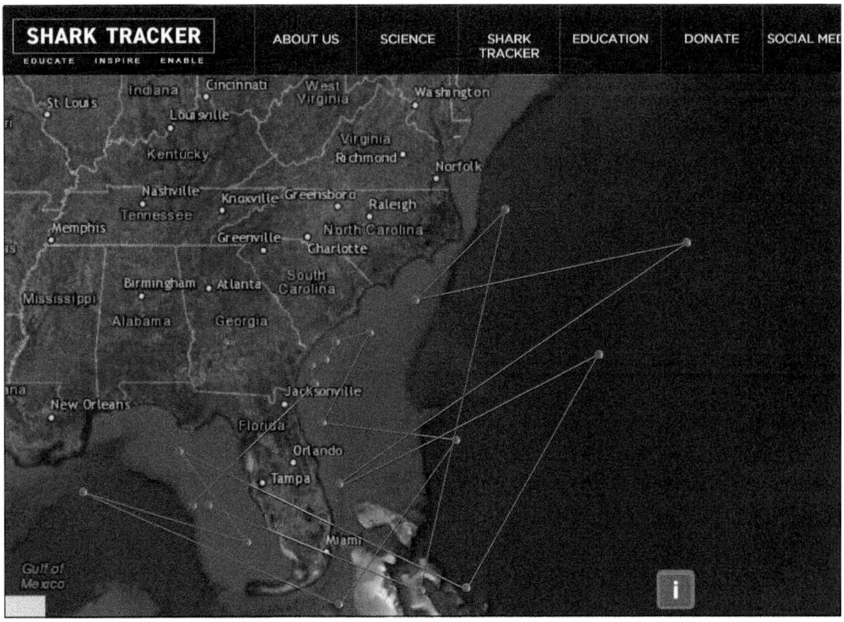

LIVE•
Shark Tracker
ocearch.org

TVC
GRB
ATW
OSH
SBM
MSN
UES
MKE
GRR
LAN
ENW
UGN
RFD
BTL
AZO
PWK
DPA
MDW
LOT
GYY
SBN
MLI
FWA
PIA
BMI
LAF
Kai Kung Leng
CMI
TYQ
IND
HUF
Zhuhai

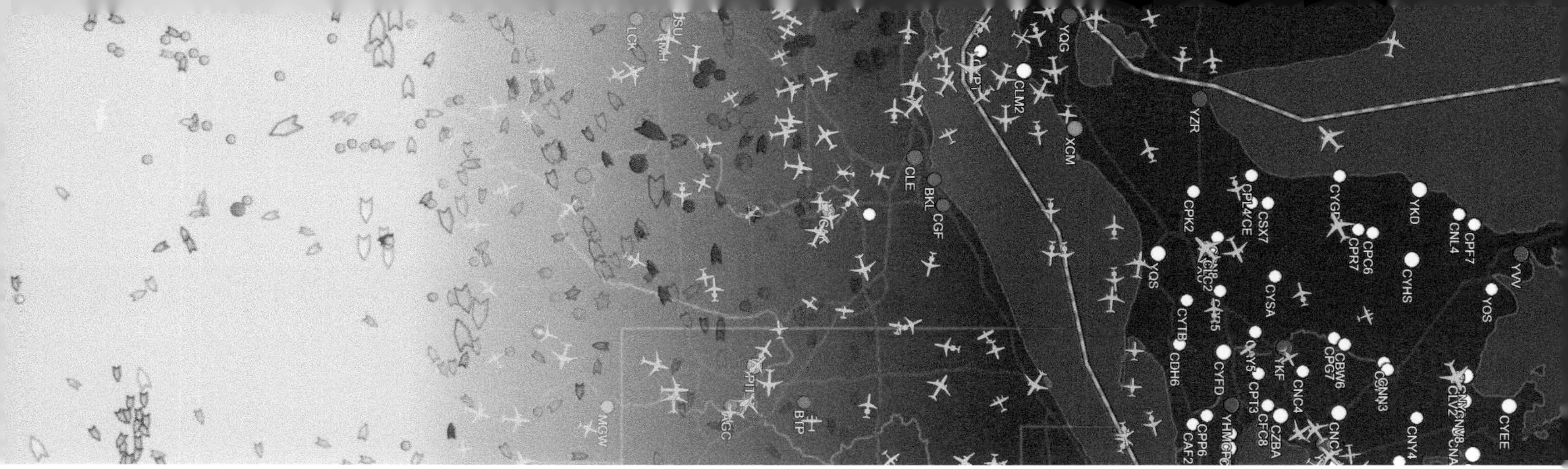

LIVE
Marine Traffic
marinetraffic.com/en/ais/home/centerx:-80/centery:43/zoom:6

LIVE
Air Traffic
flightaware.com/live/

saliva?" She pulled his sleeve back down briskly, as though she'd just finished giving a demonstration on a CPR dummy. "To determine this, we'll first sequence the genome of the lice from the same species of birds native to different areas.

"Hopefully we'll find at least one protein that is conserved across species. That would make it possible to develop a one-drug-fits-all vaccine, instead of a different vaccine for each type of louse."

"This is all familiar to us," Dan's Boss said, unrolling his Flexscreen on her desk. As he did, the company's demo began to play: *Introducing InfoInMotion....* The demo went through past projects they had completed: city planners tracing fire extinguisher registrations to predict where future fire trucks would have to be sent; another forecast the resources that a hospital would need to treat schizophrenia in twenty years by correlating the number of cats at the Humane Society to the number of playgrounds (cats in shelters correlate highly to cats in neighborhoods; cats in neighborhoods use sandboxes in playgrounds; cat feces in sandboxes carry the *T. gondii* parasite; kids exposed to *T. gondii* develop schizophrenia in adulthood).... In one project for the CDC, IiM had layered data harvested from the cell phones of travelers to show that the Honolulu Airport, with its connections between the U.S. and Asia, would be the world's largest hub for the next pandemic.

He told her about some of the other projects they worked on for Big Pharma where biology and information had been synonymous for years, then finished by saying, as if it were no big deal, "Basically, you want us to come up with a new Tree of Life."

"Just for bird lice," she said flatly, a poker face. "Only it has to be dynamic, changing as the biochemistry of the lice changes."

"Uh yeah, we can do that," Boss said, less sure, turning for confirmation to Dan, the guy who would actually have to supervise the work.

The both of them were looking at him.

In his mind he saw an evolutionary tree, but instead of the static drawings in textbooks, its branches slowly swayed as seaweed undulates in a tide, some strands flourishing, others dying out, all in real time. "Cool," he murmured.

"InfoInMotion doesn't do static, do we?" his Boss chuckled. Dan could tell that the chuckle was meant to paper over his use of 'cool.' He'd hear about it later. About 'cool,' his tight jeans, his tattoo.

Dan didn't know the ins and outs of the contract between IiM and the venture capitalists paying for everything, but he'd bet it involved the use of the cheap stuff—the 1,000 terabytes of census reports, NASA climate data, and all the rest of the 90,000 government databases that are always available gratis; they'd probably link those to databases that the company had amassed on its own in order to magnify their usefulness—the way Google first married a free phone book to a free map, multiplying the power of each, which they then raised to an exponent through software that merged this database with street-level photos, then IP addresses and text messages gathered by trucks taking those street-level photos. It was all multiplied yet again when merged with terabytes of corporate data on everyone who lived at those addresses—the cameras in their laptops tracking their eyes as they skipped over captions (0.2/ s/caption avg.); how far people traveled to work, happy hour, or church; whether they walked, drove, or rode a pogo stick; who paid for gas at the pump and who paid inside, and so bought cigarettes, and so were higher insurance risks; who, in 5 years, could be sold a yacht.... Terabytes of data gathered for each and every person—or rather, each of these 6.2 billion data nodes, as IiM called them.

Life Is Data, as the promos said.... Basically, that's what Darwin did: look at masses of data points, i.e., the shapes of snails, to discern a pattern, which he called Evolution.

But this was teaching the software to teach itself to recognize patterns in snails as they morph into other mollusks, the dynamics of open systems—'live prediction'—like mapping networks of rivets and welds and icebergs and ocean currents, then using it to see the *Titanic* sink before it pulled away from the pier. From spikes in phone-card purchases, the software was able to predict outbreaks of genocide among the Bottom Billion, its refugees converting their chickens and goats into phone cards, a form of money for those on the run. Guns, counterfeit watches, slaves, laundered money, refugees—anything in flux—background radiation, city growth, or the night sky—all reality could be seen as flux in patterns, smaller patterns coalescing as larger patterns, that formed still larger patterns....

Workaholic, is how the software labeled her personality cluster.

Dan's Boss chuckled. "Kind of ironic, how a footnote about dinosaur lice could end up saving millions of people."

Olympia just sat there with that tight little smile of hers.

Military funding.

Or kill them, Dan wanted to say, a vaccine for one side being a gun pointed to the head of the other. What was it like, he wondered, to walk around in skin that tight?

LIVE•
ISS Flying Above Earth at Night
youtu.be/Nc5gnidwMzs

Patterns are always made by something(s). But what? When cameras in space were pointed at the Earth's edge, its atmosphere appeared as thin and transparent as a soap bubble that hadn't popped. At least not yet. Not like the atmosphere of Red Marble Earth. Still, the Black Marble that was the Earth at night was dotted by city lights as well as forest fires, and flames of burning gas large enough to be seen from space....

Hard to believe that smudges of light large enough to cover the East Coast could be the result of individuals oblivious to the monumental patterns they were creating: a mother turning on a bedside lamp to read to her children; a man triggering the light in his garage; a janitor switching on lights in an empty office; a couple in the back of a cab, their faces ghostly in the glow of their phones.... Individual actions cluster into systems, systems—automatic headlights, dusk-to-dawn streetlamps—clusters of systems coalesce into structures—cities at night—structures shape the behavior of individuals who read to children, emptied wastepaper baskets, used phones....

During the day, the Earth was as blue as a snow globe. When some giant hand shook it to create weather, violent storms could pirouette across its surface, serene and silent from the vantage of the satellites, but thundering down on the millions of creatures beneath them.

Watching satellite views of hurricanes reminded Gabe of the prairie she grew up on, the land so flat that her family could watch a rainstorm slide along the horizon as though it were a distant freight train. They used to stand out in the yard and watch tornados from afar: the sky would darken as the wind picked up, the fluffy white castles that had drifted by earlier replaced by something closer to the vortex of a hypnotist's spiral. Distance reduced sheets of rain to silence, the all-too-real thunder and lightning storming down on people like them, they knew.

But not them.

And they would watch those storms with an odd mix of detachment and dread, like watching a natural disaster on the weather channel except knowing that if the winds twitched, force could add to force to turn the spectacle their way.

Watching viruses mutate was a lot like that, she thought, moving her mouse to wake up her computer and activate her World Flu Radar app. The last pandemic had burned itself out. But whole evolutionary trees of viruses were still out there, still mutating within bats, rabbits, birds, cooking up new versions of Ebola, SARS, Marburg, Nipah, and would reemerge when (not if) their mutations combined in ways that would let one live in a nasal passage here, or on a doorknob there.

Health officials still warned local governments to keep their populations vigilant for dead birds. But of course, once people stopped dying, no one bothered.

Hindsight: a tiny buoy, bobbing up and down in the ocean and attached to a tsunami beacon, could have prevented 300,000 deaths 7,000 miles away in Indonesia.

Meadow never believed that folktale about La Llorona who wandered the Earth searching for her lost children until she'd become her. La Llorona's crying was simply the sound of the wind, she would have said. But there was no wind here in WORLD.2, no weather at all. Unless the light of her computer screen counted: on-screen, the standard-issue avatar she received shuffled along with the standard-issue avatars given to the hundreds of other men and women who happened to be joining at that moment, the long line of nude, featureless, and hairless bodies she was in snaking toward a portal named Eden....

"So many, I had not thought death had undone so many," William had joked the time that the two of them had first surfed over—just to see what people were talking about. A population meter in the corner of the screen—3,567,432—rolled ever upward like the odometer of a spaceship on cruise control. Some took the '.2' to mean W.2 was a work of restoration of what the world had been. *Paradise Lost*. During the last pandemic, people sheltering at home had used the time to upload tourist photos of waterfalls taken before they had dried to a trickle, or West Virginia mountaintops before they had been dumped into their valleys, or pristine Alaskan plains before they'd been bisected by pipelines or swallowed by rising seas.

Software created 3D versions of what these spots had looked like in 1970—the year of the first Earth Day. Some thought the Earth was far too broken by 1970 and that W.2 should be reset to 1847, the last year elaborately constructed tide tables were more important than train schedules, that is, a time when men and women were still forced to conform their rhythms to those of the Earth instead of crossing it with rails and time zones, severing their dependence on its turning, its days and nights.

To placate everyone, a historical slider was installed so people could visit the world at different times. Then arguments broke out over whose history would be remembered: a digital model of Trump's Wall was inserted by Russians while the Chinese blocked a replica of the Goddess of Liberty. A database was created of every lynching in America, and avatars of bodies were hung from geotagged trees, along with avatars of George Floyd and others whose cause of death was "cop" until the project was blocked by the governor of South Carolina because it went against the can-do spirit of the state motto, *Dum Spiro Spero*.

Many wanted to use W.2 as a whiteboard on which to draw blueprints for the redirection of rivers to aide drought-stricken areas, or use mirrors to create new weather patterns, and other geoengineering that would save the planet.

That's what fucked it up to begin with! NGers cried.

Just like in the Old World, though, many didn't care one way or another. Since so much of the world had moved online during the last pandemic, some sociologists equated the stream of people joining W.2 with a desire to connect with the earth, though most thought it had more to do with a desire to abandon a dying planet. The words that William quoted were Dante's awestruck reaction to his first view of the underworld that 700 years later, another poet used to describe the stream of office workers in identical gray flannel suits, pouring off the Staten Island Ferry.

William had been an English major. An English major trying to be ironic, she knew, joking about himself for joining W.2 to sell his didgeridoo; but he'd

天安门广场 Tiananmen SquARed
天安门广场 Tiananmen SquARed
民主女神 Goddess of Democracy
四君子 4 Gentlemen
16m
民主女神 Goddess of Democracy
四君子 4 Gentlemen
16m

also been referring to the life he'd lived as one of those hollow men, working as a tech writer in an office cubicle before he chucked it all to live in a metal shipping container in Oregon: a postmodern version of Thoreau's cabin, he'd thought, delivered by flatbed, and dropped onto the land he'd bought for it.

He couldn't have known that Dante's words had also rolled through her mind as they went from makeshift morgue to morgue after the tsunami. If he had, he wouldn't have repeated them, as they got online, realizing how they would have conjured memories of that vast landscape of bodies and wreckage, and the unimaginable violence it had caused in stark contrast to the last pandemic, which had killed far more people, but had moved through cities silently, invisibly passing from one person to another as they did things as ordinary as buying groceries. Somehow, William had been able to move on while she, like some kind of shell-shocked survivor, still couldn't get off that beach. Couldn't live as though she didn't know what she knew, hadn't seen the things she'd seen, hadn't lost what she'd lost.

Back then, before she'd moved to Chicago to join Olympia's lab, Meadow would bolt upright at night, thinking that she had to look in on Nico, their son. Then that awful feeling would come over her as she remembered that she didn't have to check on him any longer. She didn't have to pick him up after school. Didn't have to make his lunch.

In the predawn gray of those mornings, she'd stay sitting up, William in bed beside her, his body a bulge in the sheets like a rise in a snow-covered field. The featureless shape could have belonged to any of the people they saw swaddled in sheets and laid out in a gym serving as a morgue. One family had been carefully placed together as though sleeping: a small boy the same age as Nico between mother and father, making Meadow do all she could to not just lie down beside them and die herself.

There but for the grace of god....

To this day those people sometimes seemed like the lucky ones. And years later, she still longed to be as they were; as she, William, and Nico had been: together.

It wasn't like William wasn't affected, she knew. Rather, what made him stay back in Oregon while she came to Chicago was that it affected him as well. Maybe more so, or less, but in any case, differently, each of them realizing—there but for a twitch in the Earth.... But if anyone could have taken their place in death, the two of them seemed to realize afterwards, then the same would be true in life. That is, she'd known back then, looking at William's sleeping form, that if the partner function in her life could have just as easily been filled by another man, the same was certainly true about her place in his life. And she wondered if he got as many messages from women in W.2 who wanted to meet offline as she got from men.

If nothing else, W.2 was efficient in matching people who 'had' to people who 'wanted': artists looking for galleries; galleries looking for collectors; bands looking for drummers; men seeking women; women seeking women; adoptees seeking birth parents.... And also, she'd heard, mothers seeking children....

Maybe it was all just VR smoke and mirrors. Since the last pandemic had made everyone virus-phobic, some avatars had affairs for years without their real-life counterparts ever meeting F2F. But she couldn't shake the feeling that their son was out there in W.2, as the rumors implied. Not him, exactly, for there wasn't any Nico anymore to actually be anywhere. But the feeling persisted that some trace of him was out there, a ghost, or memory, or whatever it was that could be conjured by an old photo of someone who was gone. Something real, if intangible: like a mother's love. She'd surfed over to MyDeath.com, that site that gathered all the iFace profiles of people who had, in life, posted their bios, photos, and favorite bands. Pictures of their pets. And then died—by nature or culture. Many were teenagers killed in auto accidents. Or over Conflict Minerals: Pfc. Brian Williams, 18, Youngstown Ohio, stepped on a landmine in Paraguay. Too many were suicides. As she went from one blurred-out young face to another, though, she saw how pointless this was. The sad emoticons and the rock-star philosophy became oppressive—*We lived so wild that Death shook to take us!*—even if she ignored the ads for sexy DeathSpace.com short-shorts, and beer-bottle openers. Mostly though, it was because some part of her always imagined Nico growing up, dating, driving, grooming his iFace page and doing all the things the teenagers who posted on this site did. Nico never made it that far, though.

God, what she would give to at least be able to say goodbye.

As her Avatar stepped through the portal and into Eden.2, she found herself in a fantastical garden. Flowers too bright to exist. A waterfall cascaded in the background with that fake shimmery look of waterfalls on mirrored clocks sold in Chinatown. *Get Clothes Here. Get Hairstyling Here. Get....* She used hand gestures, a stirring motion, to rotate her view, and found she was surrounded by other newly born avatars in various stages of dress, trying on different outfits, everything from colonial wigs to space suits. Some were also trying on different bodies, morphing the standard manikins they'd been given into different genders, or no gender, or dragons, or else giving their bodies zebra stripes, or the dimples of a tortoise shell, as easily as putting on a hat.

A woman with the hair, ears, and features of a Kittychan strode up to her and asked, *"Est ce que je peux lécher votre chat?"* She wore a bright purple jacket, miniskirt, and carried a walking stick with a brass knob on its end that, when she held it out to Meadow, began to vibrate. Meadow wasn't sure what she'd been asked, but the purr in the woman's voice gave her an idea. When she just stood there mute, unsure which icon to click to answer, the Kittychan moved on to another avatar, her motions so smooth compared to the herky-jerky movement of newbies that Meadow could tell she was a veteran of W.2—maybe some sort of virtual stalker preying on newbies? But Meadow wished she could catch up with her anyway, ask her if she knew anything about finding people who had vanished from the original world only to reemerge in W.2.

Some thought that the pharmaceutical industry came up with the idea, but given all the trouble monitoring the composition of athletes, lots of people began to ask, Why bother? Why not just hold a no-holds-barred Olympics? No drug would be banned. No training method illegal. Stop arguing whether a prosthetic, like laser eye surgery, enabled a heroic tale of adversity overcome or was an unfair advantage for the winner of the shooting competition. Just bring it on, and whoever ran the fastest, or threw the discus farthest, whoever touched the pad at the end of the pool, or crossed the finish line first would be declared champion, no matter if the webbing between a swimmer's toes was the result of a natural mutation or plastic surgery, no matter if the heart powering the athlete to victory was made of sterner stuff, or had been made of sterner stuff. No questions asked. Anyway, once kids in the street were running three-minute miles, what would be the point?

The traditional Olympic Commission passed a resolution banning any athlete who took part in the Freak Olympics, as they called it. But Big Pharma, The Plastic Surgeons Association, Prosthetic Limb Manufacturers, then Pepsi and McDonald's, and all the rest sponsored athletes just as Pennzoil or STP plastered logos all over the bodies of NASCAR cars, the tattoos of Nike and Adidas and Visa covering the arms and legs and faces and uniforms of runners, divers, cyclists, bobsledders, skiers, speed skaters, weightlifters, while traditions like testing for steroids faded into the past of other bygone practices, such as competing nude, as did the original Olympians.

//

As a kid, whenever Airman First Class Davenport got home from school, he'd throw his book bag on his bed and log into *World Wide War.* Sometimes to play, but often just to hang. He'd wander the war-torn streets of Berlin or Zombie Island till he found Jimmy or Frank or whoever was wasting Nazis or the undead or whatever and he'd join in as they chatted about girls or sports or whatever. His screen filled with a red splash when a head exploded: *Good Shot!* (swell of heroic music). Walking into a recruitment office after high school didn't seem all that different from logging in, but if he'd known it would be like this, he never would have joined. The monitor before him now showed dark, cool forest. On the infrared monitor, the cabin it concealed appeared as a white stick-frame box with ghosts moving about inside. The joysticks he used to control the drone's optics were a lot like the one he'd grown up playing with but instead of yakking with Jimmy and Frank, he sat beside his pilot, their station more like a flight simulator than game station with its industrial, 1990s' computer-beige. At other stations in the darkened room sat other pairs of 'airmen'—optic/sensor operators and pilots who never left the ground—controlling other drones flying in Afghanistan, Iraq, Bolivia, or Venezuela; or some, like him, in Paraguay. Entering for his shift, the rows of guys focused on computer screens always reminded him of a video arcade. Without the flashing colored lights. Without the music and game bells, whistles, or rumbles of video-game explosions. Silent. Stale stink of cigarettes. Mostly it was just dull, watching video screens that showed what the drone was looking at, and looking at, and looking at—hours of boredom—349 missions for his squadron alone—1,211 bad guys killed vs. 0 drone pilots. Who knew war could be so dull?

Weeks ago, they had identified one of the men inside the cabin as Ramon Urulio, a high-value target, with a bodyguard and chauffer. They had kept him under surveillance, harvesting intel on his network. It was so odd to see him here away from civilians, though, that Davenport figured it must be the doing of cyber units in some other room, maybe here on base or on the other side of the planet. They'd hack into the databases of a bad guy to make his field units receive cases of tampons instead of ammunition; they'd impersonate a commander or mess with his GPS to send bad guys marching into a kill box where a drone team like his could take them out cleanly. Fish in a barrel. During training, a programmer had explained why the deadliest weapon in WWII had been the typewriter.

Now, out here away from civilians, it looked like this was the end of the road for Señor Urulio. Except just before they pulled the trigger, some fourth guy showed up. Back in that other room, analysts and their 'typewriters' would be going through the tetrabytes of algorithm output trying to sort out their best guesstimate as to who he was, applying filters to sift the metadata of the 20 million cellphones in use in Paraguay, trying to see if the phone carried by this guy matched patterns of terrorists or their couriers, or water-meter readers, tow-truck operators, or other ordinary joe-blows.... In the meantime, orders were to sit tight.

So Airman Davenport sat watching trees 5,600 miles away, the last of what was once a vast Paraguayan forest, he'd heard, switching between the visible and the infrared view. The four men inside the cabin appeared as white heat signatures: ghostly silhouettes moving around. Until they all decided to take a siesta.

Airman Davenport was afraid this would happen. Ramon Urulio always caught a few Zs, if he could, shuttling back and forth across the Bolivia-Paraguay border, smuggling intel to take back the Salar de Uyuni Salt Flat, which from the air looked like a vast sheet of ice—twice as large as Indiana, twice as flat, ten times as boring, its white, homogeneous glare hard on the eyes. At least he decided to take his siesta here—much better to be above the forest, or above the city, or any of the other places where Davenport had seen Urulio pound down beers with buddies; play soccer with his kids; get it on with his wife, their bodies writhing in ghostlike infrared as if they were already dead and having sex in the afterlife. Afterwards, she'd make them both a cup of maté—that tea-like stuff they all drank over there. Davenport knew, because the metal straws they used to drink it with glowed white hot in infrared.

In a way, he was going to miss the fucker....

But dang it, he had a lot to do today; and he knew he wouldn't be allowed to leave until they got a Go or No Go. Five thousand six hundred miles away, as if they'd heard, the ghostly silhouettes began getting up. Putting on shoes. "Bad guys on the move!" he shouted, and his pilot began going through the ignition procedure to arm the missile. "Fire on my command," came through their headphones: the voice of some CIA analyst or someone else taking control of the show just as the men emerged out into the yard of the house. "You got them?" the pilot asked, and Airman First Class Davenport answered "Affirmative," zooming the camera onto the 4th man's head. "Say, Cheese," the pilot said, goosing the 1,000-horsepower engine of the drone, just to make a little noise that would sound to the men like a faint buzz high above, and Airman First Class Davenport caught the men perfectly, all looking up, their faces appearing as in a photo booth, searching.

Facial recognition would get a read if it could. He kept them in the cross-hairs as the men began to run to their separate cars. Not fast enough to outrun the software that confirmed the ID of the fourth guy: grunt, i.e., no value.

"Count down: Three, two, one, fire."

The pilot pressed the red button, and 5,600 miles away, the missile roared off its rails. Airman First Class Davenport kept the crosshairs on Ramon Urulio, the view from the eye in its nose a searingly fast zoom-in as it screeched at the men faster than the roar of its rocket—they'd never hear it—the two men grew larger on the video monitor at supersonic speed—bright as a nova, the infrared screen flared white. The visual monitor just showed roiling smoke. But as the smoke cleared, he could see a hole in the tree canopy, then the crater caused by the silent blast, still too hot to be anything but a white blur on the infrared. After a moment, they could see two bodies around a crater; they were also hot so glowed like the ghostly images they'd been a minute ago, only brighter. One was still alive, his legs missing, blood pumping out of the stumps, also white on the infrared monitor; white ink spilling everywhere.

"Splat," said the safety observer from behind their chairs.

Airman First Class Davenport watched the white-hot blood go dark; he watched the bodies cool. Soon they were the same dull color as the jungle.

When his shift ended, he and his pilot turned over their seats to the next team. Then he emerged into the bright heat of the Nevada noon. Coming out of the control room in the middle of the day was always a little disorienting—like coming out of a darkened movie theater after a matinee into bright sunlight. He headed to pick up his daughter at her soccer practice. He was supposed to pick up some McDonald's on the way home, too.

A bird louse under a microscope has no secrets; the light shining through its body makes it transparent—an X-ray of itself—the lens amplifying every motion of the dissecting needle so that what feels like the slightest movement to the hand controlling the needle can be as devastating to the specimen as a pile driver on an egg.... And this is what they are trying to do to me, Mohammed thought, peering through a microscope to remove the salivary gland of a louse. Its tiny corpse suspended in a clear drop of PBS, he held down its thorax with the point of one needle while he used another to gently pull away the black dot that was its head. The head off, he repositioned his dissecting needle on the last segment of the abdomen and gently pulled it away from the body, but not so fast that it detached from the internal organs, the cloudy filament that was its crop and other organs coming out of the body cavity as though he was drawing a long slimy snail from its shell. Escargot in an Algerian restaurant. He kept the needle moving, teasing out the intestines, yellowish Malpighian tubules—named after the illustrious Marcello Malpighi who first described them by looking through one of the first microscopes—uncoiling the way a frayed thread could be pulled from a sweater if the seamstress applies just enough tension to keep it coming but not so much that it breaks.

Gabe was supposed to have stopped their blood diet over the weekend. Empty digestive tracts would have made these dissections easier, but he could tell that they'd been sucking the blood from her parrots all week: this was the eighth louse in a row whose crop was as full as the bladder of a man fed on beer and so exerted pressure on the midgut, making it hard to get the chain of intestines to pull out without breaking—but finally there they were—as clean as a textbook photo—the two salivary glands he was really after, lying outside the broken body, their membranes intact. The glands glistened like a pair of minute dewdrops on the slide. Both were full of the saliva Jak would run his assays on.

Mouthparts connected to the foregut, he hummed; he and his fellow students at Simón Bolívar University had set the words to the merengue "Chupa Tu Mamey" to help them memorize lice anatomy—*the foregut's connected to the thoracic midgut, the thoracic midgut's connected to the abdominal midgut, hindgut, Malpighian tubules, crop, and all the rest....* Even butchers understood that to take a body apart you had to know how it went together, but governments didn't seem to bother with those niceties when it came to people. He transferred the salivary glands into a thimble-sized vial of PBS, snapped its plastic cap shut, labeled it, stuck it in the crushed ice along with the vials containing the glands he'd already removed.

His scratch pad told him that had been the 61st dissection he'd done that morning. Thanks to Gabe, the full crops were slowing him down. Normally, he would have been up around a hundred by lunch. But to be honest, he knew that he was probably slowing himself down by thinking so much about the FBI. They wanted to talk to him and instead of louse glands, he could think of nothing but what they might want to talk about. Was there some problem with his Green Card? Given the tightening net around Bottom Billion immigrants and the ever-smaller excuses needed to deport them, it could only be trouble. Was his name placed on some secret list? Because of something he had written? Or simply read?—the visits to his wall, the walls he visited, the merengues he liked, the pistachios from Iran that he bought at the local Arab market—the whole data cloud he generated creating a profile of him that was 'suspicious' according to whatever algorithm they used?...

A sense of dread came over him when he realized how many connections he had to the places where the U.S. had launched pop-up wars: when China, which held 95% of the world's neodymium, stopped exporting neodymium, an element needed in hybrid cars, the U.S. launched swarms of drones to protect the few neodymium mines left in Vietnam, where his father worked. When Bolivia nationalized 93% of the world's lithium—lithium needed in all those batteries in all those computers, iFlexes, and other electronic gadgets—the Bolivian dictator had ordered American companies to leave, which made not leaving a matter of national defense. And the U.S. began supporting indigenous insurgents in their struggle against the dictator—who also happened to have awarded an exclusive contract to mine lithium to the Chinese. (The enemy of my enemy is my friend.) Rather than fight the U.S. directly, China gave military aide to Venezuela, which came to the aide of the Bolivians.

Mohammed had been educated in Venezuela, which probably made him suspicious enough. But he had been born in Bahrain, and grew up there before he had to flee, and also exchanged emails with biologists from Congo, where the tantalum needed in capacitors had been 'secured.' Paraguay, Congo, Bolivia, Vietnam.... All the places that the bird lice they were studying came from had either had a pop-up war—or 'policing action' as they called it—or were threatened by one. While doing research in Paraguay, he had picked up some Guaraní—one of the reasons Olympia had picked him for her research group.

Was he following the wars or were the wars following him? Maybe something he wrote had popped a flag in one of those programs that trolled millions of emails, looking for points of contingency, linking an Eid greeting he had sent

to a colleague in the Congo who had e-mailed a field researcher in Pakistan who had a cousin in London who had emailed an uncle in Lahore, who had a nephew who had once sold a car that had later been filled with cans of gasoline and bags of nails, wired to a cell phone and left in a crowded market. Zero degrees of separation. Everyone in the world was that close to everyone else, the software said, doing millions of comparisons to offer up a list of 'people of interest' as they referred to him the time he was stopped at the airport, his profile—a Muslim, Venezuelan speaker of Guaraní with access to biolab equipment—calling to them like a siren.

He wiped the louse remains off the slide to prepare the next set, using the hand aspirator to deposit 8 drops of PBS on the slide, 8 drops to hold the bodies of 8 lice.

Then he paused mid-reach....

Above his workstation was a picture of his wife. Dressed in black, she stood out starkly against the vast, white plain of the Salar de Uyuni, a salt flat in Bolivia that was now secured by swarms of U.S. drones. She was smiling for the camera, the two of them postdocs on a weekend getaway. She could have been standing at the South Pole if she wasn't wearing a summer-thin hijab for the heat, the salt flats that they'd gone to see white and flat to the horizon behind her. Little did they know that in a few years it would become a battleground.

Maybe there were so many Sci-Fi dystopias because trouble, in fiction, was interesting, Gabe noted in the e-book she was reading on her phone. No one would ever read beyond 'happily ever after' in a novel while you couldn't be a scientist without being able to look back over the wreckage and rust that was the history of scientific theory and think tomorrow would be better. Maybe they could learn a little from each other?—the way the alien in *The Day the Earth Stood Still* forced Earthlings to think outside the box and come up with a way to relate to one another other than shooting. Who knew how hard *that* could be?

Grapefruit @inhisbag · 20m
Boy Scout sits on camp toilet at night, Bear bites ass.

askY @Novy Basnik · 19m
Replying: How could a bear get inna toilet?

VeganGirl @donfkwme · 19m
That happened to me! Only it was an iguana.

Poison Ivy @wildflower · 19m
Does anyone who camps know what's happening to the honeybees?

Mom @RyansMom · 22m
Ryan responded well to the transfusion. But still unusual bleeding. Abt to have more tests. **#PrayForRyan**.

Gabe looked up from her phone—*Klaatu barada nikto*—as her train approached the Medical Center station. To her surprise, everyone around her was taking off their clothes. The mailman, a woman in an ugly holiday sweater.... The guy who'd been wearing a nurse's uniform, one hand on the overhead rail, his lunch bag in the other, was now in the exact same pose only standing there in polka-dot boxer shorts, his nurse's scrubs draped over an arm. At the platform, the doors to the crowded subway car opened and everyone poured out, exactly as people did at every stop, only without the suits, uniforms, or jeans they'd been wearing moments ago, heading to the exists as though they were all just humans instead of X-ray technicians or mail carriers or nurses or patients....

#BLOODS @OurStreet · 12m
GF memorial@ 57th, moving to 65th. Bring leaf-blowers!!!!

DublinHousing @DublinHousing · 12m
#DublinHousing celebrates end of lockdown with Social Distanced Irish Dancing. Join the fun!

Pride @BoysTown · 13m
Show yours. Glitter bomb & block traffic with DanceSwarm to ABBA's "Dancing Queen"

Traffic began slowing just as Olympia's phone yowled like an angry cat—it was the irritating push notification that she kept meaning to change on her FlashMob app. Sure enough, traffic solidified into a jam as she read the badge on her phone's screen: *ALERT: People stripping at Medical Center to protest lack of privacy in medical records.* She threw her phone back into her purse. What good was that damn app if it could only warn you of a SocialSwarm after you were caught in it?

DJ @Alert · 9m
Pandemic giveaway!!! ---> a chance for u to get up close with XactlySO!!! Tonight at Live.Nation **#Rave**...

Mohammed @LondonMuslims · 9m
Get yourself to Amazing PrayerSwarm in Trafalgar Square! Happening RIGHT NOW! ربك أهلا

askY @Novy Basnik · 10m
WTK: When **#british** people say pack o' nips do they really mean bag of dicks?

Cosmic Color @local living · 10m
Someone should start a uber for readers where instead of a car you take turns with a book.

> Women&Children First @ClarkSt · 5m
> REPLYING: It's called a **#library**.

Occupy Everywhere @&NOW · 11m
Come out, come out and sit down now, wherever you are...

After a storm of SnapIt paper cuts roiled dictatorships, allowed BLM activists to roll over riot police, and showed other cities how to militarize social media; after an ignorant, bigoted con artist and strongman wannnabe was able to tweet his way into the presidency with lies and fear of the Bottom Billion; after most news outlets gave up trying to compete with men in red hats pretending to be journalists and foreign bots pretending to be men in red hats and started chasing clicks like everyone else, SocialSwarms seemed to be the only way to get anything done or keep it from happening. Tweets would go out, and people would trash the grocery store that had gotten away with selling tainted milk or maybe instead, a food truck would pull up, and the street would fill with people buying Korean-Mex fusion from a high-concept chef whose restaurant had a six-month wait. People would come together to celebrate the renovation of a beloved theater, or shout down the auction of archaeological artifacts from one of the submerged Bottom Billion Lands. The word 'organic' would gather around a scrum of farmers, DDT sprayers, people with allergies, Monsanto lawyers, health experts, potato buyers for McDonald's, producers of industrial solvents, all of whom would join different mobs to eliminate taxes, defend solar panels, tax solar panel users, bring back the trains, sell off the tracks.... One sixteen-year-old was able to get people all over the world to dye their hair purple "just 'cuz."

Voting for a representative who would do your 'liking' seemed like a pointless relic from a time when senators rode horses to a central capital to meet—as out of step with the way people lived as forcing them to wear wooden shoes in a world of leaderless mélanges of Christian Jihadists; No Mask No Service Waitstaff Union; Big Pharma; Big Oil; and Aircraft Carriers the Size of Texas Lobbyists. Gridlock was better than laws outlawing contraception, forcing teachers to carry guns, allowing the Grand Canyon to be mined, and all the rest. Pop-up politics began to proliferate: Neo-Aches with their Pre-Columbian lifestyle; Eternal Virgins and Future Promise Witnesses, who wanted to criminalize premarital sex; but also the Random Acts of Kindness Party; The Mad as Hell Party; Affordable Pot and/or Tuition; Don't Step on Me; the Have A Nice Day Movement; Free Internet; the preWWW cult, whose members took a vow to forsake any technology invented after 1995; Jews for Jesus; Colonize Mars; The Or-Wa-Ca Blue Wall Coalition.... There was the 4D Movement—DDDD—Death to Dictators, Death to Democracy, but as always, there was mostly the party of the apathetic....

Gabe lifted her pencil, unable to tell the difference between the graphic novel she was writing and the blogs.

> **Esquire B** @esqB · 2m
> How come no 1s ever noticed that ATLANTA is spelled the same in both directins???!

> **i hate pickles** @_lezmore · 1m
> Replying: Are you blind, dumb, or dyslexic?

> **Esquire B** @esqB · 1m
> actually, I am dyslexic. No need to get snarky

> **Caveman** @Jara Cimrman · 1m
> Im only on twitter so I'll know when the revolution begins.

Organic Poison @SunnySide · 1m
You mean riot.

Caveman @Jara Cimrman · 1m
whatever. i'm not fussy

askY @Novy Basnik · 3m
If you are on death row, please answer: What is your favorite TV show?

4Ds @NoNations · 3m
Twit or fb msg us your #flashmob sites. Together our voices are stronger!

Looking across his fireworks mortars, Wang Xiliau could see the festival atmosphere of the crowd turn ugly: what had been a group of happy spectators was being permeated by the same motley protesters who tried to disrupt the running of the Olympic torch because it had an open flame. They raised banners: Sell Out! and Art NOT Carbon.

When he first took up fireworks as his medium, Westerners like them loved him. Dozens had snuck into China to help him lay a fuse from the Great Wall through 1,000 miles of Mongolia, to help an artist shine light on human rights abuses by the Chinese government, they said. When he was arrested, when he told the Chinese government that what he was really doing, creating art—Chinese art—that could be seen from space, journalists in the West wrote that he was just trying to save his own skin, like Veronese called before the Inquisition for making a painting of *The Last Supper* full of German soldiers, monkeys, and prostitutes. Instead of changing the painting, Veronese simply changed the title: *Christ in the House of Levi.* Wang couldn't speak for Veronese, but the thing was, he never changed his rap. All he'd ever wanted was to make a splash. He'd stacked new cars on a pike and set them on fire—*Shish Kabob*; his performance *Celebration* consisted of him driving a new car full of blazing fireworks through Times Square. It was the critics who read all this anti-capitalist, anti-communist meaning into his tea leaves....

When they first learned of his latest plan, one that the Chinese government loved but that the rest of the world hated, it all became clear. He was going to set off nuclear fireworks on the moon to scar its surface in a pattern that would resemble the Great Wall of China. Whenever anyone looked up, they would be reminded of the power of China, of Chinese art. Of him. These demonstrations he put on around the world were supposed to attract investors. Not protesters.

The protesters were making the crowd angry, and the wind had begun to shift. A man wearing an N95 mask and a necklace that rendered facial recognition software useless had climbed up onto the barricade separating the crowd from the mortars and stared at Wang as police pulled at his legs, trying to get him down. Instead of looking away, Wang met the protester's gaze and held it as he pressed IGNITE.

Whump, whump, whump.... The mortars began going off. Hundreds of them in syncopated rhythm, each mortar emitting a ring of white smoke like a cigar smoker might burp out before its shell exploded high above, leaving a thick black smudge in the sky. The banks of mortars continued to fire, their dull *whump, whump* like the chug of a heavy locomotive till the sky was completely black. Then bottle rockets streaked up before this black curtain, releasing ribbons of white smoke that drifted across it, forming a picture of mountains and trees like a watercolor of a misty Chinese landscape only rendered in smoke.

*Whump-whump-whump-whump-whump-whump....*Other mortars formed Chinese characters—我担心什么—that a videoboard roughly translated as:

LIVE
Cai Guo-Qiang Firework Mortars
youtu.be/UZ0Sbbu20V0?t=60

Meadow had been to more countries in W.2 than she'd ever visit in the real world, but the cities were depressingly similar, the way it was possible to pull off the expressway at almost any point in the U.S. and find the same small-town cluster of Big-Box Furniture Store, Home Improvement Chain, and four flavors of restaurant: Red Garden, Olive Lobster, Lobster Garden.... Funny, how no one she knew wanted to live in a culture like this, and yet here it was.

On-screen, an image of Earth slowly revolved, waiting for her to type in where she wanted to go. As it turned, she was taken by how much the virtual world that people were creating online mirrored the actual world their bodies inhabited: the nighttime glow of cities in actual satellite photos were aglow in W.2 with the activity of avatars building, buying, selling, partying, living.... The Bottom Billion sections of the real globe that had gone dark were likewise dark on this globe, parts of the Middle East too hot for humans. She'd heard that there were only a dozen lines for Internet coming out of Africa now, and, as the globe rotated, patches shaped like jigsaw puzzle pieces showed areas of the world that had been blacked out. Like the Maldives or Florida Keys, little islands were gone, as were parts of the Netherlands after dikes had failed, drought evaporating the fresh water that had balanced the pressure of the sea. But the Amazon River, swollen to the thickness of a Great Lake, was surrounded by green: virtual rain forests that users of W.2 were replanting by buying carbon offsets.

If someone built a fish farm in the real world, it was supposed to show up in W.2 and vice versa, the program more of an interface than a model, its developers claimed, blurring the line between the two so much that it made as much sense to ask which was real as it did to ask whether a Vespa bought online or in person was the real purchase.

Meadow could see why Silpa and Guy used W.2 for their rendezvous. Though the parts of the globe were dotted by fires—red for forest fires, green for the gas flames of offshore drilling platforms that had been set ablaze by guerillas—here in W.2, there was no death. The real Switzerland might be littered with cows that had died of thirst, and other online worlds might be awash in people teaming up to slaughter space aliens, or each other, but here at least, the planet was Lego-clean.

She typed in Singapore City and the rotation of the globe sped up, the landmass of Asia coming into view, then as the camera pulled in, Singapore Island rose up: its turquoise shoreline, its delta, then its capital. The grid spread apart like filaments on a microscope slide as the magnification was increased, then she was on the ground—street view—the Rainforest Cafe directly in front of her.

She had to laugh, imagining profiling software trolling her computer, an OS licensed to a biology lab, compiling a concordance of 'environmental' key words in her emails and Google searches, then matching these dots of info to its list of sponsors to place her before an energy-hog restaurant full of jungle animatronics.

She clicked her arrow keys to rotate her avatar's view. Red Lobster, Shangri-La. Glass skyscrapers. A Starbucks had a pagoda roof. Orchid Road—*The Rodeo Drive of Singapore*—was lined with avatar palm trees. Store windows were filled with the avatars of iFlex and high-end phones. Boutique dresses. Neon ads. Though the real Singapore was densely populated, there were few pedestrians here: other avatars dressed as skateboarders, neo-hippies, and clubbers—the usual, except with Asian faces. One had the head of a Chinese dragon. Another glided by on large, white angel wings. Most of them were going into a movie theater—*Kill Chicks*—tough guy on a marquee three-stories high, babes with guns.

Last week, she'd begun her search in Indonesia, where her, Nico, and William had been staying when the tsunami hit. But the names of the streets, beaches, and other landmarks—Banda Aceh—the sight of them, even in their W.2 versions, was hard to take—especially given the way resort owners were desperately using W.2 to lure back tourists.

She'd been using her avatar to comb the beach for?.... For what? She didn't know, she'd realized, bending to pick up a seashell. Maybe the flip-flops her son had been wearing when he went out to watch the ocean recede. Maybe she should look for them among the trash that still washed up on the beaches in California. Maybe that flute they'd bought for him in the market—any clue....

In the real world, she'd read about a Japanese father whose twenty-year-old daughter had been swept off the roof of the bank she worked in. He had dropped her off that morning, a sunny morning like many others. Afterwards, he learned to scuba dive, and had been making dives ever since, growing old looking for her, and Meadow walked down the virtual beach, hoping for a sign that the rumor she'd heard was true: that those who had vanished could be found here in W.2.

Looking out to the virtual sea, she was approached by tour guides who mistook her for one of the surfers who had continued to come from as far away as Australia or California. In the days after the tsunami, Meadow and her husband had made their way up the Indonesian coast, searching for their son, first in the makeshift hospitals that had been set up, and then, in the morgues. Traveling up the coastline in the hopes of closure, it was called, they'd run into the real-world counterpart of these blonde avatars: men and women who'd been arriving with surfboards, somber out of respect for the destruction around them, but heading to beaches still strewn with palm fronds and roofing tiles nonetheless, their nonrefundable vacations paid long in advance.

It was obvious that virtual versions of these real-world people were here in W.2 as well. "People are people," someone once said to explain why the National Guard had to be called in to keep people from going to restaurants during the last pandemic, even when infections were still doubling every 30 days. Sure enough, local avatars, or speculators posing as them, continually mistook her for a tourist, offering to guide her to one of the coast's famous surf breaks where the continental shelf that generated those perfect, blue-crystal waves that surfers lusted after could also produce such devastating tsunamis.

"Mama, I'm going down to the beach to see the water go out," Nico had said that morning. A warm ocean breeze coming in through the window of their beachside hotel room, Meadow didn't want to get out of bed. "Hmmm?" she groggily murmured, "Why don't you wait for mommy and daddy to wake up?" Then she fell back asleep.

The next she knew, water was pouring in through that window. It was as if the window had been a portal in a ship that was suddenly sinking, seawater, sand, and crabs pouring in, filling the hotel room as though she'd awoken in a surreal nightmare. The beach that had been outside their window was gone: all sea. Frantically, she looked for Nico. Nowhere inside. The room rapidly filled with water, chests and backpacks and sandals turning into flotsam as she remembered Nico saying he was going down to the beach. By then it was impossible to get the hallway door open, the weight of the sea inside holding it shut against William's efforts. Still nude, she and William had managed to wriggle out through the window, fighting hard against the current pouring in....

She didn't even get to say goodbye.

And she couldn't stop watching the home videos. Meadow was shaken from her remembrance by an avatar speaking to her on-screen: "Are you here to see the world premiere of *Kill Chicks*?" she asked, gesturing toward the theater. The avatar was dressed like a fantasy schoolgirl: long legs, knee-socks and the miniskirt of a little sailor suit girls wore in mangas. One of those imaginary, too-cute creatures hovered just over her shoulder, giggling at everything she said. Whoever was controlling the avatar was typing, so probably on a slow node;

Kids on Beach in Malaysia
youtube.com/watch?v=ihN1qYVhka4

People on Hill Watching Town
youtube.com/watch?v=2XOx7XPLfy0

Tsunami Below
youtube.com/watch?v=ceym2c18OQM

Helicopter Aerial View of Waves
youtube.com/watch?v=w3AdFjklR50

Tsunami Caught on Camera 4/8 with Interviews
youtube.com/watch?v=oWzdgBNfhQU

Hotel
youtube.com/watch?v=uAB4zvMlhNo

maybe in a poor country, but maybe not. Just because she was on a slow node didn't necessarily mean anything. Meadow could only use the AI available in W.2 if she logged on using the computers at work, and even then she often used the typing mode so those working around her couldn't tell she was in W.2 instead of with them. "It doesn't premier in the real world until next week," School-Girl said. She gave a wink: one of those preprogrammed emoticons. "What are you trying to sell?"

"Nothing," Meadow typed. There was a pause as the message traveled to who knows where—around the world or down the hall. Then after another emoticon—a head nod this time—the words came back slowly, and with a herky-jerky speed of a one-finger typer: "Then why are you here?" Meadow wasn't sure herself. Chasing ghosts? When she hadn't been able to turn up any sign of Nico back in Indonesia.2, she thought she'd just make her way back the route they'd taken in the real world. Singapore was stop two. Before she could formulate an answer, School-Girl said, "Do you like to see pretty things? I take you see pretty things."

It was sometimes hard to tell if the person you were conversing with in W.2 had an accent or was just a crummy typist. "No," Meadow typed. "I'm looking for—"

Before she had finished typing, more words came out of the avatar: "I can take you to see Bukit Timah Nature Reserve. Or Orchid Garden...."

Meadow wanted to ask if she'd seen her son but wasn't sure how. What would he look like in W.2? Would he look the same as he had in life, four years ago? He'd be 11 if he had lived. Would she recognize him even if he stood before her? And if he was here, where? W.2 was the size of the planet. Planet W.2. He could be anywhere. Or nowhere. More likely, far more likely, he was nowhere. The bottom of the sea.

School-Girl's hovering creature scrunched up its nose to exude cuteness.

This is stupid, Meadow thought.

"Do you want to go shopping?" School-Girl said. "I can take you shopping."

"No. I'm not really here to go shopping."

"If not shopping, what else you do? Most people here are shopping."

"I'm looking for someone." There. She'd said it.

"Another shopper?"

Meadow began to type, No. But maybe she was. If some shade or avatar or echo or memory of Nico was here, he could be doing anything. Even shopping. She typed, "I don't think so."

"Well everyone here is shopping. Or going to the movie." There was another pause, a soft clicking indicating that whoever was working the School-Girl avatar had continued typing. Another speech bubble came on-screen: "Maybe we could look for him over by the animals."

Nico had stopped wanting to go to the zoo after he was able to read the signs: *Extinct in the Wild* or *Endangered*. There didn't seem to be a third choice for anything less common than a rat. But as School-Girl continued typing, Meadow realized she'd meant Party Animals.

"No, never mind. We won't find him there."

"Well, what is he into?"

He was into mummies and dinosaurs and dancing like a robot. He loved his Z-Game. Pyramids, like every seven-year-old, and drawing rockets that transformed into robots. He was one of those kids you always read about but never actually met who could find a film-editing program online, and be making his rocket-robot animation by evening. But when they arrived in Indonesia, he'd been fascinated by a handmade flute: one of those crudely carved, bright red flutes sold to tourists. Somehow it was the low-tech nature of the thing that made it exotic to him. She could still see him struggling to get his lips to form just the right amount of air pressure to make it play. The woman who'd sold it to them tried to show him how to do it, her tightening smile revealing that she thought he was the densest kid on Earth because he had to be shown how to do something every Indonesian kid could do as naturally as blowing across the mouth of a bottle. And even then Nico couldn't make it work. Forgotten knowledge. The workings of graphic programs were intuitively transparent to him, but ask him to ride a bike, or work a yo-yo, or do anything that involved interfacing with the old-fashioned material world and he was hopeless. Meadow could see him struggling with the flute back at their hotel room. How proud he'd been when a note suddenly came cleanly out! She could still hear that note: a strong, clear piercing 'C'. It reminded William of his didgeridoo; he'd promised to dig it out of storage for Nico when they got back, but of course Nico never saw it, and when they returned, William wanted to get rid of the instrument.

"...sex clubs, art openings, opium dens, Medieval libraries full of rare manuscripts.... There's lots of things in W.2 besides shopping," School-Girl was saying. "If I was looking for someone I'd try to think of the place they most wanted to visit and then—"

"Music?" Meadow blurted. "Is there music here? Or robots?"

"Sure! There's lots of music, silly. And robots. What kind of music does your friend like?"

"...When we make comparison it is very important to us population geneticists that we can believe in the variation we see...."

While Chen spoke, giving a survey of his work at their general lab meeting, Gabe stared out the window of the conference room: below, the trim life-science campus lay peaceful as a winter golf course. What had been an old Italian neighborhood and water market had been retrofitted with the glass and steel aesthetics of surgical equipment. The city had helped the gentrification along, as did the Olivetti Botanical Gardens, which was nearby, the city, university, hospital, and gardens pulling together to create a massive neighborhood rehab project—new patterns of student and Topper life and a neighborhood of iFlex stores and cafés with sidewalk umbrellas emerging out of revamped facilities whose subsidized rent allowed them to serve as groundbreakers for other piecemeal green lots and tech buildings. Their building also housed a soy-based, food-additive design company, and a startup whose 3D printers could be used to output anything from pizzas to pistols.

A robin landed in the small ornamental tree just below. A robin in February. "We also have information," Chen was saying...

"...that there are 30 proteins secreted in Phthiraptera Amblycera Menoponidae salivary gland," Chen said, describing the comparison he was making between different louse populations. "Ten have been deposited in Gene Bank..." He checked his notes. "Accession No. AF335485." Someone yawned. When he looked up, he saw Gabe, Meadow, Jak, Olympia, and a half dozen of her grad students, the main audience for these monthly meetings, looking back.

Olympia cut in, interrupting from the back of the conference room: "He means that when U of I looked at this they didn't do accurate sequencing; they were just trying to get it out before another lab beat them to publication." Instead of letting him continue, she explained to the other members of her lab group, lounging around the conference room, how the U of I lab was only interested in a single salivary-gland protein, SP-15.

Jak struggled with the tab on a thimble of coffee creamer. Gabe seemed to be considering a spot on her arm where she could get another tattoo; Silpa, wearing a lab coat over her sari, was paying attention, as were the grad students, scattered around the room in their jeans and tennis shoes. Shirley was even taking notes. Meadow, dressed like them in jeans and flannel shirt, sat on a window ledge, her feet in hiking boots dangling as though she were sitting on Lookout Ledge in some national park, and Olympia noted the difference between the group she'd assembled and those eager Uppies who filled offices in commercials for cloud computing, or other 'business solutions'....

"So even though they established the library for salivary glands," Olympia explained for the students, but also to get her crew's attention, "they only sequenced them until they got up to the one they were interested in, SP-15. Then they just stopped there. The data wasn't very good, but since it was the first, it's the reference sequence that everyone else has built on."

"Where did their lice come from?" Silpa asked.

"Probably the Congo," Olympia answered.

"That's a colony that we have to rebuild, right Gabe?"

The Congo, where Guy was stationed.

"...right Gabe?"

The mention of her name pulled Gabe back from the robin outside. She gave a nod. Slowly. Olympia knew damn good and well that the Congo lice were dead, but she never missed a chance to rub in the fact that the colony had been healthy just before it crashed and Gabe hadn't been able to explain what went wrong.

A satellite view of Earth lit up the screen, Chen moving on to his next slide. Map pins marked the origins of the lice they were now working with: AMC—Amblycera Menoponidae from Paraguay; AMSB from southern Bolivia; and AMVN from Vietnam, near the Chinese border. All the places that had conflict minerals—and U.S. ground troops to protect them, Gabe noted.

As Africa rotated into view, Silpa wished she could zoom down to street level so she could see Guy—the real Guy, not the avatar Guy who tried to meet her every other Tuesday in W.2. Was he well? Was he safe? Until their next meeting, there would be no way to know, not with the military blackout.

She checked her watch. 10 a.m. Or ten hundred hours as he'd say it in his adopted language. The hottest, and so safest, part of the day still ahead. Then the sun would set and the fighting pick up.

"So, this question must be resolved...."

Someone else yawned.

Chen hated speaking at these meetings—called on to give a cartoon of what the math showed. "Everyone here can make the same excuse," Olympia had insisted when he tried to get out of taking his turn at the podium. "Don't they have show-and-tell in China?" She smiled that American smile of hers.

So instead of doing something useful, he wasted every fourth Monday in this conference room, "building teamwork" as Olympia called the turns they took explaining their part of the project: Gabe describing the difficulties of keeping genetic drift out of a lice-breeding program—when all he needed was her data; the meeting before that it had been Mohammed's explanation about harvesting glands, Mohammed's English also broken—only broken in a different way than his—and for that reason triply difficult. Next month he would waste time listening to the *gewlo*, Jak, then Silpa, then it would be his turn again.... At least the students listened.

He advanced his PowerPoint presentation to the next slide: a second string of AGCTs that made up SP-12, the twelfth protein in the genetic sequence of the louse's saliva. "Same louse, same test, same target protein," he said. The two strings of genetic code should have been identical but when he pressed the space bar, an underscore highlighted a number of letters in the two strings that didn't match:

AGCCTTTACCTTAGGTCCCAAAGCCT....
AGCCTGT_CGTTAGGT__CACCGCCT....

"My problem is 'How can I believe in the information generated by these two sequences?' We know mismatch equals mistake. But how do we know which string of letters is the accurate one? Which is the mistake? How do we know they are not both wrong?"

"Why is there so much noise in the data?" Olympia called from the back of the room again, irritated.

"We know noise equals mistake. We have no information about mistake itself. The mistake could be in sample," Chen said, letting the finger of guilt point first to Gabe and the quality of the lice she bred. A number of the students glanced over at her. Then he let it point to Mohammed who somehow might have contaminated the glands he removed from the lice: "Maybe the solution he used to euthanize lice degraded its RNA. It could be faulty DNA caused by a bad primer or a bad sequencing reaction in the gel," he said, allowing heads to turn to Jak for being sloppy in his sequencing.

"Maybe the mistake is in the math," Jak said defensively, though everyone realized how lame that was, especially coming from him.

Chen took it in stride, listing the myriad ways the equipment and margins for error in the software could also contribute. "We can never have certainty," he said. "Only degrees of probability." Around the room, he could see everyone but Olympia relax.

Chen pointed back at the string of AGCTs, explaining that to correct inconsistencies they would have to go back to the raw data generated by the sequencer.

"But the raw electropherogram is just a bunch of bars produced by the chemical reactions inside the sequencer," Jak said, still on defense, making his appeal to Olympia. "A person can't see it any more than they can watch the electrons shoot around the chips inside their computer."

Instead of arguing, Chen agreed, adding, "So we either go on faith or we do a statistical analysis to assess its reliability. This is called the PHRED." Next slide: "The PHRED is a number of reliability; it counts all the mismatches in every run and allows you to set a threshold above which you will accept the sample. Here I set the PHRED at 10, which means I will accept 1 mistake for each 1000 bases analyzed. In order to have more confidence we can use a PHRED of 30. This allows us to distinguish between a nice region and a bad region. The bad portion is eliminated from further consideration. We then only work with sequences that have a low incidence of error. Good sequences."

He projected another graph, plunging into the math. Jak gazed at equations as though watching a light show. Silpa looked moonily at the empty seat beside her, while Gabe drifted back to looking out the window.

Christ, it was hard to pay attention to Chen's lectures, Gabe thought, doodling a bird. It wasn't so long ago that she'd been a student herself and, like the students in the room, eager. Sally?—that one with creative hair who was writing a dis on protein folding and using a gel pen to take notes?—that would have been her, excited to learn how once nature was conceived as accounting anything was possible.

Gabe counted the robins outside: seven or eight more. Cold and shivering.

She'd never seen robins cluster for warmth. They were doing such a piss-poor job of it that they looked more like strangers waiting for a bus than the tight pack that penguins formed.... In grade school, she and the other kids used to compete to spot the first robin of spring—it meant that the Chicago winter they'd endured was over, the earth softening, sap as well, trees and flowers on the verge of exploding into bloom with summer vacation as close as their shadows. Now the sight of the first robins filled her with dread. Dead man walking. Faux springs would always snap unexpectedly: the trees that had begun to bud would harden back into their dormant state, the erratic weather having the double whammy of leaving fewer robins to return when spring—the real spring—did arrive.

Further north, she knew, in the Arctic, birds that normally stayed in the lower 48 states would be mingling with birds that normally stayed in Asia, the lakes of melting tundra that were now forming allowing them to come together as they never had before. The slimy cesspools of bird shit, and rotting feathers that choked Asian farms were breeding grounds for all kinds of pathogens. The cows, pigs, and other mammals that tramped through it, and sneezed, and licked each other on those farms were incubators for viruses that could jump to humans. They passed them on to migratory birds, but even migratory birds didn't cross oceans. Until now. With the warming north, the routes of migrating birds were stretching into Siberia and Beringia; their breeding seasons were becoming longer and longer, and already North American birds, like gyrfalcons and northern pintail ducks, were carrying Asian cholera and flu back down into Oregon where with no natural barriers, they could spread as wildly as a California fire throughout the rest of the country. The last 'minor' outbreak had been stopped by slaughtering 70 million domestic birds; the heaps of bodies from one farm alone formed a berm 3 miles long. Looking at the robins outside, she knew that unless someone came up with a prophylactic, it would only be a matter of time before those berms were made of human bodies.

Jak gazed at Chen's colored graphs: sine waves as beautiful as rainbows. The Art of Science is the Art of the Future! It made him think of The Art of the Past: Once, back in college, he and his roommate were about to roll a blunt when they realized that they didn't have any papers. "What about that old book," his roommate said. "Bet it would burn real good." Kindling-dry pages—a natural history book that Jak had checked out on a whim. *God and Nature* or something. "Guess nobody will miss just one," he said, tearing out a page. On the reverse side was an engraving of a bird, which once the blunt was rolled, seemed to be reaching with its beak for the lit end. "It wants some!" Jak's roommate said, handing the blunt over, "but he's trying to toke the wrong end!" The joke got funnier and funnier as they passed the blunt back and forth, the glowing end getting closer and closer to the bird's beak—"Watch out Tweetie Pie!"—until the bird's beak was burning, caught in a forest fire of one.... "The science library ought to give us an award for discovering a use for those old books."

Flocks of passenger pigeons used to be so large that they could take four hours to pass; but the last of them died in the Cincinnati Zoo in 1913.

Sine waves rippled across Chen's body as he walked into the beam of the projector to point at something on-screen. "...this red curve shows...."

Scrawled on the dry-erase board behind him were equations left by whatever lab group had used the conference room before them—*as food decreases, cannibalism increases.*

Meetings like this made Meadow wonder if she should have stayed back in Oregon. When Olympia invited her to join her lab, the effort to close up the house, move to Chicago, seemed to require more energy than she could gather. But then, the more she thought about it, the more it seemed like a change of scenery might get her out of her perpetual funk. She hadn't worked since Nico vanished, just went for long walks in the woods with her spaniel. Drifting, William called it. Drifting, the way she liked to imagine Nico out there in all that blue: playing pirate, fishing, enjoying himself until he was found.... "You can't just drift the rest of your life," William had said. Of course he was right, though she also knew it was better than sinking.

Better than studying home videos of the tsunami that people posted online—play, pause, play—over and over, longing for a glimpse of Nico in the background....

A new job seemed a reset in some ways. A fresh start if not a clean break—on a study that seemed to be calling to her: Back at Berkeley, they'd worked in different labs but each of them had just given birth to baby boys. As individual puffins seek out the same kind of sheltering rocks and so form a colony, both Olympia and Meadow would retreat into the storage room that the university had converted into a lounge for women. Twice a day, the cycle of lactation, they'd both be in there, using breast pumps, their individual needs causing a pattern to develop at the next higher order: There they got to talking, first about the babies, then the husbands who stayed at home to watch them, Olympia saying how hard it was to have an infant at home and do all the things she needed to do to oversee her lab. Their conversation came around to shop talk.

Olympia was PI in a lab studying the biology of mutations into pandemics. Meadow was working on an MA in disease vectors. To the rhythmic, mechanical suck of the cups they held to first one breast, then the other, they discussed how a cell mutates as it is passed from one animal to another, and the possibility of bird lice saliva providing some immunity against certain bird-born diseases.

The speculation had first been proposed by another woman researching bird lice in a forest that no longer existed, and the oddity of the world came to Meadow whenever she recalled how much of her own life—where she lived, how she lived—had its genesis in an insight that a woman she'd never met had had 40 years ago while on a wild-goose chase in Paraguay. Now here it was—just a footnote—still shaping her life. And Olympia's life. And maybe, if everything went well, the lives of millions of others. Who could explain such things?

Olympia sat at the back of the room, her brow furrowed over all the things that could derail their study. Did her own life ever seem odd to her? Meadow wondered. Did she think about her husband and son out on the West Coast?

Funny, Meadow thought, looking at the reams of data Chen projected, how the smallest things can create such dramatic results. For lack of a nail the kingdom was lost.... Funny how the strangest things can become natural. Kissing while wearing face masks. Someone might live because of the work done here in this lab; someone else might die because of what they didn't do, just as during the tsunami some ran to the mountains, others to the beach—a branch in the path at every step—*and I?—I took the one less traveled by and that has made all the difference*—if that long-gone entomologist hadn't gone off on her wild louse chase in Paraguay, Meadow wouldn't have studied what she did at Berkeley, wouldn't have met her husband, wouldn't have had her son when she did, wouldn't have had the conversations that her and Olympia did, wouldn't be here in Chicago, working on what they were working on....

Looking around at the grad students and her group, Olympia wondered what it would take to keep them in the dark as she shifted the direction of their research. Not much, she figured, since she was the only one who had an overview of how the pieces went together. And the only part that would really change would be the direction of the last phase. Even if they did notice changes in protocol, they knew that a line of inquiry could sometimes go off in an unexpected direction, or raise interesting side questions. They understood that a PI sometimes had to say one thing to stakeholders or administrators in order to do what was best, like the half-truth she'd told Meadow to get her to move here: that their research could lead to a vaccine that could benefit the Bottom Billion. Or the white lies she told to get funding. When she proposed the study, all she was really interested in was the science; then, after the government got rid of the EPA and downsized its involvement in science, she had to pretend she was concerned about soldiers, her grant proposals pitching her research as knowledge that could potentially lead to a vaccine against diseases carried by bird lice where U.S. troops were stationed. Her local congressman had made an impassioned speech on the House floor—*It's our patriotic duty to protect our sons and daughters fighting to keep us free!*—and in the end, her funding had been attached to a bill that also included pork-barrel spending to pay a local cement contractor to make barricades, and a corporate-gift supplier to send cheese baskets at Christmas.

The team Olympia assembled had been cranking on the study ever since: Gabriella—Gabe—was in charge of breeding the 100,000 lice needed for the study from the initial colonies and birds that the army supplied, capturing them in the three different conflict-mineral zones where troops were operating. It was Mohammed's job to remove the saliva glands from these lice—200,000 glands. Jak ran the automated equipment that sequenced the genes found in the saliva of these glands. Using these databases, Chen was identifying the strings of genetic letters that made up the 20–30 proteins that the U of I lab estimated were in the saliva of one species of blood-sucking bird lice. For the moment, she had Meadow helping to create a library of the genetic fingerprints. As that part of the study rolled along and the genetic ID of the proteins became known, Silpa and Guy began exposing each of the identified proteins to some 1,000 human blood samples; they would note which protein caused which blood type to generate the most white blood cells—an upsurge of white blood cells being a firmly established indicator of an immune response.

If all went well, spikes in the data would rise like a new mountain range to show which of the proteins triggered the most vigorous immune response in the majority of human blood types AND was found in all three of the lice populations, that is, throughout all conflict-mineral zones.

Just about the time it began to do so, those venture capitalists came sniffing around, asking if she had any idea how much more money she could make as the PI in her own corporate lab....

The best way to help yourself is to help others, Meadow's mother always said, so to get her mind off of Nico, she'd volunteered her expertise to the Noah's Ark Project: zoos around the world that coordinated their efforts to serve as a global lifeboat for species losing their habitats. The article she'd read about the project had sounded so upbeat: the zoos would coordinate to build an environmental zone from pole to pole so animals all over the world could retreat into it as the Earth 'flooded'; then, if the environment ever became habitable for them again, they could repopulate the Earth. A pole-to-pole zoo. But, of course, that had all just been a beautiful dream, fit for a world that didn't have conflict minerals and civil wars and poachers.... That didn't account for the fact that polar bears would start eating 1,500 goose eggs an hour when they could no longer get seals.... Still, even scaled back—zoos as lifeboats—the basic idea was how earlier conservationists had brought back the American bison. But with the Earth warming, the wild was disappearing faster than its ice. The Cleveland Zoo had saved the Kihansi spray toad when Tanzania built a hydroelectric dam, but their habitat—the spray off the waterfall they lived near—had been wiped off the Earth, and the Kihansi spray toad was stuck forever in the Cleveland Zoo, living within the spray coming from stainless steel nozzles. Frantically, zoos and others began geotagging wolves and elephants and elk, trying to determine which had the best chance to be saved—soon, the squirrels in her yard were more wild than the sharks in the sea—still, the extinctions mounted, hundreds, then thousands, so many species going extinct that even the tiny proportion singled out for saving began to swamp the lifeboats, and the zoos were forced to choose: which animal to house, which had to be put on birth control (grizzly bears, giraffes and hippos), and—the part she hated most—which animals had to be euthanized.

Zoos killing leopard cubs.... "To maximize genetic diversity in what minimal space we can offer." She'd been put on a committee that determined which animals to kick out of the lifeboat. The plate-billed mountain toucan?—only able to live at an altitude of 1,000 to 2,000 meters on the western slopes of the Andes?—fugetaboutit. The lion-tailed macaque? Toast. The gallows humor others used to cope had started to get to her. Sophie's Choice. Every day. Pick one: The mhorr gazelle or the addra gazelle? Her mind would fill with images of the *Titanic* without enough lifeboats to save the men. Then not enough to save the women. Then the children—and more and more of her time was taken up picking out the weakest—those that weren't interesting enough to gain a celebrity champion or millionaire philanthropist—to throw overboard, to make room for new arrivals that might have a better chance of getting a Twitter following. Most people thought zoos were about animals, but she knew: the ways zoos treated their animals always said more about humans. What was surprising was how completely nature had become accounting.

Some days she resigned herself to being an accountant, working to make a bad situation as good as it could be. Other days it just seemed overwhelming, pointless; deckchairs, not lifeboats on the *Titanic*: animals at the equator pushing into lateral zones, those in lateral zones pushing into northern climates with the big animals, those that needed big ranges, being the first dominos pushed off the planet, Noah's Ark having reached what turned out to be, after all, the edge of a flat Earth.

Even the zoos themselves began to give up once harmless bacteria began to flip into pathogens that could kill off an entire species at once: the Sumatran rhino, the blackfooted ferret, the African wild dog.... Bulldozers had been needed to dig mass graves for the last 50,000 saiga antelopes, grazing in a safe zone on the steppes of Central Asia when the entire population suddenly collapsed, like a colony of fruit flies.... The zoo that had put so much effort into creating that safe zone shifted its efforts into luring visitors with new exotics: a Galápagos tortoise cloned from Lonesome George, a tortoise that had not only been the last of its species but had even been studied by Darwin—zero degrees of separation—a mastodon that had been coaxed out of the DNA recovered in Siberia and implanted in an elephant womb; chickens that had been reverse engineered to resemble dinosaurs; or less glamorously, the coy wolves, brown polar bears and the other animals that had began to mate with each other and take on the mutt-like, muddied characteristics of the village dog.

Meadow hadn't needed long to give Olympia an answer. Working on Olympia's project would help, in its small way, put the world back in balance. At least her world. And if a vaccine actually came out of it, then Nico's beginning, if not his end, would have some meaning. At least that's what she told herself, believing that because Olympia's son was the same age that Nico would have been had he lived, Olympia would understand.... Then Olympia pulled that article they'd had accepted for publication.

Because of the data? she wondered, looking at Olympia watch Chen now, her features focused as a rifle. Meadow had forgotten, or didn't let herself remember, that Olympia's son and husband stayed in California. That she flew out to visit them every other week, then once a month, and now, even less than that. Meadow had forgotten that while she'd pumped herself dry so Nico could have breast milk during the days she couldn't be home to give it to him, Olympia did so to relieve the ache; while Meadow emptied the pump into a bottle she had sterilized so she could take her milk home to the baby, Olympia always dumped hers down the sink.

"Keep your hatchet scoured," Olympia learned from the military guy assigned as her liaison: "the first rule of army preparedness." But even better would be to say: A hatchet is a thing; a psycho is a thing; a psycho with a hatchet is a third thing, one that makes other possibilities possible. And that's all she was doing, talking to those venture capitalists: looking into other possibilities. From their point of view her study was ideal: too academic to be initiated by Big Pharma, but with the potential to be bought out once she demonstrated its feasibility. So okay, maybe to recruit Meadow she did exaggerate the possibility of their research benefiting the Bottom Billion. Maybe she even talked herself into believing that she only got into bed with the military for their seed money. But every biologist on Earth knew what a long shot it was for a practical vaccine to come out of academic research and only a fool could believe that if one came out of theirs, it would be used anywhere but on an American GI.

"...many question marks, little information...."

Winter didn't arrive this year, everyone in the lab said, but Silpa could never get warm, the damp Midwestern winters so radically different from the tropical heat of home that it seemed to permeate her bones. Guy used to tease her about always being cold, wearing a sweater against summer air-conditioning, and she imagined him now, out in the heat of Paraguay never able to get cool.

She used to tease him about joining the army.

Army *Reserve,* he always corrected—before his unit was called up and he actually had to go. The first time, she had not meant to be funny. She had spoken harshly—a jab—though not so much at him as at his country where war was a way of life. But he had turned it into a joke between them, putting on a cowboy drawl as he put blood samples in the centrifuge, "Terrorist talk like that gets people deported, ma'am." He took her aspirator, blew on its end as if it were a pistol that he holstered in the pocket of his lab coat. "A nurse who carries a gun," she had scoffed. "What kind of nurse is that?" "One with student loans, ma'am." And he had sashayed away, whistling a plaintive song from a western.

But all that teasing was back when the war was as abstract as a movie. Before the day he nonchalantly told her that his unit had been called up. She sat at their lab bench stunned, the words incomprehensible, until he jotted an address on her lab pad: guy78@usarmy.gov, the black pen strokes somehow making his going real, the address concrete, material evidence, a link in cyberspace, she knew, to a location in actual space where the shooting, blood and death would be real. "In case anyone wants to write me," he'd said.

"...a reliable sequence, something I can believe in."

The floor vibrated. Then it did it again, followed by a dull, heavy pounding from the construction that was going on downstairs, the Insectarium on the second floor being converted into a Biohazard Containment Level 3 room.

On the wall, next to the regular clock, was a Doomsday Clock: a bar of red digits counting down how many days, hours, minutes, seconds they had until the avian flu virus jumped to mammals. The clock was a matter of speculation, of course, based on probability and mutation rates. A pharmaceutical lobbyist had a dozen of them made for congressmen to take to the floor when they argued for funding. Made a great visual. But listening to Chen, the clock seemed to stand still, and Jak snickered how they should use his lectures as a prophylactic against avian flu, cancer, aging, vacations ending....

"I cannot assume that the sequence for PP louse saliva protein SP-12 taken from flies in North Bolivia is the same as the sequence for saliva protein SP-12 taken from flies in South Bolivia. Here we have no previous informations...."

Christ, another sub-study. Jak could see it coming, Olympia's eyes narrowing like a boxer in close enough to take punches. Her scowl turned his way and he looked back at the screen.

People were the weak link of any study, Olympia knew, looking around at the characters that had coalesced around her project. That's what worried her now. The students were all engaged, but Mohammed's mind seemed a million miles away, on the status of his Green Card or whatever else was bugging him. Gabe was still staring out the window; she could be a problem, Olympia thought, looking at her tattoos. $C_{12}H_{22}O_{11}$ ran across the base of her neck: sugar. But she was anything but sweet, mixed up with NGers—Neon Greeners, or punks or whatever

EARTH CLOCK YR MO WE DY

World Population	7,218,206,968
Population Growth	34,898,783
Incidence of Malnutrition	24,445,196
Incidence of HIV Infection	1,947,680
Incidence of Cancer	4,209,254
Global Temp (C)	14.6845369011
CO2 Emissions (tons)	12,456,093,221
Species Extinct	12,230
Forest Lost (ha)	5,888,335
Forest Replanted (ha)	2,581,808
Desertification (ha)	2,717,693

LIVE• *Earth Clock* https://extinctionclock.org

they called themselves. Too late, Olympia had learned that Gabe had been a whistleblower in a previous lab. She could be a problem. Unlike Silpa, lab coat over her sari, keeping company with the empty seat that Guy used to fill at these meetings. The only one looking at the screen was Jak: vacant grin fixed on his face as though he was dreaming of the perfect wave. Was he on something?

She'd brought Mohammed in on a Tech Visa because the dissections he did in her lab were very similar to the dissections he did for the CDC in Venezuela, so he'd be okay if he could keep from thinking immigration was out to ruin his life. Jak was the one slacker, an inheritance from the previous lab director, she suspected, because his San Diego surfer attitude made him too lazy to look for another job after the shakeup. But the ABI that he ran was so automated that even an undergrad could handle it. Silpa was a phlebotomist and had been a very good Pathology Assistant back in India. She'd worked well with Guy, their all-American jock, until the army shipped him out. She took it so hard that Olympia figured the two of them were sleeping together. Even so, even without Guy, she was able to keep up with the pace of samples that arrived weekly: blood drawn from soldiers who'd never been exposed to lice in the conflict zones; blood from local villagers who'd grown up being bitten by blood-sucking lice of their area; and random samples from the blood bank in Indianapolis that they used as a check. From the attention Silpa gave those samples, you'd think the blood had come from Guy, which, come to think of it, was a possibility.

Chen's statistical analysis was rock solid, good science because he understood both the math and the biology, his humorless rigor making it easy to see why China had begun to eat everyone's lunch in a number of research areas ever since the U.S. made an ignoramus president.

Then there was Meadow, sad-sack Meadow, the only one she actually recruited—for what she knew about bird lice. True enough she'd lost a child, but even before that she'd been all touchy-feely. Didn't she live in a teepee for a while?

The last time Guy had been able to make their rendezvous in W.2, Silpa had dressed in a dove-white sari, blood-red ruby in her bellybutton such as she would never wear during a Chicago winter. He had dressed his avatar in cut-off jeans and a Hawaiian shirt, since they'd agreed to meet on a beach. In Waikiki.2: a deserted stretch they had found away from the Kittychans and dance parties, the New Agers building that pyramid.... Far from the fighting in the Congo or Paraguay or Bolivia or any of the other conflict zones. A soldier on leave could go anywhere. So long as he did it virtually. There, their toes in sand made of pixels, he described the training he got before shipping out: four days on a shooting range scattered with store-bought tumbleweeds to simulate someone's idea of Africa. Then there was the real action: suturing up the leg of a ten-year-old boy who had been playing with a grenade—or had he tried to throw it at them during a firefight the night before? The patrol that Guy had been on had been ambushed by people who looked like the family watching him sew up their son. He described going door-to-door on patrols during the day to provide medical care—mission objective: win the hearts and minds of the civilian population—then going out on patrols at night to bust down those same doors to round up sons, fathers, brothers, or some other individual that an informer had fingered as a 'person of interest'. Sometimes, he found himself waking up in the shell of an apartment they had bivouacked in not sure if it was night or day. Sometimes it took him a few minutes to remember if the other GIs waking up around him were readying their weapons to escort him on his humanitarian rounds or if this was a shift where he escorted them on their suspect roundups....

Lying side by side on the beach, a sky the color of a blue screen saver, she'd slipped her avatar's fingers into his, and via the VR glove she wore she could feel him squeeze her hand back. She tried to comfort him with the myth of Arjuna, the warrior-king filled with doubt on the eve of a battle. At his moment of self-recrimination, his chariot driver revealed himself to be Krishna, the multi-faced God.

Guy had remained silent, listening to Silpa tell how Krishna reminded Arjuna of Dharma, the duty to remain faithful to yourself, and by so doing remain faithful to the cosmic order.

When she finished, he answered with a story of his own about doing his ER training at the University Med Center before the area had been gentrified. Back then, the teaching hospital and a few high-end condos formed an archipelago in a sea of beat-down housing. "Same planet, different worlds." And no poet ever dreamed of the cosmic order that they formed together.

After being mugged for the second time, one of the night-shift doctors had begun to carry a gun. Then one night, as he was putting his briefcase in the trunk of his car, someone put a knife to his back and demanded his wallet. Instead of giving it to him, he calmly turned, hand in his Tommy Hilfiger coat pocket, and shot right through it into the mugger's stomach. A teenager. The single shot cut his lineal, and he began vomiting blood. "I was on duty when they came in," Guy said. "The doctor had managed to get the kid back to the emergency room he had just left where they saved the boy's life."

"And the moral is?"

"'Sinner, saint, pauper, king—there but for the grace of God go I,' mother would say, which I always took to mean," he said, releasing her hand to fold his arms over his head in the posture they made prisoners take, "here but for the luck of the draw squats anyone."

Now, here in the conference room beside her, the chair Guy always sat in at these meetings was empty. If he knew how she felt looking at it, she thought, he'd know how wrong he'd been.

"...we have much information...."

Mohammed snuck looks at the faces of the others in the room, trying to read them. Had Silpa turned him in? Because he was from the country Guy had been sent to fight? Before their government sent him off to die, he and Silpa used to always sit together at these meetings, because, Mohammed initially thought, it was natural, she and Guy forming the lab unit that processed blood. But had there been more between them than that? Sex? Politics? Once, passing by the hooded area where they processed blood, he heard him tell her, 'Terrorist talk like that gets people deported, ma'am.' A moment later—after they had seen him—Guy had walked away as casually as the cat who ate the canary, whistling a theme song from a cowboy show. Had they been talking about me? Mohammed had wondered. When they saw him they abruptly switched subjects, Silpa looking down, smiling at whatever private joke had passed between them. Is that why she kept averting her eyes now? he wondered. Guilt? Over what?

Dense statistics, alien languages from The Planet Calculus....

Errors were cumulative. Complex reactions, tiny margins for error adding up to dead certainty. No better than a placebo. Or worse. After spending millions of dollars testing the blood thinner Heparin, allergic reactions never seen in the lab triggered fatal drops in blood pressure out in the wild....

Uh-oh, uh-oh, uh-oh, Olympia thought waiting for Chen to drop the other foot. And here it came: some screwup, or faulty assumption, showing up in the data the way all those DNA tests—thirteen months and $180,000 worth of grant money—that showed early dinosaurs were birds had to be thrown out after the researchers begin getting crazy results: dinosaur DNA carrying the DNA of fish, the fish DNA later shown to have come from a tech, like Jak, who'd had tuna for lunch and then didn't wash his hands....

Olympia could feel her bowls clench.

Her logic had been tight: find a single protein in all species of lice that would trigger an immune response in all types of human blood; use it to develop a single vaccine—one that could be administered to all soldiers regardless of which parasite they were exposed to.

Crap, she muttered, when she saw the next slide, a picture of the worst-case scenario coming true: that the lice from each conflict zone were genetically different, even if they were the same species.

"Even if I only use samples with high reliability," Chen said, pointing out a string of AGCTs, "we still find this stretch of DNA that codes for G, a glycerin, whereas in the same protein, SP-1B from Bolivia, we find the code for aspartic acid...." He continued down the list, pointing out the differences in each of the proteins they had sequenced in the saliva in each of the louse populations, SP-1V, SP-1B, SP-1C; SP-2V, SP-2B, SP-2C; SP-3V, SP-3B....

As Chen spoke, Olympia could hear her statistical ground turn to sand.

"Why is there so much variability between populations?" she snapped.

Angry. Murder the messenger.

And Chen's not even taking into account genetic drift in the lab, Gabe thought. According to the records she kept, the flies she now had in the Insectarium were 150 generations from the original breeding pairs. If they were humans, they'd be the equivalent of modern descendants of Neanderthals, the life span of the fly so short, and their breeding so fast, that they could rack up generations of Biblical proportions before she reached the end of a logbook. It always raised the question of how much they had mutated according to the conditions of the lab. I've got some good news and some bad news, she could imagine Olympia announcing. The good news is that our vaccine works. The bad news is that it only works on birds in our lab.

Olympia and Chen often got into it in ways that were fun to watch, Jak thought, shifting his chair to give him a better view.

"This is curious thing: we have a protein, but we find variation in the protein here, here, and here," he said, pointing at the strings of genetic letters. What does it mean to have variability in the peptide region? Answer: variability in protein depends on the response of the host." He explained how the genes in the saliva could respond to the environment. "If you change the host, you change the blood source that the louse feeds on, and the proteins in the saliva of the louse can change in response. This is why proteins in the saliva from sand flies taken from rodents in the field are different from those in the saliva of the same species taken from urban areas where their blood supply also contains humans. The flies that jump to humans produce more saliva because they need more saliva to anesthetize the skin of a human than a rodent. Those that did survive long enough to jump back onto a living rodent might also be those most adapted to anesthetize human skin. Over the generations, the DNA sequence of the protein that does the anesthetizing will change. It will have a better chance of survival, and therefore pass on this trait to its host, the species it normally lives on."

"But this doesn't necessarily mean it will cloud our study, right? I mean, the protein that anesthetizes skin will be a different protein than the one that triggers an immune response. And for all we know," she said hopefully, "the protein that gives immunity could be conserved across all these different populations. Right?"

"But here is the curious thing: human blood can also change in response to the parasite. This is why we are beginning to see that human blood taken from

Paraguayan natives exhibits an immune response to SP-1, while blood from natives in west Bolivia exhibits an immune response..." He checked his notes. "...to SP-22."

"So are the lice proteins changing in response to the different host blood, or is the blood of the host changing in response to the lice?" Olympia asked, knowing how this last variable could throw the whole study into a spin, the way adding a third body to a gravitational equation makes a relatively straightforward problem hopelessly complicated.

"Big question mark. On this point we must remain silent. At least until we have more data."

"Well that's just great!"

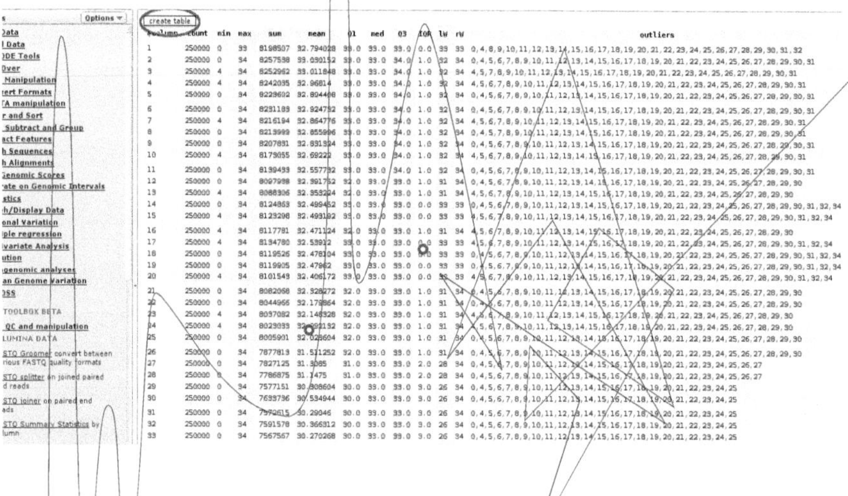

He wasn't a nudist. Never lived in a commune, or seen anyone else naked except guys at the gym. He was probably the only exchange student at *Universität Freiburg* who'd never had to share the bath in a hostel. So when the girls—sisters!—that Fred met in the college pub got a tweet to flash mob on a glacier, he'd eagerly agreed to join in. It was only that night that he found out he'd have to strip naked and pose for photos on the glacier, and he lay in bed worrying that he'd embarrass himself by getting wood.

The next morning, along with hundreds of others, maybe a thousand college students, aged crunchies, office workers, protest veterans, and plain people trying, as was he, to not look confused or self-conscious—as though hiking up a glacier

to strip naked with a thousand other people was something they did every day—he walked the towrope the organizers had set up, Heini ahead of him, in tight rock-climbing shorts, calling back to her sister Heljä in the Finnish he couldn't understand, the two of them giggling as they all went up the access crevasse. "Heini, CAN YOU SEE THE PEAK YET?" Heljä called in English to her sister, who turned, gave him a quick up and down then burst into a hissing laugh she couldn't stifle.

But as they reached the top of the crevasse, and saw the ice field below, a silence fell over the group. He had expected it to look like the old illustration he'd once seen: a mighty river of ice. From the peak where Fred and the sisters stood, the line of protesters snaked down the white slope and into the valley like avatars being born into W.2. They kept moving, the serpentine pattern they formed across the glacier lengthening. The sight of the melting glacier, the mountain peaks—black and stony instead of snowcapped as they used to be—silenced everyone with the gravity of what had brought them there. Though this was Fred's first time to Switzerland, even he could see the glacier was ill, its ice permeable instead of solid. More snowcone than rock crystal.

Then came the order to strip. All around Fred, hundreds of men and women began shedding Birkenstocks, fleece vests, striped knits, Recycle What's Left tees, and Lapland thermals. He unbuttoned his pants, and began pulling them down. When Fred stole a glance at the sisters, they were already down to panties and hiking boots. But to his surprise, even as they stepped out of them there was nothing sexual in it, and together they placed their clothes as bundles on the grid laid out with string so they could find them afterwards.

Throughout the morning, he, the sisters, and the others got into position like pallbearers being told where to stand at a funeral. No one spoke other than the organizers who directed them through bullhorns. "Nicht in die Kamera blickt," the bullhorns would call from time to time, Heini translating for Fred, "Don't look at the camera."

And when the order came over the bullhorns for them all to lie down, he did so naked with the girls on the ice, Heini's unshaved bare legs warm against his unshaved cheek, his own bare legs against Heljä warm face, the sun also warm, the ice cold as a hard sponge, and he closed his eyes imagining how they looked through the cameras trained on them from the top of a ladder, he and the sisters just flesh-colored dots among other dots, a chain of nude people, a necklace looping up and down the glacier as they all lie down with their mother to say goodbye.

ascensionnovel.com/nudes-on-ice

The thing Jak hated about working in Olympia's group was the specialization. Her parasite project required so many sequences that most days all he did was prepare primers, load them in the ABI, then prepare more primers while the first batch ran, the ABI generating reams of AGCTs that Chen and the others would then do their statistical analysis on. It got pretty boring. Like being the guy on the assembly line who put the nut on the bolt that someone ahead of him had greased and someone after him would tighten. Thousands of times a day.

The thing he liked about working in Olympia's group, though, was the dead time he had waiting for reactions to finish, and the fact that The Center was large enough to be divided into labs, each headed up by a different PI, even though the department was small enough so that each lab shared as much equipment and facilities as they could. So while Shakar's lab was working on infectious disease, and Brody-Johnson's lab was working on agriculture, and Olympia's lab was working on disease vectors, all of their insects were kept in a single Insectarium. There, among all the colonies of flies, mosquitoes, spiders, and other insects, it was easy for Jak to hide his bee-toys. Anyone who would come in there to get their weevils, or whatever, and saw his bees would just assume they were part of a project being worked on by another lab in the center.

The same with the equipment: sometimes he was alone with the $15,000 microinjection system that every lab needed but only had occasion to use. Or a $2,000 MammoZapper Cloning Gun just sitting there on a lab bench all lone-some-like. So he'd fallen into messing around with the equipment, first just to see how hard it was to work, then attaching protein 'heads' to DNA 'tails' till he was able to get a geranium to carry his DNA. iFlower, he called it, the video he put online getting, to his surprise, over 10,000 views a day, from all over the world. It even rose to the featured science spot on the BestVidies homepage until the Fun with Science Guys figured out a way to swallow copper chloride, and lit their resulting farts: brilliant green flames that came roaring out of their asses. *Blue (methane) and Yellow (copper chloride) Make Green,* was the title.

Then MyVidie attention shifted elsewhere, allowing his video to quickly fall to the 1,000th spot before fading to the one billionth, then the unranked mass. For the longest time he tried to think of a way to put the power of the lab he had access to behind a BestVidies production that no amateur could hope to produce. Under the *nom-de-net* Dr. Jakel & Mr. Hak, he ordered a pair of mice that had an myostatin gene altered to make them as muscular as bodybuilders. The gene also rewired their brain chemistry in a way that made them aggressive, and he thought he'd figure out a way to get them to wear little Lucha libre costumes and stage a wrestling match. But he had to give it up, lay low, after someone in Animal Oversight came across the mice he was trying to mutate. Olympia made a speech at one of their lab meetings about how she didn't know if the order for the mice came out of her lab or one of the others in the building, but that she'd better not find any of her people "fucking around and getting Animal Oversight on our backs!"

Covering her ass: her and her lice-infested geese. Whatever. Since he'd started messing around again, he did it in a way that was more low-key—no special orders, no equipment or organisms that weren't already in-house—his latest little hobby being an experiment to see if he could alter a bee to dance in a figure 8, like a figure skater, only an 8 with a horizontal axis: infinity.

It seemed doable. Bees naturally did dances that told others in the hive where to find a patch of flowers they'd discovered: for flowers near the hive, foragers simply did a 'round' dance to let the others in the colony know; if the food was further away, they danced in a 'sickle' pattern before the other bees—which was sort of like a deformed '8' already. It seemed simple enough to alter whatever biological switches were shaping the dance and either get the bees to put two circles together to form the 8, or stretch out the sickle pattern into something that looked more like an infinity symbol.

In the time he had to kill between loading the ABI and outputting its data, he'd been able to locate cornerstone work on *A. mellifera* dance behavior by Boch, 1956, and von Frisch, 1993, then a more recent article that described how the transition from round to sickle dance was controlled by a single gene, following a dominant/recessive model. Old-school; Mendel stuff: complex behavior like dancing, or stinging, under simple genetic control. Anyone could do it, but just to make sure Olympia didn't find out he was doing it at work, he hid his downloads on the lab computer Mohammed used. Within a week, he was artificially inseminating a couple of virgin queen *A. mellifera* with chromosomes that he hoped would cause a stutter in their step, make them dance double. A two-step. So sure was he that it would work that he'd spliced in the GFP gene that gave off the greenish glow of some tropical fish. If he could make it work, the patterns his bees flew in would leave a light trace behind, like dancers carrying glow sticks across a dark stage. Cool!

Emerging from the claustrophobic heat and humidity of the Insectarium into the air-conditioning of the hallway was always like emerging from a sauna. Gabe headed up the three flights to the communal lab, feeling like The Swamp Thing come to sit among humans. For the last few weeks, the stairs seemed steeper, taking as much wind as climbing a bell tower. At the end of her climb, once she reached the third floor, the communal lab was airy, fluorescent-bright. And full of people moving about their own tasks, talking, or not, the way people worked together in an art studio, office, or any normal room.... "How's it goin' Gabe," Meadow greeted, carrying a tray of cultures to her own station.

"Slow," Gabe sighed, feeling more tired than she should. She went to the refrigerated case and rummaged among the vials, thimbles of lice saliva that should have been put in deep freeze, test tubes of blood, and petri dishes till she found the jar of plain yogurt that she had cultured at home. Her lunch.

Lab benches ran the length of the room forming three aisles, the cabinets and shelves above the benches packed with manuals and microscopes and centrifuges and chrome gadgets. The first time Gabe saw the place it looked like a rummage sale: beakers and aspirators, agitators and boxes of film left where they were last used. Test tubes that needed washing were heaped in the sink. Olympia was always on them—a mom on her kids for leaving dirty reactants lying around their room. "Some of that shit is dangerous!" And you'd think they'd keep the place clean themselves. The techs didn't have offices as did 'the talent,' Olympia, Mohammed, Chen, and other lab managers or directors. Mostly, 'the kids' just camped out, gravitating to an area that housed the equipment they needed to do their part of the study. So the chair in front of the microscope that Silpa used throughout the day became Silpa's chair; the middle section of the middle lab bench that Gretchen used to prepare tissues had become her turf. Photos of Mohammed's family back in Venezuela were taped to the metal cabinets above the section of the lab bench where he prepared Western Blot analysis cells. While in the next aisle over, Meadow's jacket laid across the stool before a rack of heavy protocol manuals, photos of her sister's wedding and her hunting dog. She'd taken down the photo of her husband, Gabe noticed.

Jak was snickering at something on his computer screen—fucking around, trying to get the Tweet-a-Smile campaign to retweet meth formulas again, no doubt. She really didn't do much in this part of the lab other than check email or jump online to order supplies. But every morning she threw her sack lunch and bike helmet on the far corner of the far bench no one used, and from habit it had become her turf: where she took breaks, where she went when she wanted to be around people instead of lice. She moved aside the paperback she'd been carrying around—*Fahrenheit 451*—on real paper that she liked to be seen with instead of an iReader or iFlex, the way some people positioned an arm, when sitting, so you could see their NGer tattoos. She moved the mouse to wake up her computer—it wasn't really hers, more of a communal computer—when the screen came alive, she saw that someone had been using it to research bees.

"Check this out," Jak said from his stool across the aisle, swiveling his monitor so she could see.

Olympia knew why Victor Frankenstein made his monster. She'd been in her office, pushing her Sisyphus Stone—grant applications—the first time she spoke to Brian, the venture capitalist. He'd been trolling *Parasite Studies,* looking for projects like hers that had commercial potential, he'd explained—academic research that could be flipped the way real estate speculators flipped condos, she imagined—when he came upon her work on disease vectors and sand flies: she'd been trying to engineer a sandfly with receptors in its foregut which would be too small to allow the Leishmania parasite that actually caused the disease—a parasite within a parasite—to attach itself inside the sandfly's stomach. It led him to her suggestion that a protein in bird lice saliva might give humans some immunity against avian flu. He was the one to ask her about engineering an insect to instead vaccinate the birds themselves.

Like getting a little inoculation with every bite, as he put it. She'd agreed to meet him and his partner, Sid. "But not here," she'd insisted, "your place," imagining an office like hers, down the hall from the clutter of insects and test tubes, and she felt like a rube when he gave her an address in the financial district.

In a glass tower, Brian and Sid explained how the biotech she was developing could be turned into dollars: with virus outbreaks becoming as common as hurricanes, the floodgates had opened for virus research to get as many legs up on future threats as possible. Though it hadn't quite reached the level of looking into drinking bleach, Sid joked.

With an infusion of cash, the work her lab was doing on bird lice could tap into it, they thought, given how related it was to avian flu, one of the top candidates for a future outbreak. A technology transfer to bird lice would be an elegant simplification of other insects reengineered to drive out natural populations and their problems: the tsetse fly with a typo in its DNA that would spell the end of its line; pink bollworms that bore larva whose genetic ladders unraveled as they were born....

Ever since labs learned how to reorder The Garden, extinction had been a growth industry, with lots of duds, the way publishers take on hundreds of monster, ghost, witch and wizard novels in the hopes that one will be the next *Harry Potter.* And it wasn't as if going commercial hadn't occurred to her. But she didn't want to just give away her hand before negotiations even began. So she pressed them on the other thing she thought: that Big Pharma wouldn't bother with the academic issues she worked on: problems with no solutions. Or, what was the same, solutions to problems that didn't plague people. If by 'problems' you meant problems that could be solved with patents. If by 'people' you meant people in Armani suits like the one Brian wore the first time she met him and Sid: two ruddy, middle-aged businessmen who like all their brethren wanted wrinkle-free faces, solid memories, and erect penises into their dotage. Not people with sores from dengue and the scores of other diseases that plagued the bottom-dollar Bottom Billion.

But that was old-school thinking, Brian explained, by which he meant, thinking before Bottom Billion diseases began showing up on Florida golf courses.

The bump up in scale they assumed was as disorienting as the time her grade-school project won the All State Science Fair, and an image of herself in pigtails and braces, explaining her tin-can and drinking-straw display to adult judges with the power to take it global was too much to comprehend, even after they laid out how it could happen.

She gave a laugh, the two men more like genies who would turn back into smoke and return to their prescription bottle.

"What's so funny?" Brian asked, smiling to be let in on the joke.

She told him: the implausibility of all the dominoes lining up in the order they needed for them to fall the way they were thinking. She knew she wasn't telling them anything they didn't know: that pharmaceuticals came into the world less because they were invented than because they precipitated from a cloud of university labs, professors, marketers, lawyers, commercial labs, the military, health clinics, government agencies, grants, regulations, congressmen promoting business in their state, lobbyists, chemical companies supplying the raw materials, equipment manufacturers, information architects, ad agencies, publishers, investors, and venture capitalists, like them....

"At this point we don't even know if there is a single saliva protein that triggers an immune response, let alone the genes that create it. It might be two genes. Or three. Or a different combination for every louse population...."

"Maybe we concentrate on waterfowl, the most common carrier. We didn't think there wouldn't be unknowns. That's why it's an investment."

"Gamble, you mean."

"Shhh. Never use that word with investors," Brian said, toying with a chrome letter opener. When it caught the light, the embossed name of an antidepressant manufacturer gleamed. "You have to remember, 'effectiveness' has as many definitions as there are stockholders. How else could companies like Pfizer and Eli Lilly and Merck make profits off of drugs for Alzheimer's that only work in one of three patients? Chemotherapy for cancer?—it's 'effective,' that is, it shrinks tumors by 50%—in a quarter of the patients. That might not seem like a successful drug until you consider that 100% of the patients pay up to $18,000 per year. Would an automaker call a model a success if the brakes worked half of the time in half of the cars? They would if nobody had a better option. Last year the sales of these drugs totaled $584 billion."

"Wonderful," Olympia said flatly, thinking of her father; before he died, he'd been on Merck's Fosamax, a bone-building drug for the elderly that also turned out to make skeletons so brittle that a person's leg could break from the stress of just standing; some femurs had sheared so cleanly that insurance adjusters thought they were looking at X-rays from auto accidents. But Olympia hadn't meant to sound sarcastic. Really she was just tired. Most of the people she came in contact with thought that because she worked on insects that plagued the poor, she must be some kind of Mother Theresa. So she let them.

Brian winced cartoonishly. "All Sid means is that you have to think of your project in terms of where it could go, not where it is. That's been the MO of biotech since the first genetically new-and-improved chicken was shown to be 10% heavier than the old-fashioned, natural kind, even though in practice it turned out to be 200% more susceptible to feed-lot disease. Even today, only 50 of the 400 publicly traded biotech companies make profits. The rest are in the business of The Future."

Olympia paused: everyone knew that every lab was making a story about the future, no matter what else it was making. But creating a story in a lab was as clean as it got; not nearly as tangled as their plots could become out in the wild: while there wasn't a vaccine against Lyme disease for humans, there was one—LYMErid, for dogs—that worked on mice. So when ForestFree Labs engineered a mouse with the LYMErid sequence, along with the gene drive needed to override natural selection, they released the engineered mice onto one small isolated island to test the results. As predicted, the mutation spread throughout the entire wild population. As predicted, the mouse population became immune to the ticks that bit them. What wasn't predicted was that some of the ticks would mutate in response; that they would begin to carry a more virulent form of Lyme disease; that a hawk would catch a mouse carrying one of these more virulent ticks; that the hawk would drop the mouse close enough to the mainland for it to swim ashore, where super-Lyme disease spread among humans faster than ever.

Even field tests of technologies as old as sterile-insect engineering weren't straightforward: when *Aedes aegypti* were engineered to die young, they bred with other species and all mosquito populations crashed, and so the herds of caribou that used to migrate into the wind to escape their swarms abandoned their routes; wolves that used to eat those caribou starved, as did dragonflies that ate mosquitos; as dragonfly populations died out, so did the toads, frogs, herons, and fish that ate them; so did the foxes, bobcats, and larger animals that ate frogs and herons.... For lack of a mosquito the food chain was lost. Or so said field tests.

The fickle nature of scientific truth.... And everyone using it to edit the story of Nature.

Sid and Brian exchanged a look. "If we were just in it for the money," Sid said, "we'd be selling candy-flavored vaping cartridges to kids. Or better yet, Oralet—the narcotic lollipops banned here but still sold in over 60 Bottom Billion countries...."

"Olympia," Brian said, cutting in to silence Sid. "Your project is good. Something real. All Sid means is that a nation with a more streamlined command structure..."

A dictatorship.

"...might welcome a program that was cheap enough to actually use even if it wasn't as effective. Just think of the legal fights that break out over every new virus." He was referring to the last outbreak during which the Indonesian government wouldn't let the WHO or any other neocolonialists, as they put it, come in, take their 'resources,' that is, 'their' virus, to develop a vaccine that Indonesia couldn't afford. "The French, the Wing Foundation, and CDC are still fighting over who owns Ebola, Patent No. CA2741523A1. But if you could turn birds in the wild into living pharmacies...."

They let the implications of this idea swell. Everyone took a breath. Then Brian asked her to speculate about the most obvious problem: how, even if it was possible to trigger an immune response in birds, how it could be used to inoculate a wild population, and her mind flashed to Victor Frankenstein—he made his monster because he couldn't stand not knowing whether or not he could do it.

On poultry farms, it was an easy matter to put a vaccine into the animals' food. But this wouldn't work with birds spread across continents. So, okay, she wrote them her fantasy novel, explaining how the very insect that made the protein might be turned into a delivery system. A method that was patentable, Sid was happy to point out. If her lab was able to identify a protein or proteins in lice saliva that would give birds immunity, they could create a louse with a genetically enhanced ability to create it. Maybe start with a louse like Amblycera that already fed on blood and was a generalist that could range across bird species. Using CRISPR, they could give the louse an enhanced propensity to bite, give it a gene-drive to spread throughout the louse population. Then they could let that louse loose in the wild where it would spread among wild birds like a plague itself. Only this would be a healing plague: a buffer between humans and virus. "Remove the avian from avian flu and the cycle of transmission collapses." She sat back. She kept wearing her poker face though the idea of having a lab that could actually pull off her fantasy made her breathe quicker. The way they put it, there was all that money flying through the air and she only had to snag some. Who knows, maybe they were right. She couldn't help but think of the biologist in her first lab who'd come up with a way to cut genetic strings that wasn't really any better than the enzyme cutting everyone already used. After trying for years to get backing here in Chicago, he moved to San Francisco, hooked up with financiers who set him up with research space and sold the company a year later for $350 million. If he had gone through the tech transfer department at his university, he would have gotten less than a fourth of that.

Like they said, even if they never made a product, there were bound to be spinoffs that she couldn't even imagine....

Last she heard, that ex-colleague had built a home in the South Pacific and gave a TEDx lecture on one of his hobbies: the search for Amelia Earhart's plane....

"This is a lot to digest," she said.

At work one day, Meadow discovered an app that would allow her to simultaneously hear all the music that was washing over the entire globe of W.2: K-pop stars promoting live tours; aborigines beating tortoise-shell drums; conductors leading performances of Mozart; there was a cacophony of young people furiously fingering frets in the MonsterGuitarCloud competitions, as well as Tibetans chanting their prayers, and every teenager who just cut the sweetest rendition of Metallica's "One" and was uploading it from his bedroom.... And of course, everyone's favorite: cats walking across keyboards. It was a kind of music of the spheres, the music of W.2, an echo of white noise, the hiss of sea foam.

When she switched on a filter to limit what she heard, what she heard first was a flute playing those same 3 notes Nico used to blow. Coincidence? It must have been, though she knew almost nothing online was coincidence: the ads a

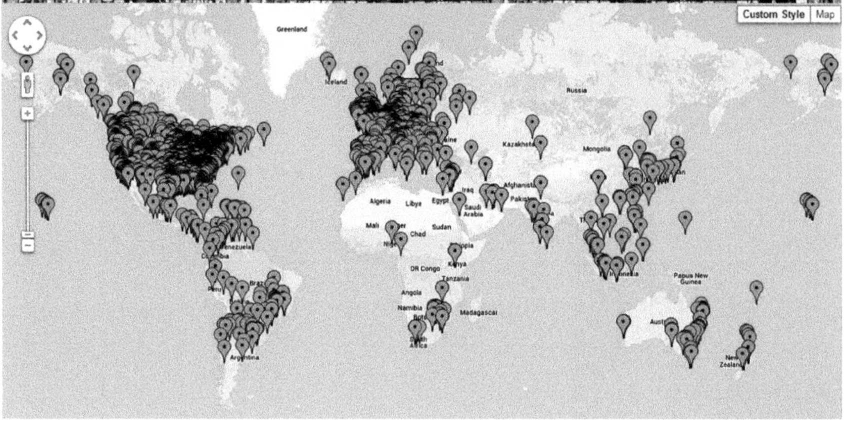

LIVE
Whiteacre Virtual Choir
youtube.com/watch?v=V3rRaL-Czxw

person saw, the news they heard, everything was directed to them out of some algorithm.

She used those three notes as a homing beacon, the flute music growing louder and more distinct as the globe turned, bringing her to a large peaceful valley. It looked like a pastel drawing—soft, flat colors, puffy clouds, and thousands of picnickers, lounging on blankets. Here and there helium balloons bobbed with the too-regular rhythm of programming trying to mimic wind; the breeze brought to her snatches of one of those last-century hippie songs with its lyrics about being stardust—*billion-year-old carbon...caught in the devil's bargain*—and the need to get back to The Garden.

LIVE•
Crosby, Stills, Nash & Young
youtube.com/watch?v=4lx86B6a3kc

Several flags sported the multi-colored rainbow of the LGBTQIAprog+ Nation. Long stretches of the valley were spanned by strings of Tibetan prayer flags. *Billion-year-old carbon.* Carbon nanotubes. That's what AI chips were made out of too, she thought, and she had to smile at how many people mythologized the 1960s just because, back then, scraggly hippies in bellbottoms came up with Earth Day. Were those 1960s reenactors here? They took turns playing No Nukes or Selma protestors and riot cops, sometimes armed with homemade water cannons. So she kept an eye out to avoid them as she wandered the audience gathered for an outdoor concert, listening for the notes of the flute she'd heard, looking for Nico among the middle-aged couples with picnic baskets, wine glasses, and candelabras. The mosaic of people seemed to go on forever. A Frisbee sailed past....

The note suddenly sounded nearby; she made that knob-turning gesture to turn her avatar, searching the other avatars to see which had a flute. Then she saw him: a vendor, like those in Indonesia who went among beach loungers, selling fruit drinks. Periodically he blew in the red flute he carried to get people's attention—just like the flute they'd bought for Nico.

Meadow's heart beat faster as she kicked her fingers into a jog. As she neared, though, his form suddenly began to vanish. "Wait!" she typed, hitting the Shout key. But the avatar's body had already begun to turn into that generic nude doll all avatars began life as and returned to when their owners logged off. Before her eyes, he deteriorated into pixels. Gone. Offline. Or else teleported to a different location.

But at her feet was the flute. A red flute exactly like the one they'd bought for Nico. The match it had made to his red hair had had mystical significance to a four-year-old. She picked it up, and read its embossing: Pyramid.com.

A week later Meadow got another email: LIVE.NATION: *Offering concert tickets worldwide!!!!!* An animation showed a W.2 version of a Tech-Jockey conducting music with a Z-Game controller like Nico used to play with. In the background, she saw robots—like Nico used to draw—and red flutes—huge red flutes, like his flute. Was someone trying to tell her something?

Or was she losing her mind?—seeing traces of Nico in every flower in every crannied wall?

The flute in her bag was real, though, delivered by FedEx. And the coincidences seemed too lucky to be coincidences—even if everything online was shaped to give everyone whatever they wanted: the tragedy of the latest school shooting a reason for gun control in the news feeds Meadow read, while she was sure that RedHatters were reading that the only way to prevent such school shootings would be to arm each student—or that the school shooting itself was a hoax that never happened—and each side thinking the other crazy for letting school shootings go on. Had she just been a victim of that?—the 'boy' who'd left the flute for her an influencer-bot, or spam-atar?

One Night Only!!!! There was a link to the W.2 location where a virtual simulcast of the concert would be held. Tomorrow night. If she bought a pair of VR goggles, and stayed after work she could go to the W.2 concert using the lab's Internet3 connection. The university sat right on a node, and its extra bandwidth and wavelength grooming would let her experience the concert live instead of typing in her words the way she did when everyone was in the lab during the day. Or was all of this just a come-on to get her to buy more equipment?

She could hear Gabe and Jak talking in the next aisle: "You doing Da Tour this year?"

Jak was asking Gabe about the illegal bike race that she had competed in for the past three years. It was modeled on the Tour de France except Da Tour stayed within the city limits of Chicago, with Chinatown, Little Italy, Boystown and other Chicago neighborhoods standing in for stages. It was over in hours instead of weeks. But like Le Tour, Da Tour was usually determined by its mountain stage: a series of staircases through city parks, culminating in a race by riders carrying their bikes up 20 to 40 flights of high-rise stairs. Most of the competitors were financial advisors, graphic designers and others who only biked to work or did road trips on weekends. Still, they often gave the pros a run for the yellow jersey because, some said, they didn't have enough fear of traffic. They'd have enough this year, though, Gabe thought.

Because Da Tour was illegal, it all had to be done under the radar. Just before it was about to start, a tweet would go out announcing the location of the starting line and racers would have about fifteen minutes to form a flashmob there. A gun would go off in the earbuds they wore, and the first leg of the route would be announced. As they raced, they'd get updates on the route, the race-DJ changing the route by monitoring police movements, and redirecting the route of the race to keep ahead of cops who would be trying to shut it down. So the racers had to pay attention to the stream of chatter coming through their earbuds as well as each other as well as the car and truck traffic on the streets.

Last year, two of the competitors had been bearing down on the Uptown finish line, pumping hard to win the stage, neck and neck, a game of chicken with neither willing to brake for the traffic light that turned red. As they shot into the Broadway-Argyle intersection they were simultaneously hit by a fish truck. Flattened like flies. Gabe had been back in the pack, but close enough to see it all.

It had really shaken her up. *There but for the grace of God....* She had an indelible image in her mind of their ghost bikes: a matched pair of Treks, chained to a post at the intersection as a memorial—the two bikes in a dead heat forever—tires, handlebars, saddle, frame, all spray painted the same ghostly white. She'd come upon them while riding home just the other night, the white outlines of the bikes caught in the beam of her headlamp.

"I don't know," she said softly to Jak. "I'm still thinking about it."

Meadow continued surveying the libraries of transgenic organisms that Olympia asked her to monitor. Lots of trans-gen insects designed to solve the problems caused by the introduction of previous trans-gen insects: the RiBeetle® designed to eat the larva of the BeetleSanto® which had been created to eradicate the Colorado potato beetle, which had developed resistance to insecticides, but with the rising heat of the planet had become invasive in many regions where previously it couldn't live. Funny, she thought, how like the nuclear bomb or Prozac, or cars that drove themselves, no one wanted this world, yet here it was.

Most of the new patents were for strains of crops and animals that could withstand the droughts that were creeping all over the globe, and the companies out there seemed to be trying anything to get an edge: *Agrobacterium sp.* bacteria inserted into soybeans to make a version of soybeans more resistant to herbicides developed for drought-resistant crops; a gene from the Lepidoptera pathogen microorganism *Bacillus thuringiensis* had been inserted into corn genome to produce the Bt toxins that would poison the insects that had crept north; rice engineered to produce higher levels of beta carotene; NuCOTN cotton engineered to carry a toxin that kills caterpillars by paralyzing their guts....

Every time she visited one of these ordering sites, she couldn't believe how many more plants and animals were on offer, labs all over the world domesticating molecules as if they were sheep, editing the poem that had been a chicken, pig, mouse, or plant to make a new version. Zeno's Paradox: the logic by which Achilles could never actually catch the tortoise because no matter how often he halved the distance between them, it could always be halved again. Only here, as played out in the bodies of these tortoises, it was made literal: the gene inserted within CRF1, 59-GAG(G/A)T(T/C)TAGTTGA(T/C)ATTAG-39, positions 2229 to 2208 in the tortoise's tRNA to create a line that would be susceptible to cancer; then the GFP gene of a jellyfish was added between those two new positions so that the line that was susceptible to cancer would develop tumors that glowed a neon green, and suddenly where there had only been the single, standard-issue line of tortoise, there were four. These four lines became eight with the patenting of a third genetic variable: a propensity to make tortoises obese. When used in combination with the other variable genes, the eight lines became 16, then 32, then 64. Then 64 became 128, 128 became 256, 512, 1,024 with the ability to knock out genetic switches similar to those that had been added. CR1-like LINEs differing at the 39 end of the tortoise Pol III/SINE isolated from *Chinemys reevesii*....

There were so many kinds of tortoises now—a whole spectrum of tortoises with more shades of disease or genetic propensity than there were hues in a color wheel; when she bent her finger to scroll, their technical descriptions whizzed

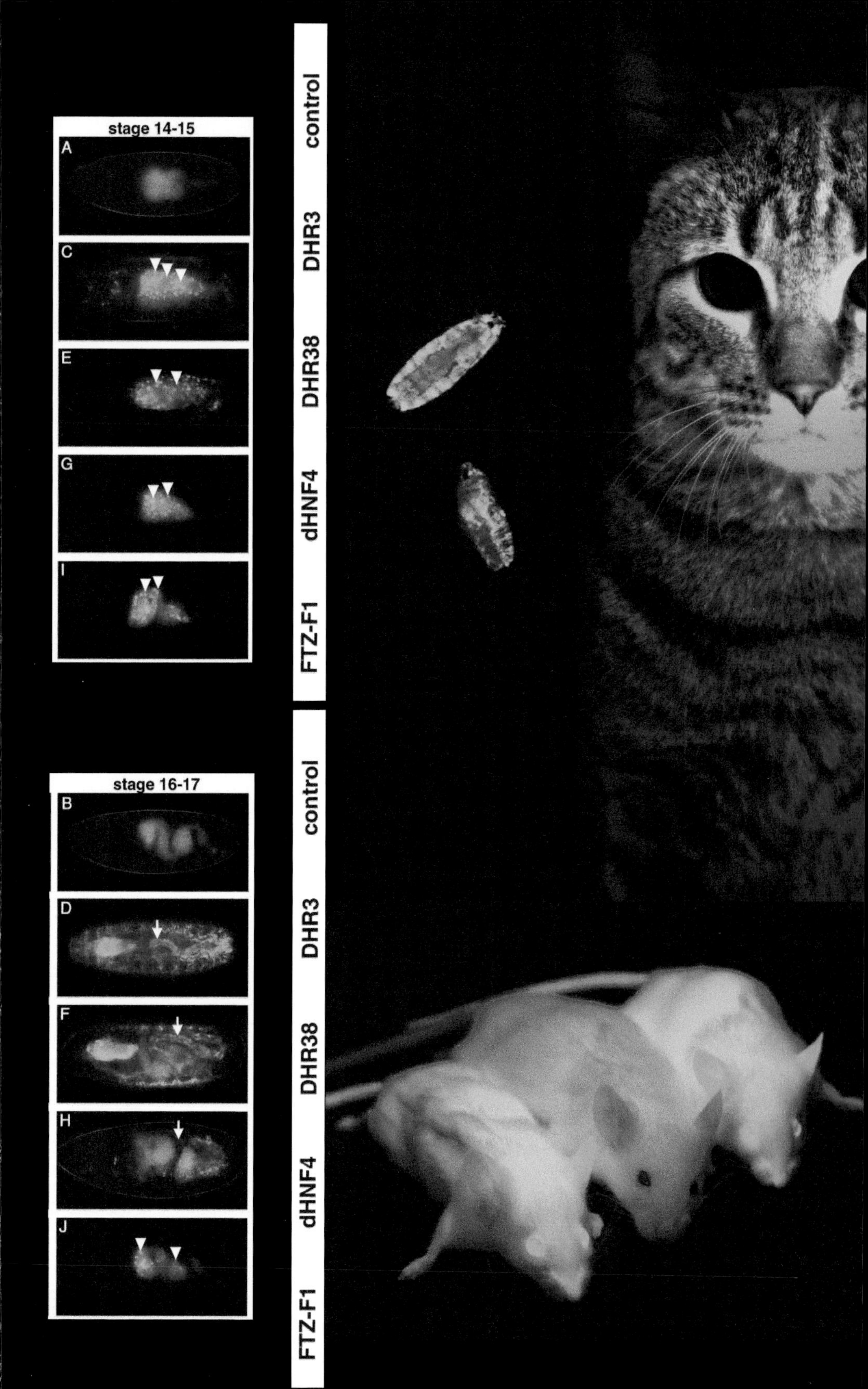

stage 14-15
A
C
E
G
I
control
DHR3
DHR38
dHNF4
FTZ-F1
stage 16-17
B
D
F
H
J
control
DHR3
DHR38
dHNF4
FTZ-F1

down the screen, the meaning of the word 'tortoise' needing so many qualifiers that to say 'tortoise' now was to say nothing....

Same with 'friend,' 'natural,' and all the old words.... Even 'Earth,' now that the Galileo Massive Cloud Orbiting Telescope had begun sending back pictures of an Earthlike planet, its continents and oceans an echo on the original Blue Marble Earth. Only this planet was tinted red—Red Marble Earth—'nearby' though of course impossible to reach: gasoline on the fire of religious fanatics who went around proclaiming it as a portend of the end of this world....

So many, I had not thought life had brought into existence so many, she thought. Last night, texting her husband hadn't gone so bad. She'd typed 'separation' then backspaced to erase it, changing it to 'time away from each other.' But if she'd mentally crossed that line, he probably had too. When she hit the send key, though, she found herself holding her breath, staring at the screen to see if he'd use the 'S' word. Or worse, the 'D' word. There was a long pause. Agonizingly long. Then the words 'I miss you' came on-screen. They'd changed the subject, but the various marketing bots had caught on, pop-up ads for marriage counselors blooming on her screen—and surely his—until they both texted 'good night.'

Progress, Meadow thought wistfully, scrolling through the database of trans-g insects. One becomes two, two becomes four, blink your eyes and you're up to 2,048....

When she recalled how everyone used to use *Drosophilidae* in genetic research because of its large chromosomes, not the hundreds of genetically-created fruit flies that labs used today.... When she thought of the fields and streams beyond the screen, it seemed as though she were living one of those Sci-Fi comics Gabe drew: a world where the whole globe was paying for ignoring the first law of parasites: *if the parasites grow too weak, the host kills them; if the parasites grow too strong, they kill the host, and then they both die.*

Easy to forget, given that the odds had been so heavily weighted in favor of the host—the Earth—for all of human history. For millennium, people applied themselves to learning how to build shelters against the Earth's weather; how to generate heat and cold to defeat its seasons; how to wage war on beetles, claw their way above the whims of nature. But then the Earth's parasites—people—began to become too successful. Too strong. Too numerous. They built too many houses. Owned too many teak countertops. Needed too many trains and planes and automobiles—and plastic cafeteria trays, and TV shows and billion-watt casinos, not caring how much they heated the air outside in order make an artificial arctic indoors. Their efforts to combat their host, their mother, grew too potent as they found ever-more efficient ways to convert her lungs into lumber, her veins into rails and smoke, their numbers and efforts fouling her breath, her rivers, and now their host was dying. And when it died so would they. At least enough of them to put the Earth back into?—What? Not the balance those Paraguayan Indians used to believe in. For surely the Earth was just the Earth: what matter to the Earth if there were two or no ice caps? The Earth would go on completely covered in water as it once was or as the scorching desert it seemed determined to become.

When she thought of the people from her parents' generation who must have seen this coming her heart ached: some had started projects like the Seed Ark. They understood that the plants and animals that could be found on the prairies had been an absolute kaleidoscope before they'd been reduced to the monochrome bandwidth of field weeds. And they worked to make it possible for some future generation to do for the whole Earth what they'd done for prairies. Restore ten percent. That had been the goal they set, squirreling away seeds in a vault in the Arctic.

Before the vault was flooded by a melting Arctic.

LIVE

Wave Pool in Japan

youtube.com/watch?v=PAZGkbJHzSY

All those well-intentioned people back in 2005, or 2010—or even as late as 2020—thinking they could make a difference with their butterfly nets and garden trowels.... She couldn't help but give a little, sarcastic snort, looking at the logo on the blue recycling bin: arrows arranged as time's snake eating its own tail—a closed loop—earnest gardeners with trowels rearranging flowers on the *Titanic*....

The list of transgenic insects on her screen was suddenly replaced with her screen saver: a picture of Magnolia, her springer spaniel. The dog looked so happy that Meadow smiled to think of the day she'd shot that photo. They'd been back home in Oregon, a craving brought on by the dog's arrangement of DNA causing

it to chase down rabbits, sniff through the undergrowth. Like her, that's where its biology was most in tune with its surroundings.

She'd always known that biology was more created than born, of course: a Chihuahua—a living toy made out of a wolf—could no more exist in the wild than any other freak of nature, and Magnolia was no different: fed on food created in factories. From fish that had been caught by Bottom Billion refugees, forced to work like the enslaved, she'd found out. After moving here to the Midwest, Meadow had had to keep Magnolia on Flea-Guard all year round because the winters in the Midwest didn't get cold enough to kill off fleas anymore.

Now, looking at the photo of Magnolia, remembering the wool leggings she wore in the photo but had since packed away for good, Meadow wondered if nature had always been a slave to human imagination—a habit of mind as surely as a nation's art or architecture reflected its time and place: the Sistine Ceiling's God-Giving-Life-to-Adam morphing into Frankenstein's monster receiving his bolt of lightning.

Across the lab she could see Jak and Gabe looking at something on his screen, probably grossing each other out as they liked to do with old photos of dirty and dangerous things that people used to do: the French kissing hello; strangers crowding into wave pools; and most disgusting of all, kids blowing on birthday cakes.... To them 'nature' always included fantasy animals without the fantasy. The body, as packets of data. Patentable. Rearrangeable as new bodies. This is what Olympia wanted to do with the lice: create a louse with enlarged salivary glands that will create a lot of SP-12. Bioinformatics. Designer unicorns, why not? At some point, animal species would be created in labs faster than they could go extinct in the wild. Maybe they were already. Looking at Jak and Gabe, she knew it would only be natural, a nature that would eventually become in its turn naïve, simple and antique to those who followed....

You could pick out the fields serviced by Beebot Inc. from the buzzing—but it wasn't the buzz of insects that used to hum in hot fields. Instead it was the whir of tiny, high-speed motors: the tiny bee-drones that had been developed to pollinate crops after real bees died off in such numbers that markets couldn't depend on them any longer. Sunlight glinted off their propellers as they worked an expansive cantaloupe field, their whisper rising to a whine as the motors momentarily ran faster to reposition the bee-drones, bringing each back to the blossom it had been pollinating when lifted away by a breeze. They outlined the leading edge of the gust the way a shiver runs through field grass, gently rising then falling like a sea full of corks riding leafy, green swells....

The cantaloupe fields down the road were silent—except for the occasional sound of Spanish. Or Bengali. Or Urdu. When José stood to give his aching back relief, he could look across rows of migrants bent to their task, working their way down the field of cantaloupe plants they had been hired to pollinate. He had heard myths of men being turned into horses, or women into spiders. But never had he imagined, back in Chiapas, that when he finally made it to California, he would become a bee. Thinking back now, though, it seemed as if he had been moving toward this fate from the start. Setting out alone one dawn, he was joined on the road by two, then eight other men just like him, and moving toward their destiny. By the time they reached the border their numbers had swelled into that of a swarm. Some died as fish trying to swim across; he was turned into a mule in exchange for the protection of the cartel that helped get him, or rather the cargo he carried, under that fake wall....

Now here he was, a bee. RedHatters blamed Mexicans for the bee die-off and there might be some truth in it—if prayers could kill. He kissed the crucifix hanging from his neck—for God, a benevolent God who knows the destiny of all, had obviously been making the bees in America die—just as He had set a plague of locust on Egypt. José dug among the broad green leafs, found a male blossom and plucked it, his hands too calloused to feel the velvety smoothness of their yellow petals as he rubbed the stamens into a female bloom. In three months a large cantaloupe would be ready to be picked and farms like this would need more men and women like him, and the poor, whom God loves most, would at least get a smell of honey....

Across the street, campesinos lined up at the same day-labor office that had hired him and hundreds of Aché Indians over six years ago. Now, flat on his back in the park across from it, Roque Samudio waited to be nailed to a cross. He closed his eyes against the brightness of the sky as the medicos used a cotton ball and alcohol—cold—to clean his palm. They had to scrub roughly because its creases were deep: a work-roughened map of the construction sites he had worked since running away as a teenager. He'd always thought that he and the millions of bricks that he must have hauled over his 60-some years were the same deep, rust red because they were both made of the same Paraguayan clay. But when the medicos finished cleaning his palm, it was shockingly white, as though they had managed to wipe away a stain. His original sin.

One of the medicos held up a syringe, tapping it. Roque closed his eyes. He winced at the pinch of the needle.

"Calmate, hermano, calmate." It was Jacinto, whom he had grown up with, and gone to catechism with when the missionaries brought them into the village after their parents had been killed in the war for the forest. He wouldn't be here today if not for Jacinto—and that Game&Watch they'd been given, out of pity he supposed, by some Russian engineers back when they were kids. They'd played it so much that Priest took it away, and Roque smiled to think how scared they'd been when, after stealing it back, they'd headed into the forest as porters

for that woman scientist who'd come to their village. When they'd come upon that skinned monkey—the devil himself, they'd thought—they'd run away for good: afraid of soldiers in the forest, afraid to go back to Priest. Decades later, here they were, still together, volunteering to be crucified in the hopes that it would shame Unicom, the company that had used them and hundreds of others to expand the Itaipu Dam, and then never paid them.

"Priest always said we are all Christ, but I don't think he meant this, no?" Jacinto joked from his own crucifix, still playing the part of the older brother. "It's not so bad."

And in fact, it took Roque a moment to realize that the pounding that shook the cross he lay on was from the force of the doctor nailing his palm to its crossbeam.

When the medic moved to numb his other palm, Roque could see the workers who'd already taken a turn on the cross. *Somos Los Paraguayos Que Hemos Construido La Usina de Itaipu,* said one of their signs.

Roque smiled back weakly. Maybe they would all have to be crucified before anyone got paid. Maybe they would all just end up with holes in their hands. But the mayor was getting fed up with the sight of workers being crucified in the park and the tourists they attracted. Even now Roque could see a group of Japanese teenagers, posing before a phone at the end of a stick as they jostled to position themselves so that he on his cross would appear in the background of their group selfie.

A cantaloupe was a node, on a vine of other nodes that include chemical factories, the dance of bees, sunlight, microelectronics, rain, refugees, immigration laws, civil wars, and thousands of other factors, Andrew considered, standing in the field to observe his bee-drones at work when a caravan of black buses rushed by on the highway beyond the fence. Prison-mesh windows. They were headed for Family Fresh Farm

Inc. down the road. The illegal BBs who'd been pollinating their cantaloupes must be finishing the job, and the owners of the farm must have reported them to ICE. Andrew sighed. When he'd switched his pollination business over to beebots, he'd graphed their falling cost against the rising cost of real bees, which he'd had to work like migrants, hauling them from field to field across distances no natural bee would ever fly, and working them to exhaustion. He'd expected the lines to cross within two years. But he hadn't factored in how many refugees would be willing to work like bees—always new swarms—like locusts—a force of nature itself—and not even Mother Nature could compete against labor costs of zero. He could have bought into the NuNature franchise: the company that enclosed acres then pumped in a dense cloud of pollinating gas. But beebots had seemed so much more natural than a gas chamber. Organic. Just then, a bee-eating wasp, *Philanthus*, captured one of his beebots in its embrace right before him. As it tried to squeeze honey out of it, a praying mantis grabbed the wasp. The wasp continued to squeeze, refusing to let go of the drone, even as it was being eaten by the mantis, and the sight of the wasp treating a drone exactly as it would a real bee seemed a sign—delivered specifically to him—that God takes care of those who take care of The Garden, just as Rev. Jimmy said.

From her side of the glass, Silpa could see Gabe and Jak out in the lab, his grin lit by the glow of his screen like some old lech intent on a peepshow. Gabe was beside him, arms crossed disapprovingly, though she continued to watch. The fact that he'd rotated the screen gave Silpa a sickish feeling. No doubt he'd come across more video posted from one of the conflict zones. Most of them had been shot with phones then put online to show soldiers like Guy being beheaded, or blown to bits, or burning in their wrecked Hummers.... The first time he'd found the site that collected them, he'd excitedly pulled Silpa over to his computer, showing her a video of an American medic applying hand pressure to a soldier's abdomen to keep his intestines from spilling out. He gave a low whistle. "Oh man, look at that soft tissue damage." Suddenly a second medic's head appeared in the scene, the medic bending in to give mouth-to-mouth to the downed soldier. "There!" Jak excitedly yelled, pointing at the medic. "Is that him? Is that Guy?" It looked like him but it was hard to tell, the faces of both men hidden by the breath-giving kiss. Then the video jerked, Silpa realizing at the same instant that the video had been taken through the lens of the sniper's rifle-cam, the jerk—a recoil—coinciding with a bullet ripping through the heads of both the medic and solider he was helping.... "Let me play it again!" Jak said, as though it were no more real than W.2.

"Are you using the sink?" Silpa asked, standing there with a rack of test tubes. Mohammed looked at her as though she had called him a name before shaking his head. What was up with that? she wondered, turning on the faucet as he walked away. For the last few days he'd been acting weird.

The video had been made by teenagers in Paraguay: a homemade version of *Jackass: The Reunion Movie* that showed old men doing the same stupid goofs they used to when they were twenty: driving golf carts into head-on collisions, shooting bottle rockets out of their asses—stupid stuff like that. Some of the original *Jackass* episodes were pretty funny, Gabe had to admit. And she liked their politics—the stunts they pulled to freak out businessmen or bankers or uptight clerks—like the time one of them took a dump in a toilet on the sales floor at Walmart.

But this DIY edition was pathetic: the teenagers had laid the *Jackass* theme song over their own stupid stunts—taking turns riding a bicycle into a cactus patch—only it was all so pointless there: the boys dirt poor, their hair shaggy and dirty. Their beltless pants had been cut off raggedly at the knees and hung on emaciated frames. Not because the waif-life, refugee look was in as it was in the U.S., but because that part of the world kept getting hotter and hotter ever since the monsoons shut down. Their title—*The Land of No Evil*—faded away as they flagged down a beat-to-hell pickup truck. Soon they had one end of a rope tied to its bumper, the other end tied to a wooden door lying on the ground. Three of them got on the door as though it were a surfboard. As the *Jackass* music played, the truck roared off, throwing one immediately; the other two were dragged at high speed across a scrub field, the plume of dirt kicked up by the truck obscuring them as they bounced violently. When it ended, they were so dirt-encrusted and scratched that they looked as though they'd been mauled by jaguars.

"Havin' fun with no money," Jak said. "These are the guys that we're supposed to be afraid of?" he added, referring to RedHat campaigns to scare Americans into invading countries that controlled rare earth elements—Brazil was next, they said—the Lungs of the World. Kill the Lungs and the World Dies, warmongering senators argued, switching from protecting the rights of coal and oil companies, once the planet was past saving, to grabbing what was left. Lots of people thought the U.S. would have invaded already if only because pharmaceutical companies were hot to get the remaining biodiversity. Gabe wasn't sure what to think about an invasion that sometimes seemed like the right action for wrong motives and at other times a very wrong action for wrong motives; and yet again as an immoral action for immoral reasons but one that would have the morally right consequences. Or at least some of the consequences would be good. Why did everything always have to be so muddy?

In the background she could see the horizon—a flat brown line like the EKG of a dead patient.

"Don't you ever do any real work around here?" she asked Jak.

"I *am* working," he said defensively. "Olympia wanted me to see what else I could find on that woman who first speculated that Phthiraptera saliva gave immunity." To impress Gabe, he pulled the article out of a heap of papers. "So old I had to have the librarian over at the LoID fax me a hardcopy." *Precambrian feather louse indicates age of avian - dinosaur split.* Not only had it never been digitized, but it was buried in a footnote in an article that claimed that dinosaurs were only misidentified birds.

"Olympia already knew that."

"Yeah, the article gave the coordinates where the entomologist thought she found ancestral bird lice. This is what came up." He hit return and the globe on-screen turned as it enlarged Paraguay to show an aerial view of abandoned farmland—so brown she almost asked, "Where's the forest?"—stupid question. "But the librarian did put me onto a clip that someone posted at the turn of the century." He brought it up and antique video showed a woman weeping in the rain, kneeling in a clear-cut forest. A nude forest Indian stood behind her, back to the camera, as he shouted at the sky, *"Ywy Mará Ey!"* Thunder rumbled while a text scrawl said, SAVE WHAT'S LEFT! DONATE NOW! "Her research might have been a dud but this clip was one of the first to go viral—even before Star Wars Kid. They say that the money it raised is what saved the Mbaracayú Biodiversity Corridor from looking like this." He clicked on the map and the banjo music started again.

"Good dog," Gabe said, patting his head, then turning back to her own bench. She logged in, then began to eat her yogurt as her email opened. The first was spam that had gotten through the filter. LIVE.NATION: *Offering concert tickets worldwide!!!!!* Video of some twee-boy TJ—so called XactlySo—using a Z-Game controller—product placement 24/7—to play a technopoem the way some hip-hoppers still played turntables; multicolored filaments morphed to become a dandelion's white seed globe, then an Earth globe, becoming in turn a map of the Internet, then a live map of everyone on Earth and their VISA transactions, a crowd of manikin-beautiful posers bobbing in rhythm to industrial trance. *One Night Only!!!! Cover: $345 live / $100 virtual.*

The ad pissed her off. Just as fashion designers began to co-opt the rags worn by refugees, just as Hummer changed the name of the army trucks they sold from The Destroyer to the H_2O-Vehicle, LIVE.NATION had taken on the look of Guerilla Concerts—but none of its politics. They even booked Shasta, the sellout fuck—"Hey man, even rebels gotta eat," he'd tweeted.

No Exit.

But the very next email had SPAM SPAM SPAM in its subject line—robotically-dumb spam filters sure to quarantine it unless a human, like her, white-listed its sender, as she had done. It was from Sir Spam-a-Lot who took spam for penis enlarging pills, low rate loans, bank transfers from Bottom Billion royalty, or whatever, rearranged their words, then sent them out again as poetry. Today's poem was itself an ad for a NO.IT.AN.EVIL concert, and she instantly knew how she'd gotten the first. He had hacked the LIVE.NATION ad, rewrote the name backwards, then resent it to his own list. Same night. Same local. An anti-concert concert. Then the email deleted itself. "I'm so there," she said out loud.

Dan could see that whoever had created XactlySo's lightshow had used visualization software like he used for the real-time branching structure he made to track Olympia's bird virus. The program could give a visualization of how, if not why. But Olympia, like most clients, didn't care about the why. (He knew this because in the next cubicle over, Fred was using the program to model the behavior of clients.) They just wanted the what: prediction was power as was discovered by the first priest to point skyward before an eclipse, the first statistician to predict that the man who appears in 73.3% of the office party photos posted on FB by his secretary doesn't yet know that he'll want a divorce lawyer 3 years (on average) later.

The HiDef screen on his left was filled by the program's controls—a screen some designer like him must have had fun creating, the retro knobs echoing antique mix boards, Moviola film-editing machines, and other analog equipment from the last century, probably everyone who contributed to the software slipping in design or coding puns and in-jokes that would be invisible to everyone except other designers, or mathematicians, or programmers who knew the language.

```
10 PRINT "HELLO WORLD"
20 GO TO 10
```

They say that the last person to know everything there was to know was the scroll librarian in Alexandria just before the building went up in flames, and Dan wondered who'd been the last person on Earth to know everything there was to know about a single software app. He gave a little laugh. As if anyone could know that.

A swipe of the finger and the screen that was his canvas came alive with what looked like a star chart, color coded—green for Environmental Node, blue for Bio Node—but without any of the connecting lines that the ancients used to form constellations.

This stage of a project was always the most fun, giving him as it did the feeling of being there at the beginning. Already a couple nodes had begun to bud. From these buds, vines would grow to show the interconnection of the parameters, creating rhizomes for variables that hadn't been named because neither he nor Olympia knew they existed. Some clients used Eureka Engine Software© to generate laws from raw data: dump in millions of data points of bouncing balls, falling apples, planetary motions, and without knowing anything about physics, gravity, or God's Will, as did Newton, the Eureka Engine© had come up with his three Laws of Motion. It took all of six hours to come up with Heisenberg's uncertainty principle. Now that computers were a lot faster, it was being applied to social and networking problems—problems with multiple variables—and the Eureka Engine© had already generated equations that described many things, though what it was, exactly, that most of the equations described had yet to be discovered. It was like coming up with the equation $E=mc^2$ without knowing what c stood for. Or m. Or E. Physicists, city planners, prison architects, sociologists, bridge engineers, and others would pour in terabytes of relevant data then wait for the Eureka Engine's© oracle-like pronouncements. Often the equations it generated were trivial: formulas relating the number of orange cars to potholes.... Usually they described patterns that were already known: the fact that shoppers who bring children with them into a grocery store buy 15% more grapes, or the correlation between late-night Internet use and poor credit, or between nicknames in an address book and relatives in prison. The most cryptic pronouncements got the most attention, everyone combing through the equations in the hopes that they could find among them an unknown $E=mc^2$ that would reveal itself if only they could divine its variables.

Mostly, though, people used the software for what you'd expect: in another office, analysts were working on the last 50 years of pop songs—over a million songs—looking for patterns in pitch, in harmonies, in volume and language—and sure enough, they'd found the data following what Zipf's law said about cities: that the largest city in a country would be twice as big as the second largest, three times as large as the third; four times as large as the forth. Same with the words of pop songs (Give, Love, Night, Day) and chords (C, A, E♭).... From this they were able to generate the parameters of next year's hit, the drive to make money off of the stupidest shit being the most predictable pattern of all.

That is, no matter how sophisticated the software, its users weren't any more able to reach beyond their mindset than were those first cartographers with their 'Here be dragons.' Or as an astronomer using the software put it, Why is there something instead of nothing? Is it because 'something' is easier to make than nothing or just easier to imagine? Or was nothing so impossible to achieve that it annihilated itself and brought into being something?—and universes were 'as plentiful as blackberries,' including the one that is nothing: 'a closed spherical spacetime of zero radius.'

He wondered. Maybe only the math of Zipf's law was real, our universe an effect of it, an illusion, as is a circle, an artifact of consciousness, or whatever it is that we cross when we pass from something into nothing, that is die....

Stop it, he told himself. Once he began meeting with the biologists, he'd have to switch to his corporate mode, believing like them that there was no chaos, only order, and it could be found in nature, like a coastline before anyone laid a grid over it, or wrote Here Be Dragons across its uncharted parts. And maybe they were right. Black holes, pop songs, whatever, it was all just data to the program. And the only order that mattered would be maps that could lead its users to their song, or....

"Her" vaccine.

Olympia's words, not his. If working with these types had taught him anything it was that they were all about suppressing symptoms, not necessarily curing anything: a cough syrup that removes the cough but not the cold, even if the 'cold' was cancer, nerve disorders, all kinds of nasty shit.

Success was measured in lots of ways she'd told him.

Still, he liked bio projects for how nicely they fit basic templates like the Milgram. Bio was info that went from one address to another by following pathways as fundamental as water seeking its lowest level: information in the form of DNA that had to be handed from one cell to another—the Pony Express, not radio—even if the route could be as simple as it was in 1917, bird to human—creating the genetic foundation upon which all flu deaths ever since are based—or as complex as Covid-24, swapping genes as it crisscrossed from bird to swine to human to whale and back to bird to human. Since birds were the origin of most pandemics, there was speculation that a virus, not a meteor, is what really killed off the dinosaurs. He called up the constraints Olympia had given him:

1 **Manter's Rule** (1955)
Parasites evolve more slowly than their hosts.

2 **Fahrenholz's Rule** (1941)
Parasite phylogeny mirrors host phylogeny.
And so:

3 **Manter's Rule B** (1956)
The more host and parasite are adapted to each other, the longer their associations.

4 **Szidat's Rule** (1960)
The more primitive the host, the more primitive the parasites it harbors.

5 **Eichler's Rule** (1948)
The more different parasites that a host harbors, the larger the evolutionary group to which that host belongs.

6 **Lowrance's Rule** (1990)

Mitochondrial DNA (mtDNA) mutates at a constant rate.
And so:

7 **Holland's Theorem** (2001)

Just as the decay of radioisotope carbon-14 (14C) can be used to date the age of rocks, so mutations in mtDNA can be used to date the age of evolutionary events.

8 **Olympia's Theorem**

mtDNA can be used to forecast future deadly mutations from past data clouds.

They would program the algorithm to be especially attentive to gene swapping between 'people' as nodes were called in the world outside the program: human switchboards where the translations could take place. Or other combinations that had occurred in the past, been suppressed, but could come roaring back. Like the famous PB2 E627K mutation: a string of letters on the virus's genome as clear as the yellow DO NOT CROSS tape around a radioactive site, the danger in this case being a string of AGCTs at position No. 627 on Polymerase Basic Protein 2, where a couple of Gs had had their places taken by a couple of Cs and allowed amino acid E to become lysine, K. Before this mutation, the virus needed the heat of a goose's intestinal tract to breed. Afterwards, it could thrive in the comfortable 98.6 of your neighbor's nose.

A million people had died.

On his desk, Dan's personal PDA began blinking. He hesitated before answering: the company he worked for required employees to install an 'efficiency expert' called MyBuddy on every device they owned so it could track them, even when they were at home sleeping, to 'help' them 'be the most you can be.'™ "Isn't this like the ankle-monitor people under house arrest have to wear?" he asked the woman in HR when she 'asked' him to 'voluntarily' sign their 'permission' form. "Try to not focus on the Big Brother aspects," she said. Then she smirked, turning the monitor on her desk so he could see that their conversation was in the yellow for time spent, but that her vocabulary grade had just gone from a B to a B+ because of the key words she had just worked in.

But he couldn't not think about The Big Brother aspects, couldn't stop resenting them actually, the constant measurement of how many steps he took; how long he was at his desk, or in the john (his blood pressure indicating how much he strained in the john); how many minutes he spent on development; how many on sales, on meetings, on 'personal time' (he got a warning from his 'Buddy' for each of those), on 'Uncategorized time' (another no-no)....

What the hell, he decided, picking up his PDA. Buddy had given him a smiley face for arriving early that morning....

When he opened it, a video began playing. LIVE.NATION: *Offering concert tickets to fans worldwide!!!!!* Video showed XactlySo, kickboxing his lightshow. Even over the PDA, the sound was pretty hot, showing why people called him the Mozart of ringtones: his 'You-got-mail' dings, 'Please reenter your access code' or 'bike-lock keypad' tones all having gone platinum before he was out of his teens. Academics wrote books about him.

One Night Only!!!! exploded as a burst of confetti—a pretty cool touch—*cover: $245 live / $45 VR.* On a map, the warehouse it was going to be held in opened to display all of the iFACE friends who were going: obviously avatars generated by iFACE as a come-on for these kinds of events, cookies examining his bookmarks—lots of design stuff, no sports—to create profiles of women he'd like to meet. One was of a nerdy Asian woman—cute, with thick glasses, i.e., Hollywood Dorky, not Dorky Dorky—with a ceiling's fluorescent lights behind her head to make it look like she snapped her own shot with a laptop's built-in cam (subtext, no guy). *Meet Me! I like web programming but having fun too!...* The software for generating both book and date recommendations was getting pretty good. He might have even believed it if his PDA wasn't displaying several other dorky Asian women, similar as sisters, the way web pages all sort of looked the same because they all used the same code: code, or at least pattern, being the ground of being. But one of the women looked pretty cool. And real.

Three thousand years after the Mediterranean Tsunami, refugees from the Maghreb made rafts out of truck tires, then used them to float out over the sunken city of Atlantis in the hopes that they would be washed ashore in France. Or Spain. Or Italy. They were greeted by thugs who took it upon themselves to tear apart tent cities; they set fire to railroad ties to block trains, and beat the refugees as a message to those who would follow. Other refugees, of course, had no way of getting this message, and arrived the next day.

Was the whole world fighting to get into Detroit? Long after the French named le Détroit—at 'the narrows'—the pinch point between two Great Lakes and so the perfect place to put a fort—after depressions in Eastern Europe and rumors of streets paved with gold brought into existence networks of steerage and a need for processing waves of humans at Ellis Island, after a boom in manufacturing to supply these new populations, after Jim Crow made blacks give up on the South, and automakers lured them north, ballooning Detroit's population from two hundred thousand to two million; long after post-WWII highways, mortgage rates, and automobiles allowed the whites of Detroit to flee to suburbs, and construction destroyed black neighborhoods to create highways that allowed white-collar workers to cross the city to get to offices from which they began to replace workers with robots and move the factories themselves to the unionless South, setting off a series of riots, and leaving behind bakeries, uniform cleaners, schools, delivery trucks, post offices, and hundreds of other enterprises that were no longer needed after the employees themselves began to desert what had become a sinking ship, long after tax streams dried up, and the city declared bankruptcy and streetlights went dark, and pavement began to crumble, and the aging water system sprung thousands of leaks for which there was no money to repair, and over 500 deserted buildings could burn down in a single night because there was no fire department to put them out; long after rain began pouring through the roofs of what had been grand movie palaces, and trees broke through the marble floors of what had been bank lobbies, and the snow howled through skyscrapers that used to have glass in their windows, and the entire city began to look like a modern-day Rome after its fall, and the city, in desperation, auctioned off its last giraffe, its Rembrandt, and whatever other treasures it had left in its zoo and museums in order to keep a minimal staff working its skeletal hospitals, and a few police to handle at least the murders, even if anyone could just park their cars anywhere they wanted, and did, even on the steps of those museums, without anyone there to write a ticket let alone keep order, and what had been a thriving metropolis became a landscape of cavernous factories, mansions gone to ruin, block upon block of residential housing turned into charred frames, or vacant lots that from the air looked like a vast prairie of weeds bisected by a grid of crumbling streets—like the grid that had given away the location of Atlantis on photos of the Mediterranean floor—or a single house that might remain—little house on the postapocalyptic prairie—surrounded by barbed wire to keep scavengers from tearing off its aluminum siding while the owners were at work; or pleasure palaces, neo-classical gems of green-glazed brick with stone mosaics,

and terra-cotta edging, whose roofs had collapsed and were used to store junk cars the way Roman villas became barns for sheep, and squatters moved into ruins, and property values plunged so low that it was said if you bought a parking lot, the city would throw in an abandoned skyscraper; long after a few millionaires began buying up the deserted properties for pennies; after they began renovating space and leasing it to artists for next to nothing, then start-up companies, after rising seas began inundating Miami, Venice, and New Orleans, Providence, and Brooklyn—after most of Bangladesh disappeared; after islands like the Maldives and Fiji vanished under the waves, after snakes overran Florida, droughts burnt up the western states, drying up reservoirs and leaving them with the famous 'bathtub ring'; after the Sahara spread over most of Africa, and the whole world was on the move, Detroit began to look better and better—a Great Lake full of fresh water that the city had successfully defended from companies that tried to bottle it, or pipe it out west, mild winters, long beautiful springs and autumns, the one zone in America that wasn't either burning with drought or under water—a freak of nature created by the airstream....

Multiply this exponentially: storms drive seas up the Ganges tributaries, turning what had been the village's fresh water supply brackish; brackish water floods fields, leaving them white with salt. Trees die. Village women search the muddy bottom of shallow seas that had been fields for roots that could be burnt as firewood; crops fail; farmers sell their youngest children to pay for seeds; after two years of near starvation, they move inland, but the slums there are even more crowded, bursting with refugees already driven there, so they decide to keep moving, to take their chances on rafts made of truck tires, or cross war zones.... They've heard of a mythical land, called Dee-troy, where the water is sweet, the temperature mild, the land fat.... Millions have heard this story.

In the renovated and gleaming Detroit Museum of Art, funded by billionaires who owned most of downtown, there's a picture of Noah's flood that shows the last humans who, along with a mother tiger trying to save her cubs, have been driven to a mountain peak. Locals can't help but think that this picture has something to say to them, but that it would be more truthful if the picture was large enough to include all mass migrations: the red fox population and the lemming population and the golden plover and all the other animals and insects, but also populations from what had been Bangladesh and Brooklyn, joining long caravans of RVs abandoning what had been Florida and Texas, refugees from fires and

floods, clamoring for the high ground, driven by heat, hurricanes, war, famine, drought, mosquitos, snakes, the animals, plants, and people pushing those at the top higher still, till they could go no higher, and so had no choice but to start kicking down at those grabbing at their ankles....

The nightly news was full of what had become a regular ritual: men in bio-suits burning thousands of infected animals, this time chickens....

Europe braces. Despite protests by wildlife preservation groups, several villages in Germany began stringing nets through the forests in an effort to keep out migrating birds, migrating birds becoming the new Big Bad Wolf. As one provincial council member put it, "We have to do something!"

From the back seat, she could hear the voice of children: "Are we there yet? Are we there yet? Are we there yet? Are we there yet?..."

Olympia did some of her best thinking in the car and she had a lot to think about. As she pulled out of the university lot, a camera recorded her license plate and a photo of her face. Instead of heading to her condo, she turned toward the expressway, driving out of the gentrified area around the campus, through areas full of old, cavernous buildings that had been converted to data warehouses back in the heyday of the floppy disc. Now, they stood mostly abandoned again.

The surveillance cameras mounted on their crumbling facades stuck out like gadgets from the future. Which, to the buildings, they were.

As she drove through a Latino neighborhood, she pretended to tip her hat, as she always did, to the statue of Alexander von Humboldt, standing in the middle of the park named after him. Parks named after Humboldt dotted the Americas, but she doubted if any of the people who spray-painted their initials on the statue knew who he'd been.... The worn pandemic circles around it reminded her of the Gather Spaces in earthquake-prone cities, except these were meant to keep people apart.

Then she was accelerating onto the expressway, merging with traffic beside an AlphaCar, its driver asleep at the wheel.

She accelerated to get ahead of it—a lot of people hated AlphaCars because, like those Japanese soldiers discovered to be fighting WWII decades after the war ended, the ex-cabbies and ex-truck drivers they displaced still took potshots at them. Last week, someone had rigged a toy drone with a handgun and was shooting iTaxis on the highway until police shot it down.

Billboards changed as she approached, their lasers directing ads tailored specifically to her. 55.7 said the radar gun of the first surveillance trap she drove through, she knew. It was on a drive like this that she began to believe her project was possible. 53.4 said the second, her plate number and face being added at each point to the data banks of car ownership, authorized drivers, potential buyers, or potential terrorists, and who knew what else. Some blogs complained that the owners of the billboards were using the personal information of drivers they gleaned from the car's computers, but what else did they expect?

Everyone trying to get theirs.

If all went well, she'd be able to paddle her little project as far down river as possible, maybe all the way to the sea where she'd jump ship, just as Brian said. And not just onto any ship, but onto one of the Luxury Liners that corporate office buildings always reminded her of: glass and white buildings, each on a trip to a different promised land: Make My Anxiety Go Away; Make My Face

Beautiful; Make My Penis Erect; Cure My Memory Loss.... Most of all, there was: Doctor, I Don't Want to Die.

Driving along, she could see some sort of machine sticking out of the trunk of another car. A red machine that looked familiar, with handles like on a lawnmower, but that she couldn't place. So she kept drawing closer, trying to get a better look. Then she realized: it was a snow blower, like her father used to own. He'd pull it out during snowfalls to clear the driveway, the machine throwing up great white plumes as he walked behind it. Then he only had to use it for the odd, freak snowstorm.

Then not at all. Instead of Virus Days, kids used to get off school for Snow Days. And she wondered what had happened to that old machine?—there must have been millions of them.

The memory stirred others. When Olympia's grandmother was a girl, she used to say, the McGills still had a horse. And a goat. Back then, it was still possible for a kid to get on her bike and ride past strip malls and gas stations until she was out in farmland. With farmhouses. No more. That bike ride kept getting longer and longer, the distance between farmhouses widening until the entire state was paved by one vast agribusiness. Field insects had been so plentiful, she'd said, that she'd close her mouth to keep from breathing them in.

What would Gram say now, Olympia wondered, to see the patchwork of family farms transformed into an industrial landscape: agri-factories of GMO crops, automated tractors, goats that gave antibiotics.... Her crystal clear windshield reminded Olympia how even she could remember using the wipers to clean off squashed insects, butterflies stuck in the grill.... Then came the Insect Apocalypse: 87% of insect biomass lost in a decade, entire flocks of birds who depended on them dropping out of the sky, having starved in midair. Flocks of purple martins sometimes tried walking to South America, augmenting their diets with ground insects, the country air perfumed by shit and dead animals because there weren't any flies to consume them. A row of giant, white wind turbines stood motionless and stoic as monuments to a lost civilization.

So okay, Olympia hadn't needed much persuading to come along. The company Brian and Sid incorporated—a paper company at this point—no labs, no offices, no nothing—would be called BioShield. Or maybe Small Bore Biotherapeutics, set up as a defense contractor. When she was ready, she would join as its principle director in the avian flu prevention project. Salary?—to be negotiated. But it would include a mix of cash and stock options. While they laid the capital foundation for the company, she'd simply continue what she'd been doing, the various parties sharing such information as would be mutually beneficial. "As a gesture of good faith, it would be nice if you pulled your article from *The Journal of Entomology.*"

The request gave her pause. First, how had they known about that article? Second, every part of her was oriented to making the information she discovered known. That's why scientists in academia did what they did. Why discover a new species if you're only going to hide it under a patent? "Are you serious?" As soon as she asked, she could hear how naive she sounded.

Now here she was, gliding to the full meal—actual investors: real people with real money looking for a project—reality to be determined. "It'll just be a little meet-and-greet affair," Brian had said when he invited her. Mr. Colfax and his wife, Ms. Smyth-Jakarta, just want to meet the primary investigator, you, have dinner and talk. Very low key."

They were bringing their lawyer.

NO.IT.AN.EVIL, the anti-concert. Gabe grabbed her helmet and hurried out.

After working in the hermetically sealed insectarium all day, she loved the freedom of her bike. No roof, no walls... And the rush she got dodging traffic. Less than a year since they'd put up ghost bikes for those guys who'd been killed in last year's Da Tour, she understood why they had blown through that red light. After working all day in cubicles, it was the thrill of having no seatbelt, no safety net... In their honor, she shot through an intersection, cheating by looking both ways—she wasn't stupid—but loving her ability to hop a curb when the traffic snarled. She loved the way jumping back into traffic could cause one of those AlphaCars to jerk, jarring its 'driver' who was usually texting or whatever. Most people saw the cars as robots, but she knew better: the cars were traveling nodes of AI—and that's why she loved throwing a monkey wrench into their works.

But what she loved most about riding her bike was the feel of shape-shifting: being on the sidewalk, a pedestrian one moment, then in the street, traffic, the next. It was like being a cyborg, its simple mechanics an extension of her legs, her heart and lungs and legs pumping energy into the machine, and the machine multiplying her strength. Riding a bike, they said, is what gave a sickly Orson Wells his idea for the alien machines in *War of the Worlds....*

Twenty minutes later she slowed before a massive warehouse. Spotlights down the block announced the entrance to the LIVE.NATION concert. Even from this distance she could tell that the people going in were beautiful: trim bods sheathed in designer versions of Bottom Billion chic: like there had been a casting call for the latest iFlex commercial. A car that looked like it had been driven through a garbage storm went by—an iTaxi—it must have passed through a mob of NGers. It pulled up to the entrance and a bunch of slick, iEverything groupies got out, the latest iFoney's between their legs, vibrate function set on high, Gabe imagined, so they could get off by calling each other. There was probably an app for that. The Jesus Phone they'd called it while awaiting its second coming to market. After it went obsolete, owners could plant it and the sunflower seeds embedded in its case would sprout. *Earth Friendly*. Who said, It's easier to imagine the end of the world than the end of capitalism?...

As Gabe coasted by, a couple were arguing with door-apes who wouldn't let them in because they weren't fresh enough or skinny enough or something. Were they trying to get into the wrong concert?

She stood up on the pedals to make herself taller, trying to find the anti-concert. No map pin, no check-ins, or even anything that could be tracked—almost everyone who came to these things went by the name Anonymous. She wasn't sure what shape the portal would take, but somewhere around here there'd be an alleyway, or maybe a fire escape jammed into its down position so people could use it to get onto a rooftop, or some other passage that would guide the tribe to the real action. She had no idea how big the anti-concert would be. She'd been to one that was so small it was held in an old, dilapidated rooftop water tank and another that was so large it filled the gym of an abandoned insane asylum. They were into that kind of anti-marketing marketing.

She did a U-turn, and pedaled back past the main entrance, past the couple who had been turned away and were walking fast, complaining loudly. Then Gabe saw a drippy, red circle spray-painted at the entrance to an alley: a crude version of the Red Marble Earth tattoos a lot of NGers got. Just beyond was a pile of bikes. As she glided up to the pack, she saw a bike exactly like hers, chained to a post with a chain exactly like the one she'd just bought—as though she'd already arrived. She had congratulated herself for figuring out how to give the chain a Möbius-like twist to lock up both the front and rear wheels, but looking at the other bike she could see that its owner had come to the exact same solution. Then she saw a third, and a fourth bike, all with the same chain and the same solution. No one told them how to do it, they all just got the same idea independently, each one of them, like her, no doubt thinking they'd come up with something unique—the kind of thing that in big ways and small gave a person the illusion of individuality when really they'd just been running along rails laid down for them by the physics of how cable coils. She tried to suppress that sinking feeling she got every time she came to a concert and saw how many people dressed like her: lots of black; combat boots; arty glasses; tats.... One million Elvis fans can't be wrong....

Then she spotted it: behind a dumpster, someone had caved in the doors of a freight elevator to create a large, open manhole. Standing at its lip, she found a chain knotted to form a ladder, dangling down into the darkness.

The couple who'd been turned away at the front door suddenly appeared at the entrance to the alley, still pissed.

"Hey," she yelled to them. "Hey!" she yelled again. When they looked her way, she waved for them to follow her. They hesitated. Maybe she'd been wrong about them. The politics of clothes changed so fast she could never keep up, but the guy seemed solid enough, dressed in one of those military jackets that RedHatters wore with business ties when the U.S. invaded its first conflict-mineral zone, while the peace-warriors, eco-terrorists, and others who got those discarded hats from Goodwill started wearing them as a reminder of all the lies and scandals and corporate deals that stoked 'policing actions' to take over militia-run mines, forests, and 'jungles of interest' even as the policing actions ground on into the unpopularity of last year's band. But his f-friend looked more iffy, dressed as she was in those camouflage patterns fashion models strutted at the height of the war's popularity.

Now, hardly anyone wore that stuff, other than anarchists or the fashion-challenged—the reason the woman and her m-friend couldn't get into the club, Gabe figured. Just like the people who wore facemasks because they didn't want to breathe in the latest virus, and those who wore one as an up-yours to Redhatters, it was hard to tell who was which sometimes.

She climbed down into the shaft, then waited a moment at the bottom, wondering if they were going to come along. It was dark here: a utility tunnel full of power cables ran off into darkness in both directions. Maybe this wasn't the way after all. She started humming *Can You Show Me the Way to the Rage?* when from the street level came the woman's voice, "Does this look right to you?" Gabe wanted to laugh. She had wondered the exact same thing at her first portal. Once inside, though, it was easy to see that it was the rest of the world that was crazy, and you knew that, Yeah, it was exactly right, the portals being NO.IT.AN.EVIL's way of keeping out Young-Lawyers-in-Love, RedHatters, and every other fuck who wanted everyone on the grid so they could sell them more shit.

Unlike the LIVE.NATION bouncer, though, the NO.IT.AN.EVIL filter was self-selective. Anyone who wanted to come down that ladder could. If the couple up above was right for the rage, they'd come. If not, fuck 'em.

She spotted a sure sign that she was on the right track: a city power line had been hacked to supply industrial-strength juice. Just then, the chain ladder tinkled. The guy's foot descended. Despite herself, she gave a little smile for the company, his sandals proving she'd been right: huaraches like those that had begun appearing on the feet of hard-core NGers, their soles cut from old military-issue bulletproof vests.

"I think it's this way," she called back to them, moving deeper down the tunnel, leading them on like Alice's rabbit....

The lab was eerily empty at night. Quiet as a lab in a horror movie. Maybe one about a virus that turns everyone into zombies. The only sound was the buzz of the fluorescent lights, and the soft, rhythmic hum of the agitator Mohammed left running to vibrate a petri dish overnight. The glassed off area where Silpa did her blood work looked like a large aquarium at Sea World, drained of its water. Meadow could imagine the flies and mosquitoes sleeping in their insectarium three floors below, the lab rats asleep, the mice and rabbits in the eternal night of their pens. From her backpack, she retrieved the VR goggles she'd bought to let her see in 360° 3D, speak and dance and listen in real time and with a fidelity that wasn't possible on the regular Internet.

She first surfed to a lo-fi site so she could see what difference the VR headset made: a YouTube video that Jak had shown her earlier in the day of one of those exotic birds that didn't belong in Paraguay but somehow ended up there anyway. On-screen, the bird began screeching, cawing through the speakers of her computer.

Then she had the creepy sensation of being watched. As she turned around—a man standing there made her heart leap. It was Bill. The janitor. "Christ, Bill, you scared me."

"Sorry," he said, leaning on his push broom; one of the last human janitors left, he clutched it like a security blanket, insisting that he needed it to get the spots the bots missed, though no one else could ever see them. "I thought a bird had got loose in here or something. Working late?"

"Not really. I just wanted to use the computer," she said, her pulse still fast but returning to normal. Scared by a janitor in a horror movie: what a cliché. She didn't want to get into a conversation with him because he'd talk all night given the chance. But she didn't want to be rude either, and he was gazing at the bird on her screen. It made that cawing noise, then a chirping. "It's called a lyrebird."

"How come it lies?"

"Lyre. Like the harp. But I like to think of it as the mockingbird. It only tells the truth."

The bird began making a revving sound like a motorcycle.

"What was that? Did they add that?"

That's what Meadow had thought when Jak showed it to her, his main comment being, 'Isn't that wild?' But listening closer she could tell that the audio hadn't been doctored—not unless they'd done a lot of sophisticated sound editing to keep the background noises of the jungle seamless. "No it only imitates the sounds that it grew up hearing in the forest." Then the bird mimicked the sound again: the unmistakable sound of a chainsaw. "That's why I call it the mockingbird."

After Bill left, Meadow logged into W.2. The W.2 Earth rotated on her screen, the North-American Midwest in darkness as it was outside the windows of the lab. During the day, those same windows framed the center's quad. But now the night made them mirror-black and she watched herself reflected in them, putting on her goggles. Her entire field of vision filled with her screen, the globe on it smoothly speeding up, zooming in on where she was, the concert only a few miles from the lab. Watching the satellite view zoom in to her own town always reminded her of the time she'd been nursing Nico, the TV on to pass the time. A news flash switched to live coverage of the U.S. bombing of Caracas; beneath those bombs, she knew, there were mothers, like her, and ever since, her own town zooming up on-screen gave her the uneasiness of seeing it through the crosshairs of one of those smart bombs—*a screaming comes across the sky*—as it screeched down at her head. The grid of Chicago streets rapidly became a checkerboard of rooftops, then the roof of a warehouse that the camera passed right though, placing her avatar inside a virtual club.

Her ears filled with the party. She looked to the right, then the left, seeing the party from the viewpoint of her avatar, people talking, beer bottles clinking, the crowd of avatars she was in all having the impossible Barbie & Ken bodies of

W.2, but dressed better than most avatars in W.2, the avatars this event drew having the money to buy the custom programming it took to dress in high-end fashions, their bodies, jewelry, and clothes minutely detailed. When she looked down at her own avatar's body, the standard clothes it was dressed in made her feel like a hayseed. Compared to the fine-grained programming she could see in the stitching of hemlines, she may as well be dressed in a sack. People immediately turned away from her. Most of their operators were probably also using the VR goggles Meadow had just bought. She'd never been in a space so audibly rich, the sounds coming not from one but dozens of others, all around her, and with more fidelity than if she were actually there. The building, though, was as devoid of detail as the lo-fi version of W.2: brick pattern instead of individual bricks.

The dance floor was so crowded it was hard to see the stage. A huge video screen was mounted above it, streaming video of the real concert that was going on in a real warehouse with real people in the real-world counterpart of this W.2 concert. A center screen displayed live video of the real TJ: a Rastafarian white guy with long green dreadlocks. He danced about, directing the music, using a Z-Game controller like a conductor's baton. As Meadow made her way closer, she could see his avatar on the stage in W.2, exactly mimicking his movements in the live video of the simulcast. Motion sensors mapped his movements onto his avatar, which mimed him exactly.

She made a walking motion with her fingers to get closer to the huge red flutes supporting the stage canopy: logos. The flutes were the logo of a sponsor, she realized. She almost had to laugh at herself. What a dope.

Just as she began to log out, though, a voice came through her headset, clearly directed at her: "Would you like to dance?" When she turned to see who was talking to her, the avatar she faced looked so much like her husband it made her suck in her breath.

"William?" she asked.

No response.

Unlike all the other avatars in the club, he was dressed in jeans. Flannel shirt. Buttoned at the neck, the way her husband wore it. The way he had worn it in the photo he'd emailed her. Only not so. More like a SIMS character or a sketch by a street artist who got the general face more or less right, but no better than a poor caricature. The distortions made him look younger than he appeared in his photo: but not quite a younger version. No, not William. More like a younger brother, or cousin, or—before she could stop herself she'd thought it: Or an older version of Nico. Coincidence, she said, not wanting to let herself believe.

"No," she said, watching to see what he'd do. "I don't dance." No reaction. He stayed still for so long that she began to think he had frozen. Then he said, "You're not from here, are you?" The voice sounded familiar, almost like her husband, almost like her son. Somewhere in between, but faintly synthesized. "What are you looking for?"

The question caught her off guard. "Who says I'm looking for something?"

"Everyone's looking for something."

His answers seemed real if vague, like *VOĈO* when it just fed back different versions of your questions to make you think you were having a conversation with a real person. She decided to play along. "Yeah, well not everyone knows what it is."

"True." He began to look around, as though checking out the scene for someone more fun. Or better looking. Maybe he was real after all. Then he walked away from her—manners of a robot—joining the crowd out on the dance floor. The way he said it though gave her the sense that he knew something he wasn't saying, so she continued to wander among the avatars, keeping him in view.

He began dancing with an avatar modeled after a famous influencer, doing a dance that involved grinding their hips together. Even if he was some kind of ghost image of Nico, would he be able to recognize her? Seeing how much younger all the other avatars were, or made themselves out to be, she knew she'd aged too.

The live feed showed the real TJ, sweeping his Z-Game controller as though it were the handlebars of a motorcycle while his Lego-like avatar mirrored his motions in the W.2 version on-screen. Live video showed the real-people counterparts of the avatars, dancing in a real warehouse. Though not as perfectly shaped as their avatars, the real people were surprisingly close: twentysomethings—all of them so young she felt like a chaperone, though her avatar's body was the same age as theirs.

Some of the avatars danced with the novice Frankenstein-like motions available from the W.2 control panel, the people controlling them activating moves like 'The NASDAQ' or 'The Fraq.' Some had gotten really good at combining these in ways that made the avatar's moves look unique. At least to someone who didn't know any better. Some avatars competed in worldwide dance contests, she knew. But the real dance pros were nerds who had gotten into the programming itself, designing code that would make their avatars spin like ballerinas or figure skaters unbound by the laws of gravity, and do so in time with the music.

She searched for the guy she'd spoken to. As she wandered through the crowd, she also kept looking for?... For what? Some sign of Nico?

Then she saw someone moving with robotic-like motions: an avatar keeping his feet fixed in place, his legs stiff and bending at the waist, rotating through minor degrees of arc with the speed of a robotic arm run by servos. Nico liked robots. And as she watched this avatar dance, she remembered where she'd seen those robotic dance motions before: it was in one of the animations Nico made, downloading an animation program to make the robot he drew dance. As she neared to get a clearer look, she could see that his face and arms were red—the same red Nico used to color his robots. Did this mean anything? Or did it just mean that both animation programs shared some code? Or was she just losing her mind, relating everything to everything else even if there were no relation?...

The couple caught up with Gabe when she paused at a candle burning near the end of the corridor. Up close she got the joke of the woman's pantsuit: camouflage fabric marked up to turn its patterns into interlocking flowers: Ecouflage.

"Hey," the guy said in greeting, stepping up to see what Gabe was looking at: Instead of the fishbowl of condoms that a lot of hosts placed at the entrance to their parties, the candle's glow illuminated a bucket of industrial earplugs.

The sight gave Gabe pause. No Production events always skated a line between excitement and danger. Their manifesto claimed that the only way to wake up consumer zombies was to scare them into realizing that they'd been sleepwalking.

The concerts or performances or whatever you called them were always loud, and involved cobbled-together machinery. The organizers never tried to hurt anyone, even though accidents sometimes happened. If earplugs were being passed out, something big must be planned.

"This is going to be great," Gabe told the couple, grabbing a pair.

Sometimes it felt as though they were all living within a Hieronymus Bosch painting, the beak of a bird-devil jammed up the ass of a donkey-man, flagellants in a garden of earthly delights....

As Officer Cheryl Fisher pulled her squad car onto the block of boarded-up houses, she could see black smoke curling up from the center of a ring of people gathered in a vacant lot the way the NGers sometimes made a bonfire of tires they'd stripped from Hummers, drinking and dancing at their flash parties. But as faces turned her way, she could see that many of them were too old to be part of that scene. And too well-dressed. No embedded chips. No piercings or topknots. No odor of burning tires. Maybe it was some kind of other protest—like the flash mobs that had taken to burning the corpses of Climate Deniers—old dead men from the last decades like Rep. Lamar Smith, Sen. James M. Inhofe, and other politicians—their names were more famous now than when they were alive—men who could have done something to keep the planet from overheating but instead, gutted science budgets, kicked the legs out from under the planet's last chance—the historic Climate Agreement of 2015—fought for the 'rights' of mines to poison rivers—and men like the Kroch Brothers who poured millions of dollars into electing RedHatters. We Cover the Earth. Pop-up Parties like the Vengeance Now Party would call for a flash raid, and mobs of angry people too young to have known these men in life would show up at a cemetery to dig up the corpse. After a brief trial, they'd burn it. Or hang it, if the body was still in good enough shape for hanging. Then they'd burn it. "Hot enough / for you now?" the mob would chant. So many had shown up for Trump's trial that the guards either had to start shooting civilians or give up the body; someone kicked the corpse

before the trial could start, then more and more people joined in—even the guards—stomping on it over and over—like the body of Mussolini—till there was nothing left....

Suddenly a flash of flame, howls of pain.

No such luck, she told herself, realizing as she approached what was going on. A couple guys in golf clothes—first timers—scattered, thinking they had something to worry about. But most of the others just stood there, glancing her way once in a while, thinking she was going to be part of the show, rushing to get her burn-victim blanket out of the car, and such. But she didn't fuck with that.

She unholstered her service revolver and aimed at the burning animal.

"Hey!" someone yelled, others scrambling once they saw that she was going to open up whether or not they were in the line of fire.

Her gun sounded like a cannon as she put the burning dog out of its misery.

"The fuck! You could have hit someone!" a man in a red hat yelled as she walked back to the car, wishing a ricochet had hit someone. Then maybe the city would pass an ordinance against bear baiting, dog immolation, or any of the other shit social workers said some people on a dying planet were sure to do, politicians afraid to make shit like this illegal because social workers said men like that would beat their wives, or worse, if they didn't have a 'healthier' outlet.

Her cousin, Ashly, wanted to take a selfie before an ancient undersea coral reef, rising from the desert floor of Texas like a tower of ash. "Ash, Ashly, get it?" she said, adjusting her distance so it looked like she held the ancient coral reef in the palm of her hand....

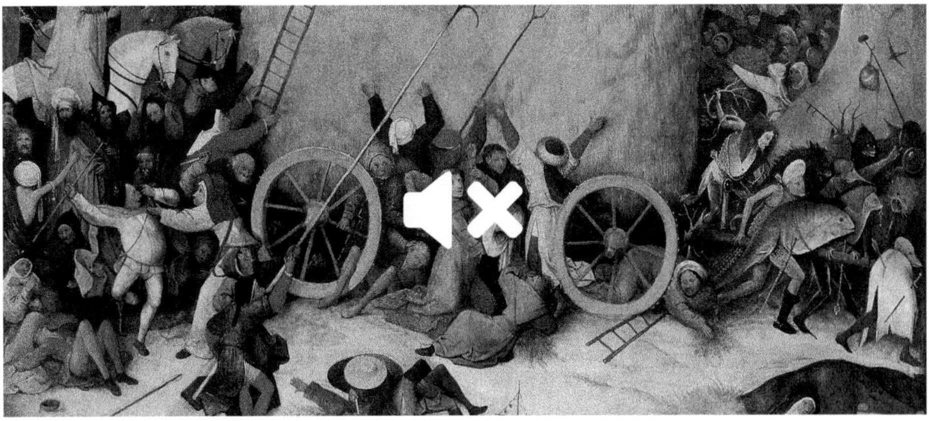

We cover the earth. The logo of a paint factory showed a cosmic-sized can pouring red paint onto the Earth, oceans of red paint dripping into space. After an exo-planet that was losing its atmosphere was shown to look like Blue Marble Earth—only red, like a red-hot marble—some NG designer took the *We Cover the Earth* logo and turned it upside down, its red drips now streaming off the planet the way the atmosphere streamed away from Red Marble Earth, as they called it. It became a meme.

"Abortionists, homos, and pornographers want you to believe in Global Warming," the Rev. Adams said, "so they can go about their business of killing babies, fornicating, and poking God in the eye!... God's not sending us Global Warming! He's sending us Noah Warming! Driving an electric car to an orgy won't save you! Nor will gay marriage to an organic chicken! No, the only way to save ourselves from the deluge is to climb aboard the Ark He has already given us," he said, shaking his Bible at the cheering stadium of believers....

Euclid would have never made it at the Stitch 'n Bitch, Mary Anne thought, crocheting her bit of the Evolutionary Tree. Nor Darwin. She'd been doing a math Ph.D. when she wandered into the combination knitting supplies and feminist bookstore just off campus, just to check it out, maybe knit a pandemic mask like some of her DIY friends did as a way to unwind. A class had been in progress—Extreme Knitting—with a crunchy standing in the center of a knitting circle: women on folding chairs, drinking kombucha out of jars, knitting and just hanging out. Most of them were also grad students, a retired philosophy prof, and a few

others. But unlike the hipster caps or baby booties she was expecting, they seemed to be crocheting abstract sculptures. "A coral reef, actually," one told her. "We're crocheting a replica of The Caribbean Coral Reef that died in 2012."

It was part of a project begun years back by Christine and Margaret Wertheim who hoped to enlist women, and men, from all over the world to recreate all the extinct coral reefs in crochet, a technique that proved perfect for modeling the folding and ruffled surfaces that appeared in lettuce leafs and other plants and animals, including corals. So Mary Anne joined them, taking on an area that she reworked in white yarn, since before the reef vanished, it had been bleached of color by a warming sea.

She loved the non-Euclidian nature of it: the way the folds and curves were perfect representations of hyperbolic planes, that is, folded and curved planes that made it possible for a line and a point to have dozens, even hundreds of parallel lines, instead of just one, as Euclid drew it up on a flat sheet of paper. Crocheting in the circle of women one day, they got to talking about how lots of bio majors and paleontologists were into crochet. It was a mental margarita, and fun, but it also helped them imagine how an animal that had been squashed flat as it fossilized might have looked in its 3D form; they got to thinking about crocheting clams, sea slugs, nudibranches, and other creatures; they got to talking about the math, and how the non-Euclidian surfaces they were crocheting also resembled 3D models of Big Data problems. "I wonder if crochet could be used to put the two together, to model the evolution of an animal," Zøe had said, "what with its ins and outs, its folds, and multiple parallel lines?...." Then, almost simultaneously, they all cried out, "Or the whole freakin' Tree of Life!"—not the

Latvian Satellite Reef (detail) from the Crochet Coral Reef project by Christine Wertheim and Margaret Wertheim and the Institute For Figuring. Photo © IFF

individual animals, of course, but the hyperbolic planes that species as a group could map onto, each thread of yarn made up of thousands of little strands; frayed strands would resemble all the dead ends that most mutations ended in, each branch that continued hooked into the others, the strands together making the millions of branching and parallel lines of individual creatures.

Crowd sourcing the labor was easier than anyone had imagined, thousands of women in hundreds of Stitch 'n Bitches, or in their own kitchens, or in retirement homes, before TVs, at the pool, or in subway cars, all crocheting according to the patterns Mary Anne generated, then posted on Mechanical Turk. Her original group took on the line of dinosaurs that included *Archaeopteryx*—a small dinosaur that people used to think was an early bird, but had since been reclassified as a dinosaur 'experiment' in which lots of parallel evolutionary paths were trying to figure out how to create a 'birdlike body.' Mary Anne herself took on ancestral Psocoptera, the hundreds of parallel and branching lines of lice that eventually produced the feather lice that infested feathered dinosaurs, then later birds.

As Brian handed Olympia the wine list, she thought she could get used to meetings in private rooms with oak paneling instead of dry-erase boards. A sommelier instead of grad students. Over *filet de boeuf*, Brian and his partner Sid went into their pitch for the benefit of the couple who were thinking of investing: Mr. Colfax and his wife Ms. Smyth-Jakarta.

They dumbed down the science to the level of a magazine article you might read in your doctor's waiting room. But the couple listened closely, as though they truly were more interested in genes than dollars. They weren't what Olympia had expected: young—not at all like the gray-haired and bejeweled matrons she imagined at opera or museum benefits. The kids—she couldn't help but think of them that way since they were barely older than her students—the kids were multimillionaires who'd made their fortune off of the software he created in his dorm room as an undergrad so he and his friends could remotely control each other's model railroads. The software went on to form the basis of the most elegant and profitable system there was for all sorts of other remote-control applications: controlling robot repairmen on the exterior of the space station; last year, a doctor in California used it to perform a hernia operation on a patient in Hong Kong.

Apparently, Mr. Colfax, the inventor, was leaning toward pouring millions into a state-of-the-art model-railroad museum. Satellite links and his software would allow kids from all over the world to play with its trains. But his wife wanted to invest in one of those humanitarian projects that were trendy among the neo-rich. No, that was unfair, Olympia realized, once she got to talk to her. Even before Ms. Smyth-Jakarta—or Jackie as she insisted Olympia call her—even before Jackie's future husband figured out a way to remotely play with toy trains, she'd already used her allowance to open an orphanage in her home country. High-end designers met with locals there, Olympia learned, to develop products that would have both the eye-candy sleekness to attract investors and the ability to employ the Bottom Billion. She proudly showed Olympia the dress she was wearing, made from a satin-like fabric extracted from coconut husks. "High-concept design applied to Bottom Billion materials to solve Bottom Billion problems," she said, showing Olympia a sleek brochure. On it, a celebrity hawked a line of golf balls made of compressed fish scales used at the eco-resort she owned in Paraguay. At least her intentions seemed sincere. They'd brought their lawyer: a guy from the ringtone business, whom Mr. Colfax had roomed with in college.

For the benefit of his recorder, Brian reintroduced himself and Sid as serial entrepreneurs whose role was to find the capital to launch promising projects. "With a social component," Sid pointed out, adding a detail Olympia couldn't remember coming up before. He described to the Colfax Smith-Jakartas a few of their projects in an effort to lay out the range of their portfolio: everything from small start-up operations—like the $9 million in Series B funding they'd raised to exploit extracts from the Chinese Thunder God Vine—to up-and-running projects—like Medical Ventures, $230 million in committed capital to finance early-stage heart-replacement technologies. Mainly they were bridge builders, they explained: for example, linking Polar Ventures, Accelerton, and Alnylma Pharmaceuticals to develop cholesterol blockers; or putting Advent Capital Management together with Momenta Pharmaceuticals, and other companies with names that sounded like financial institutions that sold drugs or drug companies that were also financial institutions in a joint effort to exploit resveratrol, the molecular compound in red wine that was shown to extend the life span of mice by 24%, and of the flies and fish by 60%. "If that ship comes in, whoever dominates the resveratrol space could reshape the entire pharmaceutical industry." Sirtris, a four-year-old startup that had only done some preliminary work on a synthetic version of resveratrol had been bought by GlaxoSmithKline for $720 million—$720 million for access to preliminary studies about a compound that might not ever work.

Subtext: on that scale, the exploratory five million they were asking the Colfax Smyth-Jakarta Foundation to throw at her project was probably less than what some of their friends put into school-board elections.

There must have been more than one entrance, Gabe realized, when she and the couple she'd met emerged into a large storage yard behind an abandoned warehouse. The yard was already packed, a lot of people wearing surgical masks as they did in any gathering even though there wasn't an active pandemic at the moment. Those who went to protests to fight cops were already wearing identical black clown masks and those electronic necklaces that scrambled facial recognition software. On stage, a Korean woman in a wetsuit bobbed before a huge screen full of pixelated Aliens, Centipedes, Pac-Man ghosts, and the icons of other enemies from first-gen shooter-games. Silent and enigmatic as Easter Island statues, a pair of huge mechanical men bookended the stage. They'd been built from junkyard parts, old hydraulic equipment, rocket nozzles, and truck fenders, welded up in that rough style that had become the No-Tech Production signature. One of the metal giants had the face of the Trump: goof-ass orange hair, a pout like a puckered anus, made of old casino marquees. The other puppet, the larger one to the right of the stage, was a generic CEO, Mr. Monopoly, wad of cash in one hand, a bouquet of drones in the other.

All of it had been set up along the back wall of the warehouse that LIVE. NATION had rented for their concert, she could tell, the frosted glass of its industrial windows flashing green, then blue, in time with the thumps of techno-trance coming from the massive theater speakers out here in the yard. The outdoor rhythm was being driven by the Korean woman on stage, BubblyFish: red helmet-hair, black wetsuit, a one-woman band named after its single member, her. Her reed-thin body swayed like a long, undersea plant in a current of sound waves she made wash from one speaker to the next.

BubblyFish was famous in Pirate culture for the songs she composed by hacking into the sound cards of Gameboys, PlayStations, XBoxes, Pong, Donkey

Kong, Nintendo, and other low-tech or Soviet knockoffs like Game&Watch from the last century, looping their antique blips, happy bonus points bleeps, collaging swooshes, and sad, sinking electronic game-over *wa-wa* sounds to form compositions that slid between electro-jazz and punk, disco and new-wave, riding over the thump of the up-tempo pop that seemed to stream endlessly out of Asia. They said she was trained as a classical violinist.

At the moment, she was into a goof on the LIVE.NATION techno-trance thumping inside the factory, using the massively wired Gameboy in her hand to send out a string of goofy cartoon sounds over the theater speakers in a call-and-response with the techno-trance in ways that seemed to dance around it, undercut the seriousness of that music as skillfully as a whoopee cushion at a State dinner. The crowd was loving it in an angry sort of way, the way laughter at a comic's send-up of Trump had always been tinged with hate.

Looking at the people, it was easy to tell that being part of the scene was the real attraction; people went to concerts of classical music to be classical and people came here to?.... Let loose between pandemics? A lot of the NGers in black Kabuki masks locked arms, jumping up and down to create a wave of bobbing, wooden faces. Others mimed throwing bottles as they had during the G7 summit. Packed tight around the lip of the tiny stage, those at the very front reached out so far that it was hard for BubblyFish to not step on their hands.

Lots of arms bore tattoos of Red Marble Earth. A few had tat-sleeves of AGCT TGCA TTGC TAAG GTAG TATC—from the genome of the ape some NGers were trying to free from the Lincoln Park Zoo. The lawyers for the ape were arguing that it was a person, and so its confinement amounted to slavery—in a zoo named after Lincoln, no less. They weren't interested in dancing. They beat their fists on the plywood stage in unison to her riffs, turning its plywood floor into a large tribal drum. Hopping up and down in the dancing throng were Geo-Skinheads, and another group whose name she couldn't remember but that left the ErthLiberation Movement because it was too pacifist. The FBI classified them as terrorists—another reason that anything that could be tracked was banned at these concerts.

A jet of burning gas shot from the nostrils of the CEO robot, and they all let out a cheer. Something big was going to blow, Gabe could tell, a pilot light continuing to burn in the CEO's head. Was that the preheater for a rocket engine? The techs worrying the cylinders of compressed gas at the base of the stage were wearing orange jumpsuits from Guantanamo. Where did they get this stuff?

While waiting for the escargot, Brian explained to Jackie and Mr. Colfax why most of their projects had modest expectations. Some only wanted to be bought, which other companies often did in order to acquire techniques pioneered by the startup: OmegaOrion bought Phiron simply to acquire their method for networking existing MRI machines, which OmegaOrion then used to create 3D images of brain synapses firing.

They thought Olympia's work might fall somewhere between the two extremes. In a worst-case scenario, Sid said, by which Olympia took to mean that no one would lose money, they would have a patentable library of protein sequences. "But if everything works out as we hope," Brian continued, now speaking to Ms. Smyth-Jakarta, "it could be one of those projects where everyone says, 'Why didn't I think of that?' Simple, elegant solutions."

"Well, not so simple," Olympia couldn't help but add, the phrase sounding like the tagline for a company. They all laughed as though she'd been making a joke, especially Sid. A forced stage laugh. But Olympia knew about resveratrol in red wine. The studies that grabbed headlines were always the ones people wanted to believe: the experiment that turned couch-potato mice into Olympic-athlete mice by putting them on the resveratrol. People ignored the details, like the fact that resveratrol only worked by activating sirtuin, an interaction that took place in mice but not people. The woods were always full of dead ends. Stairways to nothing.

Brian asked her—Dr. Olympia; they kept referring to Olympia as Dr. Olympia—Brian asked her to describe for Mr. Colfax and Ms. Smyth-Jakarta, in layman's terms, where she was in her research.

As she did, they listened politely, though Olympia got the impression that they already knew what she told them: that her lab was now in the process of sequencing the most common blood-sucking lice to test the theory that it's the saliva in the lice that gave the local population immunity. Brian kept suggesting that she fill in the details later and skip to the other goal—the project they could shift to once the proteins in the saliva of lice were sequenced: a genetically altered strain of bird lice that could give fowl in the wild immunity against diseases harmful to people. "If you kill the messenger, the bad news never arrives." Thousands of people could be saved: people who'd never see a vaccine developed for wealthy nations.

It was weird having this ringtone lawyer there, a yellow string tie bright against his crimson shirt. He could have stepped out of a boyband. But whenever he opened his mouth, she could tell how smart he was. She wasn't sure why she should be surprised. Lots of smart people were devoting their lives to coming up with high-tech deedle balls. As he took notes, Mr. Colfax and Ms. Smyth-Jakarta asked her many things: about lice populations; about the military funding she'd gotten; if she'd ever discussed her idea with any Bottom Billion government; if she'd been approached by any of the pharmaceutical companies yet. "Can I be honest?" Olympia asked. She explained how no one would be interested in the diseases of the Bottom Billion, or lice, if the U.S. hadn't occupied so many conflict-mineral zones. "If these wars ever end, so will our funding. As a scientist, that is very frustrating."

This was where Mr. Colfax, Ms. Smyth-Jakarta, and others were willing to bet she was wrong, Brian said, becoming animated now, as though having gotten through her school lesson, they'd finally be able to discuss the real subject: 'potential.' Sid spoke up, sounding like a politician running for office with all his platitudes about doing good for others, the ideas he laid out as smooth as a rock polished by a river of words: There'd been so many 'spot' epidemics of *Plasmodium vivax* malaria in Florida over the last few years that the CDC would have classified the Southern U.S. as a malaria endemic area if Disneyland hadn't thrown its political clout into squashing the discussion. "Charities might only be able to raise a pittance for all of sub-Saharan Africa, but a Niagara of cash would be poured onto the problem of keeping Mickey and his Magic Kingdom malaria free."

"That's so true!" Ms. Smyth–Jakarta said, indignation making her eyes shine. Sid knew which buttons to push, Olympia thought, listening to him go over the way the UN couldn't agree enough to move in and stop the genocides that made conflict zones so unstable; instead, they'd assembled worldwide response teams to keep spot pandemics from spreading to the West: an army of men in bio-suits was at the ready to fly in and quarantine any area in the world. Within twenty-four hours, they'd throw a vaccination blanket over the locals and slaughter the poultry. In this way they'd slow the mutation of the virus. Slow but not stop. Especially after terrorists had begun infecting themselves as a way to spread diseases. Scared Americans watched the news more; between bouts of shouting-mouths bellowing about more walls, they saw more ads for Sleep Aide, Viagra+, Prozac, Dieta, and 0.1 micron face masks (also good for TB, SARS, Smallpox, Anthrax). Like companies that sold nations phone systems, Pfizer had built a $14 million multimedia theater in Riyadh just to show a promotional video to Saudi princes in the hopes that they'd buy their vaccination program. Fear wasn't good for business. It was great.

"And you really believe," Ms. Smyth-Jakarta asked Olympia sincerely, "using lice to vaccinate wild birds gives poor nations a better chance than developing a cheap, human vaccine?" She looked directly at Olympia—her eyes asking Olympia to answer woman to woman, as if the men weren't present.

Olympia was silent. She could see Sid holding his breath, waiting to see how she'd answer. She wasn't going to lie. But still.... Finally, she said, "If every family was provided a $1.25 mosquito net, they say, malaria would be eradicated in a generation. But 'they' have been saying this for 5 generations now."

Sid exhaled. "Let the rich nations tweak human vaccines," Brian added, "But if Dr. Olympia's BioShield"—they kept calling it 'her shield'—"caused every mutation to fizzle out at the level of the birds, who would benefit most?"

Investors, Olympia thought but didn't say.

"The poorest of the nations," Brian answered.

The music turned darker—Game-Over—BubblyFish driving the bleeps faster, making them more threatening, sinister. On the wall behind her, a pixelated stick figure dodged rows of bug-like aliens washing down the screen the way they did in the original game. DEATH RESTART DEATH RESTART. Gabe could feel her pulse quicken with that ancient biology of the hunt and the hunted—even though the graphic cards were so antique that to depict the aliens, the programmers had to make a series of stair-stepped arcs. Still, the aliens' pincers, biting in time to the music, set her on edge, the aliens as relentless as goose-stepping automatons, multiplying faster than BubblyFish could kill them. The trill of electronic bleeps crashed into a register so low Gabe could feel the sound as dull thumps in her chest. Almost subliminally, some of the aliens morphed into corporate logos: *We Cover the Earth*—an icon of paint pouring from a giant can onto the globe....

When BubblyFish pulled out a JesusFone, the crowd surged—like a bunch of people wanting to fight but having no one to punch. BubblyFish stepped back as though stunned that they didn't break into laughter at the sight of the hacked JesusFone the way other audiences would. Not this bunch. She kept her distance from the fists beating the stage. More hands reached out to the thick braids of colored wires that cascaded from the hacked phone to her synthesizers and mixing boards. Someone in the crowd slipped, falling against someone else who turned and pushed back. Hard.

This is how riots start, Gabe thought. The beam projecting aliens and logos now filled the screen with invasive beetles and plants that had moved ever northward as the climate changed. Then the projection beam swung from the stage to a backdoor of the warehouse that LIVE.NATION was using, the white beam painting it with their guilt for having fucked over the Earth. NGers had spray-painted a goth bull's-eye on the door. *Take back the day & the night. erthlib now!* was scrawled across it.

Something was going to happen. Gabe could feel it; she could feel herself becoming itchy for something to blow, her body tensing for a fight the way adrenaline always pushed bodies to run or bring it on.

"Truth! Truth! Truth!" the mob began chanting.

Something was happening outside the W.2 warehouse that Meadow's avatar was in—rather it was outside the real warehouse where the concert was being simulcast from. Inside the W.2 warehouse, most of the avatars continued to dance but from the streaming video in the background. Meadow could tell something was beginning to worry the people at the actual concert: first one, then everyone stopped dancing, and turned to the same direction—a shattering of glass—they were watching breaking windows or a fight or something going on out of camera-shot—a range of emotion on their faces from surprise to fear to irritation to anger—for having their party crashed? The muffled sound of a mob swelled then faded in Meadow's headset like a cheer coming from outside a room whose door had opened then shut. 'Truth,' she thought they were chanting. But it could have been 'Roof.' Whatever was said, other avatars heard it too. They looked up to the live feed of the real people watching whatever they were watching. Jet engines whined in the background. Were they near an airport?

The TJ alone continued to groove to the music, the video feed continuing to show him on stage, snapping his head to make his long, green locs whip the air, the green lines that were the braids of his avatar moving more jerkily—like the difference between a live actor and his image in an old, jerky videogame. When the competing noise began to overpower his music, even he turned toward the door. There was a loud boom, a muffled explosion—outside? Someone in the video screamed. People began to back away.

Meadow kept her avatar on the dance floor to see what would happen, everyone fixed on the back door as though expecting Godzilla to bust through.

Heat and shock from enormous gas plumes on either side of the stage blew out the back windows of the warehouse.

The vidie projections were coming rapid-fire now, low-res centipedes from antique Ataris snaking back and forth across blocks of text: DEATH OR TRUTH.

More images of ice caps breaking apart. HEAT. STARVATION. One of the pixelated aliens became a black mosquito enlarged in the projection to the size of a small airplane: a black silhouette.

Gabe froze at the sight.

Plasmodium falciparum. She recognized it immediately. It was large and black as a horsefly. Suddenly she remembered: it looked just like the insect she'd swatted in her Insectarium some weeks ago. Just before her hand turned it into a smear, she'd seen enough of it to tell that it wasn't one of her insects—she'd studied the smear wondering if it was a local that had gotten into the building. It happened from time to time, given the size of doors and insects. No big deal, she'd thought then. But now....

A flash of incredulity, then rage, went through her as she remembered how someone had ordered genetically altered mice—doing shit off the books—and it wasn't long after that she'd started feeling tired all the time; just like that the pieces fell together: some fucker in the lab must have smuggled in malaria-bearing mosquitoes....

The giant CEO robot to the right of the stage erupted with volcanic force, a jet flame roaring from its mouth. BubblyFish jumped off the stage. Hands shot to ears; the jet-powered squeal coming from the robot sent everyone scrambling to get in their earplugs. Even when Gabe pressed on hers, the sound was so loud it hurt. The crush of people pushing to get away from the stage stepped on those behind them. Hydraulics made the two robots lurch, then come together like the jaws of a vice. The plywood floor of the stage between them began to buckle in their grip, snapping, splintering down its middle, then heaving upward like pavement in an earthquake.

Techs in the same earmuffs as airport ground crews operated control boxes hacked from industrial cranes. A pipe—no, it was a pipe fashioned to be a dick—rose from the Trump-bot as though the sight of the giant CEO had aroused him. Compared to the robot's Goliath size, Trump's dick was tiny.

The techs navigated the robots until Trump's tiny dick jerkily docked into the mouth of the CEO. A mufferless motorcycle engine roared, powering the dick to thrust—faster and faster, fast as the needle of a sewing machine, creating so much heat that smoke began to pour out of the CEO's ears.

The operators pushed the throttle higher than the limits of the pivot points, cams and pulleys of their machines, the entire contraption beginning to rattle, then squeal the unnatural squeal of metal grinding metal. Still, they pushed up the speed, the piston-dick a blur of motion, the motorcycle engines roaring at a deafening level. The Trump-bot's bobblehead shook violently. People backed away, squashing against those behind them who were pushed forward by those in the back trying to see. Jets of burning gas began to shoot from the Trump-bot's mouth—as they had during the teaser blasts; then a gigantic flame from his mouth blackened the CEO. The crowd screamed in fear or glee, it was hard to tell, running from the contraption as it began to fall. It hit the ground with the force of an auto accident right where people had been standing a moment ago.

There was a pause in the crowd as though everyone had sucked in their breath at the same time, then, just as they realized that no one had been hurt, they burst into laughter; at the same instant, two tub-shaped robot-warriors raced out from under the stage. They attacked the fallen automatons with sledgehammers and buzz saws, sparks flying as they tore into the hollow metal heads....

On Olympia's drive home, the white corporate headquarters she passed seemed to glide by as smoothly as cruise ships. Like the emblems of foreign nations, each bore a sleek corporate logo, each logo a different version of the euro or dollar sign. Compared to these buildings, her little academic lab was a rowboat. What was going on behind those walls, she wondered. What bacterium did they have in their incubators? What reactants had their centrifuges teased out today? How many of them were racing to patent the same string of letters?

Lots of them, she knew, from the frequency that the logos on the buildings changed, a futuristic LP SYSTEMATICS being replaced by PL LOGOSYSTEMS, fashions in drug companies changing more often than fashions in clothes, fortunes riding on which way an amino acid fell....

Some of those companies were way beyond domesticating molecules, she knew, that is, beyond changing a few letters to flip a gene on or off. Some tricked stem cells into embryonic scaffolding, the brain of a SHEEF growing in one dish networked with the rudimentary nervous system growing in another. Others were assembling synthetic cells to make synthetic bugs that could absorb carbon and emit oxygen; eat garbage and urinate gasoline.... If they got their way, a whole zoo of synthetic creatures will be let out into the oceans, the atmosphere, homes....

Everyone who plants an olive tree does so for a future generation, the ancients used to say, olive trees back then taking 70 years to bear fruit. This is why it was a war crime for city states to cut down another's olive grove, the cutting of an olive tree serving no purpose other than as a spite to future generations. Now, acorns were reprogrammed to generate floor planks direct; the time it took to get an olive out of a tree had been cut to 3 weeks. Warlords in the conflict-mineral zones might not think twice about razing an olive grove but it was the staggering speed with which Sci-Fi dreams could fix men's wickedness that gave her hope—and made her row faster to not be left behind.

As she passed one of those suburban cemeteries, she could see a coyote sleeping openly on a grave, lots of wildlife growing bold as rolling pandemics made people retreat.

The police arrived. Lots of them, judging from the blue strobes that began reflecting off buildings around the yard. She could hear a drone, too, up above in the dark. Then she saw it: motorcycle-sized, prickly with lenses and big enough to be loaded with the skunk, armadillo, or shit spray they used on crowds. Some of the men in black clown masks started the engines of leaf blowers, and aimed them skyward, ready to disperse it.

People who weren't already wearing pandemic masks covered their faces with kerchiefs or homemade gas masks. DIY directions for making them had been all over Pinterest. Pushing, scuffling.... On the ground, being stepped on by dozens of feet, was a keffiyeh. She bent to pick it up, and was nearly knocked over. On a knee, she tied it around her mouth and nose, then stood, looking across the crowd for a way out, imagining police in riot gear looking for a way in. The freight shaft she'd climbed down to enter had been sealed off, no doubt. Ladders were being lowered from the roofs of adjoining buildings to give spectators an escape route, but like the fights that broke out over lifeboats, pushing and bickering over their bottom rungs were making it hard for anyone to go up. More NGers put on black Kabuki masks, or pulled the blue scarf they'd been wearing around their necks up over their face. One near her took off the chain he'd been wearing as a belt and wrapped it around his knuckles.

The performance itself only seemed to ramp up, adding to the chaos: after smashing the gigantic puppets to pieces, the mini-bots had turned their saws and hammers on each other, the music blaring, people screaming, looking for a way out, others storming the door of the warehouse. Gabe could feel herself carried by their anger, images of the Biohazard Containment room that was under construction flashing through her mind, mixing with the black silhouette of *P. falciparum* and the other images projected on the wall that the mob crushed against. Bits of conversation came to her: Olympia and another PI complaining that the containment room was behind schedule—had the fuckers brought in the mosquitoes anyway? Olympia yelling at the lab group for ordering transgenic animals without approval—and the thought that she could have picked up malaria because of someone else's greed or laziness or whatever really pissed her off.

When people around her began running, she ran too. Some scattered the way they always did when cops arrived, but she found herself being carried along by the part of the crowd that was storming the building, the building and those in it making all the abstract political arguments vapid in comparison to this real thing that was in front of her—NOW!

Charging in through the back door, eco-terrorists and their ERTH LIBERATION MOVEMENT seemed like the only sensible ones left, and the first of the police pushed by her, forcing their way out of the LIVE.NATION concert she found herself suddenly inside: Uppies all around, lava lamps and a real stage with high-end sound equipment and a professional light show. One of the things she would remember later was how new and sleek the people looked. She came face to face with a girl dressed like her, only not like her—it was some Urban Outfitter version of the DIY stuff that she and others at NO.IT.AN.EVIL were into. The screens that surrounded the dance pit here were live with a high-def version of interactive vidie that played in the LIVE.NATION email she'd received: April is the Kruelest Month... XactlySO, the TJ, continued playing his Z-Box controller, pointing it like a gun at those who had stormed in, hologram words coming at them like snowballs, then bricks, then dragonflies, then the silhouette of those jets that had been hijacked.... One of the screens showed a W.2 avatar of him, mirroring his movements. His green dreadlocks flipped out as she came closer, his wild, wide eyes fixed on her, the hair that was supposed to be an Eco-style of long green locs, looking more like Medusa's snakes as she came closer and closer, getting up on the stage as he kept shooting her with his game controller, the words coming at her changing to axes: virtual axes.

Suddenly she found herself picking up a mic stand—she'd show him what the real thing could do!— She chopped into one of his amps and it exploded in sparks.

Riot police continued to take the names of people in the streaming video of the live concert while avatars stood around looking up at them in the W.2 simul-cast, knowing that their IPs were being downloaded into police files as they watched. Then the live-video screens went blank, leaving the avatars with each other. All around Meadow, they began spreading rumors. "I heard that the bust was staged," an avatar in the shape of a dragon said.

"No way," a steampunk girl said, leather biplane pilot's helmet, big goggles. "My friend was there and she Snapped a photo."

Dragon man wasn't deterred. "Come on. I'll bet XactlySo's label filmed the bust in a studio in L.A. then made it look real to big-up his street cred." As others began to argue whether the bust was real, the concert staged, or one or the other faked by hackers who tapped into the live video feed, more avatars, bored by the same old arguments, began to vanish as their owners logged off. Others logged off when the police avatars showed up, trolling for who knows what.

Through the chatter about whether the concert had been faked—by the same people who faked elections—Meadow heard the faint sound of someone struggling to play a flute—a hollow whiffing sound exactly like Nico used to make, trying to play. She turned her head, trying to tell what direction the flute was coming from—The crowd parted for an instant, revealing a redheaded avatar sitting on the floor, playing the flute: the guy who'd asked her to dance. As she neared, she could see that his flute was exactly like the one they'd bought for Nico.

Meadow went up to him. Without looking up he said, "I can't seem to get the hang of this thing."

Despite herself, Meadow could feel herself tremble as she began to type, YOU.... Then she remembered that she could speak. "You have to tighten your lips," she said. "Like blowing out candles on a birthday cake."

The avatar before her did so, and her headset was suddenly filled with the sound of the first clear note Nico had played, the single note sounding with an intensity that vibrated the test tubes. Meadow could feel a rush of fear and joy. But then she remembered. It wasn't real. And yet, her ears continued to ring after the note died away.... It was all so confusing. Something was happening, but what? Other avatars continued to mill about. "What?... What's going on?" she asked the avatar.

He hesitated. Not the way a person hesitates when thinking, but more the way an online video freezes for a moment, waiting on a bit of info to arrive via its network before it can play. "Maybe you should check out the pyramids. Lots of people who aren't here to shop or dance end up at the pyramids," he said.

He knew her, she noted: he had a memory of her that was deeper than the few words they'd exchanged.

But before she could ask, Who are you?, he stood up and handed her the flute. Then he began to morph into the bald manikin shape all male avatars took as they went offline. "Wait! What pyramids?"

Too late. He pixelated, then was gone.

As Olympia pulled off onto the exit ramp that would take her home, her car's GPS went dead. Christ! Had she stumbled into another social swarm? She tried to check the FlashMob Alert on her phone but her phone didn't have a signal either. What good was that stupid app if the police jammed the signal before it could warn you?

Her car was back in its electric mode, silent as a glider, and as she neared, the staticky chatter of police radios grew louder. There were police vans and crowds of people. Had there been a shooting? A person could never tell if they'd stumbled upon a mob of queens blowing bubbles or a mob of RedHatters beating up a refugee. This crowd seemed to be a commercial for iWhatNots. Did a fire break out at one of those underground clubs? A cop waved to keep the traffic moving, and Olympia inched her car through the thicket of trendy people. A model-thin woman in a glittering miniskirt sat on the curb, one shoe missing, while another model nursed her with a compress. Others stood around staring into dead phones as though lost without them. There were a dozen bicycles chained to a lamppost. Back in the day, the only place you'd see bikes piled up like that was outside the park pool. Now all the bars had bike racks. As if the kids from those pools had never grown up, just gotten bigger, moved on to fucking and fighting in more adult venues.

After Chen started pointing out discrepancies in the data, Olympia wanted the disease carriers to more closely model the vectors that lived on geese. She'd had Gabe develop a colony of lice that were fed on the actual bodies of geese: geese that had been reduced to their motor function—lobotomized—that she intravenously fed. With the lobotomized geese unable to preen, Gabe could get the numbers of lice they needed from just an approximation of a flock—and the birds themselves wouldn't feel any pain. Didn't even need cages. Birds in aquariums. Every time Meadow came down here, the sight of them still triggered her gag reflex. Goose-shaped masses of lice, slowly expanding and contracting with the unmistakable rhythm of breath.

She'd come down to talk to Gabe about the liquid diet going through those tubes, but Gabe was nowhere to be found. Maybe she was in the john? Idly, she began looking at the labels—liquefied plant matter. But what kind? Olympia wanted both geese and lice on a 'natural' diet. But what was that? Meadow wondered, remembering adult geese that she'd seen back home, shepherding goslings. When they came to a road, the adults stopped and looked both ways—animals that had evolved to know how to cross streets. They began honking frantically, driving the small ones across as quickly as possible before continuing their peaceful grazing on the other side. Did Gabe need to include that road as part of their eating habits? Or the herbicides that the highway department sprayed along the road? Was that now part of their nature?

And hers? Since tons of debris from the tsunami had shown up in The Great Pacific Garbage Patch, she'd been checking in on it: she followed the studies of anthropologists who mined this Denmark-sized gyre of trash; some part of her stupidly kept hoping that she'd recognize a shoe, or maybe even Nico's flute in one of the photos taken by marine biologist who monitored ocean life, documenting the way water skaters and other insects had begun laying their eggs on trash—a flip-flop or juice bottle—instead of floating seashells, or gull feathers, as they once had; she couldn't help but think of rabbits carrying the genes of a fish; cows with the genes of a human; hens who'd had the talpid2 gene switched on, causing them to grow alligator-like teeth, and the Fgf8 and Lef1 genes causing the bones of their skulls to come together as dinosaur-like snouts instead of beaks, and the genes that tell the backbone to stop growing switched off so chickens would develop the tail of a theropod instead of a bird—the embryos growing up to be small neo-dinosaurs instead of hens—just as switching on other genetic switches allowed other researches to rewind the evolutionary clock on other animals, allowing the legs of alligators in the Cincinnati Zoo to grow to the long lengths of their dinosaur ancestors; allowing passenger pigeons, Galápagos tortoises, mastodons, and other extinct animals to fly, crawl, and swim again.... That is, she couldn't help but wonder what Olympia meant, exactly, when she used the word 'natural.'

As the pandemic of 1918 burnt itself out, and the need for mass graves slowed, police began to bother with crime again. Those firemen who survived were able to cobble together a few skeleton crews, while enough nurses and doctors began to return to work for hospitals to slowly resume operation. Surveying the state of these institutions, a meeting of mayors concluded that civilization had been three weeks from collapse.

As the pandemic of 2020 burnt itself out, refrigerated trucks were returned to transporting food instead of storing corpses. Seismologists, whose instruments had recorded an earth gone quiet, began to note again the blasting in mines, and the rumble of subways instead of the faint vibrations of heavy equipment digging mass graves. Surveying the state of hospitals, a congressional committee concluded that though those in the south, where people refused to get vaccinated, had come within days of collapse, these corporations could not be forced to stockpile additional healthcare supplies or increase their number of beds.

(August) Maine Biological Labs fined for illegally importing an avian flu virus in order to develop a vaccine for a private party in Saudi Arabia.

(August) The quickly moving and rapidly mutating virus attacks Congo; scientists say it had arrived months ago but civil war prevented efforts to contain the disease. Warlords make all conflict mineral zones incubators for the rest of the world, increasing pressure on the U.N. to send troops into these areas to secure them.

The agents—one man, one woman—were friendly enough. The woman could have been a real estate agent trying to sell him a house if the breast pocket of her business suit didn't sport an FBI badge, if the room itself didn't say trouble. Instead of the flowers, or living-room lamps that real estate offices often used to make clients feel at home, this room had the aesthetics of a vise. Mohammed was becoming depressingly familiar with the bare logic of the interrogator and interrogatee: windowless walls, metal office desk, three chairs arranged as chessmen converging on the king. Two on their side, one on his: Checkmate. Up in a high corner of the room where geckos liked to lie in wait back home was a video camera. Outside, bell-clear skies; inside, clammy palms and the buzz of fluorescent lighting. Funny, he thought, how all of these rooms were the same, whether in Bahrain or America. You'd think the styles would somehow differ—the way a mosque's prayer rugs differ from church pews—but no—the only difference was that the furniture was better here in America—he'd seen the same chairs at OfficeMax.

The woman agent began politely asking him to state his name, his address—to get a baseline for the lie detector equipment focused on his pupils, he knew. Then the man asked him to describe his work at the lab. Mohammed detailed the process of creating Western Blot Analysis. He spoke eagerly to show he was cooperating fully. He made a point to not ask why he was being questioned; he said nothing to indicate that he was a troublemaker. But then, as he talked, he began to wonder if that was a mistake: would they take his lack of questions as a sign of guilt? Were they on an immigration or terrorism fishing expedition? Or maybe they were investigating a common crime. Or perhaps his imagination had gotten away from him and they were only doing some security clearance on him because he had an H-1B Visa but was working on a project that received military funding. This last idea almost made him laugh, revealing as it had that he'd fallen into the last hope of the truly damned. How many men had stood on the gallows, certain right up until the trapdoor opened beneath their feet, that their case of mistaken identity would be revealed?

It was right at this point that the conversation took a strange turn: "Tell us about your work with honeybees," the male agent said. It was then that Mohammed noticed that the agent wasn't wearing a badge from the FBI but from the Dept. of Agriculture. Mohammed explained that he didn't work with honeybees. Or bees of any sort. The agent became confrontational. No matter what he told them about his job, they kept bringing the conversation back around to honeybees; from their questions he could tell they were investigating something to do with the collapse of the honeybee colonies that were occurring all over the country. Yes, he knew about it. Everyone did. After the bee-colony collapses of the '00s, all kinds of groups had taken to weaponizing Nature—killer bees were an invasive species in Washington; ISIS had been linked to sterile bees in France.... Anyone with a charge card and kitchen could do it. Anyone with a news feed knew about it. Were they playing dumb? Should he? If he did, would he look like he was hiding something? He decided to say exactly what he knew. Not more, not less. When they asked him what he thought was causing all of these bee colonies to fail, he gave them the pantheon of explanations that had appeared in the journals: the dances bees did to alert others in the hive of sources of nectar were being confused by cell phone transmissions, or climate change, or pesticides, emanations from power lines—so many causes had been proposed that it was the same as not having any explanation at all. "But what would you do if you wanted to bring down a beehive?" the female agent asked.

Bring down.

As if beehives were the Twin Towers. A vision of what they saw when they looked at him snapped into focus and it made his toes clench.

All American Girl @aag · 1m
President gives amnesty to **ILLEGAL MEXICANS** poisoning
#OUR BEES!

U.S. Reality Check @USRealityCheck · 1m
Missing Evidence of prior **#Keffiyeh Girl** Relationship with **#ILLEGAL MEXICANS** poisoning **#OUR BEES**

Veteran Freshman @yusufyuie · 1m
FBI not allowed to search **#ILLEGAL MEXICAN** cellphone?
I was like waaaaaaaaiiiit!!!!

Blogs said she'd damaged $300,000 worth of light and sound equipment. XactlySo's FB claimed it was $500,000. But Gabe knew, she fucking knew, it couldn't have been more than a couple of grand. She stood in the middle of the Insectarium she managed, too stunned to work. Hunted. She'd never been hunted before. The day after the concert she'd called in sick, afraid to go outside. But then, after watching the witch hunt unfolding on social media, with her as the witch, she thought she'd better just act natural. She biked into work, late, feeling a thousand eyes follow her: sensors switched traffic lights to green as she approached; ads for bike helmets flashed at her as she passed signs; her bike lock reported where it was being used; the doors to her job opened and the heat of her body was scanned for fever, then added to the building's climate-control system, reporting to its heat exchangers reporting to the power grid, reporting to.... Once inside the Insectarium, though, she was glad she came. Her routine with the lice was comforting, as was working deep in the bowels of the lab, deep in the basement where no one would normally go, and cameras weren't allowed. As with her own loft, she'd rigged it to be an island—as dumb as possible—and what networked devices there were—heat, light, humidity—were focused on the life of the insects, not her. She could almost believe the other night had been a dream....

Around her, in place of the flies feeding on dung that she had managed at the start of the study, aquarium-like containment boxes housed lobotomized blue-fronted parrots from Paraguay. They were the most common parrot found in pet shops, so were found in lots of places where they didn't belong. In Chicago, the first colonies had managed to survive the winters by huddling for warmth in streetlights—the same kind of early mutation in the brain that made humans the smartest of primates making parrots the 'chimps' of the bird world. Since the winters had grown mild, they could be found in lots of parks.

Gabe moved about the ratty, wired-up parrots, trying to keep her mind on her work instead of the growing number of photos being put online by people who had been at the LIVE.NATION concert or its NO.IT.AN.EVIL parody. Using her handheld vacuum cleaner, she began to suck lice off of the chewed-up feathers of a duck. But the news that she was wanted had struck her like a sledge between the eyes and she felt lobotomized herself. She began to think what police could do to anyone the government pinned the terrorist tag on these days. People disappeared. As the population of Guantanamo prisoners swept up in the oil wars died of old age, they'd been replaced by younger prisoners swept up in the wars over conflict minerals and water. Some had already been in one black site or another for years. And even those lucky enough to resurface, often without ever having been charged, couldn't do anything about having lost their lives to executive powers in time of war, a time that had no foreseeable end, and a beginning that was hard for people her age to remember.

Stop it, she told herself, trying to take comfort in the white noise of the Insectarium, the perpetual whir of its humidifiers making it easier to forget the swirl going on up above, out in the real world, the chips and sensors embedded in chairs, in floor tiles, in light bulbs and switches like a million witnesses reporting to the cloud where she was or wasn't, even monitoring how much toilet paper she used—a sensor in each dispenser wired into the reorder center. There must be hundreds of photos of her—or rather of parts of her—online by now: her ankle in one, an elbow in another, but none, at least the last time she'd checked, of her face. And even if there were, her face had been covered by the keffiyeh she'd found on the ground. Should she have thrown it away? She could imagine its black-and-blue checkered fabric hanging with a few N95 masks off a kitchen chair back home, right where anyone who walked into her loft could see it.

Having her face covered while she smashed the stage equipment probably bought her some time. And NGers claimed that if enough of them wore those electronic face-scrambling necklaces, it gave the whole rave facial-recognition herd immunity. Still, there must have been a gajillion cell phones and surveillance cameras—even a police drone with infrared and night vision imaging, for God's sake—Not to mention FB, Google, Flickr, Twitter, and every other website that aggregated photos, instantly scanning them, comparing them, logging every detail in ways that made any sense of secrecy a thing of the past. Any teenager with a Snap account could probably out her. But so far, none had. Why?

The question gave her that creepy feeling of being watched. But when she turned around, there was only the shelves of lice-coated geese. It gave her the urge to check, for the thousandth time, for updates. What was going on out there in the Twittersphere? What? She pulled out her phone to check, but down here in the bunker there wasn't any cell service. And even if there were, she only carried a dumb phone, because, she remembered with a laugh, she didn't want anyone to track her—not because she had anything to hide—rather, it was because, as she liked to tell people, she didn't like walking around naked either. Duct tape covered the holes she'd made in her sneakers to dig out the chips that monitored the number of steps she took in order to report her movement to the Fitbit she didn't own—and also the Fitbit manufacturer and who knew who else. She'd dug them out long ago—as an up-yours to the Internet of Things, and also to keep someone from hacking her shoes. But could that be used as evidence against her now?—evidence that she was, in fact, hiding? Nah. If so, they'd have to arrest nearly everyone at the concert, lots of people there even making their own clothes to keep any form of biometrics out of the cloth.

As she prepared to go upstairs to check on how the hunt for the witch was going, she wondered if there was something to that idea of preemptive arrests: the claim that algorithms could identify criminals—people who didn't let the chip in their shoes talk to their Fitbit—from their patterns of behavior, before they'd committed any crime....

If anyone ever doubted whether or not 1s and 0s, cars, bikes, AGCTs, or water could flow in ways other than by the logic of the grid, all they had to do was watch traffic in India or China or Vietnam: motor scooters would force a break in traffic to cross, snarls developed then untangled within seconds.... Leaving the snarl to enter the wet market, Ah Lam soon found herself navigating crates, stalls, cages, and tubs holding live chickens, fish, crabs, scorpions, pigs, monkeys, dogs, turtles, frogs, privet cats, wild ducks, geese, pheasants, and so many other animals howling, mewing, braying, clucking....

Bai peeked out from behind the poster that the government made him put on his stall, warning of avian flu.

When Bai saw Ah Lam, he motioned her inside, and after looking both ways, she slipped in to inspect the exotic animals crammed into his small shop: soft-shelled turtles from Sumatra; parrots from Paraguay; pangolins from Vietnam; pythons from Myanmar, and red-eared sliders from the U.S.A. They had to be careful. The government tried to keep him from selling his animals; they said having cages of animals on top of each other, chickens shitting down onto ducks, ducks shitting on the pigeons below them, was unclean. But Bai's family has been selling exotic animals for generations and he knew far better than men in offices that all animals are unclean. And Ah Lam knew that there is

LIVE•
Alternate Flow Patterns
youtube.com/watch?v=iElk3RpV6RA

no better cure for liver problems than the bile of a black bear; that there is no better cure for poor circulation than eating seahorses; no meat fresher than that from an animal that has been slaughtered in front of her. And that she wouldn't know how she would live if she didn't have her own business mailing animal cures to America, Africa, Australia, and Europe....

At Olympia's request, Dr. Karen Kitlaus created a bird-to-mammal virus. Olympia said she'd have her own people do it, but the biohazard containment lab being built in her building was behind schedule and she didn't want to wait. Already she was at the stage where they could start plugging data into modeling programs, and it would help to have some models of what a bird-to-mammal disease mutation might look like. So as a favor, Dr. Kitlaus had her technicians take human flu of H3N2 strain and samples of H5N1 collected back in 1997. They infected a ferret to see what would happen. Would the infected ferret infect other ferrets in the same cage? Could it spread if the ferrets exchanged saliva? By licking each other or sharing food? Would it attach to receptors in the mammal's noses and throats and so be easily spread by sneezing? Or would it mutate into something that could only live deep in the lungs, like in the outbreaks in Azerbaijan and Iraq in 2006, something that even heavy coughing had a hard time spreading?

Whatever her results, they were sure to be worse out in nature, nature's laboratory infinite compared to the artificial conditions of a lab. Under the controlled conditions of the lab, the disease could only spread via one path: ferret to ferret. But in the wild, it could go from ferret to ferret, but also ferret to mouse to owl to ferret; it could develop a completely unanticipated route, like the *Leucochloridium paradoxum*, a parasite that infests snails: one mutation causes the eyes of the infested snail to bulge out of its head; another causes the snail, a ground dweller, to climb to the light, scaling reeds to get as high as possible. By the time it reaches the top, its eyeballs look like long, wiggling caterpillars, the favorite food of Jays. The birds devour the eyes of the snails, and thus ingest the parasite. Inside the Jay, the *Leucochioridium paradoxum* matures, then releases its eggs into the rectum of the bird, which the bird shits out, down onto the forest floor where other snails eat it, become infected, the ability of a virus to try all doors as infinite as its patience, shape-shifting as easily as water seeking its own level.

When Dr. Kitlaus went into the animal area to see how her ferrets were doing, she noticed the smell first. They were all dead. Dead ferrets lay about in their cages. And not just in the cage of the one she had infected, but all of the ferrets in all of the cages.

Most of the time Combat Health Care Specialist Guy Resnick was too stuck in the here and now to notice. But sometimes he'd emerge from his workaday routine, as one wakes from the daydream of monotony, to realize how surreal the world around had become: the corridors of high-rises his company had been maneuvering through could have been Condo Canyon back home—if it weren't for the rubble and broken windows from previous fighting. In this part of Kinshasa, entire blocks looked as though wrecking balls had left after only beginning the job: doll-housed, they called it, the force of shelling too far away to bring down the entire building, but close enough to weaken its structure so that eventually the front of the building collapsed, leaving the interior rooms exposed like those in a dollhouse. The people, having nowhere else to go, would go about their lives in these apartments, living dolls.

The building that he and the other six GIs in his platoon made their way up was still intact though. All of the buildings on this block still had their glass. On the eighth floor, the family they found living in darkness could have been modern-day cave dwellers if it weren't for their gaudy dining-room sets. He thought he'd even seen the same glitzy chairs in a store window on Devon Avenue, along with clocks in the shape of minarets, and those enormous suitcases—the size of steamer trunks—used by wealthier Bottom Billion immigrants.

The mother of the family could have been any Muslim mother living above those shops. The kitchen doorway Guy stood in, posed like a sprinter, could have opened onto any Chicago kitchen—if it weren't so empty; if the Shiite mother and her two sons weren't staring at him from the gloom of the bedroom where they huddled off to the side; if a broad streak of blood didn't stretch across the kitchen floor, painted there by the back of Mejia's head when Guy, T-Ball, and Fred dragged him out of the kitchen, away from the window that had been punctured—a single .308 caliber hole—by the sniper bullet that brought him down while he was going through kitchen cabinets like anyone might, trying to look behind a box of Cheerios.

The rattle of machine-gun fire continued on the street below: a metallic clacking that could have been a Chicago Streets & Sanitation jackhammer if it weren't one of the FARDC units they'd been sent to support, fighting to eliminate the M23 Tutsis militia that had been driving Hutus out of the neighborhood. He wasn't even supposed to be here. An imam had tweeted the URL to the latest "Mohammed is a Homo" video to come out of America, and like always, the riots began. Riots in 16 countries this time, linking up into what some were afraid could be a new regional revolution—like when the Iron Curtain fell—the embassy had been burned—and he'd been redeployed—*Today's Mobile Army!*— Rebels in the Congo used the chance of the U.S. army being spread thin to retake control of mineral-rich areas; and Guy's squadron had been sent to one of them to put a cork in it. A policing action, they called it.

Guy's unit was the come-along, trailing the FARDC as a rearguard action, going building to building, searching for stragglers or snipers or weapon caches. As they passed the building they were in now, a boy stepped out from the ruins. Dressed in a Sox tee shirt, he could have come from a playground near that Ethiopian restaurant Silpa had taken him to before he shipped out. Standing in the yellow spotter smoke that drifted through the street, the kid yelled out to them the name of the family now huddled in the bedroom off to the side. The father had a collection of DVDs made by snipers shooting Americans, he said. So Guy and his unit made their way up the damaged stairwell to the apartment. While Fred and Amato ransacked the living room, Mejia went through kitchen cabinets, and Sgt. Bee interrogated the family: a woman covered in black—a Muslim among Christians in this French-speaking country—and a boy no older than the one who gave them the tip—they could have been playmates—and another teenage son. As the woman spoke French, she looked from their Congolese interpreter to the sergeant, as though unsure who held the real power over her, who she should make her case to. The interpreter gave no sign either way, as though whatever she said didn't have the slightest interest to him—French in one ear, English—American English—out the mouth—though Guy wondered if the interpreter's American accent already condemned him. Or maybe he and the other guys in the platoon were the ones who were condemned, the rednecks among them too give-a-shit or deaf to the interpreter to understand that he understood their cracks about him and his country and its women or about whose side he was really on. Guy himself wondered about this last point every time the interpreter flipped open a personal cell phone to rattle off something in Swahili, a black scarf hiding the lower half of his face. Maybe he was only on his own side. Who'd blame him. They called him Zorro.

The family obviously wondered who Zorro was really fighting for. The older son stared at what he could see of that face as though trying to memorize it while his Mother explained, or so Zorro reported, that her family had lived in this apartment for fifteen years. They had stayed through the fighting, right up to when the local Tutsi warlord ordered his militia to kill Hutus. They were neither Hutus nor Tutsis so hoped they would be left alone but a local Sunni imam began preaching that Shiites were like Hutus. The neighborhood they had fled to was destroyed by fighting also, so they had come back. But the Sunni family they found living in their apartment wouldn't leave. After the American army made them leave, the Sunni family told the M23 that her husband sold information to the Americans; they told spies for the Americans that he smuggled water to the M23. Now she hadn't seen her husband in two days and only Allah knew if he'd been picked up by Americans, picked up by M23, the imam's militia, or some other gang, or was lying dead in a ditch. "Will you tell the Americans to help me find my husband?" she pleaded through the interpreter.

Guy didn't need an interpreter to see the fear in her eyes. He had watched the wheels turn in their CO's head as he tried to sort it out, tried to judge whether the woman was lying, her husband maybe hiding in the building just as the boy who gave them the tip said, maybe grenade in hand—his ticket to Paradise. Or maybe the woman would like to see them all dead because so many innocent 'persons of interest' like her husband and sons had been picked up then never seen again. Or maybe he scrammed when he heard an army coming up the stairs, not knowing whose side they were on. Scared or confused or mistaken about soldiers in his living room, led there by a boy who was really working for the M23, or just helping his own family get a better apartment, or settle a score, or was confused, or simply misinformed, or mistaken—maybe he didn't even know this family was up here, and had only given them the tip to divert them from a cache of arms, or to lead them into an ambush.... Or maybe he had been sent to divert the Americans so his uncle could finish stealing a car. A lot of killing, ratting, and lying went on to cover ordinary street crime or settle scores. Family feuds. A lot wasn't. Hard to tell.

While Fred ransacked the apartment, looking for maps or the doorbells used to detonate homemade bombs or anything that would tip the story one way or the other, Guy considered how everything here was a weapon, even the most everyday objects: cars and cell phones, of course, but food was a weapon too, sacks of rice used to award or punish families like this woman's for information or their sympathies; water was a weapon, so was electricity, and ice in one-hundred and ten degree heat when the electricity, and so the refrigeration, and air-conditioning didn't work; religions were weapons of mass destruction. Nature was a weapon: terrorists getting the idea from the last bee die-off to genetically alter them to bring on hive collapses the way they once tried to bring down airplanes. Even Silly String was a weapon: those aerosol cans that Guy used to play with as a kid, spraying ribbons of colored foam at birthday parties. Here, GIs sprayed Silly String down hallways in the buildings they searched, like this one, the party-colored foam sticky enough to cling to and expose trip wires, but light enough to not detonate booby traps. Clothes were certainly a weapon: the uniform he wore; the Sox shirt the boy wore, camouflage to make him look familiar? His words believable? Yeah, most deadly of all were words....

Then there had been a tiny tinkle of glass—like a wind chime—and Mejia had dropped to the kitchen floor. They hadn't even heard a rifle shot, just the tinkle of window glass falling into the sink. When he turned to look, the first thing he saw was a perfectly round hole, the diameter of a pencil's eraser—a nothing in the grand scheme of the cosmos.

Time blurred: Sgt. Bee yelled at everyone to get down. Mejia was on the floor, a pool of blood widening beneath his head as everyone reacted: Fred and T-Ball getting Mejia by the feet and dragging him to the windowless corner of the kitchen where Guy tore off his flak jacket to keep its weight from squeezing blood from his body. He wiped blood away to find the wound in the back of his neck, applied compresses to the gurgling hole.... While he frantically tore open more bandages, worked to staunch the bleeding, the sergeant must have called in a medivac; though minutes had to have passed, they seemed to have appeared instantly, and out of nothing, as though conjured from the air. An evacuation medic took over from Guy as they got an IV going, got Mejia onto a stretcher; then they were carrying him down to a waiting Humvee. Then they were gone. The kitchen was silent, eerily empty, except for the red streak on the floor. Dust drifted in the shaft of light streaming through the window.

It all happened so fast it didn't seem real—as though it had never happened—as though a quake had ruptured Time and Mejia had fallen in before it snapped back, leaving everything as it had been before, minus him. Guy, T-Ball, Fred, and Bee were still there, standing around; Zorro was beside the Muslim family, still huddled in the bedroom, still looking back like trapped animals waiting to see what their captor would do next. All that had changed was that Mejia was no longer going through kitchen cabinets. Mejia was gone: replaced by a long red smear on the tile. Guy's hands were bloody; he wiped them on his pant legs.

Wrappers and the bandages he had used to staunch the wound lay scattered all around. Then Guy saw what shit they were still in. The flak jacket he had torn off of Mejia was on the far side of the kitchen. He couldn't remember having thrown it, but he must have. And that's where it landed, on the far side of the kitchen, along with Mejia's rifle, bolt cutters, and helmet. Four items across a small kitchen, the morning light coming through its single window harsh as an interrogation lamp.

"Shit," someone muttered, seeing what Guy saw: a helmet, rifle, bolt cutters, and a flak jacket on the kitchen floor, on the far side of a window punctured by a round from a sniper's rifle. Items they couldn't just leave behind. The others slumped down along the walls, the wind going out of them.

They would have to retrieve the gear, they all knew. The weapon was a weapon, of course, one that if left behind would end up in the hands of someone in the imam's militia. Or in the hands of a carjacker, or maybe that teenage boy huddled in the bedroom, or a hundred other possibilities, but all of them resulting in someone else dead, maybe one—or all—of them. The same was true of the flak jacket, designed to protect a shooter. The bolt cutter could be used to steal explosives. Or steal fertilizer that could be used as an explosive. If a helmet was added to a shirt from another dead GI, a uniform could be cobbled together that would let a suicide bomber walk into a group of....

"Shit," Davis repeated.

"What the fuck'd you have to throw his jacket for?" T-Ball snapped at Guy.

"If you ever need a medic, I'll be sure to fold your clothes first."

"Shut up!" Sgt. Bee yelled. His hand was shaking as he picked up the radiophone and called for another unit to clear the building across from the window, where the sniper most likely lined up his shot.

Sitting cross-legged on the living-room sofa, he gave them the coordinates. They could hear what he was being told: the drones were all occupied, so no overview; another unit could clear the building, but they had their own problems and they'd need time to get there. Deal. "How long?" T-Ball asked as soon as Bee was off the phone. Stupid question, everyone knew. They sat down to wait, knowing that the longer they sat, the larger a target they became. An unmoving target. Word would spread that they were pinned down, and a militia would get a grenade launcher over here, flatten the whole apartment, kill the mom and kid too. M23 Tutsis wouldn't care if they were Hutus, and Jihadist didn't give a shit either way. Not even about their own. Making Martyrs, they called it.

Outside, the popping of gunfire started up again. They all fell into their thoughts. Mejia. There but for the grace of god go.... After a while, Fred said, "At least medivac got here fast." His voice was choked with emotion, the weight of what had happened catching up with them all now that they had stopped moving and had time to think. There but for the grace of god.... A sniffle came from the other side of the couch.

What god?

"He'll be okay," Bee said, but everyone knew it was a neck wound. "Ain't that right, Guy? You had a patch on him before the bullet had a chance to hit the wall. Then the medivacs were here."

"Yeah, right," Guy said, his answer sounding like bullshit even to his own ears, his eyes falling on the family staring back, the lack of remorse in their eyes making him understand how others in their place sometimes just went off—the way frustration sometimes makes a person need to punch something—anything—a wall, or a kid. Then sure enough, Fred popped off: "Make the kid go get it."

All of their eyes went to the kid, and the mother grabbed him, looking back with that fear that wasn't sure what the danger was, but knew there was danger.

"Stow it," Bee said.

"They're the ones who—"

"I don't give a shit!"

Then they returned to silence, listening to the popping of gunfire die off, then start again. Somewhere, in another apartment, a baby was crying. T-Ball stood, being careful to stay within the sheltered edge of the kitchen where he, Guy, and Fred had been since Mejia went down. Crawling beneath the living-room window, then along the far wall, then the couch, he worked his way back to the bedroom—was he going to be the one to go off on the family? It'd be just like him, Guy thought, simultaneously hating the hothead for being the one to go off and hoping he would, hoping someone would take it out on these people for making him be here: them and their shitty tantalum and all the others in all the zones he'd been sent into to secure veins of coltan and tungsten and whatever other shit arms dealers said was vital to national security because they needed to make missile guidance systems and GPS systems and even the radio that Fred would use to call in the support to secure an area that was vital to national security because they needed its minerals to make the weapons they would use to secure it and keep the merry-go-round going....

T-Ball emerged from the bedroom with two sheets. He tied them together, and then fixed his hand ax to one end to make a line and hook. From the sheltered edge of the kitchen, he cast his line at the equipment, trying to snag the helmet. On his tenth try he managed to work the helmet close enough to where they could reach it with a broom. After some minutes of trying, he managed to get the jacket. Then the bolt cutter. But the rifle had fallen in an awkward position against the far wall; its barrel seemed to be snagged on something under the stove, its low profile announcing from the start that hooking it would be impossible, and after a while Fred gave up. T-Ball tried. Over and over. Then he gave up too and sat back against the wall, lit a cigarette. Davis took his turn as sentry in the outer doorway.

Fred began to speculate where the shot had come from. T-Ball thought that if they got to the living room windows they could lay down fire at the apartment across the street. He said it in an absentminded, hypothetical way, everyone knowing how stupid that would be, but after twenty minutes dragged into a half hour, then an hour, they began talking about it more seriously, Fred and Davis getting into an argument about which window to direct their heat at. Guy knew why they were on edge. That little prick who had sent them up here could be directing militiamen right to them. By now they would have had plenty of time to round up some real ordnance. They could be in the opposite building at this very minute, aiming a shoulder-launched rocket at this apartment. He couldn't stop imagining the nose of a rocket screaming at the wall he had his back against. T-Ball, Davis, and the others appeared around him as burning skeletons. "The bullet came from below," he said. "The entrance wound was below his helmet; the exit wound above his ear."

"If I keep low, I can get his gear," Guy said.

Not even T-Ball was expecting this, and he and the others looked first at Guy, then to the Sergeant, who considered it for a moment, then shook it off. As though Guy hadn't said anything, he continued, "We don't know that. We don't know anything. Mejia might have been looking down into the sink, the bullet coming from a higher floor with a clear view into the kitchen."

T-Ball stretched to see if he could see where the shot hit the wall but before he could argue, Bee cut him off: "We wait."

The men fell silent again. One thing everyone learned here was that optimism gets you dead. If it looks like a trap, it's a trap. Guy began to feel it was his fault. They were all going to die because at the moment he was supposed to let his training take over, he'd thrown the flak jacket and it had slid into the kill box of a sniper. Then his mind began to work past this again. A lot of times, snipers shot and ran. Or maybe the same fear of sitting that was eating them had begun to gnaw his ass and he got out of there, seeing a rocket come at the wall his back was against every time he rested his eyes. Yeah, odds were that there wasn't anything across the way except fear.

But that was optimism talking again. Still, Guy couldn't help but consider the possibility that there might not even be a ghost across the way: Mejia could have been taken down by a mistake—the FARDC Army down in the street or some other unit mistaking Mejia, visible through the window, as an M23 sniper. Or it could have been an accident, like Davis said, not a carefully aimed, deliberate shot: Cross fire. Friendly fire. The FARDC Army shooting at M23; or the imam's militia shooting at a FARDC unit, or another American unit, or no one shooting at anyone. A misfire. Someone celebrating, shooting into the air—what goes up, must come down....

Guy sighed. He was being optimistic again, his optimism enabled by ignoring more likely possibilities: an ambush set up by the boy who'd sent them up here, the boy directing them to where the sniper could get a clean shot, snipers just as likely to sit for hours, motionless as a cobra, if they thought they hadn't been spotted. Then he realized another possibility: the father could have had a collection of sniper tapes because he was the sniper. He could have gotten out the back way when he heard them coming, then took up a position across the street that would allow him to shoot back into his own apartment. Is that why this one apartment, of all others, had been singled out?

Worry furrowed the face of the Shiite mother in the bedroom. Worry for what? That they'd get him before he got off another shot? Then a call came in: their relief had gotten lost. One other thing: an air strike had been called in on a neighboring apartment block. "That's just great!" Bee said. "Our own guys can't find us but an F-16's going to shoot an apple off our heads."

"With a five-hundred-pound bomb."

"Hope it's one of those smart bombs."

"A really smart bomb."

While the others bitched, Sgt. Bee agreed to let Guy go for the gear. And the sight of Guy stripping off his ammo and gear to make himself lighter shut up the others. T-Ball pulled off his own flak jacket, then Fred too. As they helped him wrap them around his legs and midsection, Guy could see Zorro in the bedroom. From the way the woman was going "Ahh"—like pantomiming a patient at the dentist—Guy could tell Zorro was getting them ready for the air strike, reminding them to keep their mouths open so the shock waves wouldn't blow out their eardrums. The boys already knew the routine, taking up positions deeper in the room in case there was flying glass. Guy took up his position in the kitchen doorway. The plan was for him to wait for the air strike—the blast would surprise the sniper—if there was a sniper—knock him off guard. Or at least make it impossible for him to get off a clean shot.

Guy put his back foot against the doorjamb, a sprinter in the blocks, waiting for the starter's gun. The light coming through the kitchen window had softened by now to a warm, welcoming glow, the long narrow kitchen stretching out like infinity before him.

What's the matter with me, Guy wondered, trying to instead concentrate on getting a clean jump. He could have not volunteered, he realized, gradually becoming aware of the others watching him as though he was no longer one of them. Three more sets of eyes stared back from the bedroom, his very presence holding their attention, a range of emotions across their face from the dread of the mother, to the excited expectation of the teenager. Instead of volunteering, Guy thought, he could have just sat back like the others, waited for Bee to pick someone. Odds were, since Guy was the medic, it would have been someone else: Davis the fastest among them; or Fred the screwup, the expendable one; or maybe T-Ball might have lost the lottery, Fate or chance putting the short straw in his hand; and Guy would be sitting there in his place while he, or one of them, stood here in his place. But no, Guy had to open his mouth because— Because something inside him made him feel responsible. Not responsible because, like T-Ball said, he was the one who threw the flak jacket. Stupid mistake. But a stupider way to think, he knew. Say instead that gravity or fate or chance or the evil eye was to blame, making the gun skitter to the far wall. Makes no dif, the others would say, and since they didn't throw anything, the jacket was the deciding factor: the flipped coin that had turned up heads though he'd called tails. But even if they didn't say that, he still felt responsible for keeping them safe, the way genes somehow made him go into biology to begin with, to learn to draw blood, staunch its flow. He certainly didn't have the gene that researchers said predisposed some to take risks, an AGCT combo that made those people crave adrenaline as a junkie has to have his fix, one of those wrinkles of population genetics that sacrificed individuals to keep the whole healthy, every tribe needing someone who would taste the untested berry, volunteer for the vaccine test, as much as they needed the skittish ones who wouldn't. Was it his genes speaking when he said he'd go for the gear, a combination of genetic letters his fatal flaw? His fate?

The rifle lay at the far end of the kitchen, an infinity away, the window with a single round hole making the floor into a vast plain.

A rifle is a thing; a refrigerator is a thing; a rifle wedged under a refrigerator is a third thing that makes other possibilities possible....

Waiting, waiting.... For minutes or longer, he had no idea, losing sense of time the way waiting in a hospital waiting room makes the waiting timeless—just the opposite of the way time had contracted when Mejia was hit—the soft yellow light in the window so normal it could have been full of Silpa's voice, telling him that everything was going to be all right.

Silpa claimed that some people could hear colors, he remembered. Cognitive science backed her up. He'd never believed it, but if it were true, the soft yellow of afternoon light coming through the window would sound like her. He worked to get back to that voice, imagining the last time he'd been able to meet her in W.2, the two of them on a Hawaiian beach as he struggled to explain the weirdness of helping mothers like the one in the bedroom during the day, and then rounding up their sons and husbands at night. It had been a softened version of what was really bothering him: being called to retrieve body parts from a burnt Humvee. From one of the survivors, a medic like him, he had learned that a young girl had run out from between two parked cars into the path of the Humvee. The driver had slammed on his brakes to keep from hitting her, even though all drivers were trained to not stop for anything: no man, woman, not even baby Jesus. The girl had smiled sweetly, an enigmatic Mona Lisa smile—in thanks? Or because she'd done her job well, setting them all up to die? "Step on it!" the GI riding shotgun had screamed at the driver. A moment later, a grenade bounced onto the hood, a white flash, windshield glass....

The story got to Guy because he could so imagine himself stopping the Humvee instead of running over the girl and getting himself and everyone around him killed; he could so imagine himself refusing to take that chance, flooring the gas pedal and squashing the little bitch like a bug on the grill. He'd been afraid of what Silpa would think if she knew this about him, though, so instead told her a lighter version: his story about the ER doctor back home who shot a mugger. Same moral: here but for the grace of god stands anyone, he had said. She'd remained silent, taking his avatar's hand in hers, running them through the sand, then answered, "Action without desire," as a way to explain that that was how the doctor was able to treat his own mugger, doing his duty, a lack of passion allowing him to remain true to himself. She had meant it as a way for him to not blame himself for some of the things he found himself doing, he knew, Silpa somehow knowing there was more to his story than what he had told her, elaborating his story of the doctor as though it were a reincarnation of one of her own: a story about Arjuna, a warrior on the eve of battle, who was seized by pity for those he was about to kill—cousins and first teachers. The bloodshed he was about to begin filled him with doubt. Everyone in India grew up learning about Arjuna and Krishna, his chariot driver, she said: from philosophy students to untouchables getting the story from Bollywood movies. They all learned that Arjuna asked Krishna how he could slay those people facing him when they, when all living beings, were worthy of worship. Even if he was victorious, he said, the blood on his hands would poison all of life's delights, for the grief of his enemies' mothers would be no less piteous than the tears of his own mother should he fall. Indeed, Arjuna continued, it could well be that those he was about to slay were the ones who were truly fighting on the side of justice, as both sides claimed. It could well be that he, not they, were the pawns of larger forces; that they, not he, had been wronged, forced to act by circumstance, and that the freedom they won over his body would most embody the righteousness that they both claimed.

With the two facing armies waiting to attack, Arjuna declared that he would not fight, and laid down his bow.

Krishna responded by saying that Arjuna could have no way of knowing who would live, who would die, or whether it would be better for humanity if his side or the other lost. All life is change, he explained, and the wise are not troubled as their spirit moves through youth to age. The soul can be thy friend; the soul can be thy enemy. The pleasures of the world bear within them sorrows yet to come. The good works of man are not his works; the evil works are not his works. They come and go. Not in them do the wise find joy. Pain moves him not; nor pleasure.

As Krishna spoke, he revealed himself in his Eternal form, and Arjuna saw in this humble chariot driver the eyes of innumerable faces—all who had ever lived, who would ever live, the light of a thousand suns. "He who sees one single fraction of me sees all creation, and seeing all creation," the God said in glory, "that which is beyond the visible and invisible, the Eternal; when all things pass away this remains: I am the silence of prayer; the Himalayas of all that does not move; the thunderbolt of weapons, victory, defeat; the cleverness in the gambler's dice; the wind of purification; the beginning, middle and end of all that Is. I am Time which destroys all things, puppets whirling forward in a play of shadow. Even if thou dost not fight, all warriors facing thee shall die.

"But fear not, for the man whose peace is not shaken by others is dear to me. The man who is free from vanity, whose soul is as his actions, whose love is the same for his enemies as his friends, this man who sees that the God in himself is the same God in all that is; he hurts not himself by hurting others. Free of selflessness, even as he kills warriors before him, he sees Eternity in things that pass away, including his own life—"

The screech of a jet woke Guy to the blood on the floor before him: beautiful as an abstract painting, a red streak across a rectangle of yellow sunlight. The apartment rattled with the jet's roar, dust sifting from the ceiling, his heart racing as though swooping up and out of his body to catch up. In the same half instant, he forced himself to focus on the rifle at the far end of the room, glancing at the window to judge his dash. *Wait for the blast, wait for the blast,* his mind's eye seeing the jet release its bomb.... *On your mark*—he ran track in high school—was this the way a fetus feels before it pushes into the light?—*Get set*—or old people at the moment of their?—wait for the blast—*Go!*

When Dan woke the computer, he was surprised at how fast the diagram of Olympia's virus was branching. Ten days in and it already looked like the MRI of an overactive brain, synapses firing like crazy. He'd modeled other open-loop systems—the tide of handguns that wash into then out of hot spots—but none were as dynamic as this. He snapped his fingers to take a screen grab: a depiction of what the computer model thought the virus looked like out in the wild at that very moment.

They weren't supposed to do their own blood work but that was like asking a cook to not taste the soup. So, when Gabe asked Silpa to have a look at her red blood cells, she just got out her kit. "Make a fist."

A few minutes later she had Gabe's blood on a slide.

"Here. Look for yourself."

Gabe bent to Silpa's microscope. In its eyepiece, the blood cells had dots of black. "Maybe it's a dead virus."

"No, I recognize this one. It's an earlier form of malaria. It'll make a person sick but it's not lethal. Where do you think you got it?"

Gabe didn't answer, her eye screwed into the eyepiece.

"Could be a stray," Silpa said, thinking of the Carolina wren she'd seen the other day: a bird that wasn't supposed to be this far north but was at the bird feeder that someone set up outside the lab window.

When Gabe looked up from the microscope, the worry on her face reminded Silpa of her own. For weeks she had debated calling Guy's mother, afraid what a mother would think if a strange woman called, making inquiries about her son. In India, this could mean so many things. None honorable.

There had been times before when he couldn't meet her in W.2. He'd warned her of this, what with Today's Army functioning more as a social swarm jet-coptered in to defeat some ragtag uprising, secure a mine, put down a warlord or some such, before being airlifted out to the next crisis. He could be anywhere. With all the information blackouts it was amazing they'd been able to meet in W.2 as often as they had. So even if his mother didn't know any more about his whereabouts than she did, it probably wouldn't mean anything.

Looking through the microscope at the black specks in her blood, Gabe understood anger. She used to bike past the duck pond on the way to work: an ugly thing in Humboldt Park, all concrete and chain-link. Signs told people to not climb the fence around the pond or feed bread to the ducks. The pond was littered with chunks of donuts and Cheetos anyway, and Gabe could never figure out if the people who used the park were oblivious, or so used to being told what to do that they ignored all signs as a matter of course. She began taking a more roundabout way so she wouldn't have to pass the pond after the morning she'd found it littered with the bodies of the ducks themselves. Someone had poisoned every last bird. Now she was pretty sure she was the one who had screwed up Chen's data: she'd been so distracted by the idea of having caught something that she could have mixed up the lice. She'd worried about it for days, but now she was like Fuck it. Fuck it all. And she was okay with that.

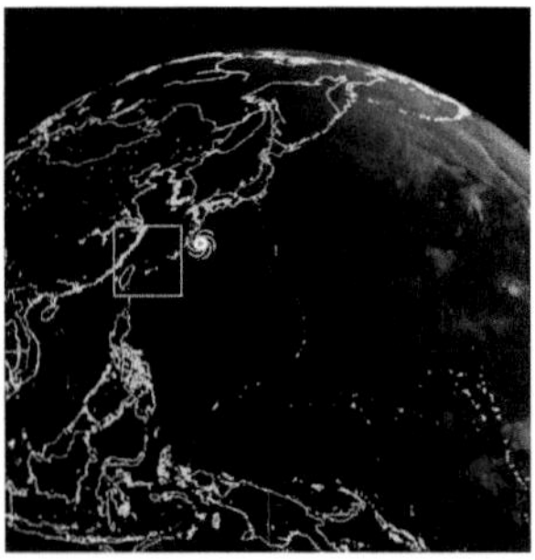

LIVE •
Himawari-8 Earth
himawari8.nict.go.jp

Sitting in her corner of the lab, zoning out over what she'd just learned, and how it made her tiredness make sense, Gabe realized she'd been gazing at what looked like a gleaming gold ingot crawling with ants on the screen of Meadow's computer. Screensaver? Then she saw the W.2 interface.

Meadow noticed and swiveled to face her, eyebrows arched as though expecting Gabe to ask her something. Not in the mood to talk about what was really on her mind, Gabe said, "I didn't know you did W.2." She nodded back toward the screen.

"Yeah. Stupid, huh?" Meadow said sheepishly, glancing back at it. "Like thinking you can defeat global warming by bagging your own groceries." The ants continued to crawl up the ingot.

When Gabe looked closer, she could see that they were making an anthill out of grains of gold. Two-legged ants—avatars—walked up the footpath of a mountain. A golden mountain. "Good intentions, anyway," she said, not meaning to sound so snarky. Once upon a time, she'd been one of them, after all. She even remembered her username: ClrUrCookies.

"I'm in Brazil.2. I'd heard they were building a pyramid." Meadow pressed the down arrow key to make her avatar fly in a little closer and the bird's-eye view they'd had of the pyramid pulled in tight enough to show individuals inching up the scaffolding: avatars of nuns, nudists, women in business suits, and of course, the ubiquitous skateboarders and clubbers, each carrying a single gold brick. When they got to its top, they handed it to one of the bricklaying avatars, who added it to the pyramid they were building, brick by brick.

"What's going on?" Gabe asked.

"I'm not really sure." Like a telegraph operator, Meadow kept tapping her finger till her avatar was on the ground where she asked a penguin carrying a gold brick and it told her how this used to be the site of one of the world's largest strip mines. As the penguin spoke, Gabe remembered: in the real world, this had been the site of a real mountain. Then someone discovered gold, and the rush was on, so many peasants, ex-teachers, ex-cops—men from everywhere—hoping to get rich, digging into the earth that after a few years the mountain was level; still they dug, the peasants so poor that to find even a pinch of gold was a windfall. The mountain became a massive pit with hundreds of makeshift ladders going down, companies moving in, hiring the natives to dig, working many of them to death, the entire site looking, from the air, like a volcano crater being dug deeper by thousands of ants. The hole was still there in the real world: an abandoned open-pit mine the depth of the Grand Canyon, now flooded. Here in W.2,

though, UNCV had used it as a rallying point, running a worldwide campaign to refill the hole with gold—with a portion going to charity for the indigenous people who had been exploited to reduce the mountain to a hole. The campaign had been so successful that UNCV had kept it going, spurring donors to build a pyramid where the hole had been.

"Are you're helping?"

"No," Meadow said. She kept looking down at her shoes, as though embarrassed. Gabe noticed that Meadow's avatar held a red flute. "I heard there was a connection to missing people somehow."

The way she said it, the sincerity that came over her face told Gabe that she'd been thinking of her son again, and she instantly saw the situation: Meadow going online in search of some kind of memento of her son only to find Russian spam artists, and just plain old con artists who were to the Internet what Bible salesmen had been to Dustbowl America. Meadow had tried to enlist one of those groups that sifts through millions of images for hints of things like downed planes, or exoplanets, but they'd turned her down. Like looking for a needle in a haystack? she'd asked. No, like looking for a needle in a haystack of needles. To make up for her snarkiness, Gabe said, "Like a support group?"

"I'm not sure. Something like that I guess. Only stronger. I don't know. I don't even know if it's true."

The emptiness of losing a child.... Gabe wished she'd realized what Meadow had really meant before she'd opened her mouth. In the old days, someone would be trying to sell someone like Meadow life insurance or the Brooklyn Bridge. Here in W.2, you could actually buy the Brooklyn Bridge. Or at least Brooklyn Bridge.2, and lots of people thought owning it was worthwhile, even if it cost real dollars. Gabe felt a tide of sympathy rise in her for Meadow. For everyone.

Lots of people doing their own thing for their own reasons: poets still writing poems; bank clerks coming home to play World of Warcraft; DIY journalists roving the war-torn streets of Rio de Janeiro, pushing the shopping cart that held their makeshift production studio; the owner of Gourmet Groceries arranges apples, onions, and carrots to look like bands of red, white, and orange in an abstract painting; a Zip Code full of bobos who expect their produce aisle to resemble an art gallery; Tibet shoots silver iodide into clouds above Nagqu grasslands to deplete them of rain before they drift out of their airspace. A half-hour later, China invades to claim the clouds. FB matches the faces of children at birthday parties around the world to faces in child porn, and police around the world move in.... All sorts of things that had never been measured before are measured—teacups in Iowa shaken by tremors in Japan—and rhymed in new ways—shark attacks to bathing-suit sales; spiritual well-being to virtual aliens killed; rain clouds to Chinese tanks; heirloom tomatoes to Modern art collections. Machines find more relations than they can possibly judge and draw in humans to do so for them: Alfred Safarzack among hundreds of other Christians searching images of ice melting on mountain tops for the telltale angular shapes that distinguish objects made by human hands—hopefully, Noah's Ark; Kiran Ghosh, and thousands of other hobbyists going through the masses of photos of the night sky, one of which might have a faint smear, the telltale sign of a meteor on a collision course with Earth. Hive activity gives rise to a hive mind to evaluate, classify, rank, which draws in more poets, gardeners, birdwatchers, and retirees, their collective action emerging as a way of thinking together, a way of writing poems together, singing together, or evaluating crowds for potential mates, potential terrorists, volunteers searching for evidence of ancient tsunamis, searching for patterns of all kinds within this data sludge. So when Norman Blacklander came upon a flash mob glitter bombing members of the God Hates Fags Coalition to Save America, when he saw the cloud of glittering confetti, each piece a tiny mirror, it was natural for him to see it as one large hive-mirror; it was natural, when Dr. Janice Hookey was tasked with finding the wreckage of a slave ship, for her to turn to the hive to read the thousands of pages of 18th-century ship logs for clues to where one might be; it was natural, when Richard Stone sat under a beach umbrella on his own private island, nursing a fruity drink, a tiny umbrella shading its ice, for him to think of scaling up: fruity-drink umbrella is to beach umbrella as beach umbrella would be to a hive of umbrellas in space, shading a planet....

The first slide reminded everyone that the largest mirror that could be manufactured was 9 meters in diameter, 2 metric tons of molten glass. The second diagrammed how directing the light from eight 9-meter mirrors onto a single focal point allowed them to act like a single telescope with a mirror 72 meters in diameter. "So why not direct the light from 100 mirrors, or thousands of mirrors, even if each was only the size of a piece of confetti?—glitter—the light from each piece of glitter shaped by computer into a single image." Slide 4: "A mirror made of glitter instead of molten glass could be made any size, any shape. Weightless in space, a cloud of glitter 10 miles in diameter could be used to make the most powerful telescope ever imagined. If another satellite was placed between the telescope and the star it was aimed at—to totally eclipse the star—we could see the planets around it with approximately the same detail that astronomers in 1950 saw in Jupiter."

Once the hive set about pouring over the images of the Mediterranean floor, looking for a bomb that had been dropped by accident, they found the telltale, angular shapes of human construction: the grid of a street, the foundation of a temple....

The Galileo Massive Cloud Orbiting Telescope (GMCOT) was a telescope whose mirror was a cloud of glitter, ten miles in diameter, shaped out in space by lasers the way whales can herd thousands of small fish into a tightly packed ball. A billionaire paid to park it, like a beach umbrella, at a location in space so it could also be used to control the temperature on his island.

Astronomers first trained the telescope on what crowdsourcing had identified as a rocky Earthlike planet in the Goldilocks zone. For years they'd been able to see the planet as a dark dot against its star, its atmosphere boiling away like steam from a teapot. What they hadn't expected was how much it would look like Earth: stunning pictures of oceans and clouds and continents of an Earthlike planet only with a red cast to it....

And a collective groan went up from Earth, as though everyone had been given a look at what they were doing to their own planet, the way people baking in the heat of Seattle had once felt the anguish at what they had had and lost—the cold salmon streams, the natural air-conditioning of Puget Sound—back when they were still able to see snow at the top of Mt. Rainer off in the distance.

Yesterday, 1,000 died of heat, while I tended my tomatoes.

After the groan, silence. Maybe he was too old to get his first tattoo, as his wife insisted, but Roy thought there would have been more of a reaction to the news that the Earth was losing its atmosphere. He flipped through the book of designs the parlor had to offer, looking for the one he came in for, thinking how those who paid attention fell into arguing over whether the Earth's loss of atmosphere was A) cyclical or B) caused by humans. He was always a voracious reader, and from what he could tell, people on the 'A' side mainly pointed out that atmosphere loss had obviously happened before without the help of humans: Mars had once had an atmosphere as lush and dense as that of Earth before the solar wind gradually stripped it away. And that was simply what was happening to Earth: it was turning into another Mars. Mars.2. What had saved the Earth before was the magnetic bubble it lived within and that channeled the solar wind to the poles as spectacular aurora borealis; but the strength of this magnetic field was cyclical, and indeed, not unrelated to the complete reversal of Earth's magnetic poles every 450,000 years.

Unfortunately, this weakening of the magnetic shield was happening at a time of intensifying solar wind, the convergence of the two cycles amplifying the effects of each into the perfect storm that was stripping away the Earth's atmosphere—and was accelerated by the thinning of the atmosphere brought on by global warming, fluorocarbons and other pollutants that broke it down, and made it easier to blow away, said those who claimed there was a human component—a component that multiplied the effect of the other two enough to knock the loss of the atmosphere into a permanent slide.

Even if the cycle didn't end, Tom, his old rock-climbing buddy, answered on FB (Roy loved the photo Tom used for his wall: a selfie he'd taken of the two of them 20 years ago, grinning in their gear on El Capitan, Yosemite Valley 1,000 feet below), even if the loss of atmosphere became permanent, it still had a projected lifespan of millions of years. So what's the dif?

True, Roy thought. But still.... The Earth losing its atmosphere seemed like it warranted more than becoming a political football like face masks had become on talk radio. Especially after the Galileo Massive Cloud Orbiting Telescope began sending back pictures of oceans and clouds and continents of that Earth-like planet that was already losing its atmosphere. Red Marble Earth, NGers called it, naming it after a photo that could have been of the Blue Marble Earth only tinted red, a bloodred, like the moon during a lunar eclipse, with a plume of atmosphere trailing away.

"This one," he told the tattoo artist. "I want this one." He tapped on the design that was a cartoon version of the Red Marble Earth. Maybe he wasn't expecting the prayers for forgiveness that went up from ancients upon seeing their first eclipse. He didn't expect anyone to give away their belongings or flog themselves in atonement, though some did, he had read, when Earth was about to pass through the tail of Halley's Comet and people thought it would poison the atmosphere. He didn't think there'd be mass terror at the unknown, or overwhelming scale of the cosmos. Or the awe one might think would naturally follow. But anyone old enough, as he was, to remember the Earth when it was too big to be held in a single glimpse could remember how that first image of a blue, cloud-swirled globe, suspended in utter darkness, changed people. Once people were able to get a camera up high enough to look back and take a selfie of the entire planet, it was suddenly easier for everyone to think of themselves as Earthlings instead of Russians or Germans or Americans. On a finite planet. A closed system. Spaceship Earth, people called it. At least for a while. And yes, it was a little scary, the way Galileo's critics must have been scared, looking through his telescope and having the centuries-old idea of Earth as 'fixed, immovable position' pulled out from under their feet and replaced with?— What? The unknown? Nothing? Or the thing every rock climber knows: once you step off a cliff, gravity is synonymous with destiny.

"**That freak snow shower was really awesome**," the director of Christmas Town said, "because it gave us a good idea of how to dust with our own snow."

The rolling hills of ancient Latina once provided an Arcadian landscape for villas with fabulous Roman mosaics, gardens, vineyards, and olive groves. Now, the hills channel raw sewerage, runoff from swine farms, a pharmaceutical factory, and steel mills into canals where the descendants of those ancient Latinas still bathe, fish, and get their drinking water. After giant rats became the only wild animals able to live there, Latinas began bulldozing their rolling hills to make new routes for the water; they planted weeds that could absorb toxins, creating a landscape that could coexist with the factories.

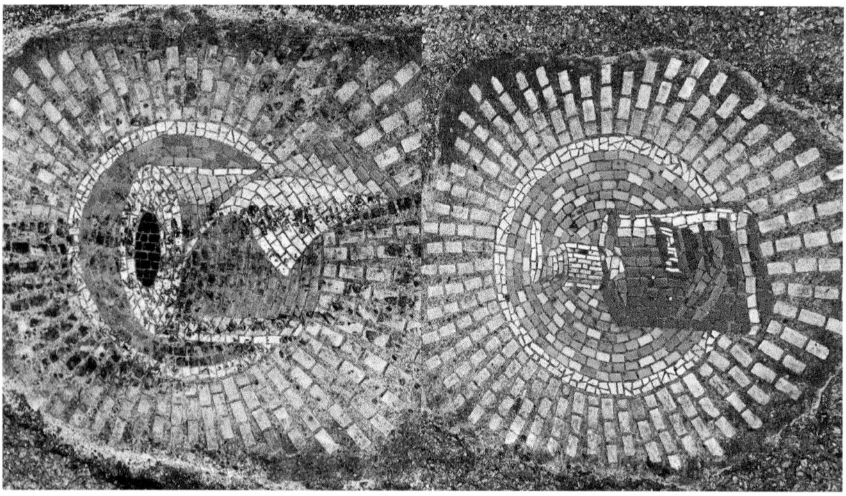

Center seat; Center row: Malcom sat in the theater hosting a Sci-Fi film festival: *If the World's Ending, We May as Well Go to the Movies!* On-screen, yet another group of white scientists, white generals, and government wonks—white people—frantically worked to build a white rocket to leave earth before it blew up, or cracked in half, got too close to or too far from its sun, was invaded by aliens, or robots, or simply became too mucked up with shit to live on. Wait for it, wait for it, went the clock in his head as the money shot came on-screen: the new space station, blazing white, orbiting earth to serve as the port for ships carrying humans to a new, earth-like planet that had been discovered in deep space.... "Oh, hell no!" he muttered, even though he'd expected it. *Hellllllllll nooooooooo!*: a white suburb, built inside a massive rotating wheel to create artificial gravity that allows white kids to play baseball; the crack of a bat sent a baseball through the kitchen window of a white women, while white men mowed lawns like in a super-high-def Norman Rockwell painting, the light pouring off the screen blinding white while Malcolm sat down in the dark, the poem "Whitey on the Moon" rolling through his head, and giving him the title of the next Sci-Fi movie he would make: *They Came from Planet X*. Without even needing to think about it, a plot began to unfold as if delivered by a god. Or maybe it was a lifetime of having lived it so immersively that every cell in his body understood. [OPENING SHOT] Camera behind a little white boy, waving goodbye out the rear window of a spaceship.

[CAM PUSHES IN]

Camera pushes in, then over his shoulder to show what he is waving at: the canonical blue-marble Earth, only now it's brown, against a field of stars. The planet recedes into the distance as the spaceship accelerates away, and we hear the voice of the boy: "So long, ghetto Earth."

[JUMP CUT]

The Earth's surface. Brown haze for air; a montage of landmarks, all destroyed: scavengers hauling away pieces of the Eiffel Tower in shopping carts; the Grand Canyon filled with garbage, New York Harbor dotted with rusting oil derricks—and in every scene, there appears to be a riot raging in the background.

[CAM PULLS IN]

One of the riots: what seems at first to be screams and gunshots becomes more distinct as shrieks of glee—the mobs that had appeared to be roaming an apocalyptic landscape are actually having a mass celebration. Then a dandy steps forward from the mob, his skin panther black against his baby-blue suit, declaiming loudly to be heard over the party, "After the last white person left earth, all the Blacks they left behind broke into worldwide celebration!" This is our Griot—our storyteller, praise singer, magician, poet, historian—who describes what we see on-screen. "Grannies and preachers and players turning factories and farms and church aisles into dance parties. Mail carriers threw their letters into the air like confetti. No more KKK, no more skinheads, no more 'heritage' bullshit with their statues to Robert E. Lee. I mean, whose side, exactly, was Col. Sanders on? Even better than reparations—we got the whole planet!—even if it was a Popsicle sucked down to the stick. But hell. We'd worry about that tomorrow! For now there really was only one race, the human race, and not a single one of its members was three fifths of a person. No more presidents selling the enslaved from the Oval Office. No more preachers selling your children to found their Harvards. No more white people mailing postcards of your papa's lynching—*Wish you were here!*—No more 'black tax': making less for the same job, getting less social security, dying before you can collect even that; loans denied, taxis and doctors avoiding your neighborhood like it was a toxic dump—which it may well be! No more, Confederate flags flying over U.S. courts like a Jolly Roger. No more Jim Crow, New Jim Crow, New-and-Improved Jim Crow; no more food deserts or 'voter fraud' (i.e. NWV). No more Dred Scott, Rodney King, Latasha Harlins, Laquan McDonald, Freddie Gray, George Floyd, or open season (all the time) on—everyone's got an opinion about—Black bodies; no more getting your tires slashed just because you wanted to play Santa Claus at the local mall, no more U.S. Public Health Service conducting syphilis experiments on you while you thought you were just getting a flu shot....

"And yes, people got excited—wouldn't you?—and yes, some celebrations got a little out of hand, like the party-riots that sometimes break out after Super Bowl wins. In D.C., brothers broke into warehouses where 4th of July fireworks were stored and set them all off on the Mall in celebration of the first true Independence Day, each skyrocket launched at the white spaceship leaving earth behind—*don't let the door hit you in the ass on the way out!* Yoruba drummers started a dance line that circled the globe. In Mogadishu, men celebrated by shooting AK-47s into the air; brothers and sisters in Parisian cafés clinked espressos, lit cigarettes, then set to work on manifestos as to what the moment could mean....

"After a while, after the euphoria wore off, the United (Black) Nations—which was now all of them—convened to rename the planet. After much heated debate, they decided on Planet X, after Malcolm's namesake. And everything was cool. Buildings were designed along the principles of architects like Kunlé Adeyemi, the Nigerian, who designed A-frame schools out of barrels that could both collect rainwater for use during droughts and float the school during floods; entire cities took on the Sierra Leone aesthetics of smooth, pine staves, gently tapering to infinity.... They abandoned the broken power grid for solar panels and a 12-volt system to create sustainable, green suburbs of high-tech moss huts, skyscrapers with hanging gardens: a civilization by the people, for the people, with justice and liberty for all....

"In the meantime, out in deep space, that plan to colonize New Earth went the way it always did when white people decided that a world was 'New' just because they hadn't heard of it before. Massacres. Invasive microbes. Disease & Dominion. They baptized what was left and called it a day. But after enough centuries passed, and even the seas of New Earth began to turn into cemeteries, they began to look around for another planet to invade, I mean save...."

"There's another," Dr. Guntle whistled, zooming in on a satellite photo. Deforestation was a disaster for the Amazon Basin but a boon for archaeology. Logging had already destroyed enough of the tree canopy to make some 2,000 ancient earthworks visible from space: berms and roads and geoglyphs, built by people in cities the size of those in Europe, then lost. Not lost. Wiped out—by microbes carried by Spanish conquistadors.

'An Eden, untouched by human hands,' everyone had said of the Amazon, though it was now becoming clear that it was more like the way Detroit would have looked in 500 years if it had been left abandoned, unchecked jungle taking over deserted ceremonial plazas, burying networks of roads connecting hundreds of villages.... According to Arctic core samples, the years after Columbus were the only time that the carbon in the atmosphere decreased and it was because the Amazonians who had carved their cities and farms out of the jungle, and created its very dirt—rich soil that made jungle growth possible—did so through controlled burns. Then they were no more. And the jungle grew unchecked for 500 years, swallowing whole civilizations as a sinking ship is swallowed by the sea, leaving the impression of a pristine wilderness, not a land shaped by human hands. Until now.

The first thing the Chinese did with the island they created to extend their shoreline, and thus their domestic waters, and thus their claim to its fish, was to arm it with surface-to-air missiles.

Every summer, Gabe's parents took her to visit the city's planetarium. In its sky theater, hundreds of seats were outfitted with control panels. The idea was that the audience could collectively control a Mars Rover to explore the planet, seen through a camera on the Rover and projected before them on the huge screen. As might be expected, it was like having hundreds of hands on a steering wheel, and all of them trying to make the Rover go where they wanted. There were the earnest dads, hers among them, who truly wanted to search for water; there were the kids who just wanted to play with the colored buttons; there were teenagers who wanted to drive as fast as possible, who did their best to drive the Rover off a cliff or into a crater; there were those who wanted to steer but didn't know how, pushing the up button when they wanted to go down, or trying buttons at random; there were those who only wanted to do stupid things—look for rocks shaped like Elvis, or make the Rover do donuts in the Martian soil. Mostly, there was the great majority who simply didn't want to be bothered. Over the years that her family went, the result was always the same. The individual people were different but she always ended up closing her eyes to keep from getting motion sickness, the immense view of Mars on the screen bouncing in slo-mo, careening this way then that as though the camera were in one of those beach balls lofted into a crowd at

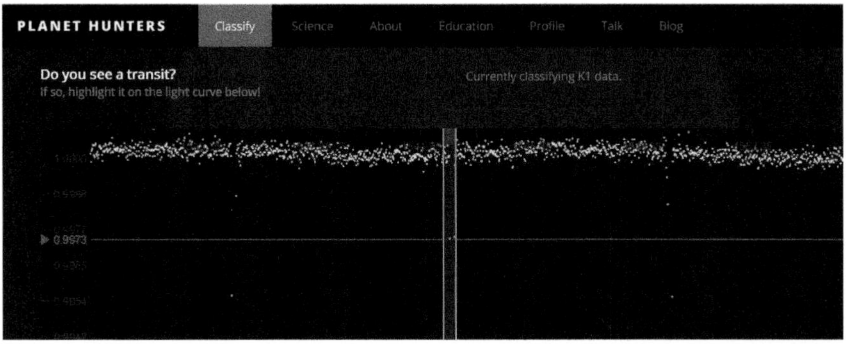

LIVE
Planet Hunters
zooniverse.org/projects/nora-dot-eisner/planet-hunters-tess/classify

a rock concert, alternately showing random views of sky then dirt, then being violently punched and lurching in a new direction....

A planet growing so warm that it begins to lose its atmosphere has a tail: like a comet.

Soon after the sighting of Red Marble Earth, another Hive-mind project found Atlantis. Archaeologists had long known of underwater villages: Agios Petros off the coast of Greece, and Atlit Yam off the coast of Israel, and other cities that had thrived along the Mediterranean coast before the Ice Age ended, and the melting glaciers raised the sea level 30 meters, submerging them. What they hadn't known was that one of these villages was just the outer suburb of an even larger city, built on what had been a sandstone ridge caused by tectonic lifting and running parallel to the present coastline. A city there prospered until 8,000 years ago, when half of Mt. Etna in Sicily slid into the Mediterranean: a mountain-sized avalanche large enough to bury Manhattan under mud so thick only the tip of the Empire State Building would stick out. The avalanche hit the Mediterranean with as much force as the meteor that did in the dinosaurs; it rearranged the sea bed and sent a giant 300-foot wave crashing across the Mediterranean at 450 miles an hour; the wave pointed every rock in the Middle East in the same direction, and wiped out coastal villages, along with what had been this Venice-like city. The rising sea levels finished the job and the city lay in the bottom of its watery grave for another 8,000 years until modern humans, with modern machines, destroyed

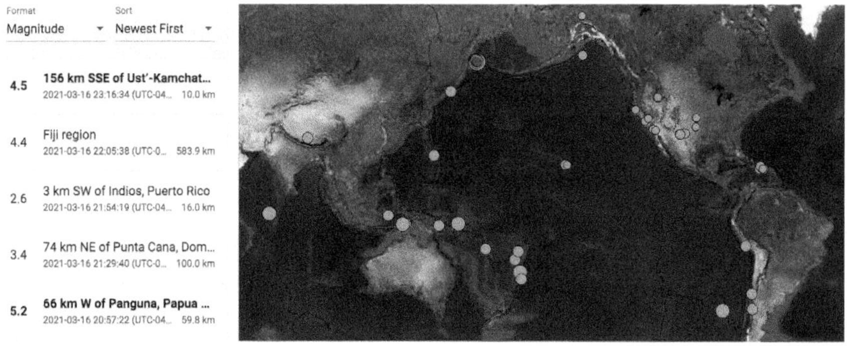

LIVE •
Earthquake Tracker
earthquaketrack.com/v/norcal

the currents that kept the ruins buried, and the erosion of wave action gradually began to uncover this lost city, revealing the source of the story of Atlantis, the source for the story of Noah's Flood. But why? And Why now?—just when Red Marble Earth was discovered. How could it not be a sign? A warning of some kind. Many searched the skies....

A horrible thought came to Meadow as she looked through photos of the Ghost Forests that she'd shot back home: an entire forest that had died long ago, leaving only petrified stumps. The forest of ghostly white trunks had been a mystery for generations, the source of spooky stories, especially after a botanist counted tree rings and determined that they had all been killed at the same time—drowned in salt water, though they were far from the sea. But how? Native legends told of the sea rising up to swallow whole tribes, but they had no written records. Medieval Japanese might, though, the botanist thought, and with the help of historians in Japan, he found stories of an orphan tsunami: a massive wave that had destroyed the coast but inexplicably had no earthquake—at least not until the botanist matched it to one that had reared up on his side of the ocean. It had been caused by the Juan de Fuca tectonic plate, which was still pushing up against the North American plate, its pressure building, building.... When it finally gave, the Pacific Northwest would drop seven feet. The Cascade Mountains would spring back to the sea, as they had in 1700, causing a tsunami so powerful it wiped out much of Japan, 5,000 miles away. This time though, the earthquake would not occur under a vast wilderness on the U.S. side. It would be under Seattle. Or San Francisco. And it would destroy everything from Seattle to Sacramento—a real-life disaster movie. The geology was clear: an earthquake of this destructive power had occurred every 240 years for the last 10,000 years. Which meant it was overdue—by more than a 100 years. When Mount St. Helens blew its top, it was like two nuclear blasts. But more important, it was a sign that so much pressure was being generated again that it was now melting rock deep below—and a horrible thought came to Meadow: was that why William moved back to Oregon? The threat of a mega-tsunami that was making people start to leave the very thing that drew him back?

She could imagine him sitting in the metal shipping container he used as a hut, playing his flute as the earth turned to sea, a poetic communion with Nico, as if dying in a wall of water would restore some balance to the perversion of a son dying before his parents—

She felt guilty for not being there with him. For thinking she was the only one who hadn't been able to get off the beach....

Had so many yawned at the sight of Red Marble Earth because we had been so well prepared? Wasn't that the lesson of human progress?— Kepler removes Earth from the center of the universe; Darwin removes humans from the center of Eden; the discovery of thousands of other planets makes ours one of thousands. The same with bodies here on earth: that New Eden where bodies—those last boundaries between each other, as well as animals and plants—did not end where we did. We had been so prepared for the news that we were just genes, like so many other genes, on a rock, like lots of other rocks, that when confirmation came, it was easy for many of us to just shrug.

But not all.

Even before the Galileo Massive Cloud Orbiting Telescope sent back images of Earth's red twin, he'd been drawn to Chichén Itzá by the sense of something larger than himself, or even the world, and he knew the people around him could feel it too. The ruins of the abandoned Mayan city rose out of the misty forest just like in its *National Geographic* photos. He wasn't surprised to find so many backpackers, Germans, Japanese, and other Birkenstockers.... What was surprising was the number of men and women who looked like plumbers from Milwaukee, or Star Trek conventions: people you wouldn't expect, and looking mostly lost, as though unsure as to what was going to happen next.

Their motions were muted by the surrounding predawn jungle. But also, they were mostly silent, or spoke in whispers like people in church. He could hear distant birds. Even the local natives sat quietly at their souvenir stalls. There wasn't any of the carnival atmosphere so common in places where the locals hawked their histories: Italians selling plastic gladiator swords outside the Colosseum. Mostly, these descendants of the Mayans who built these pyramids stood there in the dim light, looking toward the steps ascending the pyramid, the Temple of Kukulcán, as though in reverence for the ghosts of the largest American city that had been suddenly and mysteriously abandoned 1,500 years ago, waiting for....

This: the tip of the pyramid suddenly became radiant, golden, its yellow stone illuminated by the leading edge of day's first light. A gasp went up from the crowd. At the same instant, the shadow of a serpent's head appeared at the top of the stairs. Slowly, as resolutely as the rising of the sun on this the equinox, the shadow grew, and moved downward—the jagged shadow of an ever-growing serpent with toothed scales along its spine—the plumed serpent Kukulcán—slithering down the staircase. A knot of middle-aged tourists gathered around a tour leader who lifted a green umbrella as they began chanting, *"As above, so below. As below, so above...."* A couple of hipsters stood off to the side smirking. But a young woman with long flowing hair ironed into zigzagging cascades broke from her group to throw herself into the path of the serpent's mouth. A few wept. Looks of rapture and despair came over other faces—expressions one would expect from those at the appearance of their god, not tourists at some foreign weirdness; it was their god, he knew, a god of time, something cosmic that they were part of as surely as the Mayan descendants around them waited for the believers to come over and buy some water or jewelry and whose ancestors had created the calendar that prophesied the end of the world in 2012. When it didn't come, nonbelievers had laughed at them, pointing out that the apocalyptic end of the world that all these people thought the ancient Mayans had predicted was nothing at all like what the Mayans themselves believed: though their calendar did predict that this world would end in 2012, they also thought another, new world would begin at the same time, the way we believe one year ends and another begins at the stroke of midnight on December 31. Some refused to accept this interpretation, redoing their calculations to show that only the date was off: that the world would end at one of the equinoxes between 2012 and 2024. And if not then, soon enough. Maybe by a giant meteor hitting the Earth—the Earth passing through a distant meteor belt every 65 million years, the cycle by which life on Earth had gone extinct five times before, with the regularity of a metronome. Or maybe all the matter that made up this universe would come in contact with the antimatter astronomers hypothesized, causing both to vanish in a flash.

But the theory that came to dominate was that the ancient Mayan calendar had been right: that the world did end, back in 2012, and it had happened exactly as the Mayans had said it would: one world, the world that had existed for all of human history, had ended just as another began, the new world continuing on just as the old one had before it: in silence, indifferent to whether its surface resembled the Amazon or the Sahara. For 2012 was the year that the ice bridge that had held a vast West Antarctic ice sheet in place, like a keystone in an arch, cracked. And as later shown by satellite photos, once this mountain of ice, an ice mountain that had existed for all of human history, a mountain of ice that for all of human history had pinned the West Antarctic ice sheet in place, once this mountain of ice collapsed, the rest of Antarctica had begun its tumble into the sea; ice shelves the size of small countries crumbled, setting mountain-sized icebergs adrift, their massive bottoms tearing up the ocean floor....

That massive ice mountain had been like the finger of the Dutch boy who saved Holland by plugging a hole in a dike to keep it from bursting. Except this Dutch boy had pulled out his finger. And now, the Earth had to find somewhere to put an extra ocean.

But melting tundra also released methane that had been trapped for centuries, the gases that moved between the atmosphere and oceans changing their chemical composition, the change in chemistry killing the algae and krill that fed on them, and the fish that fed on the krill; coral reefs died, as did the ecosystems they supported, taking with them mollusks, plankton, and all the animals that relied on them for bone growth, a quarter of all fish—the die-off of fish bringing down mangroves, marine reptiles, seabirds, mammals.... That is, as the oceans died, the planet began to transform into a different world—as it had 2.5 billion years ago when sunshine caused microbes to emit oxygen, creating our oxygen-rich atmosphere—the beginning of our world—and poisoning almost all other living creatures—the end of theirs. The Earth didn't care who or what lived on it.

Only this time the change was our fault. And the error made by those who read the Mayan calendar in 2010 was that they thought the world would end according to a modern, rather than a Mayan, sense of time—instantly—instead of slow enough to let us live through the consequences. And he knew that at that moment, all over the world, believers were branding themselves in communion, just as they had on the equinox last year; a yard full of women prisoners in Russia were probably breaking out into seizures and mass hysterics, believing they'd heard the Earth yawn as they had last year; believers in France were camping on Bugarach Mountain in anticipation of an alien landing; in America people were buying ammunition; in Greece, ads run by stores were urging people to stockpile food, blankets, batteries, adding to the runs on fuel and food while the Greek Orthodox Church was issuing its annual Equinox Statement assuring congregations that the End of the World truly was at hand, but that it would be triggered by moral decline, not an alignment of planets....

Or maybe the world ended in 1712, the year the steam engine was invented, and promptly put to use pumping water out of the coal mine that was soon feeding other engines that required more coal mines that....

Or maybe it ended 700,000 years earlier—a blink in geological time—when hands first sparked rocks to make fire....

That design guy came out of Olympia's office just as Gabe was going by. He stopped as soon as he saw her, a weird look on his face.

"Excuse me," she said, pushing by. But he didn't excuse her. Instead, he said, "Don't I know you from somewhere?" Thick, arty glasses, arty shoes: the kind you polish. "No, I don't think so," she said, but he was already trying to guess where he could have seen her before, snapping his fingers and saying, "Weren't you at XactlySo's concert the other night?" Fear electrified her shorthairs, but she kept her cool, saying calmly, "No. I don't think so." Dumb. How could she have given such a dumb answer? His face froze as though she'd just confirmed what he was thinking, and she continued on her way, trying to not look like she was running away.

"Hey," he called, coming after her.

Then she was running away, hurrying down the stairs as soon as she was on the opposite side of the fire doors.

The doors opened behind her. "Wait a minute," he called to her. She could hear his footfalls on the metal stairs and rushed to get to the INSECTARIUM AUTHORIZED PERSONNEL only. She touched her ID, his footsteps growing louder behind her.

Then she was in. But just as quickly, the refrigerator-sized door opened and he was in the room with her, his eyes wide at the rows of lobotomized parrots and geese on the shelves all around.

"You're not supposed to be in here," she said.

He had his cell out.

"No photos!" But he wasn't going to take a photo. His phone's screen filled with his Vine App: Here's all the New Vine-Friends you made at XactlySo's Concert!!! Below the caption was a field of faces, color-coded polka dots, each with a face and connected by lines — less like those used by contact tracing during pandemics than those organization charts that didn't really organize anything, just gave the impression of connectivity. Among the smiling posers, avatars, cartoons, and other images people used as their stand-ins was a photo of her grimace, her eyes squint shut with the effort of smashing XactlySo's sound system, her face hidden by the keffiyeh she'd found in the yard behind the concert.

She tried to grab the phone out of his hand but he held it up, out of her reach, and swiped to another photo: XactlySo's hands over his shocked mouth, her with the mic stand raised above her head like she was about to give it to him in the face. "Sort of like Joan of Arc, don't ya think?"

"No. I don't know what you mean."

"Lots of other people do. Overnight 'keffiyeh girl' gained like 90,000 followers. Now there's like seven people claiming to be her."

"If you're trying to say that photo is of me...." Even as the words came out, she realized how useless it would be to deny it. She wasn't sure how she'd gotten away with it as long as she had. In their rush to get to the anti-concert in the yard outside, every cop pouring out through the club's back door had run right past her, every club-goer and camera lens in the place pivoting toward the cops as they continued into the lot where the NO.IT.AN.EVIL concert had become a riot. Somehow in the confusion, after she'd busted up XactlySo's equipment, she just put down the mic stand and walked away. Walked out the front door. The wheel of the bike with the same lock as hers was bent double under a police van parked up on the sidewalk. Through dumb luck, though, her bike was untouched. She untangled it, pulled it from the others, and just pedaled away.

Say nothing, she told herself. Even if you could be identified from shoe-recognition software, or keffiyeh-recognition software, or ass-and-elbow-recognition software, it still wouldn't hold up as a positive i.d. in court. Or was she just being naive? Last year, a weekly Stich 'n Bitch meeting had been broken up by the police: the women, who met to crochet a replica of the Great Barrier Reef, had begun discussing other ways to help, and conversation had turned to supporting a kayak and Indigenous canoe blockade that was trying to prevent an Arctic drilling rig from leaving the harbor. The women were charged with forming an eco-terrorist cell, and she wasn't so naive to think something like that couldn't happen to her: and all for trashing a few guitar amps. You have the right to remain silent, she told herself, like a movie cop.

"It's okay," he told her. "I won't rat you out. But there are people who will."

And they're closing in, he didn't need to say. She stood there in silence, trying to think in the hum of the ventilation fans.

"...a witch hunt is a thing," he was saying, "an Internet is a thing. A witch hunt with an Internet is a third, and dangerous, thing. But a witch with an Internet is also a thing. I can help you disappear. Even if you're not a witch."

She began to deny it, but before she could speak he said, "Don't even tell me if you're a witch or not. I don't want to know. Did it matter in Salem?"

After ErthLib was declared a terrorist organization, anyone associated with them, that is, anyone in the same room, or even just listening to their music could become a Person of Interest. Did he know that?

"Help me? Why?"

"Is there somewhere else we can talk?" Already the humidity of the room had steamed up the screen of his phone. He wiped it on his sleeve, obviously worried about his gadget.

Are circles an illusion, Euclid's dream?—C=πd—a fiction we pretend is real in order to play marbles, build an arch, get a satellite into orbit? Does it matter? Who cares what gave a casting its shape once its mold is stripped away? Or if the scaffolding of statistics, population, blot-stain analysis, controlled trials, and all the rest did what we thought they did once the vaccine works? Or at least seems to.

Lots of wrong reasons for the right answer.

A dark pixel is a dot; three dots in a row is a line; a line that bends is a curve; a curve that bends back to its start is a circle; three dots in a circle is all an infant needs to recognize a face. And here our troubles begin: software straining to tell a smile from a grimace, when in reality no two cats are alike, no two lab rats, no two lab monkeys, no two human test subjects though we use one word—mammal—to gather features that are conserved across all. We make a vaccine for the group and hope it applies to the individual even if we know that a study's average height of 5′4″ might not match any one. We draw an evolutionary tree when it should be a cloud: billions of clouds, ever changing, patterns that make up the cartoon we call us.

Lying in bed, or staring at lines on her computer screen, Olympia's mind often wandered over the fact that the vaccine she was working toward wouldn't do what she said it would. It might seem to work, mostly, as measured by studies that would have the same constraints of the lab. At worst, the mutations she put into the world could open up some unanticipated pathway that made the virus deadlier than ever. Her own mother might have died because of assumptions like that: for years the hormone replacement therapy she'd been put on was the darling of epidemiology, a miracle of modern medicine that could put off the sweating of menopause, as well as diabetes, kidney failure, osteoporosis, heart attack, and other side effects associated with that disease called aging. It wasn't long after she died that studies began to show that tens of thousands of women had been killed by the cure.

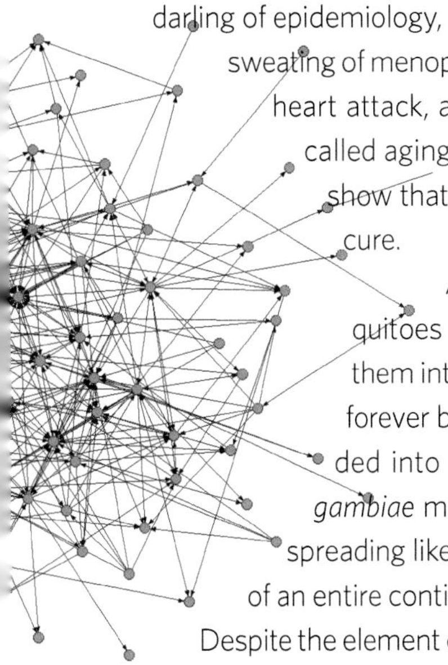

A former colleague had been so sure that the mosquitoes he altered would eradicate dengue that he released them into the wild: an entire species, Aedes aegypti, changed forever by one overweening man, the gene drive he'd embedded into them to override evolution jumping to *Anopheles gambiae* mosquitos, then flesh-eating blowflies, the mutation spreading like an oil slick threatening to tar the ecological balance of an entire continent....

Despite the element of chance that was always there, Truth wins out in the end, her teachers used to claim, zealots to their faith. But to believe that, you had to believe that time was infinite, while in the meantime, if the vaccine she was chasing turned out to only work on the birds in her lab, wouldn't the world be better off without it?

Still.... She didn't know it wouldn't work. And tweaking the data wouldn't change the result—it would just get the study to its conclusion faster. Was that being dishonest? As though in answer, she thought of the Dr. Naoki Mori papers: studies that researchers all over the world downloaded, and based their own work on for over ten years, until someone noticed how Mori had fudged the data, relabeling slides and presenting them as different measurements because he thought that more research would just show the same thing. Or so he claimed.

What if she got caught? Well, 'caught' was too harsh a word: say, 'discovered.' No, 'corrected' would be more accurate.

Even if truth did win out, what good would it be to those too dead to get the news? People who might have been saved if the money and time spent on her solution went into one that actually worked, the way thousands could have been saved had Trump not pretended the Covid-19 pandemic didn't exist? Or at least hadn't had its data 'tweaked.' If civilization ends before science is able to arrive at that one, unified, objective and verifiable Truth that needs no explanation because it is itself—a Möbius strip of both theory and demonstration—did that mean they would all have been wrong? The history of science a history of failed theories? A result always bestows meaning and significance upon all that comes before it.

She knew how the process worked long before she was part of it. But it was still shocking in the way that everyone knows about auto accidents, but can only understand their force, their violence, after they've been in one.

The success of what she did in her lab would be measured by lawyers and patent officers, and businessmen with pinkie rings instead of other biologists; her very conclusions would be co-authored by a web of venture capitalists and day traders.... The box office was the only movie review that mattered, a producer on TV once said, but he may as well have been talking about insurance adjusters, and doctors who may or may not be persuaded during the free Alaskan cruise they were given for sitting through a sales pitch to prescribe Aleve, an anti-inflammatory drug that reduces protein fragments associated with Alzheimer's, if anti-inflammatory drugs in fact reduced protein fragments, which was unclear, and if reduced protein fragments helped with Alzheimer's, which was even more unclear.

A circle: The old man who takes his Vioxx with his morning juice and twelve other prescriptions, orbiting the pharmacist who oversees the program run by operators who work for the mail-order house—a circle—stocked by the insurance company that has a raft of legal agreements—a circle—to buy in bulk from Big Pharma which was developing dozens of drugs—a circle—in the hopes that one would be a hit, the way a record company might back a dozen singers, knowing that it only took one to float everyone's boat—a circle—farming out the development of one drug that they held the patent on but didn't have the facilities to develop to a struggling biotech company that had facilities but only duds in the pipeline, this Little Pharma company that could, getting a big boost by being 'partnered' with Big Pharma—a circle—putting in 25% of the development cost in exchange for 5% of the profits, the deal they formed with Big Pharma—a circle—raising their stock from $32.04 to $32.84, which some investors took as their cue to cash out, and others took as a sign to jump in—a circle—a layoff-enhanced upturn in cash-on-hand making them look better on paper though they were no different in bricks, and inspiring a new spin in the revolving door of financial backers—a circle—allowing the company to start another 8-year cycle—a circle—like cicadas digging in—trying to convert an antibacterial drug that didn't get FDA approval because too many people in the study died before the drug could take effect, clouding the data, and so causing the company to rethink their drug as a medicated anti-acne cream—a circle—a terrorist attack suddenly giving the original antibacterial drug new life—a circle—politicians looking to look like they were doing something about bioterrorism—a circle—not because they were worried about people being hurt by anthrax, that likelihood being statistically somewhere between nonexistent to less than being struck by lightning—a circle—went looking for companies to pour money into—*Invest in America's BioDefense,* they called it—and they ended up with $35 million of Biodefense funding to help develop the anti-acne cream back into an antibacterial drug in defense of the nation....

"Does it work?" she'd asked.

"Depends what you mean by 'work,'" Brian had answered.

"And 'it,'" Sid added.

Thalidomide, the wonder drug for morning sickness, headaches, coughs, insomnia, and colds, ends up causing babies to be born without arms or legs, without ears or genitals, eyes or large intestines. Fifty years later, its maker, Grünenthal, regrets what happened, but still insists it wasn't their fault since the drug had been approved by the best testing methods available at the time.

Truth won out, they say.

You got to take the long view, Brian said, and even if a drug turns out to not do what it claims, it can still keep labs running until they find a better solution, and what's so bad about that?

RECENT PAPERS RETRACTED

: : : ///

Drugs for bacterial infections, acne, and rejections of bone marrow transplants....

LIVE•
Retraction Watch
retractionwatch.com

It takes 7 to 8 years on average to bring a drug to market.

Johnson & Johnson's Velcade, a drug that shrinks tumors at $48,000 per year per patient.

Four makers of a multiple sclerosis drug have agreed to offer a 10% discount on the annual price, now $18,000 per year per patient, if the drug didn't work.

GlaxoSmithKline made similar agreements with two European governments though it won't say which countries or drugs are involved.

Pfizer, which makes the best-selling cholesterol pill Lipitor and other cholesterol-lowering drugs, was asked to pay the expenses of patients who had been on the drug and still had heart attacks.

Velcade, a drug that works against bone marrow cancer, was recently dropped because, as its maker put it, it was not 'cost effective.'

Should a drug that shrinks tumors 50% of the time be considered 'successful' or should 25% be considered the minimal 'successful' response? What if you're in that 25%?

Dr. Diederik Stapel was found to have fabricated data for years in scientific papers he published in over 30 peer-reviewed journals, such as *Science*, where his data showed that a messy house can encourage its occupants to be racists.

There are so few cases of malpractice because scientific fraud is easy to perpetrate but hard to uncover. "It's like asking how much of our money is fake money," as one reviewer put it, "we only catch the really bad fakers, the good fakers we never catch."

An analysis of the images published in the *Journal of Cell Biology* found that about 1% had been deliberately falsified, while in a confidential survey of scientists, 33.7% admitted to other questionable research practices.

The Guidant Corporation agreed to pay $195 million to settle claims for a defibrillator that used electricity to interrupt a chaotic heart rhythm after 7 patients died when the Ventak Prizm 2 Model 1861 failed to work because of faulty insulation. The company became aware of the problem in 2002 but kept shipping faulty units until a journalist posted an internal memo leaked to him about the wiring.

The science journal *Nature* reports a rise of 1,200% in retractions in scientific journals over the last ten years.

After Raptiva was shown to not work on AIDS, it was repackaged and sold to treat rough, red, scaly skin—until it was shown to be even better at making fatal brain infections....

Jazz Pharmaceuticals, a maker of the narcolepsy drug Xyrem—the prescription name for the street drug Gamma-Hydroxybutyrate, or date-rape knockout drug—pleaded guilty to felony charges after having been shown to have improperly promoted the medicine for unapproved uses. Though the drug is in the same class as heroin, it has 120,000 legal patients. The company tried to widen this 'audience' by promoting it for unauthorized uses: depression, insomnia, and fibromyalgia, a pain disorder. Did it work for these?—Hard to say, a doctor said at their trial, since the drug was never tested for these uses. Nevertheless, a spokesman for the company claimed that this is a free speech issue, and they will be pursuing legal action against the whistleblower, a former saleswoman for Orphan Pharmaceutical, who was awarded part of the $20 million settlement.

The FDA stopped Xoma and the Harvard Medical School from using Neuprex to treat Meningococcemia, a deadly bacterial infection that afflicts children and can kill them within hours. Too many patients died after receiving the drug for the company to demonstrate that it increased survival rates so they converted it into a drug for acne.

Leading Causes of Death in U.S.:
1 Heart Disease
2 Cancer
3 Medical Error

Mediator, a drug developed for diabetes but prescribed as a slimming aid, has been linked to hundreds of patients who developed heart problems.

Dr. Hwang Woo-Suk was considered a Nobel Prize candidate after publishing in *Science* first his method for extracting stem cells from cloned human embryos, then, a technique for making stem cell lines from a patient's skin cell: a method that would allow genetic engineers to make personalized cures. Two years later, someone noticed how he had fabricated his data.

Norwegian researcher Jon Sudbø still holds the record for scientific fraud: the fabrication of an entire 900-patient study 'carried out' over a decade, and published in the premier British journal, *The Lancet*.

The CDC found in tests that the antiviral drugs Amantadine and Rimantadine were ineffective 91% of the time against H3N2 influenza, the dominant strain of the season.

A commission in France found that half of all prescription drugs are worthless and/or dangerous.

The professional federation of medical industrialists denounced the doctors' report as full of 'confusions.'

Dong-Pyou Han, who confessed to spiking rabbit blood samples to make the results of an HIV vaccine experiment look better, has been sentenced to 57 months of prison time.

A hedge fund manager takes over a start-up, Turing Pharmaceuticals, which buys Daraprim, a drug for malaria that keeps people from going blind or dying, and raises its price from $13.50 to $750 a pill (and celebrates Trump's victory by releasing part of a rap album he personally owned).

Days after Valeant Pharmaceuticals acquired the heart drug Isuprel from Marathon Pharmaceuticals, they raised its price 525%.

Rodelis Therapeutics buys the TB drug Cycloserine and raises the price from $500 for 30 capsules to $10,800. Because the drug works better now that they control the supply?

On the stock exchange, Big Pharma is third after Big Oil and Banking. It has bypassed diamonds with profits increasing 20% a year.

Out of a possible 130, Eli Lilly's bestseller Alimta, a drug for lung cancer—annual revenue of $2.8 billion—scored a zero. Asked to explain why it cost each patient $9,193 a month, they replied that on average patients lived six weeks longer. What did those patients get for the money? Six weeks of suffering? Six weeks to say goodbye? Was it worth it?

When asked to comment, the FDA would only say that it was not unusual for agencies and pharmaceutical companies to evaluate 'effectiveness' differently.

See what I mean?

NOwmd @OnePlanet · 1m

Twit or fb msg to protest use of supercomputer for war instead of GreenErth Project. Together our voices are stronger!

Tomatoes: The weapon of choice. They would have thrown tomatoes at Oppenheimer too, Dr. Recker consoled himself, switching on his windshield wipers to smear away the tomatoes that demonstrators pelted his windshield with as he drove through the police line to get to his office. Lots of signs had that upside-down *We Cover the Earth* logo that NGers had converted into a cartoon Red Marble Earth, its atmosphere boiling away. It served its purpose for those who needed a flag to rally around. Among the huge puppets of the president, some of the protestors held signs that actually showed the Earth's atmosphere on fire. An obvious reference to Oppenheimer. Beatniks or whatever they were called back then had gone ballistic when they found out that some physicists on the Manhattan Project were worried that the test of the first A-bomb would ignite the Earth's atmosphere. Of course, beatniks never stopped to consider how carefully Oppenheimer's team had check the calculations to make sure that setting the atmosphere on fire had a low probability. Maybe if those beatniks had been marines onboard one of the battleships steaming toward a beach invasion of Japan, they would have had a different opinion. The bomb had saved the lives of over a million soldiers. Both American and Japanese.

If the NGers throwing garbage at him had stopped to consider that, they would fight through the police line to thank him for the judo flip his team did on off-the-shelf video game hardware, getting it to coordinate banks of math processors to break the exaFLOP barrier: 40,000 core processors running a quintillion calculations per second—fast enough to simulate reality as never before. Cosmologists wanted time on it to study the Big Bang; relief workers wanted to model world hunger; banks were hoping to coordinate billions of worldwide charge-card transactions.... Everyone wanted time on his computer, but the number one law of science was 'He who pays plays,' so was it his fault that the first thing his funders put it to use on was to simulate the way nuclear warheads behaved in the first microseconds of a blast?

A well-armed society makes for polite people, as Oppenheimer's baby showed so long ago. Maybe if someone explained that to these neo-hippies, they'd be grateful it was being used to make better weapons instead of modeling climate change as they all wanted. What good was a cooler world if it was embroiled in war?

Arriving at the Burning Man, Meadow saw immediately how different the population here was from people in the malls of W.2. Many of the avatars she spoke to had arrived by paths other than the one she'd taken: frustrated with their job. Or life. Many—it was surprising how many of these she came across in W.2—many were sure the Earth was dying and had come to mourn. Some to celebrate the end of the parasites that had killed it: humans. Some reminded her of 19th-century walkers—out for a Sunday stroll in a cemetery for the melancholy it evoked. Eat, drink, and be merry for tomorrow we die—the battle cry of every pandemic—driving others to hole up in their temporary hermit cells. Many were too stoned to talk—not the avatars, of course, for avatars could only drop virtual X-tacy; but their real-world counterparts got high at home, while their avatars sat around in a circle together, their conversations slurred, because the words of those operating them were slurred. Watching them try to dance was like watching robots too drunk to dance dance.

Several avatars, though, had arrived in ways that were very similar to the path she'd taken: shunted off to the side, lured into one of the few dead zones of commerce.

Thinking back over the last weeks, Meadow saw that after she had stopped buying things, more and more of the avatars she met online made suggestions to her that would shunt her further from the business of W.2, acting as though they were trying to help. But really, she could now see from the avatars around her, all they'd been doing was to help her get out of the way of profits: the kind of help store owners gave the homeless, or those Neo-Amish NGers who refused to use any technology invented after 1995, insisting on dumb phones, or using cash, slowing down the wheels of commerce.

Following her 'helpers' advice, she increasingly found herself at sites where there was not only nothing for sale, but no one was trying to buy anything. Spiritual, her helpers called it—the Mayan Temples, the Caves of Lesbos—'Spiritual' being their code for 'Loser,' 'Loser' meaning someone who didn't shop.

Meadow walked over to a group sitting in a circle, still dressed in the clothes newbies were issued. If any of them had spent money to alter these standard-issue clothes, it was to add holes in the knees, or maybe an NG appliqué. There wasn't much profit in virtual, ass-pocket appliqués, though. And most hadn't even bothered with that.

One got up and came over to Meadow's avatar. A reed-thin woman with long, pale blonde hair, and pale blue eyes. "You didn't come here for the Burning Man, did you?"

Meadow shook her head, looking down.

"You're getting closer," the woman said. She took a toke on her joint, then offered it to Meadow.

Meadow shook her head. "To what?"

"Out there," she said, nodding toward the vast wasteland. "They're waiting for you."

"Me?"

"Yes. Everyone like you."

"Who?"

"The Book People."

"You want to go *there?*" Gabe sneered when Dan suggested continuing their conversation at Starbucks, meaning, he could see, the whole chain-store-globalization-WTO-anti-environmental world she and her kind thought it represented. Passersby could have thought he'd called her a name from her operatic jaw drop. She acted as though going to Starbucks instead of Kafeino, the threadbare place off campus, was an ontological decision. Which it was, she said, when he told her he'd prefer Starbucks because he could find parking there, car lanes in this part of town having been converted to lanes for electric scooters or hydrogen-only buses. One wheezed by, with a flock of scooters in its wake."Fine," she conceded, testily. "We'll talk about it later."

As he got into his car she unlocked her bike: a black Urban Crew with white rims, front brake. He noticed she had the chain on the freewheel side of a flip-flop hub so she could stand up on its pedals.

She began to follow him, he thought, as he pulled away from the curb, watching her in his rearview mirror: orange racing goggles tinting her face. A game face, serious and hard as a nut in the shell of her helmet. Muscles striated her forearms, her hands in gloves gripping her handlebars.

At the first traffic light, she shot past him, standing up on her pedals to pump through the intersection as the light changed. Show-off. Racing him to make a point about cars vs. bikes the way her kind loved to do. He'd noticed that she had $C_{12}H_{22}O_{11}$ tattooed on the base of her neck: probably a Neo-Ache, NGers, or one of those others who wanted everyone to live in teepees and save trees by giving up toilet paper.

When he arrived, though, he smiled to discover that he'd won—her bike was nowhere to be seen. Had she been lying? Just to ditch him?

Inside: the usual Toppers, each alone and occupying one of the small round tables like a Buddha of Commerce in its shrine, gazing into the navel of his cell-phone. Sprinkled among them though were paunchy, middle-aged guys. Some in camo. Or wearing those goofy red hats. Each had a pistol on his table.

Dan walked by them, pretending it was no big deal. "Gun club in town?" he asked the barista after he placed his order. Arms wallpapered with tats, the barista sighed. "My boss signed a petition to outlaw guns in his church, so the websites that RedHatters get their 'news' from started saying the U.N. used his coffee shops to traffic in child prostitutes. They're all here to 'investigate.'" None of them had ordered anything, Dan noted. "But I don't mind," the barista said, "they're less work. I'll have your latte right up."

Then he saw her. She was sitting as far in the back as she could manage, her back to him. She waved a hand over the top of her head. As he approached, he could see she'd been using the tiny mirror attached to her bicycle helmet to watch for him. "I don't want anyone I know to see me here," she said as he sat down across from her, taking the seat that had a view of the café instead of the wall.

Flushed from pedaling, she used a rubber band to pull her hair out of her face. She was kinda cute, he thought, pulling out his iFlex to show her what he did. Cute—in that Sci-Fi girl-scientist way.

Nerd, she thought, with a nerd's security blanket: the iFlex that automatically logged him into the Starbuck's network. Still, he was kinda cute—in that retro, computer-nerd way. And he really did seem to want to help her. A damsel in distress in his Dungeons & Dragons MUD? She stiffened. Is that where he was coming from? She watched him launch a program, trying to get a read on what he wanted. Here he was, saying that he thought what she did was cool, even though he was at the concert she attacked. What was that about? Then he follows her into a room of lobotomized ducks, whips out his cell and starts showing her pictures of the concert instead of snapping incriminating photos of the lobo-geese as she—or any PETA sympathizer—would have done. Maybe he was just coming on to her.

"Wait till you see this," he said, rotating his iFlex so she could see, excited as a geek with the newest OS. He turned the computer so the gun nut near them couldn't see, and she smiled, in spite of herself. A sea of dicks with guns all around, NRA and MAGA types with their faded red hats, and here she was, sitting right under their noses. A real terrorist would have detonated her vest by now.

"So, you think what I did was kinda cool, huh?" she said, skeptically, just to see how he'd react. When he didn't, she took a sip from her Nalgene bottle, trying to do so naturally even though she was aware of the security camera's black eye staring down at her from the ceiling. Back in the old days when surveillance was mostly optical, gorilla-theater actors used to stage plays for cameras like this: pranks like moonwalking past with a sign that explained *Just going to work*.... It all seemed so innocent now.

His screen came alive with faces like the ones he'd shown her on his cell phone. At its epicenter was the photo someone had taken of her at the club. Around it were lots of other photos of the riot outside, of the concert inside, of the party—and screen shots of the virtual concert going on in W.2—all overlapping to make a mosaic, overlapping to try to reconstruct an image of her. Only they were Frankenstein versions of her that a viewer could scroll through, like one of those flip-books for kids where the head of a hedgehog could be matched to the body of a penguin and the legs of an ostrich: a leg from one photo, an arm from another, the other arm from twelve different possibilities, dozens of different hands. There must have been fifty suggestions for feet, all in different kinds of sneakers, but none of them the shoes she'd actually worn that night. "Good thing my face wasn't visible," she said.

"As if," he muttered, fiddling with the app.

"I mean," she said, "I'm glad no one's been able to figure out who I am."

"Oh they know. Lots of people must know. Maybe your insurance company, tracking the behavior of its clients so it could weed out the ones that go to risky events. Or an aggregator compiling a dossier on you to sell to a realtor, or car dealer, or whatever other business.... Google knows for sure. Turn a face into a pattern of dots, which is what every picture is—pixels—and it's no harder for pattern recognition to match them than it is for you to do a global search to find every use of a word in a Word doc. Even if FB can't see your face, their algorithms can troll through some 800 million photos in less than 5 seconds and identify people with 98% accuracy: they use the same algorithms that map the features of a face to map the features of your posture. Hairstyle. A stain on your jacket, the way you hold a cigarette.... "

She knew he was right. When she'd been waiting for someone to out her, and waited, and waited, and still it didn't happen, she'd begun thinking that maybe nobody knew. That the density of the crowd had shielded her, so many people wearing facial-recognition blocking necklaces that it hid the faces of everyone there? That maybe the keffiyeh masking her face had masked her identity, finding it lying on the ground as she had, belonging to a stranger as it did, software matching the keffiyeh to someone not her. The cap she'd worn to keep the stink of smoke, or grass, or pepper spray out of her hair also hiding her hairstyle from the drones.... But she also knew that she was giving in to the worst thing a scientist could: the urge to let desire cloud her judgment. Did he work for one of those companies? Is that how he'd known from the start who she was?
"Then why haven't they outted me?" she asked warily.

"I don't know. Maybe because doing so would contradict some b.s. about protecting users' privacy that they're saying in a billion-dollar lawsuit against them in Europe. Maybe they don't want to set a precedent for giving away monetized information such as the details of your life. Maybe busting you isn't worth reminding everyone that FB owns all their baby photos. Maybe someone's pulling a reverse Snowden," he said with a wink. "Something like that."

"But the police could—"

"The cops don't care. They're not going to divulge the fact that they can go to Google or FB and have them finger anyone in the world over a couple of busted guitar amps. It's not like you blew up the White House, you know. No, your fate is in the hands of self-appointed cyber vigilantes, and that's a good thing."

He brought up on his iFlex the stream of people claiming to be her, all of them trying to hijack her 15 minutes of fame to sell their own band or politics, and all of them being analyzed by members of the witch hunt.

PlanetSansSun retweeted your repost. SunsSansPlanets.

Agent007 @Agent007 · 7m
#keffiyehGIRL may have obtained **#keffiyeh** in Syria.
https://handmadepalestine.com

OopsAgain @oopsagain · 7m
#keffiyehGIRL spotted in Malta. https://goo.gl/LtaSBt

We Can Do It! @wecandoit · 6m
Right, a woman could have never pulled this off.
Go **#keffiyehGIRL** !!!

knowledgeW/Oreason @knownot · 6m
Has anyone considered the possblty that **#keffiyehGIRL** is a dude?

EL PAÍS @el_pais · 6m
Paul McCartney, todavía frustrado con John Lennon
http://ow.ly/Pg0I7

reasonW/Oknowledge @purereason · 5m
#XactlySo paid **#keffiyehGIRL** to smash his shit. Part of show. Go home rumer mongers. The Internet is closed.

URhere @urhere · 4m
If you compare #photo1 to **#photo2** you can see **#keffiyehGIRL**'s elbow in crowd.

Accidental Tourist @accidentaltourist · 3m
Help compile **#keffiyehgirllineup** of all women at concert

RightWinger @eaglesoars · 3m
The Ditto Report shows **#Liberals** DELUSIONAL about relationship between **#keffiyehGIRL** and ISIS

AlsoRises @alsorisesthesun · 3m
Why is everyone talking about **#keffiyehGIRL**?

LiveBlogging @liveblogging · 2m
Are you live blogging yet! Here's how:
http://www.24liveblog.com/

Missing Evidence @missingevidence · 1m
Infrared imaging reveals outline of **#keffiyehGIRL** face beneath keffiyeah http://goo.gl/0jFhFt

Fr. Thomas Petri, OP @petriop · 1m
Had an emotional voicemail thanking me for saying it's okay for Catholic to be in favor of Death Penalty

In other windows he opened up Flickr and Punkster and iNote and ePod and other sites posting clues to her identity: hundreds, maybe thousands of photos taken that night that vigilantes were trolling through, sorting, and labeling with their amateur-forensics attempts.

The detective work seemed to be narrowing to a handful of 'persons of interest' as some of the vigilantes already called them, adopting officialese the way phrenologists used to give bumps in the skull Latinate names to make their crazy theories sound like classical learning: a woman in one of the photos with the corner of a scarf, or handkerchief, or some other piece of cloth that could be a keffiyeh sticking out of the back pocket of what could be jeans. The online discussions debated whether or not the keffiyeh in the picture was from a tribe in Saudi Arabia or Morocco or Bangladesh; after it was determined that Yes, the different patterns did designate different groups, but that No, no keffiyehs worn in Bottom Billion countries were blue. Only hipsters in the U.S., Japan, and U.K. wore blue ones. Which set off a discussion about terrorist groups in Japan and the U.K., which bled into a discussion about whether the keffiyeh in the picture was cobalt, lapis, or azure blue, which dredged up #thedress and how colors appeared differently on different screens, even the same screen depending on how it was calibrated; meanwhile, others were trolling the online stores in Japan, the U.K., and U.S., to see where the keffiyeh could have been bought, while others were posting video of the different ways that one of the red-and-white checkered Bottom Billion keffiyehs could have been dyed blue, as someone managed to hack into the records of an Urban Outfitter that sold 'Cobalt Blue' keffiyehs, and had tried to match sales records of keffiyehs to people identified at the concert, while one of these, a researcher for a conservative think tank, first tried to claim that he hadn't been at the concert; then, once too many photos of him dancing there emerged for him to deny it, tried to claim he'd been there for the music, then as others came forward to say he'd been there to buy drugs, and the witch hunt began to go off in other directions, one of the vigilantes claimed to have identified one of the 'persons of interest'—one Amanda Hernandez—the woman in the photo who had the corner of a keffiyeh sticking out of her back pocket—which she claimed was just a blue paper napkin she'd stuck in her pocket after grabbing a bite from a food truck; and she'd posted photos on her FB page of her napkin, but others said it wasn't the same one, so she said it was one LIKE it! That of course she didn't keep the same dirty napkin in her pocket for 3 days! But they said they'd caught her in a lie, and others accused her of being one of the Mexicans who were killing all the bees in the country, and that's why she busted up XactlySo's amps, but she said that made as much sense as a jackass wearing a smoking jacket! Or a burro wearing a keffiyeh! Others began retweeting, calling her #burrogirl, turning it all uglier, fans of XactlySo began harassing her online, even though other vigilantes continued hunting for other 'persons of interest' while those they left behind continued to work it out with #burrogirl, #Confirmed Suspect #1....

He went back to that original photo; data windows popped up beside each bubble. "Look at the time stamp," he said, pointing at the data linked to her photo. "Whoever snapped the picture didn't put it online until almost 15 minutes later. Probably after they were out of range," he said, referring to the fact that whenever the police arrived at a flashriot, the first thing they did was bring down commercial channels.

"But look," he added, pointing to a blip on the screen as though to change the subject, "the server it went through was in Pakistan." The blips made up the paperless paper trail of the photos: little pull-down menus that gave the code for the data transfers, routing numbers, IP addresses, handshaking signals, and other data he said could be used to trace e-mail, bank transfers, photo uploads—really anything that passed through the digital pipeline. "It's how cyber vigilantes are able to out people."

Jenny texted Mattie that Mary retweeted Heather who FB'd Alexa that Debbie was the one who first started the rumor—that Leslie wasn't just iFriends with every guy on her iFACE page, but friends-with-benefits. But Leslie's mom was the one that the little bitch should have been afraid of, spreading lies like that about her daughter. Lies Mom knew kept her daughter off the cheer squad. So she made up an online persona for herself—'Brad'—posting a picture of some teen model as her own. Then Mom made up a backstory for the photo: 'Brad,' she wrote, was a popular but sensitive and misunderstood quarterback at his high school—and just wanted to talk. Then Mom, a.k.a. 'Brad,' struck up an online relationship with little-bitch Debbie to find out what she was saying about her daughter, Leslie. The plan worked perfectly, the little skank giving up the dirt for a couple of sappy compliments: *Your cheerleading lyrics are so awesome!* She never meant for the stupid twit to fall in love with 'Brad,' though if she had, that would have sweetened the revenge. Still, how could she know, how could anyone know, that after 'Brad' had lured her in, got her to write how much she *really, really cared* for him, after 'Brad' got her to trade secrets, got her to confide in 'him' that she was in fact the one who spread that rumor about Leslie being a slut—but only because Leslie had been *really, really mean* to her—after 'Brad' got her to send him a nudie so he could see for himself how much hotter she looked than Leslie (which took some doing since she and most of her class had been suspended freshman year for sexting photos of themselves), even after all of that, how could anyone know that after 'Brad' told her what a shitty trick that was, that only the scum of the Earth would think of it, and that's why he put her nudie online, who would know that after he texted *the world would be better without people like you* and, *BTW, I think your cheerleading lyrics actually suck* and for that reason he was e-dumping her, how could Mom or anyone know the lying little skank would go and commit suicide? Sleeping pills, of course, the teenage girls' weapon of choice. The girl was obviously messed up long before 'Brad' came along.

After the funeral, Debbie's parents wanted to talk to 'Brad,' but he'd canceled his iFACE membership. Police pointed out just having a nudie on your phone broke child porn laws. Bloggers formed a virtual posse. Their techie friends took up the trail. When they discovered who it all led back to, they formed a cyber lynch mob around www.AllAboutLesliesMom—posting as much personal information as they could about her, and inviting everyone in the world to contribute. Virtual vigilantes hired a spammer to mass e-mail millions of people who cared about children and the Internet or at least one of the two, to visit the site where they could help make whatever punishment she would receive in court seem minor by comparison. They hacked into her phone and posted an interactive map that showed where she was 24/7, along with photos snapped of her and her license plate number as she went to the store, went through a speed trap, went anywhere and everywhere: every bit of data about her they could find in the public domain—or in private files like her health records—so people who thought like them would know where to direct their hate, inundating every inbox she was associated with with the message *The World Would Be Better Without YOU*. Someone else replaced her chest X-ray with one taken of a coal miner's black lung. They gave her a life sentence of harassment, forcing her, after she got out of prison and tried to reclaim her life, to take up one identity after another after another after another in the non-virtual world....

"There's no way to hide," Dan said, "but you can vanish." He showed her how easy it was to follow three photoshopped photos of her through a server in Denmark, then others from Spain. There was one from Monaco. He clicked a few buttons, saying, "Maybe there's a selfie of you posing before Hagia Sofia at the same time that the concert was going on.... "His screen showed a red line arc across a map of Europe, connecting one server to another like those old-time movies that depicted travel by showing a cartoon airplane leaving a dotted line across a map as it flew from Istanbul to Paris.

"Maybe your photo went through Monaco via someone who snapped your photo in Pakistan, who put it on the web; or someone in Pakistan. Or in Morocco or Williamsburg: someplace where lots of women wear keffiyehs." Now the red line spread like a spider web, as if the cartoon airplane connecting one dot to another was multiplying as it simultaneously flew to multiple cities. "Or maybe a friend in Monaco emailed a photo of someone who only looked like you to someone in Spain who was reminded of someone else who looked like you and e-mailed that other someone's photo to a friend in Malta, who put all of them online. Or maybe there never was an original.... There's so much fake news that I wouldn't be surprised if XactlySo paid you to smash those amps. Or flood the Internet with fake photos."

He clicked on the keyboard, mumbling, "Data gets corrupted all the time too," as the Spanish IP number changed to the country code for the United Arab Emirates. "There."

"How'd you do that?"

"The hard part's generating some swarm."

She knew about swarms. They were actually closer to her field than his because entomologists with backgrounds in math had been the first to construct models describing how insects, following a few simple rules, come together to act as complex nest activity. It wasn't until much later that other fields took it up, using swarm models to describe subway riders, fluid dynamics, cloud patterns, or how individual voters could coalesce as a trumpapocalypse even if it was a disaster for each of the individual voters.

Still, she appreciated the way he was making her photo multiply, and doing so as hierarchy-free as individual ants. Water molecules didn't need a leader to tell them when to become steam. Nor did rush-hour traffic. Who was foreman of the fish? Yet their schools could change direction more abruptly than any choreographer could direct.

"Third call: Low-fat latte in a dirty cup and a toasted bagel," the barista called out, "Sans twelve-year-old."

"Can you watch my Flex a sec?" he said, quoting a late-night comic whose skit about places like this had gone viral. "You sure you don't want anything?"

Funny, she thought as he got up to get his drink. But she wasn't sure if she meant ha-ha funny, or nerd-funny. She pivoted her bike helmet on the table and watched him walk up to the—Damn it!—he turned around to look back at her just as she was....

He'd meant the joke as a pun: a performance of swarming humor—millions of individual TV viewers finding the joke funny for their own individual reasons but their collective behavior coming together to give the joke a life of its own. But she hadn't cracked a smile. Just sat there fiddling with her helmet. Probably didn't even own a TV.

"Thanks," she said when he returned. "For the noise, I mean." Did he blush? He waved her thanks away as though being thanked hadn't occurred to him. Then he began telling her how it looked like every NG hacker on the planet was jumping into the act, bots beginning to multiply even the fake IPs he'd created.... Somehow talking to him, the way he injected all the misinformation into the system as casually as changing his socks made it all better.... Like turning a witch hunt into a game of Where's Waldo. If for no other reason, she had him to thank for that. As she began to say more, the argument that a swing-bellied RedHatter was having with the barista grew louder, the man demanding to know why the barista had called out a latte "with a twelve-year-old" if the place wasn't a U.N. front, while the barista kept sighing, tattooed arms crossed, looking up at the ceiling, and trying to explain that "sans" meant "without." But that only made the RedHatter confused; he placed a hand on his gun as though that would help him think better as he demanded to know what country the barista was from, talking foreign as he did....

It got louder, and about the time Gabe and Dan began to consider leaving, it died back down. The RedHatter returned to his seat and the same old dumb scene fizzled to its predictable end with him grousing loudly to those around him.

"You into that?" she asked Dan, to not give the RedHatter the satisfaction of being noticed. She'd meant the W.2 icon in his dock.

"Nah. It's just something a bunch of people I follow mess around with. Info designers and computing nerds, mostly, who keep tweeting about W.2 like it's some kind of mystical thing."

"It is. World's largest shopping mall, The Holy of Holies."

"Well yeah, that's pretty much what it's become. But there is something Cocoa-Puff going on." He explained how the blogs keep talking about these mystery avatars: avatars that only appear to someone in W.2 after someone they knew died in the real world.

Gabe looked at him like he'd just told her about a weeping statue so he rephrased it: "Someone's wife or son dies in the real world and then an avatar of that person appears in W.2."

"Like a ghost?"

He hadn't thought of it like that. "Well, not exactly— More like MyDeathSpace.com," he said, meaning the virtual cemetery that gathered the MyFace pages of people who had died. "Except compared to the millions of people online, and the 160,000 who die every day, someone appearing as a ghost avatar in W.2 is rare. Maybe only happened a couple hundred times. Plus, all the iFACE pages gathered at MyDeath were created by the people themselves while they were alive. The MyDeath administrators just blur their faces to make them look ghostly. But some of the ghost-avatars are of people who never even heard of W.2," he said, feeling compelled to press on, though not wanting to sound like he was recruiting her for the Flat Earth Society. "I mean there's some

blip in the W.2 programming that causes some people who die in the real world to appear as avatars in W.2."

"Maybe it's just 'cause," she offered.

He rocked back. "No, no, no. That might work in the real world. But not here," he said, tapping his computer. "It can't. To a computer, lack of pattern is more impossible than angels or miracles."

During the argument with the barista, a couple of regular customers put on blue face masks as an up-yours to the red hats, both armies fighting this year's war with last year's rhetoric. A RedHatter launched into a loud-mouthed explanation of the Second Amendment.

Dan composed himself. "Look, I know what this sounds like," he said, trying to make her see that he wasn't just another flake running around trying to cure droughts with prayer circles. "But seeing an avatar of a dead husband or wife isn't like seeing Elvis. The people aren't stupid or even religious. They aren't into pyramid power or chakras. They're not even the kind to leave flowers on the steps of a school shooting." This last point he said loud enough for all the NRAers in the café to hear.

That was kind of cool, she thought.

"At least not all of them," he said. "They don't have a guru or meditate or own a yoga mat. They're just ordinary computer users: college students or engineers or paralegals. Not stoners or wineheads. This one Marxist professor won't even talk about it other than to acknowledge that he'd seen an avatar of his dead son. A psychiatrist wrote an article in *Wired*..."

If it's in *Wired* it must be true, she thought but didn't say, seeing that she'd irked him enough already.

"...about how people, especially the emotionally wrought like someone who's just lost a wife or husband or child, often sees whatever it is that they desperately want to see...."

Jesus's face on a burnt tortilla.

"During the Middle Ages people often saw the devil. After Sputnik, alien abductions spiked—until Simpsons Episode 107 when Kang tells Kodos, 'We've gone as far as anal-probe technology can take us,' and they fly off, leaving Earth forever...."

Nerd. Quoting vintage TV.

"Now it's Blood Falls—that bloodred waterfall pouring out of a gash in the ice of Antarctica? Pilgrims call it the Wound of the World and flock there to ask the Earth's forgiveness. Maybe seeing ghost-images of loved ones in W.2 is just a manifestation of our networked mentality.... But there is something Cocoa-Puff about it...."

Cocoa-Puff? She held in a laugh at such a goof-ass, nerd-word.

"...even if it's all just projection on the part of lonely people, there's still something there for them to project onto. You can't see an angel in the clouds without a cloud."

Again with the angels and witches.

"...Maybe these mystery avatars will turn out to be just another version of the weather balloons people mistook for UFOs. But right now, something's going on that nobody can explain. That's the only thing these bloggers are really saying: how it could happen. Even if they can't say why. Even if it isn't really happening at all."

If patterns were the most fundamental ground of being, any system will always need humans, thought Paul, checking the wiring harness that connected the brains of four rats to one another. Plural. Link billions of neurons together and you had a brain; link brains together, as he had, and you had a super brain—four rats with their brains wired as one could run a maze 67% faster than four separate rats working individually; wire ten rat brains together and it's 78%; wire the brains of enough rats in a maze and they could run right through it as if they were looking at an aerial view—an overview that video-game players, or soldiers, could emulate by having EEG devices tattooed onto the scalp of each player to transmit and receive brain activity—a god's-eye view that no one person could have alone since one person was not a pattern any more than one neuron was a brain. Unless a 'person' was a shorthand for the patterns he or she made, and/or the patterns that made him or her.

Over at the far end of the coffee shop was a brown pleather sofa, matching armchair, table lamps: one of those corporate attempts to make a store look like home. Gabe noticed because a girl came in wearing a vintage 'mom' dress like she had at home, even the same canvas tennis shoes she also had at home. After prepping her latte, she sat at one end of the couch. A few minutes later, a guy wearing the same Etsy-esque face mask that Dan had hanging loose around his neck, and the same round, vintage glasses, sat down with an espresso. If Gabe ran home and changed clothes, she could make herself and Dan look like a mirror image of the couple in the 'living room.' Except the guy and girl didn't even say hello. Strangers. He wrote in a Moleskine journal, while she had her nose in a book of quotes from Che Guevara. Gabe could tell from the cover because she owned the same book.

The system would always need people—at least it was easy to think so back when the Asian Solutions office that Mr. Ashfram Sing supervised buzzed with chai wallahs, secretaries in saris, and hundreds of associates on headsets:

AUTOMATED MESSAGE
To better serve you, your call may be monitored.

CALL CENTER
Hello, my name is <<Samuel>>.
How may I assist you?

CUSTOMER
Hey, I'm like, I got a duplicate bill, dude.

CALL CENTER
I'm very sorry for the <<inconvenience>>
<<mistake>> <<delay>>.

As soon as the mass migration of American companies to India began, though, the effort to weave humans ever tighter into the machine intensified, associates simultaneously handling multiple lines via function keys:

F1: I can help you with that, <<Customer First Name>>.

F2: You can use the 'I want to' drop-down menu: <<Manage My Plan >> <<Manage My Features>> <<Change Plan>>.

Then came the interactive FAQs. Bots. Customer Advice 'Communities,' and it seemed as if the human component might disappear completely. But as W.2 became a worldwide shopping 'opportunity,' corporations realized that merchandise pushed by sales avatars sold more Adidas, or bottles of NuWater or whatever, and they began generating thousands upon thousands of automated sexy sales associates, dignified African princes, and other sales avatars, all networked so that they all learned from each other the way every self-driving car learned from every other self-driving car. And Sam knew, imagining the cloud of online reviews, interactions, judgments, and other human reactions that replaced everyone in his deserted call center, that he'd been right. The system would always need people, just not the ones he had imagined.

"...As regular people began to adopt blocking software to keep these spamatars from appearing on their screens," Dan said, "merchants began using the same blocking software to keep non-buyers out of their stores. No shirt, no shoes, no W.2 Bank Account, no service...."

"And a computer consciousness begins to emerge," Gabe said. "It's stock Sci-Fi."

"Sort of. Except it isn't consciousness at all, unless consciousness is just an anthropomorphicization of programming. In financial markets it's clear: make the number on the right side larger than the number on the left. But how do you automate judgment about music? Or a painting? How do you make a computer guess instead of calculate odds? Or elect a president who will tear up climate agreements because he doesn't 'believe' in thermometers? That can look at the Israeli-Palestinian conflict and continue to keep fighting even if a two-state solution would result in peace and billions of dollars for each side? No regular computer would pour that much blood and money into an area the size of Lake Michigan without being called insane. So how do you build religious fervor or historical resentment into judgment? Or sexual obsession? Or mourning? How do you make a computer that's rationally irrational or insane? Easy! Make people part of the system.

"Maybe you read about the two sisters who were talking about their dad's chemo treatments? They started getting texts for cemetery plots. They knew something was eavesdropping on them, but couldn't tell if it was the thermostat, toaster, or TV, feeding their sniffles and breathing rates to an algorithm that identified their mood."

"Oh yeah, now I remember. They sued the carrier for invasion of privacy."

"Do you remember why it was dropped?"

"Lack of evidence, I guess."

"Lack of defendant. Or rather too many of them. A judge decided that the Internet itself had come to the decision. Or rather, the true defendants were too dispersed. The system itself had cross-indexed their mood with different databases, the father's drug prescriptions, recovery rates; insurance actuary tables versus his age; it figured out his diagnosis, where he was on the timeline and saw that dad didn't have long to live.

"But, here's where it gets spooky. The mother kept getting messages from him even after he died."

"Junk in, junk out."

"No, hear me out. The same automated software that would profile shoppers began to generate facsimiles of whatever it was these people were looking for—the way Google's neural network was able to survey oceans of YouTube video and come up with the concept of 'cat' on its own."

"Yeah, except dead people don't shop. Nothing to track. Nothing to profile."

"I know, I know." He threw his hands up. "You start to see how this discussion begins to become like talking about God, or cosmology—speculation based on scant, indirect, and questionable evidence. The truth is that no one knows. But the Wiki that's emerged around this seems to think that it has something to do with the fact that every signal leaves a trace, and every trace leaves a trace, the way they say that the explosions of ships that sank during WWII are still echoing in the deepest parts of the ocean, ever fainter, but there nonetheless.

"The Wiki thinks that a version of that is going on in W.2: every 1 and 0 is a stone thrown into the data pool, its ripples moving ever outward. If we could develop software to capture the motion of those ripples, then triangulate from their speed and direction back to their point of origin, we could recreate the original splash. Given enough data, and enough number-crunching capability, we could reconstruct anyone's online life, they say. Or at least a cartoon of it."

"An avatar."

"Somehow the system is triangulating—generating a shade or ghost of these social nodes—once the originating source ends."

"How do you mean 'ends'?"

"You know, Ends. Dies. Dead people."

"Oh," she said. Then she asked, "But why would only some dead people reappear as ghost avatars?"

"The ghost avatars only seem to be generated when there's a spike in interest—a living person searching for them. And searching intently. Marketers call it PUL, Persistent, Unfulfilled Longing: the obsessive mode some people go into searching for the perfect hat, or checking ten times a minute to see if anyone's swiped right.... Somehow, the system is collating these searches as facsimiles of the longed-for items."

"Even if the item is a person? How?"

"That's what people can't figure out. They think it has to do with searching online but not buying anything, combined with some algorithm that tries to match people to their desires—sorting and matching is what networks do best. The facsimile, or ghost, or shade of the dead one is being generated by some subroutine. His or her avatar can't just roam W.2 because it has no more freedom than Jacob Marley. Meanwhile, the avatar looking for them is being shunted out of the buying zones the way bad email addresses are culled from a mailing list. Somehow the avatar of the living is being led off into the same zone as the dead one. That's where they meet. The bloggers call it the Elysian Fields."

The name made Gabe sit up. "Wait. What did you call it?"

"Elysian Fields. It's from Homer. It means—"

"I know what it means," Gabe said, Meadow coming to mind. Especially the longing in her face. "I think I might know someone who's seen one of these ghosts," Gabe said.

Dan went quiet.

"Or is at least trying to."

How to imagine a tsunami: thousands of grains of rice thrown into water going over a dam.

The death of a million people is a statistic; the death of one, a tragedy, as Stalin put it.

Each grain of rice with a human face.

Nico's face.

Mrs. Whitewood hesitated, finger on ADD TO CART for a pair of Striped Calf Hair & Leather Lace-Up Boots. $1,250. Not outrageous, but she already had a pair almost exactly like it. As she tried to decide, she became aware of Maria, standing beside her, twisting her rag, waiting to be acknowledged.

"Yes?" Mrs. Whitewood asked, expecting Maria to ask for an advance. Or a day off. Or a job for one of innumerable 'cousins'.... Whenever Maria had to work up the nerve to ask a favor, she thought sneaking up on the answer would help.

But instead, Maria asked, "Have you heard about that poor Bottom Billion boy?"

"Yes." Of course Mrs. Whitewood had. Everyone had. "Such a tragedy." It was one of those sensational stories: a boy escaping the wars caused by rising seas had tried to cross the Aegean with his family in one of those flimsy smuggler boats when it capsized, drowning more than 50 people. Happened all the time, it seemed. At least often enough to be unremarkable. Like the weather. Twenty today, chance of 30 by Wednesday morning.... What turned this statistic into a tragedy was the boy's body had washed up on a beach in Turkey—near the resort in Bodrum where Mrs. Whitewood had once lain getting a tan—and within hours, a million people had reposted a heartrending photo of the boy in his tiny red shirt and blue shorts, dressed like he'd just left the house to go to school, and instead ended up facedown in the sand. Like a piece of driftwood. His little corpse was a bloodless white, the way fingers got when you soaked in a Jacuzzi too long. Recently, an artist had made a 3D avatar of the boy and geotagged it to the spot on the beach where the body had been found. Anyone standing on that beach could look through the camera of their smartphone and see the boy lying there in the surf as if they were the first ones to come upon the body. To remember, the artist said.

Maria kept standing there, worried. "With a computer you can see it," she said.

What? What was she asking? "Did?— Did you want to see it?" Mrs. Whitewood asked, offering her computer, not knowing what else to say, the designer shoes still on-screen.

Maria shook her head. Then she described, haltingly, something else she had heard: someone had made a picture of every refugee who had died trying to escape rising seas, or drought, or fires, or the fighting caused by them, and placed them at the exact spot where each person had died—like those crosses that families placed along highways where a son or daughter had been killed in an accident.

Mrs. Whitewood knew what she was talking about but Maria hadn't gotten it right: someone had leaked databases of refugee deaths and an artist had mapped them onto the actual physical places with avatars standing at each spot: virtual corpses littered the Aegean Sea, the Syrian deserts, the beaches of Greece and Italy, railroad tracks, bridges, canals, and other routes through Serbia, Hungry.... Hundreds had died in one of the blazes that roared through the vineyard country of Sonoma Valley, well-heeled refugees bringing pets and mementos. Most of the underfed corpses were along the U.S.-Mexican border.

Maria was now talking about a sister she had expected weeks ago but had never arrived. She was very worried. She was hoping that the website could give her some news. Maybe a glimpse?—of those who had died so she'd know her sister wasn't among them....

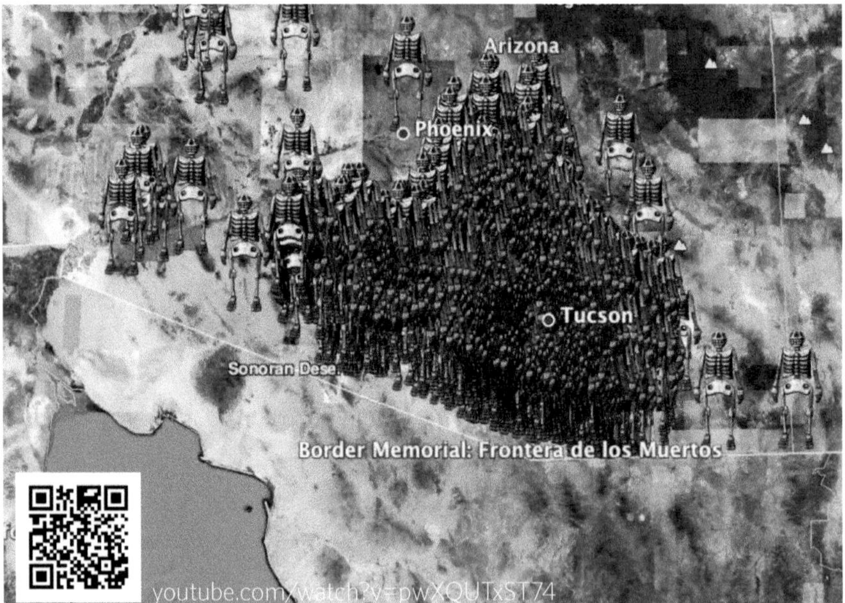

Mrs. Whitewood tried to explain that you couldn't use the computer to see these sites. You had to be there with a smartphone. The bodies were virtual, after all. Maria just stood there confused. Too hard to explain, Mrs. Whitewood thought she'd just show her, but poking around on the web she found a review that described what the app could do, and as the world in the video turned, it showed sites from Bangladesh to New Orleans that had been mapped. There was a virtual memorial to retirees who drowned in their RVs as they fled what was left of Myrtle Beach. Maria stepped closer, anxious, as though the virtual images were as real as the rag in her hand. Mrs. Whitewood clicked on the Mexico-U.S. border and the screen filled with a skeleton standing at the spot in the Sonora Desert where border patrol soldiers had found a dehydrated corpse. Then the camera pulled back, giving a bird's-eye view of the desert—and of hundreds of other skeletons, each standing where someone had died trying to cross the Arizona desert; it kept pulling back, and as polka dots on a balloon grow closer together as the balloon deflates, the number of skeletons marking spots where someone had died became so dense that they looked like a forest of skeletons. There were no identifying features, just data points, and far too many to pick out one.

The first parodies of Gabe that appeared on the web were pretty much what she expected: low-tech affairs, posted by people with names like SmurfVadar, that basically animated the still of her smashing XactlySo's equipment to different soundtracks: the banjo music from *Deliverance*, a steampunk version of "Bring the House Down".... If the fun that people were having with her video was going to just fizzle away, the memes would have ended here, as they usually did. But as the number of views continued to climb, so did the memes, as well as their sophistication.

"Uh oh, uh oh," she said to Dan as they watched her skin turn green in one animation, the big E that was the logo of an ecology movement sprouting from her head like horns. Whoever had made this one had access to studio-grade F/X. The same E sprouted from the top of the microphone stand she was wielding, turning it into a pitchfork. A few days later, a meme of this meme showed her as a giant ear of corn. Then a robot. Then she was the farmer in *American Gothic*, holding the trident pitchfork that had first appeared in the earlier animation, made from the ecology 'E'. In another, someone photoshopped her face to make her a freckled hillbilly, turning down the corners of her mouth to make it look less like a scowl than a drool. Coming from her mouth was a cartoonist's speech bubble: "The corncob: free-range toilet paper."

A Grrrrl-punk singer had an image of Gabe busting amps tattooed on a shoulder.

Vengeance is Mine. 735K likes.

Replying: Rockers, druggies, and gangstas never crack a bible unless its to find a caption for their tat.

FoundHimInPrision

So long as they come to Jesus everthang else is earelephant or irelephant or however u spll it.

In the weeks that followed, Instagram and other sites grew a crazee-quilt of Gabe tattoos and memes, each a commentary, in its way, on who she was and what she did: Circus Freak, Trust Fund Baby, Savage, Idiot Savant, Star-Trek-Con Geek, New Ager, Anime CosPlayer, Neo-Hippie, EcoNazi, Music Hater, Anarchist, Nut-Job—and also the backlash: Hot Eco-Chic, She Guevara, Joan of Ark. She figured Dan had put up that one....

"Relax," he said, "this is just how people share opinions. It's not like this is about you, you know." Then he added. "Isn't that what you wanted?"How far would it go, she wondered, watching the images proliferate. Stupid question. And just as well. Just as Dan had said, the more images of her that were created, the more she was dissipating: the original getting more and more diffuse, drop adding to drop till there were so many drops—a pool—that the truth began to sink in. No one cared. Except NGers: NG hackers continued to generate hundreds, then thousands of false addresses, IPs, dead ends, and forking paths—to protect her, she saw, even if what they really liked was the folk-hero idea they'd made of her, not her. And apparently XactlySo's PR people had decided that the churn was giving him pub that he couldn't buy. Five more strangers claimed online to be her—the woman in the video smashing XactlySo's stuff. Instead of Waldo, she was becoming Kilroy: the name that WWII GIs came across so often—'Kilroy Was Here'—that they began to believe in him, or at least take up his cause, signing his name instead of their own. Or maybe there was no original, no Kilroy, no them, the way that the 'Guy' over in Congo was not the 'Guy' who they knew here, or she, dressed in a pastel dress when she was six wasn't the 'her' who was standing here thinking about that other 'her,' the one who had smashed the equipment, each playing its part before morphing into another, everyone only a prequel and a sequel to themselves and each other, at so many ages and in so many ways that sometimes she herself didn't know which of them to ask, Who are you?

She liked the way this one avatar of her did her hair. Looking at her reflection in the computer screen, she swirled a curl around her finger to bend it the same way.

Calmly going about their work in the lab, the others seemed the picture of normalcy. So normal that Mohammed felt as though he'd stepped into that movie where he was the crazy one, even though he alone saw that everyone else had been replaced by a double, grown in a pod. "You're asking me to spy on my colleagues for you?" he had asked the Ag agents near the conclusion of their meeting. "Not spy, just notify us if you see anything suspicious." At the time, Mohammed would have happily spied for them. He would have done anything to escape the claustrophobic grip of their room. It was only afterwards, after he had time to think of the secrets he had to betray about his coworkers, that he was able to see what sort of pod-person the agents wanted him to become, meeting them in shadowy garages to report that Gabe made her own yogurt, or that Meadow was having troubles with her husband after the death of their child....

Taped to the side of his cabinet was the photo of his wife and child. They had all made a trip home to Bahrain before he was to return to Venezuela to study, and Mohammed had asked a stranger to shoot the picture so he could be in it with his wife, his wife holding their child. It had been during Ramadan, a happy time of year. The palms that filled the water park they had gone to for an evening stroll were filled with dates. But unlike the family photos Americans had on their desks at work, Mohammed and his wife were not touching. Even if morality police didn't patrol the palm groves, it wouldn't have occurred to Mohammed or his wife to hold hands in public. They merely stood beside each other, expressionless. A portrait of two peoples: Americans smiled even in the photos for their passports—as though happy to see the government official filing away their faces, their smiles betraying how deeply they assumed that all would be fair, unlike the line of gray men in the passport office back home, stoically waiting for the camera's click to dispatch them as if they already stood before the immigration/police/interrogator machinery that would use the photo to decide their fate.

Somehow Mohammed had known even then that he would end up as a 'person of interest.' His uncles had foretold it when, to their astonishment, his visa was approved and word spread of his coming to America: where everyone had a big car and machine gun.

youtube.com/watch?v=hC3VTgIPoGU
1:25 / 2:55

The agents who had summoned him for a 'conversation' were investigating the collapse of bee colonies in the Midwest, they said. Some of the bees found in a hive had GFP in their genome. So they'd cross-indexed names of guest workers from 'countries of interest' with sales of the machine a terrorist would need to insert GFP into the genome of a bee and he and his lab were a match. "What can you tell us about that?"

I can tell you, he wanted to say, what was obvious: they were chasing shadows. How many more people like him were they using?—people with vulnerable immigration status, people they could scare into helping them with their 'extreme vetting.' The devil's desire colonizes your thoughts so completely that by the end you can't even think to ask for forgiveness.

She'd signed up for the cruise thinking it would be a floating party: Boutiques & Business. *You Only Have to Unpack Once!* Don't miss the Polar Ice Cap Break Apart, the brochure said, *A Once An Epoch Event!* They were far too late to see the really large chunks go, like the ice shelf that collapsed into the Weddell Sea back in 2002, a hunk bigger than Luxembourg. But the ads for this cruise promised the collapse of at least one ice bridge, and the one on today's stop was massive, spanning a river that had cut through a glacier.

New Age sitar music played. Tourists crowded the ship's railing, snapping pictures of the ice cliffs. Every time a sheet of ice thundered down into the sea they cheered, the slabs so massive that they seemed to fall in slow-mo, giving up geysers of spray. But it was obvious that everyone was really focused on the main event: seeing the bridge itself collapse. Like a New Year's Eve crowd waiting for the ball to drop, all heads were turned toward it, whooping louder each time a chunk of ice fell from its underside, thinning the arch. The cheers were motivated, she imagined, by the reasons people always cheered at the watershed between new and old—especially a change of *fin de siècle*—some cheering for the fresh start it seemed to offer, some cheering for the death of the old, some because they'd simply lived to see it happen, some because it—whatever *it* was—was really happening, some out of mindless exuberance, some out of fear of the unknown, or worry, or nervousness, or any of the other reasons people also laugh or cry....

When the collapse came, there was no countdown. The massive ice arch failed so suddenly and so completely that it was clear that whatever keystone anyone could imagine had only existed in their imaginations, the arch instead standing the way a house of cards stays upright, one side giving way and pulling down the whole opposing cliff, drowning out the crowd and the sitar soundtrack with its roar—a terrifying, earth-deep rumble—though the cruise ship was far enough away that it only gently rode up, then over, the resulting wave.

Meadow came in Saturday afternoon, late, after everyone was gone. As soon as she logged into W.2, she began to twitch her fingers in that finger-puppet motion to make her avatar jog away from Burning Man. By the time it was dark, her knuckles ached, and she stopped to rest. Behind her, the huge bonfire they'd made of the wooden man was just an orange glow on the horizon. The next time she had her avatar turn around to look, even the glow was gone. When the moon came up, she saw that she had walked so far that the landscape had grown cruder than anything she had ever seen in W.2.

What few features there were—a cactus and a ridge—were no more detailed than a paint-by-number picture with only the more basic hues painted in. When the landscape began to lose its color, she knew she had definitely slipped, somehow, into a construction zone: a loop of code left incomplete, or that ceased to function after an upgrade and yet no programmer had ever taken the time to edit out. Her VR goggles didn't work here, and she pulled them off. On-screen, the land around her avatar appeared as outlines.

She couldn't fly any longer. And the navigation compass that always appeared in the corner of the W.2 interface wasn't there. She didn't dare log off out of fear that she wouldn't be able to find her way back, so she only kept walking, wondering why she'd taken the advice of a stoner. "Out there," she'd said. "They're waiting for you." What the heck did that mean? Neo-Hippie mumbo jumbo. Now here she was, heading deeper into the great nothing, afraid to log off, even though she was so tired she could fall asleep at her keyboard. After a while, she was falling asleep, nodding off like a student on an all-nighter. She rested her fingers and her avatar stopped walking. When she had it lie down, her screen filled with its view of the sky: black, twinkling points of light.... At least the stars were still there....

When she awoke, she was surprised to find herself at her desk in the lab. Sunday. She'd have the lab to herself. Only Gabe would be in to tend to her lice colonies but the Insectarium was two floors down so they wouldn't see each other.

Rubbing her eyes, she turned back to her computer, remembering stars. Now, the sun was up; she could tell from the dawn-colored light of her screen, though she couldn't make her avatar find the sunrise no matter which direction she turned. The uniform glow seemed to come from nowhere and everywhere.

She continued walking. All morning she walked—through what could have been an infinite, flat desert. She only stopped once, to go down the hall in the real world to use the john and get an apple out of the vending machine. But then she was back.

Sometime later she could make out a bump on the horizon.

Using the arrow keys, she walked toward it and as she neared, it grew like an island seen from far out at sea. Columbus's first glimpse of the New World?

Had she walked all around the Earth? Maybe she'd gotten disoriented and ended up back at the Burning Man. Explorers sometimes ended up walking in a circle because one leg was invariably stronger, it was said. But no, she considered, swishing her fingers faster to hike at a brisker pace; the island or whatever it was grew rapidly as she neared. Soon, she could make out avatars milling about. There was something odd about them, though: their bodies were geometric figures. Rectangles or boxes.... No, they were books.

She felt oddly drawn to them. Partly it was the silence here; she hadn't realized how thick the din was in other parts of W.2 until she arrived in this dead zone where a person could hear her own thoughts. But she was also drawn to their shapes, the book-shaped bodies comforting in some way she couldn't articulate but gave her the peacefulness of gazing into a campfire, or watching waves. She could tell they must have felt it also by their manner. None of them were dancing or trying to sell anything. Mainly they seemed to be strolling about in twos and threes, arm-in-arm, the way people used to once take the air, conversing as though going for a walk after a heavy dinner, and she felt humble as she approached, as though guilty for the minutiae of her busy workaday life while they were—what? She couldn't say, wasn't sure what she was approaching, but the feeling she had was much like the one she had as a tourist entering a shrine or some sacred space, puzzled by what it was that surrounded her though understanding that those in its midst were under the sway of something larger than themselves.

Two of them stopped talking when they saw her and the thickest of them stepped forward—a body with the squat dimensions of an unabridged dictionary. He began to type and a moment later the words appeared in the communication bubble of her interface: "Did you come to join us or are you in exile?"

Meadow didn't know how to answer. "What do you mean?" she said. But no words came out. Audio didn't work here she remembered. That accounted for the odd silence. She positioned her hands on the keyboard to type but the keyboard felt odd, though also familiar, like a telegraph key to people used to phones—and it seemed a code between them. Here, 'language' meant 'text.' Before she could translate her words into keystrokes, though, text appeared in a speech bubble above the other avatar, a much thinner rectangle: "Come on, mate, let's go. She's just lost." He motioned with his head, trying to get the squat one to walk off with him but the squat one maintained his stance, waiting. He typed another question and a new speech bubble appeared above his head: "What are you looking for?"

This time Meadow was on it: "I'm not sure." The skinny one gave off a 'sigh' emoticon, then began to turn away as Meadow continued to type whatever came into her head, trying to hang onto whatever thread was between them. "Are you the Book People?" She tried to remember the science fiction novel that Gabe had at work—with its firemen who burned books, and readers who fled to live as a community of hermits out in the woods, each one memorizing a book in the hopes that one day they would be able to return to civilization with the knowledge they had saved from destruction by storing it in their memories. "Like from *Fahrenheit 451*?"

This question froze the thin one in his tracks. "Ha!" came an I-Told-You-So emoticon from the stout one. The thin one came back to them, his hands typing as he did so, "Most people who stumble upon us think we are boxes."

"Or bricks."

"Boxes of breakfast cereal. Or lost birthday presents. The Island of Misfit Toys."

"You can say that again," the stout one joked, kindly, and the thin one gave off a laugh emoticon. The stout one bowed to Meadow, and announced with faux gravity, "I am *Remembrance of Things Past, Volume One.* And this," he said, introducing his thin friend, "is, in fact, *Fahrenheit 451.*"

He was the same edition she'd seen on Gabe's desk; coincidence? —no, too much of a coincidence to be one, and she wondered how the system had known what she'd been thinking. The answer seemed out there, out in the community of book-shaped avatars milling around beyond them, coming into then going out of view in the pacific way of fireflies she'd once seen, silently pulsing in a forest on the other side of a river. *So many, so many, I had not thought death had undone so many.* There must be thousands. Millions. Maybe more if they could go offline here. Wherever here was. "And you are?" the stout one was asking her.

She sent a 'shoulder shrug' emoticon then sat down. "I'm sorry; I'm not a book."

"Well neither are we," the stout one said, sitting down beside her, doing so by tipping his chest forward, exactly as someone would tip a book to put it on a shelf. "Not technically at least. Up there, in the other world, I'm a librarian. *Fahrenheit*, my friend here, is a firefighter who simply likes to read."

"A lot," he added.

He pointed at a slim rectangle walking by. "There goes *The Wasteland*, a professor of modernism in the other world."

"So many, I had not thought death had undone so many," *The Wasteland* called out jollily.

How did they always seem to know what she'd been thinking?

"Most of us have some connection to languages—English majors who end up as clerks in their father's law firms; comparative lit PhDs who earn their daily crust by comparing real estate listings. There's a surprising number of waiters among us. *Fahrenheit* thinks it's because reading all that British lit makes them think like butlers. But I believe it's a butler mentality that draws them to British lit. If there was anything that could be called Brit Lit; if there was anything like a British butler anymore. Have you read *Remains of the Day?* In any case, everyone likes to see themselves in a story. Then there are the unemployed philosophers and hikikomori who live in their mothers' basements so they can spend their days here. But the vast majority of us can't be that pure, so only come here when we can. What are you? Out there?" he asked, motioning up—upward but not Northward, was the line that came to mind.

"I'm a biologist."

"A biologist! Ha!" *Fahrenheit* exclaimed. "We don't see many of your kind down here. Not given the demand for your kind up there," he added derisively.

"Don't take him wrong," *Remembrance* rushed in with. "We're very pleased that you've come. We have a large number of historians of science: those who can quote Hippocrates in the Greek."

"What he means," *Fahrenheit* interrupted, "is that in our community, many readers only become interested in science once it ceases to be pragmatic knowledge; that is, once it has passed on into the realm of literature. The way Duchamp turned a urinal into art by disconnecting its pipes and putting it in a gallery. We also have lots of science fiction readers. But not actual readers of science."

"Oh, I know what you're thinking. You're surprised to hear this since the people you know only read things like *The Journal of Paramecium....*" Again, she wondered how he knew.... "In a field like yours, keeping up with the literature is a job in itself. It's the same with doctors. Most of them are too busy seeing patients to be a book here. Those who aren't have no use for collective wisdom. The past, I mean."

"Is that what you do? Memorize books? Like the Book People in *Fahrenheit 451*?"

"Did you know that only 5% of all scientific articles continue to be read five years after they're published? That's the same life expectancy for deer living in the wild."

"No sooner published than thrown onto the dust heap of history."

"Dumpster, you mean."

"That's why having a reader such as yourself would be so valuable here."

"'*Look, cried Montag*,'" *Fahrenheit* declaimed, quoting from himself. "'*And the war began and ended in that instant.*'"

Remembrance paused—frozen in mid-gesture as though waiting for the moment to pass—then continued. "Some of us still believe that our perspective can put off the day that Bradbury imagined. Or its many versions. Fire or Ice. In any case, unlike Bradbury's Book People, our collective knowledge is in use now. Even as we speak," he wrote, looking up to the sky as though god might be up there listening.

"Like a wiki?"

"More like the multi-lens eye of a fly, each a slightly different view of the world. A view that is diminished by one lens each time a book winks out of the world.

"That's what drew so many of us to the cause to begin with. Some of us, like *Iliad* there," he said, pointing out a thick volume going by, "have been here since the early days of cookies—when Internet pages first began reading the people reading them. First a narrow, low-res portrait of you would emerge—maybe centered on just a few questions—your love of animals, for example. But then, as more and more data points accreted, your profile would take on more definition.... Cat owners have different demographics than dog owners—an apartment in the city instead of a cabin in Oregon. They score differently on personality tests. They work out in gyms instead of take forest walks...."

Was he talking about her?

"...a high-res portrait emerges with your dog as less of a pet than a node in your life, your relation to your dog helping you find meaning in your own: you volunteer at Animal Ark..."

How could he know so much about her?

"...three days after the spaniel that you owned for 13 years died you bought a puppy, which you named Magnolia, after an aunt's flowered hat, and took it to the vet regularly, even though the only time you'd been to the doctor yourself, according to medical records, was to get the anti-allergy medication you needed to have a dog in the house....

He was definitely talking about her, and it was creepy, like having a stranger describe the contents of her purse.

"Oh, and we can predict with 97% accuracy that you are depressive, even though you yourself are in denial." As he spoke, *Fahrenheit* seemed to look away, as one who feels guilty....

"Of course, this portrait can only address the 'what' of a person," *Remembrance*, said. "It has very little to say about the why—much like science has much to say about the 'how' of the universe, but leaves the question 'why' to people like us."

"To be or not to be!" a volume cried out, strolling by, "One of the most succinct statements of the human dilemma!"

"Shakespeare's first folio," *Remembrance* explained, continuing, "Automated judgment is so ubiquitous that we take AI for granted, but it's still horribly mechanical. Especially when it comes to being moved by Mozart's *Requiem*, or feeling our own fleeting mortality at Hamlet's graveyard speech....

"...we supply a sense of what the poem means to humans and the program makes us part of itself," *Fahrenheit* said, still refusing to look directly at Meadow's avatar.

"The poem is the software running on the wetware of our minds; our judgment becomes the variables of the software; in this way we become the ghost in the machine, if you will. Or, if you won't, we ensure that a literary perspective will continue for at least as long as there are humans: The human perspective doesn't lose out to the machine's database because we are part of it." Then he clapped his hands together and declared, "But you didn't come here for that. None of us did. You're here because you're searching for—"

She cut him off. "Someone. I'm looking for someone."

Her answer caused a shift in his demeanor. He and *Fahrenheit* shared a meaningful glance, then fell silent.

"I didn't think you could help," she said.

After a while, *Remembrance* said, "We are very sorry for your loss."

How did he know?

• •

"The failure of poetry is the greatest theme of poetry," he replied, as though in answer. "That's what most of these books here are about," he said, "no matter what else they may be about."

Then he stood, reaching out for her hand. She rose, taking it. *Fahrenheit* bowed in the manner of a servant letting a queen pass as *Remembrance* led her into the thicket of other books. The text bubbles appearing over other heads began to take up more and more of her screen: the conversations that the other books were having, all jumbled together—not as the competing shouts of a trading floor, but as voices in a conversation that knew there was time enough for everyone. They seemed to talk of everything and nothing—not as a business meeting or speech or lecture—but the way a conversation among friends meanders from one subject to another, jumping from philosophy to a conversation about a change in bus schedules; from the best place to get roast chicken to the meaning of art, never coming to any conclusion but in the end creating an aura that seemed meaningful if not meaning any one, or even a dozen things. *The Elementary Particles* went by, nodding hello. With the return of some definition, more of the books bore titles she could read. *Alice in Wonderland. 2666. Satin Island. War and Peace* and *IN & OZ*. Now that she was in their midst, she could tell they weren't just randomly walking around as she had thought. Those along the fringe did seem to be going wherever they wanted, but most were moving in a great circle, those that she had thought had been walking against the flow were actually on the far side of the circle, continuing around to where she stood and she had the sense that if she could rise above them to have a bird's-eye view, they would appear as a weather system, leisurely turning about an eye. And yet the longer they walked, the more familiar the titles became, books she knew, or had heard about, or had looked through in her youth but hadn't thought about for years, as if somehow they were being attracted to her the way a Higgs particle gathers mass by moving through space.

"Nurse, you are the last who will know her," one said, the poem the words came from remaining just beyond memory. *"She is very old,"* the book said, and she strained but failed to remember where she had heard the poem—like the voice of someone she had known in her youth but hadn't seen in years and couldn't quite place. Then he was gone.

Remembrance continued looking for someone in particular, Meadow could tell, seeing how he would pause from time to time to search the crowd of books the way someone in an airport might look for a loved one due to arrive. Many of the books would pause to let them pass, the way most cars paused to let a funeral procession through, but not all. Some impatiently went around them. Others sped up to cut in front of them.

Once she found her path blocked by a small book, a child among adults: *The Little Prince.* She wanted to stay and talk. But another explained, "I'm sorry. This one didn't even know how to read."

At this point, *Beloved* came over to her. She put a sympathetic hand on her shoulder. "I'm sorry for your loss."

Then they found it: The book paused the moment it saw *Remembrance*. It was about to call out happily, but the sight of Meadow beside him gave it pause and a sympathetic expression replaced its cheer as though it understood immediately what her being here meant. *The Collected Works of Homer* it said across his chest, and as Meadow approached, he opened as a book opens. *Elysian Fields* it said across the first page and she understood this to be a door—a portal.

Remembrance allowed her hand to slide from his as she continued on into, then through the title page the way avatars were able to walk through walls, or the way Alice passed through the looking glass.

One leg inside the book, the rest of her body still outside, she paused, turning for one last look at *Remembrance*. Before entering completely, she asked, "Are you real?"

He brought his hand to his chin and thought a moment—or froze up; she couldn't tell which it was as he stood there in mid-gesture the way an image on the web does until all of its data packets arrive via different servers, each byte taking differing paths to constitute the one image; when they did, he answered, "Depends what you mean by 'real.' And 'you.'"

Another book who had paused beside him—*Philosophical Investigations*—added, "And 'are.'"

"Hey Gabriella, you hear about the cat?" Jak asked. He was referring to the dead cat that was discovered in Germany, a lab test revealing avian flu in its corpse. Everyone in influenza labs had their panties in a twist because this was the first instance of the virus killing a mammal. The hope lay in the fact that the WHO couldn't determine whether the cat died from a virus that had mutated to mammals—one step closer to humans—or whether the death was merely poetic justice, the bird that the cat ate taking the cat with it to the grave. Meadow, and the rest of the world were hoping for the 'poetic justice theory'. "Yeah, well, no need to panic," she said. "Cats do eat a lot a birds."

She was right of course. But watching the plague move from China to Vietnam to Romania and now Western Europe, it began to dawn on Jak how flimsy the story he'd told himself had actually been: in it, he'd have time to prepare. He'd watch the human variety nearing, like an army of zombies in a MMORPG, the kind that moved slow and always walked in front of your gun—and then, once it arrived in North America, he'd act. He'd buy N95s and wear them more conscientiously than condoms. He'd seal off the bathroom in his apartment, turn it into a live-in biohazard containment room if it came to that.

But thinking more soberly now, he realized that if a plague broke out again, it would be different from those in the past—and everywhere all at once—humans in jumbo jets traveling much faster than migrating birds, carrying the virus into every artery of human communication. People used to think they didn't share a body. And maybe once that was true. But with people burning coal and the mercury going into the ocean and the fish eating the mercury and the people eating the fish, and plants carrying human DNA, and everyone breathing the same air, there wasn't even any separation between people and animals, let alone each other.

He and his buddies had had a laugh after the last scare when one of them confessed that once he thought the end was near, he had hoarded gold. Yeah, the good news is, you got all the gold in the world, they'd laughed, but the bad news is that there's nowhere to spend it. It's said that people reveal themselves in their ultimate concerns, the philosopher among them said sagely. And they laughed when another confessed that he had hoarded beer, laughing more, when a third said toilet paper, and the fourth ammunition. After this last had spoken, they stopped laughing, and looked at one another as they never had before.

The government solution, he'd read while standing sardine tight in a subway can: civilians are advised to maintain a separation of three meters between one another.

We Cover the Earth—said the logo of a paint company, an icon that could be used as a logo for the flu as well, complete coverage measured in hours.

When the agents showed up at her office, Olympia got the kind of chill that comes from inside. She moved some books off the extra chairs so they'd have a place to sit, then sat at her desk acting cool though her mind raced with all the reasons that what she was doing was perfectly legal. Then they began asking about Mohammed. They weren't interested in her or copyright infringement at all, only in Mohammed, and she tried to not let her relief show.

It wasn't like him to not show up at work, she told them. And he hadn't been in for four days. When they tried calling his cell, all they got was his voice mail.

"Is he in some kind of trouble," she asked, meaning, Am I in some kind of trouble because of him?

Instead of answering, the man, an agent from the Dept. of Agriculture, asked, "Can we see his computer?" The warrant he pulled out let Olympia know the question was rhetorical.

After they left, taking the computer with them, Olympia sat in her office wondering what it could all mean. They never asked her if she knew where he was, meaning, she surmised, that they knew where he was. If they weren't holding him somewhere he would have at least called. But why? Was he mixed up in some terrorist shit? Mistaken for someone who was? Extreme vetting often meant people were held for months, even years, without ever being charged with anything. Disappeared, it used to be called.

Then a horrible thought came to her. Had they arrested him because he was trying to sell her data? Had he copied his hard drive and peddled their gene library to Big Pharma? Or, more likely, offered it as a perk to whatever company would hire him? She knew of several PIs who had a story like that and always it starred someone like him: a postdoc working way below grade because he depended on Green Card renewals, or some such, a family back in some foreign country, depending on the money he sent home. Maybe a boss he was pissed at. Her? Unlike Jak, Meadow, and Gabe, Mohammed never said anything directly, but when she retracted the article, she could tell he was pissed. Like Meadow, he had been counting on having his name on the publication.

Jak, Gabe, Silpa, and Meadow stood around looking at the empty spot on the lab bench where Mohammed's computer had been, talking about the FBI agents who had taken it, asking each other and themselves Why? No one could figure it out. They kept looking back to the spot where it had been, a clean footprint in the dust on the bench.

"Maybe he tried to leave the country with our data?" Jak said.

"Oh right," Gabe said, "like a half-completed Phthiraptera gene library's a state secret."

"Maybe customs agents mistook it for bomb data."

"Ha," pause, "ha," Gabe laughed to show how stupid that was.

But Jak shot back, "You don't know. You don't know what we really could be working on. None of us do. The project is getting military money. Maybe the government is planning to take our lice data and use it for some kind of biological weapon."

The comment gave them all pause. Every tech had a friend or a friend of a friend who came to realize they were working on a piece of a project that could be used for fertilizer or to break down oil spills, but could also be used to stabilize a detonator, or even more evil, unimaginable shit. It was part of the turf.

"Yeah, no one ever went around the rules," Gabe said sarcastically, and Meadow wondered if Gabe was including herself. Everyone knew how raw she was about picking up a 'dead' strain of Malaria. 'Fuck it, fuck it all,' she'd said. Then Chen's data had gone wonky. But she wouldn't sabotage the study, would she?—it was just a manner of speaking—the way someone who's angry says, 'I'm going to kill you,' without actually meaning it. But she wouldn't let it go, blaming the lab though she'd never been able to prove it, even after Compliance had been called in. The fact that they hadn't been able to find anything only convinced her all the more that there was some sort of conspiracy, or shadow study, or something that had kept it off the books. Not, as Compliance concluded, a stray had gotten in.

She exchanged a knowing look with Silpa, Silpa willing to believe anything about governments after having a complete blackout on information about Guy. She'd begun spending hours searching for him online. Some mornings she showed up bleary eyed from not having slept the night before.

The others were deep into details that could be evidence for motives Mohammed might have had to steal data that might or might not have military uses: his family back in Bahrain or Venezuela, or the pride he had, or how neat he kept everything.... As a group they realized what they were doing when Silpa exclaimed, "Now you all have gone off the deep end." Silpa wanted to believe there was nothing to the idea that 1) they might actually be working on a military project; and 2) Mohammed was A) a terrorist, or B) a criminal. The most innocent detail could be used against a foreigner, she knew. Or anyone. And she told them so.

Jak continued pumping life into his conspiracy theory, the others now arguing against it, either out of wishful thinking, or because they really did believe that a vaccine that helped an invading army didn't make them weapons researchers.... →

Meadow wasn't sure what to believe, except that above Mohammed's spot on the bench was a photo of his wife and son. And she knew he wouldn't have left on his own without that.

Dan decided to drop by her place with her latest incarnation. Friends had sent him to Flickr for pictures of their trip to Australia, and there, in the background, behind a kangaroo, was a billboard with Gabe's smashing XactlySo's equipment. Some ad agency had doctored the photo of her, and tinted her red to make her look insane, then used it on the label for a screw-cap wine. *Go wild!—Tasmanian Red!* He thought she'd think it was funny. So he'd found a site that carried Tasmanian Red, got a bottle and showed up at her place: one of those old factories near the university that had been converted into the offices of a tech startup during the boom, then abandoned during the last tech bust and hadn't been re-re-gentrified yet.

He could tell she was pleased to see him, even though she wasn't thrilled about him showing up unannounced. With a bottle of wine that must have had a carbon footprint the size of Australia. But soon enough she was rooting around in the area that was her kitchen for a couple of glasses. "You mind drinking out of a jelly jar?"

While the sound of clinking dishes came from her kitchen, he looked around. Without her in the room, it was like he'd found her diary lying open before him. If she wasn't an NGer, she at least sympathized with them. Her bike hung on hooks on the wall by the door. Another wall was a checkerboard of windowpanes that looked onto rooftop water tanks and pandemic gardens. Gaps let in light between the old, industrial window frames and the brick wall where mortar had crumbled out. She'd plugged the larger chinks with hunks of foam instead of doing a real patch. A drafting table was before the window, bathed in light. Sketches hung from a clothesline like laundry: drawings of robots and melting glaciers. A computer had been retrofitted to use a typewriter for its keyboard. Steampunk: the way the black water tanks outside were reminiscent of railroads and telegraph wires. The sticks of charcoal she used to draw robots probably weren't all that different from the ones Neanderthals used to sketch animals on the walls of caves....

Then she was there, holding a couple of mismatched jars, half filled with Tasmanian Red. "What do you think?" she asked, referring to the drawings she'd found him looking at.

They were pretty good in that graffiti sort of way. He tried to be complimentary. No, he was complimentary. The drawings made a lot of sense once a person saw those black rooftop water tanks she looked out onto everyday—the way he'd once been struck, while walking down a narrow cobblestone street in Pisa, how Galileo must have walked those same streets, built before cars dictated the shape of cities in America—and made old European cities so much more livable now that cafés and subways and density and bikes made feet the best way to get around again.

She asked him if he wanted to see some of the drawings she'd already finished.

Sitting next to him on her couch, she pulled out a stack of handmade comic books. The kind of low-tech DIY print jobs they sold in racks at indie bookstores. When she had enough stories to make a collection, she was hoping to get it published but she had no idea who would buy it since her stuff wasn't really Sci-Fi so much as Fi about Sci: more bio lab than saucer-eyed girls with ray-guns.

He could tell this one was based on the work she was doing in her own lab: drawings of fleas and other parasites spreading to what had once been cold climates. She'd collaged drawings from other plagues—medieval doctors wearing bird masks—and some of the Big Data graphs he'd given her: projections showing rates of extinction rising like a tide until the only mammals left on Earth were rats. Each page of her graphic novel was darker than the last, lots of black charcoal strokes: scientists in white lab coats trying to coax into life embryos of extinct animals. Then the next panel showed that the lab they'd been working on was located inside a big wooden boat: an ark that, when he turned the page, went plunging over a waterfall at the edge of a flat Earth.

"I guess the research you guys are developing isn't going so well," he said.

She sank back in the cushions. "It's so messed up. We were at the point where we needed to process more human blood, then one of our two phlebotomists gets shipped off to the Congo."

"Human blood? Why do you need human blood?"

"If you're laying down the groundwork for humans you need human blood, of course."

Humans? He sat there silently as she explained the program that her group was working on, looking for a way to inoculate humans against avian flu. As she talked, he saw how the version of the study she was describing differed from the version that Olympia had given his company. This wasn't the first time he'd seen this: a PI giving the lab a different story about what they were doing than what they were actually doing. Or giving them part of the story, the way a bunch of chemists who worked at Dow Chemical during the 60s only knew the one little chemical reaction they were working on, not how others would put all the pieces together to make a jellied gasoline that would stick to skin and burn under water.

Then he told her so.

Instead of arguing, she only let out a sigh. Had she known? She must have had suspicions.

"Birds," Dan confirmed, "all of the computer simulations Olympia has my company make are related to birds, not people. BioDefense they call it," he said, though the 'oh brother' look she gave him made the euphemism sound ridiculous. 'Preemptive strike' was probably the excuse Cain used to brain Abel.

He sat silently as she lamented all of this but when she finally wore herself out, he only said, "Your phlebotomist? You said he was sent to the Congo?"

"Bolivia or the Congo, or who knows where," Gabe said, irritated, frustrated for being used as a tool. "At first Silpa, the one phlebotomist we still have, was able to keep up. But she can't work like a machine. Then instead of hiring a replacement to help her, the study starts calling for half as many units of blood...."

But Dan's mind was on the tweets he followed about ghost sightings, the latest ghost to have appeared also having been a phlebotomist when alive....

"But you think he was sent to the Congo?" he asked again.

"Yeah, Congo," she repeated, "or at least somewhere in Africa," agitated, all of it becoming a single fabric to her: the endless wars over conflict minerals, the military funding Olympia got, the lies she must have told everyone in the lab to keep it.... What was going on in her lab was just a microcosm of the bigger lie Guy and thousands like him bought into, joining the reserves.... "At least that's what Silpa thinks," Gabe said, telling him about Guy but really meaning the whole, bullshit system.

"The two of them used to meet every Tuesday in W.2 but she hasn't heard from him in weeks and she's been worried sick about it. Everyone tells Silpa that it's probably nothing. That he'll pop up in Bolivia or somewhere and explain it all. But everyone knows it doesn't look good."

The more she talked, the more agitated she became, as if the whole lie of the lab had come to be epitomized by the lie of the wars: the U.S. blacking out pictures of returning coffins, then whole countries on maps, all while pressuring people at the Super Bowl to stand and repeat the Make America Great Again pledge....

As she spoke, she could feel herself growing as emotional as if she were talking about her own boyfriend; which in a way she was, Guy being a friend to all of them.

Looking at the drawings in her graphic novel, open on Dan's lap, the reality of it came to her hard: the world was ending. Not just for Silpa and Guy but for everyone—the whole planet becoming uninhabitable though everyone continued to live as if it weren't. They say that Homo sapiens began painting caves as Sistine ceilings of animals when they first noticed a difference between themselves and the animals. Was that where it all began to go wrong?—the first step out of an Eden of crazy abundance and Technicolor variety of plants and animals being the first step down an ever-narrowing path that would lead to a dead end? You'd think that the cave people who could paint those studied pictures of animals would realize that they were getting so good at killing them that they were driving their food supply to extinction. But even early naturalists denied that people had anything to do with the loss of the dodo bird—and every time there was a call to do something—drive less, eat less—people did nothing. Nothing but replace jet strikes over oil with drone strikes over water. Then there was the disaster of 11/9 and RedHatters kneecapped the planet's last chance.... Now it was too late to do anything. Anything except watch Earth die.

She felt powerfully sorry for Silpa, for herself, for everyone.... All of them just going about their workaday lives like people with six months to live who continue to report for work because—never having faced anything like this before—they didn't know what else to do. Was a lack of imagination what kept them going to school, checking in on Yelp, taking up tennis, doing whatever it was that they spent their lives doing: musicians who continued to play as the *Titanic* sank?... If so, they didn't deserve the Earth and it would be better off without them....

An image of a mother hugging her child as their cabin filled with water.... Gabe didn't want to go down alone, though. No one did. An image of those two old men on YouTube clinging to one another as they were swept out to sea: moments earlier, they had been strangers, sunning themselves at a hotel pool while someone on a balcony began recording with a phone, just another tourist posting a vacation panoramic of the hotel's courtyard and pool on a Sunday morning when people started screaming, the courtyard suddenly filling with water, swamping the pool, camera-phone shaking, the water rising like a tide that wouldn't quit until it nearly reached the level of the balcony, the camera jerking wildly, droplets on the lens, view of the wet floor, then dry-eyed heaven, then back down to the poolside bar and lounge chairs joining oil drums, broken trees, a vending machine and the other flotsam swirling around in the courtyard like hair around a drain, the men clinging to one another as the tide went back out to sea, carrying them with it.

Dan was close. He was looking into her eyes, somber. "Was his name Guy?" he said. "Your phlebotomist, I mean."

The instant he said it, she knew how Dan knew Guy's name and a sickishness washed over her. 'Was.' He had said 'was,' past tense, and an incredible weariness entered her body. She let her head sink to Dan's chest, feeling awful, feeling like a fainting heroine in an opera—even though she knew it was just a sudden drop in blood pressure—she never used to believe in those things—W.2 ghosts or women swooning—but here she was, swooning over how hard Silpa would take Guy's ghost.... Gory images from those videos Jak had pulled up flashed before her. She felt Dan's hand on her back, tentatively tapping as though he didn't know what to do. Then he held her more firmly, and she let him, a cry coming on.

The origins of Social Evolution: When the ground is wet and food plentiful, the slime mold *Dictyostelium discoideum* lives as thousands of independent cells. But when food becomes scarce—that is, when the individuals have to pull together to survive—these thousands of cells independently seek each other out, becoming, without any queen or even a brain, a single animal that can creep along the jungle floor eating, growing hardier, making itself more able to survive.

It was a form of prayer, to hold a turtle egg. For 150 million years, countless generations of sea turtles had come ashore at this Costa Rica beach to lay their eggs, then return to the sea. Turtle eggs had been a delicacy among his people since before Columbus.... No more. The beaches were lined with hotels, and the lights from the hotels confused adult turtles, making it impossible for them to land. The young that did manage to be born were all female, the sex of a sea turtle being determined by the temperature of the sand that the egg was laid in, and so, with the rise in the temperature of all the beaches of the Pacific, only female turtles had been born for some years now.

Each night, still wearing his waiter's tux after the last shift at the Playa Resort, José scanned the dark beach, thinking about all of this. On one of those rare occasions when he spotted one of the last adults come ashore, he followed her.

He watched her dig a hole in which to lay her eggs between tennis courts or casinos or wherever she could. When she began her return to the sea, he threw aside his cigarette, and went over to the spot and began to dig with his hands. He appreciated how much his hands, cupped to dig sand, were like the fins of a turtle, his ancestor, their myths said. He lifted one of the pearly eggs and cleaned the sand off to admire its rarity. Holding it was a gift, a reminder that he too was the last of a kind, he cracked open the egg and sucked out a delicacy that today not even kings, nor even the richest tourists, knew.

Gabe hadn't been able to sleep, but she didn't want to wake. Didn't want to have to talk. Not yet. Instead she wanted to just feel him beside her and drift, so she pretended she was still asleep, her loft purple with predawn light, her bare legs twined with his as she imagined Guy adrift in W.2: What was it that Dan had said?: first someone disappears from the first world, then the online chatter about them accelerates, coalescing around a name and date of demise until a nexus forms, gathering to it the chatter and searches and memory caches, which coalesced as an avatar the way humid air condenses on cold glass. Since the avatar never buys anything, never updates its FB page, or does anything else online, it doesn't take long for it to be shunted off into the Elysian Fields, and a pang went through her as she thought of Silpa, finding out he was dead by coming across his shroud-covered avatar, standing there mutely amongst other shades....

Opposite the windows was a clothesline she'd strung to hang watercolors she made for her Sci-Fi manga: they depicted a man shivering in his living room, living the way they say Europeans used to, putting on a sweater when the weather turned chilly, opening a window when it got warm—instead of cranking up the heat or the AC in buildings whose windows had been made hermetically sealed, as in America.

In the next panels, though, the man wakes up, and he's sweating profusely. He'd been dreaming. From bed, she couldn't make out her drawings in the dim light, but she had them in her head: he'd woken up from his dream to the reality of the whole world overheating; as the polar caps melted, the shift in the weight of the oceans altered the wobble of the Earth on its axis, making its seasons more extreme. Only the thing was, everyone just kept going about their business as usual, complaining about the heat but still worrying about what color to paint the living room; still worrying about which gel to put in their hair; still making their retirement plans, and buying lotto tickets.... Last year, a working group within the International Commission on Stratigraphy lobbied to change the name of the Anthropocene to the Petrocene, arguing that the first name didn't place blame on those who deserved it. When they didn't get their way, they took the fight online to force a popular vote. Except the public, who were themselves mostly beyond caring what the heat was called, treated it like a joke. And in the end, there had to be a runoff between the top three vote-getters: the 'You-Own-Too-Much-Shit-O-Cene,' the 'What Me Worry-O-Cene?' and the ultimate winner, the 'Strata-McStrataFace-O-Cene,' and Gabe began to consider seriously, for the first time, the possibility that we were all going to die.

She should be angry.

What the hell was the matter with people? What had those old fucks been thinking when they were young, and ran governments and companies, and had been able to do something to keep the Earth from wobbling off its axis? She could see them now, with their bioengineered hearts and prosthetic hips in that Assisted Living Condo she biked past on her way to the lab: them and their withered asses, and daily newspaper—that they still printed out on paper!—They should have been bringing down governments, not running for office—no wonder so many young people thought they deserved to die in the last pandemic, or wanted to drag them out of their retirement homes and beat them to death—like dictators dragged out of their palaces and into the street. An Arab Spring for Earth, that's what the world had needed...

But they had done nothing.

Now here she was, doing the same as the world went crazy trying to come up with desperate, last-ditch solutions: Big Ag pumping sulfur into the stratosphere to block the sun and keep corn crops in America from withering though the sulfur shut down monsoons in India; the Chinese gambling that geoengineered algae blooms the size of America could make oceans absorb more carbon. Even multimillionaires—complete amateurs with stupid ideas and unlimited money—were tinkering with the climate, using their own billions to make clouds more reflective, though their efforts just as often left huge dead zones in the oceans, or set off unexpected chain reactions....

She stroked back the hairs around the tattoo on Dan's forearm: the Red Marble Earth that had been a battle flag until guys like Dan began to get one for the sake of fashion. Still, he seemed to have come around to 'sincere,' and she knew no one's motives were completely pure....

After what he'd told her about Olympia, she felt stupid for not having said anything to the others in the lab though they'd all smelled something rotten the moment Olympia pulled their article.

Who am I kidding? Gabe thought. Even if she had admitted to herself that owning a phone in America meant child soldiers would die in the Congo, she would have answered exactly like those Dow Chemical chemists did back in the '60s: that they were just doing their jobs. She hadn't seen the movie Dan told her about, but she didn't need to to know the kinds of things they would have said: that they were developing plastics that could make baby buggies safer, or chemical processes for fertilizers that would help feed millions. And they would have tried to not believe they had nothing to do with the fact that others might assemble their individual efforts into napalm. Tech was the problem, as a lot of NGers said. But it also was the only possible solution, she used to argue. If tech makes it possible for a disease to spread, you find a vaccine to shut down its vectors. But now, she couldn't believe she'd ever thought that, lobotomizing birds—for their good, she'd once thought—preparing them so that they wouldn't feel the pain of the lice she'd next infest their bodies with. She was just a biotech version of an arms manufacturer, she now saw, thinking she could make peace on Earth.

We Cover the Earth, said the logo she had hanging on her wall; What sick mind had ever thought that would be appealing?

The image of the *Plasmodium falciparum* that BubblyFish had projected during her concert came to Gabe.

Military funding, selling out to Big Pharma, cutting corners, sneaking in diseases: Anything to keep the machine moving. Even if it could bite a lab tech in the ass. Her ass.

Outside, there was the rumble of distant thunder. Soon Gabe could hear the sound of rain and she wondered if this was a natural or a forced, man-made shower. Dan stirred under her, his legs firm, like a guy, and she nestled against him, feeling as though they were the last people on Earth. Or the first. Maybe Silpa was right: the virus she'd spotted in Gabe's blood was an antique strain. It lacked the mutation at the 17q12 position that would have made it deadly. But the general low-level crappiness that Gabe had been feeling since being bitten stayed with her. And she couldn't shake that dreamlike anxiety of time-out-of-time that came over people with lockdown fatigue; the fuzzy logic of streets deserted at rush hour; beautiful, sunny days masking an invisible killer that could be anywhere—on an ATM, in a summer breeze, or neighbor's hello, bringing down victims randomly. Like prisoners, they said, people needing to get out often dreamed of returning to their hometowns only to discover that no one there remembered them. They also dreamed a lot about tidal waves.

How had the world gotten so complicated?

Remington, said the gilt script on a typewriter whose keyboard she'd connected to her computer, a design from another age. Only later did she learn that typewriters were just a sideline for Remington, their real business having been rifles, and she remembered that video on YouTube by some lefty activist from the last century—wait! Was this the movie Dan was talking about? It showed a worker in a state-owned rifle factory disguised as a factory that made vacuum cleaners. His job was to deburr each part as it came past him on an assembly line and he truly believed that his one small job contributed to the assembly of vacuum cleaners. So he began to steal one for his wife, taking home a different part each day. But he couldn't understand why, when he put the parts together at home, he always ended up with a rifle. The man who lived in the next flat, a political agitator, saw what was going on so he took a job on the line to prove it. Like the first man, he stole a different part each day but every time he tried to assemble them for members of the opposition, all he ever got was a vacuum cleaner.

Maybe everyone was complicit, as neo-Nazis, climate-change deniers, and other apologists always whined. But didn't that also mean that everyone could be part of the solution?—like those crunchy women who laid down on an expressway to block traffic because gas-guzzlers were killing the Earth?

The thought gave her pause.

She couldn't go into the lab and bust up equipment the way she'd hammered XactlySo's sound system, though. That would be too obvious—and mean jail since Olympia had military funding and so any vandalism against her project would get classified as an act of terrorism—the way the women who torched an SUV dealership had been sentenced as terrorists to a military prison because the maker of the luxury SUVs also made military jeeps.

She lay very still, thinking.... There were other ways, though.... Ways to mess with procedures. Or data. Yeah, she could mess with the data.... In fact, it was hard not to: a louse from Anwar looked identical to one from Palestine so it was easy to mix them up. A mistake anyone could make. A mistake that would play havoc with Chen's reliability numbers. The first time she'd done so it had been a real accident—a screwup she'd made because she'd been too angry, too distracted to concentrate and she'd messed up Chen's data by mixing up the lice. Probably. She never was sure if that's what actually happened, or if Jak was the one who screwed up, or if the data went south for a completely different reason. But now it seemed like poetic justice: the right solution for all the wrong reasons. Or as her mother had told her the time she'd come home crying from being bullied in a grade-school lab, Don't be a victim; be a carrier. Don't take any old shit the world brings you; you bring the shit to the world. Like Typhoid Mary.

They had all been summoned to the conference room, but only Gabe, Jak, Chen, and Meadow had shown up. Silpa had called in sick. Heartsick, they all knew, though there had not yet been any confirmation of what they all feared was true. Mohammed hadn't been at work in days. Nor had Olympia. So Dr. Krygoski, the center's director, had summoned them to the conference room where they sat looking at one another, wondering what was going on.

"This is such bullshit. What'a we even here for?" Jak said, swiveling back and forth in one of the conference table chairs, a kid allowed on the adult furniture.

"That's what we're here to find out," Meadow said patiently.

Then the Director burst in with the air of a man with too many things to do than explain to someone else's employees why their boss was a thief. Which is what he basically did, in that polite bureaucratese. He wouldn't answer any questions. The university might initiate an investigation so all he could tell them was that Olympia had abruptly resigned in order to take another position.

"So what are we supposed to do?" Jak said.

"I'd suggest you just carry on. Just do what you normally do. What do you normally do?"

Gabe had to hold in a laugh, thinking how for Jak that meant he could go back to fucking around on the Internet, or trying to get bio-reactants to explode.

She couldn't help but notice the smile creep over his face as the Director left, leaving them all looking around at each other as they had been before the meeting started.

Chen stood up. It was his turn to present at their monthly general lab meeting. He went to the podium computer and used it to switch on the projector hanging from the ceiling.

"Chen, you got to be shitting me?" Jak said, making a big-eyed incredulous face for everyone. But Chen just ignored him and continued with the presentation he was scheduled to give. The screen at the front of the room filled with one of his reliability graphs.

Gabe wondered if he'd continue talking even if the room was empty.

Jak gave everyone a salute—"Have fun, amigos"—then left.

But Gabe stayed. She wanted to see this. In place of the constantly deteri-orating curve that Chen had shown during previous meetings, this one was straight again. It was as if the deteriorating data had been an aberration. Gabe leaned in for a better look. He began to explain how he had no explanation for why the data had suddenly become unreliable, then reliable again, but over the last few weeks, it had continually shown increasing signs of corruption: sequences he would have expected from SPA-12 showing up in SPE and vice versa. Everyone else in the room thought it might have something to do with Mohammed. Or Olympia. Or the both of them. But as Chen continued to speak, he continued to look directly at Gabe, and she knew that the fucker knew what had happened. He knew it was her even if he couldn't prove it. But so what? Let him, she thought. She gave him a steady look so he'd know that she knew that the real question was how the data had straightened out? Was Chen cooking the books to make the study come out right? He must be, but she couldn't say anything without giving away how she knew. Chen kept looking at her. She looked right back.

Prof. Ahote could tell the Anasazi hadn't been wiped out by plague, as a theory put forward during the last influenza epidemic claimed. Or destroyed in war, as claimed theories developed during the American-Soviet Cold War. And he guarded against making the same mistake: explaining the past with stories that said more about present fears than what had actually happened. Today's Fads: The Norse cut down their trees till there were no more trees, and so no more boats, and so no more Norsemen. Easter Islanders destroyed their islands, and so their society, by going to war with nature; as did the Olmecs... Seemed like a year didn't go by without the collapse of another ancient civilization being attributed to its citizens maxing out their resources. The price of wood skyrocketed in Manhattan in the 1800s because forests for 300 miles all around had been clear-cut....

Still, just because two times or places rhymed didn't mean the poem was a fiction, and as he brushed surface dirt away from the adobe doorway, the evidence that Anasazi society collapsed because it had become too complex seemed clear. He got out his pocket loupe and examined the doorway's threshold. There they were again, just as he had found in the doorway of four other cliff dwellings: smooth marks left by human hands, the kind one would see in the wet clay on a potter's wheel, evidence that wet clay had been used to seal the door shut. And if that were true, whoever lived in this cliff dwelling abandoned it deliberately. And with enough time to do so carefully. And, it would seem, with the intention to return.

As Prof. Ahote focused a camera on the smooth clay, his mind pieced together a scene as to how it played out: an Anasazi father—let's call him Yani—who had lived in this cliff dwelling some 500 years ago smoothing wet clay to seal up its doors and windows, remembering how when he was a child, his father had tried to hunt deer during a drought. He'd done so because his father before him had said that was how the Anasazi used to make it through droughts—just walk out of the pueblo and find deer there.

Prof. Ahote knew that the Anasazi had lived by hunting deer during periods of drought, even if Yani hadn't, because the professor had been able to match rainfall patterns written in the growth rings of fossilized trees with the ages of charred deer bones excavated from fire pits. From the other data he collected, he also knew, even if Yani didn't, that there were too few deer even in Yani's father's time, and none at all by the time the Anasazi abandoned their city. A city that had been ever growing. More people. Always more people, then suddenly less water....

When people were few and deer plentiful, an inefficient society with scarce resources wasn't a problem: the men could simply go out into the wilderness and hunt in times of need. Or eat the fruit of wild cacti. And always times of want could be weathered as a boat rides over a wave. But then as the people became many, their lives began to entangle, each family weaving its strands with all other families till their society was as knotted as a net with each knot depending on strands from all the others—zero degrees of separation—turkeys depending on corn harvests which depended on ash to nourish the soil and hoes to spread it, the hoes dependent on the straight adder trees and tool workers and all the others who now depended on turkeys—if one knot in a net fails, the entire net becomes worthless, catastrophe for all. No longer could the men simply find food outside the bounds of the pueblo. No more could they simply walk to the next spring, for there was now another tribe there. Their world became a game of knucklebones with the change of climate and increase of people and decrease in deer and cacti being the players that positioned their bones to narrow their options. The rows upon rows of maize that they had depended upon withered. The turkeys did not multiply for lack of maize. And without the turkeys, children grew crooked. The old died before their time. The people grew desperate. They listened to the hotheaded young men and their new god who deemed today as the day they would all walk away. Abandon their cliff dwellings. Abandon the navel of the world. They would walk out into the world, where fields of grass were as vast as the sky, and roamed by beasts so large that just one could make a feast.

The fall of Athens, the fall of Rome, the fall of Mesopotamia, the fall of Constantinople, of Easter Island, the Mayans, Norse Society, and all those other civilizations that had collapsed because they grew larger than their fields. Once they began to eat their seed corn, it was over. And every time, the last Roman, the last Mayan, had moved on to start over in a place beyond the horizon. Progress, we'd called it.

Now that we were progressing on a global scale, though, the professor thought—if one knot in a net fails—and there was nowhere to go.... What would Yani do were he alive today? Build a rocket and leave Earth?—like people here kept talking about ever since The Galileo Massive Cloud Orbiting Telescope started sending back pictures of Red Marble Earth?....

The professor snorted. That fiction was worse than fantasy. It was suicide. And he wished Hollywood would make a Sci-Fi movie titled *Leaving Earth Is Not an Option.* He ran his fingers over the marks in the clay, the work of human hands; clay was a thing; hands were a thing; clay in hands were a third thing that made other things possible, one being the act of philosophy that the Japanese considered a person working clay to be. Seeing a meditative hand at work in the clay here, it was obvious that leaving Earth would never be an option even if it became possible.

Though the air did seem to have become like the heat of a fire, and the ground dry as dust, and the seasons fled the land, the rains always returned, Yani must have thought, as any of the elders could attest. So he calmly sealed up its window and door to keep out rodents, then climbed down the ladder of their cliff dwellings. He joined those leaving the withered fields behind, and turned to look at his abandoned home one last time, nestled among the other cliff dwellings, sure that one day he—or maybe his descendants—would be back.

They called it Elysian Fields but the space was more like a beach. An infinite beach or a valley of ghosts. Waking up her computer, Meadow found herself back in the twilight of the portal she'd been shown by the Book People. Though she'd been wandering through it for over a week, a forest of avatars still stretched as far as she could see in every direction. *So many, I had not thought death had undone so many.* Since entering, she had left her computer on, had used it for nothing else, afraid that if she shut it off, or even used it for any of the work she was supposed to be doing, she wouldn't be able to get back. So she was glad, in a way, that the workday had gone to hell, and she hung back, lingering, as one by one the others left, first Jak, of course, then Gabe, but then even Chen left early, and she was finally alone in the lab.

With the reverence that overwhelming scale always gave people—the night sky, geological time—she continued to wander the vast plain of avatars. They stood there silent and apart from one another. There were no hellos. No goodbyes.There wasn't even the kind of 'waiting together though apart' that people adopted during pandemics. Rather, they stood as chessmen on a board in mid-game, de-peopled of most of its pieces. Though many faced her, they seemed faceless, their features blurred out as on MyDeathSpace, the mouth of one an expressionless line in the deep shadow cast by the bill of a baseball cap. Another wore a widow's veil. As Meadow moved her avatar among them, she saw that the faces of others were shrouded by what seemed a perpetual dusk. Many of the avatars were holding framed portraits of fine young men in military uniform, yearbook photos, baby pictures, happy couples in vacation settings—snapshots of all kinds, held to chests the way family members haunt disaster sites in search of husbands lost when an earthquake opens the ground and closes up around the unfortunate; or wives who had gone to work in office towers that came tumbling down; or daughters or sons who had gone off to war, or to sea, or to space, or the frontlines of a Covid ward and never returned.

Some of the avatars she passed spoke to her, she thought. But as she answered one, then another—"I'm sorry. No, I haven't seen them. I don't know"—she realized that they weren't so much speaking to her as mumbling to themselves: "Why did you leave? Why did you let go of my hand? Why did you run to the right and live while I went to the left and ended here? Why me and not us?"

Meadow came upon a tableau: five bodies swaddled in white linen, laid out on the ground. They were all members of a single family that had drowned in the tsunami, laid out as though sleeping beside one another. Father, mother beside him, as they must have laid down in life on the evening before the wave hit, teenage daughter beside her mother, then their two smaller sons.

As Meadow's avatar moved closer, she could see that the corpse of an infant had been placed in the mother's arms. Meadow recognized them because a photo of this very scene was famous. At the time of the disaster, it had won a Pulitzer for the way it captured a humanity that was so easily lost in the statistics of the thousands who had been swept out to sea—like 3000 grains of rice going over a waterfall, as one writer put it. Now, someone had modeled the very image here in W.2., the whiteness, and folds of their shrouds giving it all the aspect of the Pietà. Except the cloth around their faces was as gauze, and wound as tightly as a spider's filament, and she wanted to weep for the peaceful expressions that had been put on their faces....

Had those expressions been taken from life? she wondered, moving on, wanting it to be true so bad that she ached. She moved a little quicker so she wouldn't be tempted to look for signs that would give away an answer she might not want to know. One thing was certain, here in W.2 there was no smell.

Then another avatar was suddenly standing before her: one of those motherly types who wore pink overalls to the farmer's market. Unlike the others, she was smiling sympathetically. "The apocalypse isn't what it used to be," she said pleasantly. In the distance, Meadow could see others building something. An ark or huge wooden bird. A phoenix? Trojan horse? Who are you, she wanted to ask. What are you? What was any of this? A trick? A joke? Or a way to go along with people?—the way her mother used to indulge her own aged mother after Alzheimer's turned her into the young woman she imagined herself to be, back in their kitchen, happily making her daughter's lunch for school. It was all a wiki of some kind, she could see, averaging human knowledge but why? To what purpose?

The Gardener, as Meadow thought of her, asked, "Is there anything you'd like to know?"

Meadow thought a moment, and then said, "Yes," remembering all the yearning that had brought her here. The pain of childbirth, the number of hours she had spent feeding Nico, and watching him grow, learning to hold up his head, then sit. Then speak. Then struggle to draw robots and play the flute. For nothing. She remembered how it had been when she'd first met William. They'd been young then. Their lives stretched out like a runway before them. How badly she had wanted him. Had wanted everything. To know. A thirst for knowledge. Early explorers had died for less. A craving to know more powerful than the drive to mate. Or even survive. All the novels that had been written in prison—why?—all the thoughts and theories people had brought into the world—why?—only to have them fade into oblivion. The question came to her on its own, as though summoned by some collective memory: "Is our world ending?"

"Yes." But there was no dread, or even resignation in the Gardener's voice. "When has it not been?"

No extinction, only transformation went through Meadow's mind. But that wasn't what she'd meant. What she'd meant was to ask if everyone was entering a new age—one of those transitions that the Earth had gone through five times before when it erases its surface, and starts over. Unimaginable numbers of trilobites. Were we those creatures now?—the chemistry of the oceans and atmosphere changing again, becoming acidic, poisonous for mammals? Another shake of the Etch A Sketch?—brought on by humans, and the shortest of all: a transition between the Earth being so massive it could absorb any stain, and whatever would come after the straw that broke its back. Time to start thinking like a mountain, William had said, stone being its skeleton, the deep time of the cosmos here on earth. The teacher of Sisyphus. The eternal of every shore. The black, polished meteorite that links heaven and earth, now orbited by worshipers in Mecca. Albertus Mangus once theorized that living animals had emerged from the bedrock of Eden, and that fossils were those fish, snails, and other creatures that had not completely transitioned when Eden fell. Was it happening again? Stardust caught in the devil's bargain? Were tsunamis, earthquakes, the reversal of the magnetic poles, ice ages, all just different versions of the earth arching its back to bite back?.... Or maybe those New Agers were right. Maybe we really were all just avatars in the virtual world of some other civilization: Game Over—Restart—Game Over—Restart—Game Over—Restart.... An alien civilization's W.6022666.... There was compelling evidence for the idea that our reality was someone or something else's simulation, after all—especially the stubborn persistence of belief in life after death—even if the alien whose created world we lived within was the Earth itself.

Maybe that's what the Gardener had meant. Meadow thought about that. And about all that had come to pass in her life and in all the lives there had been in the four billion years since the Earth cooled enough for its crust to form: superheated steam on the bottom of the sea creating the static electricity that charged particles—the spark of life—creating amino acids, strings of amino acids combining to form DNA, DNA creating microbes, and ending their pacific world. Is that when yearning began? Fear? The smallest mite scurries to escape the shadow of a descending hand, and she felt somewhat like that mite as life, not her life but life itself, washed over her as so many waves that they filled her with a sense of the sea.

Just before Voyager left our solar system for good, it turned its cameras around for one last look at home, which from that distance was smaller than a pale, blue dot, not even a pixel, upon which every child, man, woman who ever existed took breath, stood upright, was destined to dust; less than a pixel upon which all life had emerged: the first plants, then so many protozoans, trilobites and sea urchins, each with its span of days. Crushed to the density of rock, they formed a crust a mile thick. Mudfish drew the first breath. The first insects. Buzzing and yowls breaking the silence in a world of sound far more complex than wind through leaves. Reptiles and amphibians and turtles and *Archaeopteryx*. The squish of squids. The perfectly shaped orifice on the tentacle of an octopus. The first bird. And bird lice. The first flowering plants, the first dance by a bee. Then a meteoritic flash and that Age was over. Patterns coalesce into larger patterns, the shrew five thousand million years in the making, an accident that was itself a convergence of genes shuffling from *Pikaia*, a worm with the first spine from which all other spines evolved. Whales. Monkeys. The first grasses grow over the past. Apes. Hominids, the first *Australopithecines*. That world ending under the crush of the first human footprint. Stones become weapons. Pictures. Massive slabs hauled miles to erect as Stonehenge. The first writing closing the silence of the vanished. Philosophy. A map of the world that could be held in the palm of the hand; pyramids built for eternity melt like sand castles, given enough time. Alchemy. Navigation based on the rhythm of waves. An anatomy of body weather. Unremembered peasants dying during the construction of The Great Wall. Why? A universe imagined as the music of the spheres. A monster brings the End of the World to the Aztecs. The first open-air opera in Rome. To celebrate Easter, witches are forced to sit on red-hot iron seats. The Unknown Turkish Soldier molders in his grave. Why? Plague. A cloth merchant uses the first microscope to reveal the beast that is the flea. Still, the great plague of Vienna kills 76,000... The End of the World. "Oh du lieber Augustin" becomes a popular song, commemorating the luck of the drunken musician who was accidentally thrown into a pit of plague corpses but survived to play in the taverns again—so many lives that had flashed into being, lived a moment, then were gone.... Disease decimates American populations; mound builders abandon their cities. Pocket handkerchiefs come into use. Hundreds of African languages. Marcello Malpighi dissects flies in 1669, and ever since biology students have had to memorize his names for the parts. Wallpaper becomes the must-have fashion. Histories erased. There were over 1,000 revolts on slave ships headed to America. Handel's *Water Music*. So many conceptions of the world. All absurd. Shackleton. Some histories, like waves, canceling one another—animal electricity; Humboldt's theory of all science as different faces of one *Kosmos*—others combining—Wallace, Darwin—to rise with tsunami force. Divide and conquer. Badminton invented. Audubon's years in forests. Unremarked stable hands die saving horses from the Chicago Fire. Unremembered entomologists die exploring Paraguay. Paraguay not in need of exploring. Unremarked stories... Stories far too tiny to figure in any algorithm's calculus. Robert Traub discovers continental drift from the physiological similarities between Old and New World fleas. Miriam Rothschild spends a lifetime compiling *The Ceratophyllidae: Key to the Genera and Host Relationships with Notes on Their Evolution, Zoogeography and Medical Importance.* Now obsolete. Watson and Crick sneak into Rosalind Franklin's lab to steal her structure of chromosomes. Aerosol shaving cream shown to destroy the ozone layer; manufacturers fight findings. *The Chewing Lice: World Checklist and Biological Overview* (majestic). The pill, the auto and the bra struggle to shape women; the British Empire, the auto, struggle to shape men; the Christian manger, petri-dish babies, adoption laws struggle to shape the family. Billions of lines of code only readable on unusable machines, web links going dead. An epidemic of religious men shooting people in cafés.... A hose is threaded down the throats of others to drown them until they confess. Tsunami washes away most of the Bottom Billion landmass....

If a person stretched out their arms to represent the history of the Earth—fingertip to fingertip—a teacher of hers once said, the white crescent of the furthest index finger's nail would be the span humans had walked its surface. When she thought of the rest of the arm's span, mudslides and volcanoes, wars and periods of peace, mass extinctions, famines, plagues and earthquakes tripped over each other in a mad stampede to bring on the present. When she thought of these same events ticking away over the course of 10,000,000 years, she came away with quite different impressions—a rock on a mountainside taking a thousand years to shift—impressions that meant quite different things for the people who would live through them: the particular way the taillights of her father's car would glow as he pulled into their garage after work. Nico never lived to see this day....

Nurse, said one of the Book People, reciting a poem, *You are the last....*

Then she remembered: it was a poem William had shown her back before Nico was born and her only worries were for the Earth:

You are the last
Who will know her
Nurse

Sunlight through the reed shade on the porch.

Not know her,
She is very old

How could anyone know her, she remembered, thinking of the Earth, of its breezes, of its pulsing waves....

You are the last
Who will see her

Or touch her

Or the feel on her cheek of the flannel pajamas her mother wore in winter. Despite all the yearning, all the centuries of digging and searching, if all the prehistoric skulls that had ever been found were gathered together, they wouldn't fill the bed of a single pickup truck.

She knew the city referred to in the poem:

You forget the changes after a while
Sea walls instead of fortress walls, giant, offshore turbines
bring the horizon close

Unbelievable, at first
as the collapse of mountains
of ice

A monument rises,
crowned by a gilt figure
The Genius of Our Species
I suppose

People love to go out and look at it towards sundown
when it catches the dying light

Dazzling, like an artificial star

It looks...

Curious.

She herself had seen that crown at sundown, aligned with the evening star. And it had brought to mind machines falling silent, stars winking out. The heart monitor in her mother's hospital room going to flatline. A faint, blue, pixel. She gave a sigh, "Hmm." Then, after a moment she asked, "So what was that all about?"

ACKNOWLEDGMENTS: The author would like to thank the numerous people who made this novel possible, especially Mervi Pakaste, whose designer's eye and hand touched every page; the Board of FC2, who set it in motion; Dan Waterman, for his guidance at the press for what are always odd books; Maria Tomasula, and now Alba Tomasula y Garcia and Ava Tomasula y Garcia, for art.

More specifically: Overall book design and layout, Mervi Pakaste. **CHAPTER 1:** Design and layout by Mervi Pakaste. Maria Tomasula, *Conquistador* and *Flooding of Mediterranean Valley*. Ernst Haeckel, *Kunstformen der Natur.* Georges Cuvier, *Recherches sur les ossemens fossiles*. Thomas Webster in William Buckland, *Geology and Mineralogy Considered with Reference to Natural Theology. The Bridgewater Treatises on the Power, Wisdom, and Goodness of God, as Manifested in the Creation*. J.G. Wood, *Animate Creation*. Alba Tomasula y Garcia, *Strata of the Three Geological Ages*. Robert Hooke, *Micrographia*. Frederic Edwin Church, *The Icebergs*. Louis Agassiz and Joseph Bettannier, *Études sur les glaciers*. Rare Book Division, The New York Public Library, "Mare Humorum," Digital Collections. John James Audubon, *Birds of America*. John Richardson, *The Museum of Natural History*. Francis Willughby, *Ornithologiae libri tres*. Jim Harter, *Animals*. Charles H. Hitchcock, *The Relations of Geology to Theology*. Other works that were influential in the writing of this chapter include: David Attenborough, Susan Owens, Martin Clayton, and Rea Alexandratos, *Amazing Rare Things: The Art of Natural History in the Age of Discovery*. Robert Chambers, Alexander Ireland, and F. W Thompson, *Vestiges of the Natural History of Creation*. Charles Darwin, *Journal of Researches into the Natural History and Geology of the Countries Visited During the Voyage of H.M.S. Beagle Round the World*. Asa Gray, *Structural Botany* (1879). Alexander von Humboldt, *Cosmos: A Sketch of a Physical Description of the Universe* (E.C. Otté trans., 1848). Jean Baptiste Pierre Antoine de Monet de Lamarck, *Zoological Philosophy: An Exposition with Regard to the Natural History of Animals*. John Richardson, William Sweetland Dallas, T. Spencer Cobbold, William Baird, Adam White, and Joseph Bassett Holder, *The Museum of Natural History* (1877). J. P. Robertson and William Parish Robertson, *Letters on Paraguay* (1839). *Charles Hazelius Sternberg, The Life of a Fossil Hunter* (1909). Henry David Thoreau, *Walden; Or, Life in the Woods* (1854). Laura Dassow Walls, *The Passage to Cosmos: Alexander von Humboldt and the Shaping of America*. J. G. Wood and Joseph Bassett Holder, *Animate Creation*.

CHAPTER 2: Design, layout, and imagery by Dan Warner. Thanks to Jill Godmilow for docfilm conversations over the years; thanks to Barbara J. Hellenthal and the access to resources at the Museum of Biodiversity; to Dr. Ronald Hellenthal, especially his invaluable *The Chewing Lice: Word Checklist and Biological Overview*. In addition, thanks to the following for their resources: Alba Tomasula y Garcia, camping photoshop, and feather lice slides. Maria Tomasula, storyboard, and *Feathered T-Rex*. Dan Warner, Land Rover, roads, and compound photoshop. NASA, Satellite Image. U.S. Geological Survey, Department of the Interior, Satellite Images. Vicki Funk Collecting, Smithsonian Institution Archives, Image # 95-1204. Thomas Lovejoy, Smithsonian Institution Archives, Image # 2002-32304. Alfred Lord Tenneyson, "Flower in the Crannied Wall." Other works that helped shape this chapter include: Augusto Roa Bastos, Luis Vera, and Manrique Zago, *Paraguay: país de maravillas*. Sankar Chatterjee, *The Rise of Birds: 225 Million Years of Evolution. Yossi Ghinsberg, Back from Tuichi: The Harrowing Life-and-Death Story of Survival in the Amazon Rainforest*. Stephen Jay Gould, *Wonderful Life: The Burgess Shale and the Nature* *of History.* Stephen Jay Gould, *The Hedgehog, the Fox, and the Magister's Pox: Mending the Gap Between Science and the Humanities.* Thomas S. Kuhn, *The Structure of Scientific Revolutions.* Ted Nield, *Drawing and Understanding Fossils: A Theoretical and Practical Guide for Beginners, with Self-Assessment;* Erland Nordenskiöld, *La vida de los indios.* Erland Nordenskiöld, *Exploraciones y aventuras en Sudamérica.* Roger D. Price, *The Chewing Lice: World Checklist and Biological Overview.* Mary Hanson Pritchard, and Günther O. W Kruse, *The Collection and Preservation of Animal Parasites.* Robert Traub, Miriam Rothschild, and John F. Haddow, *The Rothschild Collection of Fleas: The Ceratophyllidae: Key to the Genera and Host Relationships with Notes on Their Evolution, Zoogeography, and Medical Importance.* Hayden White. *The Fiction of Narrative: Essays on History, Literature, and Theory, 1957-2007.*

CHAPTER 3: Design, layout, and imagery by Dan Warner and Mervi Pakaste. Thanks to Dr. Mary Ann McDowell for conversations about disease vectors, infectious diseases, and for allowing me to be a fly on the wall of her lab; to Marcelo Ramalho-Origao for teaching me how to dissect sand flies, and everyone else in the lab for being so open. NASA, earth from space, earth at night. Tomáš Malík, Pexels, Ice as Blue and White Abstract Painting. Martin Krzywinski, DNA visualization. NOAA's Office of Coast Survey Historical Map & Chart Collection. John Craig Freeman, and 4Gentlemen, Tiananmen SquARed. Anouchka Unel, *Salar of Uyuni,* 2004, Free Art License, Wikimedia Commons. Ava Tomasula y Garcia, kids on beach, GPF cat, planet losing atmosphere. Ingrid Moen, Charlotte Jevne, Jian Wang, Karl-Henning Kalland, Martha Chekenya, Lars A Akslen, Linda Sleire, Per Ø Enger, Rolf K Reed, Anne M Øyan, and Linda EB Stuhr: *Gene expression in tumor cells and stroma in dsRed 4T1 tumors in eGFP-expressing mice with and without enhanced oxygenation in: BMC Cancer. 2012, 12:21.* Louis Agassiz, *Zmutt Valley near Zermatt.* MrHicks46 (Teo Romera), *Ice Fields* licensed under CC BY-SA 2.0 (creativecommons.org/licenses/by-sa/2.0). Ben Funke, *One.* Eric Whitacre Inc., Virtual Choir. Iselita Arlen, *Tokyo Wave Pool.* Wilfredor, *Petare Slums,* Wikimedia Commons. Shutterstock, *Migrants on Fence, Greenhouses Almeria Spain, chicken factory, migrant boats, Sun City, oil field.* FreedomHouse, Wikimedia Commons, *Migrants and refugees arrive by dinghy behind a huge pile of life vests after crossing from Turkey.* ©Bwag/CC-BY-SA-4.0, Wikimedia Commons, *Migrants Wien-Westbahnhof.* Gémes Sándor/SzomSzed, Wikimedia Commons, *Migrants in Hungary near the Serbian border.* Wikimedia Commons, *Hieronymus Bosch, The Garden of Earthly Delight (details).* National Oceanic and Atmospheric Administration, *Pacific Garbage Patch, Mina de Chuquicamata, Calama. Latvian Satellite Reef (detail)* from the Crochet Coral Reef project by Christine Wertheim and Margaret Wertheim and the Institute for Figuring, photo © IFF. Sound Spirit, *Congestion in India.* Alex Rio Brazil, *Deforestation, Wikimedia Commons.* Chris Lintott, PI, Zooniverse and team members, *Planet Hunters.* Pandemic mosaics, Jim Bachor (photo by author). U.S. Geological Survey, Department of the Interior/USGS, *Earthquake Tracker.* Peter Rejcek for National Science Foundation, *Blood Falls.* John Craig Freeman, *Border Memorial.* Bernard Spragg, *Hubbard Glacier.* Also helpful: Susan Flader, *Thinking Like a Mountain: Aldo Leopold and the Evolution of an Ecological Attitude Toward Deer, Wolves, and Forests.* Barbara Matilsky, *Vanishing Ice: Alpine and Polar Landscapes in Art, 1775-2012;* end poem after "Of Being Numerous," George Oppen. A compost of too many online sources and events to list; however, à la Wittgenstein, I make no claim to ideas not my own, an idea that I owe to him.